BEATRICE COLIN

Beatrice Colin was born in London and raised in Scotland but has lived in New York. She has worked as a freelance journalist, writing for publications including the *Guardian*, and a playwright, writing radio plays for the BBC. She lives in Glasgow. Her most recent book, *The Luminous Life of Lilly Aphrodite* was a Richard & Judy selection and has been translated into seven languages.

Also by Beatrice Colin

Nude Untitled

Disappearing Act

The Luminous Life of Lilly Aphrodite

THE SONGWRITER

BEATRICE COLIN

JOHN MURRAY

First published in Great Britain in 2010 by John Murray (Publishers)
An Hachette UK Company

First published in paperback in 2010

1

'Over There' (1917) was written by George M. Cohan and published by the William Jerome
Publishing Company

A CIP catalogue record for this title is available from the British Library

ISBN 978-0-7195-2392-2

Typeset in Goudy Old Style by Servis Filmsetting Ltd, Stockport, Cheshire

Printed and bound by Clays Ltd, St Ives plc

John Murray policy is to use papers that are natural, renewable and recyclable products and
made from wood grown in sustainable forests. The logging and manufacturing processes are
expected to conform to the environmental regulations of the country of origin.

John Murray (Publishers)
338 Euston Road
London NW1 3BH

www.johnmurray.co.uk

To Paul

Under every no lay a passion for yes
that had never been broken.

Wallace Stevens

1

If only, thought Monroe Simonov, if only love was like a Pianola playing a roll. If only it was a piece of card all cut out with dashes and holes and slits that you could thread into the slot and turn, once, twice, three times. Then all you'd need to do was sit down and pedal like mad to make the keys play and music pour out perfectly every time.

Monroe found his reflection in the tarnished mirror above the bar, his twenty-four-year-old face, his dark hair swept back, his pale indoor skin with its Sunday afternoon tan, and finally his eyes, eyes that she had once told him were the colour of Taconic Mountain slate, whatever that was. Today his face didn't feel as if it belonged to him. Certainly it didn't reflect the real state of his crumpled heart.

At the end of the counter where he sat, the gaslight was a slightly brighter shade of dirty yellow than the walls. The murmur of one-sided conversations was punctuated by the clatter of dishes by the short-order cook and the clink of glass on glass as the barman poured out shots of Scotch, or sloe gin, or bourbon. The wooden counter had been worn so smooth by countless elbows that the varnish was almost all rubbed away. And although the ashtrays were always on the point of overflowing, no one ever seemed to have a match.

Outside, the sun had just set and the sky was clear and blazing and beautiful. If he walked out now, Monroe considered, turned right and looked past the illuminated sign that read *Vacancies*, if he looked out further, much further than Hoboken, he could watch the day fall into the west. What time was it in California? Morning time? Lunchtime? Early afternoon? He hoped she had found a decent place to stay. He hoped she'd slept well the night before. He hoped she missed him, sometimes.

The waitress was standing in front of him, a coffee pot in her hand. Her eyebrows were raised into a question: *WhatcanIgetya, wantmorecauffee, readyforthecheck?* Monroe had no idea what she had just asked him so he took a wild guess.

'Sure,' he said. 'Fill me up.'

The coffee fell in a single stream, a black stripe, a dash of tar against the ivory of the cup. He threw it back in one swallow and grabbed his hat.

'Any new songs?' the cashier asked. 'Any new songs you can let us have for free?'

'Only the ones in my head,' Monroe replied.

The cashier laughed as he handed him his change. 'That's the problem with you guys,' he said. 'Too much going on up there.'

It was already October but Manhattan was still baking in the heat of an Indian summer. At that time of the evening, however, the air was edged with cooler currents. Everything was in shadow, the harsh angles of the buildings and the geometry of the grid all softened by the blue wash of nightfall. And yet on Times Square, the night was ablaze. The electric illuminations, the flashing bulbs of the Petticoat Girl and the Corticelli Kitty signs, the theatre hoardings, the cinema kiosks and the moving headlamps of dozens of taxicabs would all burn until long after closing time. As usual, the streets were choked up with people from out of town who had come to gawp at the lights and to spend their savings in the Irish bars and the overpriced restaurants that lined the square. In all that joviality, in all that hilarity, in all that extravagance, it was hard to remember that in Europe a war was being fought.

Monroe headed south down Broadway, past the Flatiron Building on Fifth Avenue and onwards to West Twenty-Third Street. Here, the rush-hour traffic, the tramcars and the elevated trains, the horse-drawn cabs and the private cars, had started to thin out. A couple of booths lit by strings of bare electric bulbs sold pretzels and chestnuts on the corner. Groups of construction workers, their eyes dizzy with height and too much coffee, crouched in doorways and waited for their lift home. A white horse pulled a cart towards the Bowery, its load of seltzer water bottles clanking gently in their wooden crates.

Skirting the edge of Chinatown, he strode towards the Court House and up the ramp of the Brooklyn Bridge. The wide wooden walkway for pedestrians and bicycles rose above the tracks of the electric tramcars and the road until it hung suspended above four lanes of traffic. Most of the office workers and clerks who lived in lodgings in Fort Greene or Carroll Park clocked off at five sharp and had crossed the bridge a couple of hours before, and so he was almost alone as he paced towards the Brooklyn side, his hat pushed down hard against the wind.

Suzette Kinross had been a speciality dancer at Ziegfeld Follies. He had known her for four months and been in love with her for three. She was from Halifax, Nova Scotia, but lived in an apartment hotel for women in Midtown. At first he had laughed at her sing-song accent and the way her wiry auburn hair would always escape from the pins she used to flatten it. But then she had danced in his room after they had shared half a bottle of Irish whiskey and he had started to see her in a completely different light. He still kept finding those pins everywhere, those pins and single strands of copper-coloured hair that had caught what little sun found its way into his room and held it.

Of course, when she told him she had been offered a part in a moving picture, he was thrilled and excited and insistent that she should take it. She threw her arms around him and licked his ear with her sharp little tongue the way she did when she wanted their embrace to 'lead to something'. That something caught them up and swept them along to a place where there were no borders, no barriers, no limitations, only the rush and tremble of what he thought was a perfect affinity.

'Be careful,' she had whispered.

Afterwards when they lay breathless and damp with their legs and arms all wound together he noticed she was crying. 'What is it? Are you all right?' he asked. 'You did say you were safe.'

'It's fine,' she replied. 'I mean, it'll be fine.'

3

'Then what is it? Why are you sad?'

'It's just . . . it's just . . .' she whispered. 'Would you marry me? Would you marry me tomorrow if I asked you to?'

He laughed; he had thought she was joking. 'You're crazy,' he said. 'We only just met.'

And when she didn't respond he took her hand and kissed it.

'It's a nice idea but it doesn't even give me enough time to get to the tailor's to order a new suit,' he said. 'But if there was ever a reason,' he added softly, 'I'd do the right thing. Is that it, Suzette? Are you worried I'd run off?'

'No!' she answered, her voice rising in pitch at the end of the word in that comical way it always did. And then in fits and bursts, in stops and starts, she told him that the film was being shot in California and not in a studio in Astoria, Queens, as he had supposed.

'What?' he said and let go of her hand. 'You might as well tell me you're going to the moon.'

He had sat up then, got out of bed and without another word he had pulled all his clothes back on.

'Monroe?' she had called out.

He tried to stay calm. He tried to keep his temper but still it was about to boil over. And so he walked across to the second-hand piano he had paid three weeks' wages for and which he'd had to hire eight men to lift up the stairs, and started to play Mozart at twice its normal speed.

'I'll call you,' she had said as she had gathered up her clothes and dressed. 'And I'll write and stuff.'

He had only stopped playing when he heard the front door close. And then he had listened to the click of her heels recede along the street.

It had been two weeks now and he'd heard nothing from her. He didn't know if she was dead, or dying or, even worse, that she had dropped him. And stuff. He should have made her clarify what the 'stuff' was. If it was telepathy then he wasn't receiving.

At the first pier, Monroe stopped and looked out over the East River. Two boats were unloading their cargo on to the wharves on the far side, the reflection of the longshoremen's lanterns bobbing and drifting in the black water. Beyond the boats, further out in the New York harbour, a single ocean liner drew level with Battery Park on its way to one of the Hudson piers. Over half of the moorings on the piers were vacant now. The threat of being sunk by a German U-boat had brought almost all sea traffic to a halt and only the most determined passengers now made the trip across the Atlantic. But they still came, new immigrants mostly, from Greece, Italy, Ireland and Turkey, from Macedonia and Scotland on any ship sailing, safe or not. Although some brought their wives and mothers, their daughters and their grandmothers, the majority were single men, men who had nothing more than a change of clothes and a willingness to do any job, anywhere, as long as they were paid in cash. The passengers in first and second class, should there be any, would be allowed to disembark on to Manhattan almost immediately. The rest, who'd made the trip in steerage, would be ferried to Ellis Island where they would spend several days being 'processed'.

Monroe Simonov himself had been carried on to one of those same ferries from steerage. He was the third but sole surviving son of Clara and Nikolas Simonov, and had been born in the middle of the Atlantic Ocean on the SS *Bohemia* in the late spring of 1892. He nearly failed to make it to New York harbour and everybody thought he was going to end up as one more piece of hand luggage to carry on to Ellis Island inside a tiny coffin that the shipping company would, they had been informed, supply on request.

Monroe had been born to a mother who was so seasick she couldn't nurse. At first he had cried with such a piercing, strangled kind of wail that any offers of milk from other new mothers, and there were another forty on board, were not forthcoming. But Monroe had been lulled by the sound of the swell and the pull of the Gulf Stream; as his tears dried and his sobbing was quelled, he was taken to the breast of a former wet-nurse who had never quite dried up, and saved.

At a few days old he was obviously far too young to remember his first sight of the Statue of Liberty, but his three sisters had told the story so many times that eventually it had become fixed in his memory like his very own: the greenish tinge of the lady's mantle, the thorns of her crown, the sense that she was so much smaller than they had been expecting, more an over-large statue stuck on an ugly block of rock than the huge monument they had imagined.

His family came from a province called White Russia. It was a place that made big statements; its lakes were as large as seas, its forests as dense as knitting and its wild animals so fierce that they could bite you in two or kill you with a paw. In his parents' memory, at least, it was a brutal place with no room for the frivolities of city life; you worked until you dropped, you kept a promise, you loved your wife, and you drank until you forgot everything you'd just pledged. Honour and remorse lay west and east respectively and were there when you fell asleep and there when you woke. When rumours of pogroms reached the village near Kiev where they had lived for decades, however, his parents had decided that there must be a better way to live. They sold almost everything they had, which wasn't much, borrowed what they could and announced their decision to emigrate to America. Although they said, *until we meet again*, rather than *goodbye*, they left in the full knowledge that it was unlikely they would ever return.

With three young daughters and another child on the way, the family had taken the train from Kiev to the Polish border, another to Warsaw, one more to Berlin and a fourth to Bremen, where they had boarded ship. Of course, they had hoped that the birth would wait until they reached America, for reasons of both safety and citizenship, but five days after they had departed from German shores Monroe's mother went into labour and after just four hours of pain so severe her screams could be heard on the first-class deck, the baby was born in the middle of the night in bunk 24 on Deck E.

Despite the fact that the family were Jewish, Monroe's mother was insistent that they name him after a Scottish bo'sun who had been present at the birth rather than a figure from the Old Testament as was the tradition. Somehow the bo'sun's first name and surname became confused and the baby was named Monroe instead of Hamish. Even when the mistake was pointed out his mother remained resolute. New land, new name, new life, she had said at the time. The euphoria didn't last. After twenty years in the Land of the Free, she sailed back east to Palestine, with her daughters, one son-in-law, a trunk full of old clothes and an urn full of ashes.

Monroe sent her a third of his wages every month, while she wrote him long rambling letters which, until the war had broken out, had urged him to emigrate, to marry the nice Jewish girl who lived next door, and to help her tend her newly planted orchard of lemon trees. They both knew that he would never consider any of her plans seriously, but still she kept asking and still he kept on saying, *perhaps, Mama, perhaps.*

From the Brooklyn Bridge, Monroe watched a tugboat chunter up the river. A silver biplane buzzed overhead. And then, as the sound of its engines faded, he could make out the faint strains of a zither coming from a teahouse in the overcrowded slums of Chinatown. A couple approaching from the Brooklyn side of the bridge slowed their pace a little when they saw him. But when they deduced by the cut of his clothes and the affable nod of his head that he wasn't about to beg for a spare nickel or rob them of their pocket watches, they relaxed and continued their conversation.

'Not with a man like him, you dolt.' The woman laughed.

'But she has a penchant for revolutionaries,' the man replied. 'At least that's what I heard.'

They passed by, the tick and rhythm of their shoes leaving behind a pattern in Monroe's head. The pattern became the time signature of a melody, the melody became the suggestion of a symphony and in snatches he heard the bass, the slide of the string section and the blow out of the horns. At that point in his life Monroe would have claimed that music was the language he dreamed in, it was in the warmth in his blood and the rhythm of his breathing. Even his heartbeat, he liked to imagine, was a hammer hitting a string.

One of his earliest memories was the sound of his mother's voice singing songs in Yiddish, songs like 'Bayn Obsheyd' and 'Tum Balalaika'. And the first time he saw a piano, he climbed up on to the stool and managed to pick out those melodies note by note and phrase by phrase. The child should have lessons, somebody said, and so after much discusssion and a redistribution of the housekeeping money, the family agreed to eat chopped liver instead of beef so he could learn the piano.

With his fingers on the keys and his eyes on the music in front of him, he stumbled through his first lesson and quickly claimed that actually he'd rather have the beef. When his teacher, a retired Episcopalian church organist, who lived with her five cats and a baby grand piano, played him the tunes the way they were meant to be played, he was stunned. He could hardly believe that in the simple overlap or quick progression of notes were melodies, chords and rhythms he had never imagined existed, that this construction of wood and string, of felt and ivory, that sounded so frightful when he played it, could be made to produce such a beautiful sound.

The more he practised, the more he pounded away at the piano in the freezing cold Salvation Army hall where his mother had organized that he could play every day, the more he realized that learning to read music was like learning to read all over again. But instead of words, the notes, the time signatures, the adagios and minuets conveyed different kinds of meanings, meanings that could express emotions and moods he could feel but couldn't yet understand. It was as if those long-dead composers, Chopin and Bach and Mozart, were talking to him alone. And he wished then that he could have just a fraction of their articulacy, just a fraction of their ability to capture something fleeting and transient and write it down.

It could have been only a few seconds, it might have been several minutes, or it might have been an hour before Monroe came back and found himself still standing there, alone on the long stretch of wooden walkway below the cat's cradle of cables that spanned the Brooklyn Bridge. And even though he could still make out the music in his head, its exuberance and epic melancholy, it had become intangible, vague, and the more he tried to catch it the more it eluded him, until he finally had to admit that note by note and phrase by phrase, it was gone, the notes, the pauses, the sharps and flats all dispersed into millions of tiny reverberations over Lower Manhattan. The temperature had started to drop, the wind was rising, and so he turned up his collar and headed home.

Home was a fourth-floor walk-up on Joralemon Street in Brooklyn Heights. It was an apartment so narrow that only one room was ever blessed with any light. The other rooms, the tiny bedroom and the cupboard that his landlady optimistically called 'the kitchen', had no windows and were almost permanently dark. The fact that all the walls were painted in heavy brown gloss only made the problem worse.

'Mr Simonov?'

It was impossible to creep up the stairs without being noticed. He'd tried it many times.

'You had a call,' shouted his landlady, an elderly Italian who liked to be known as Nonna Maria.

Monroe hesitated on the stairs. At last. He should have had more faith in her. Why hadn't he walked home faster? Why had he stopped for so long on the bridge? What had he been thinking?

'When?' he asked. 'Did she leave a message? A contact number?'

Nonna Maria came out on to the landing and looked up at him before she spoke. 'He didn't leave no note,' she said softly. 'Think he was trying to sell something.'

That night, no breeze reached the Heights from the river. A lone mosquito droned, looped and then was silent. As he lay awake he tried to remember every inch of her: the curve of her neck, the hollow of her hip and the tease in her voice. When he had kissed her she seemed so experienced, so at ease with her body, so open to the suggestion, when it posed itself, that he presumed that she had done this all before, that she was a modern girl, that sexual relations were nothing more to her than an extension of kissing. She knew what she was doing, didn't she? Although he never told her, she was his first. Maybe she knew as much as he did, and that was nothing at all, maybe she was more serious than he realized, maybe he should have said, yes, yes, I'll marry you tomorrow. And right at that moment, as he felt the tiny stab of the mosquito's sting enter the skin of his shoulder and he slapped the spot just a fraction of a second too late, it dawned on him that he might have lost the very thing he hadn't even understood was his to lose.

9

The mosquito buzzed just beyond his left ear and then was silent again. It would break his mother's heart, he kept telling himself. It would break his mother's heart if he married a girl who wasn't Jewish. And he tossed and turned and lay hopelessly awake. But then, as St Ann's bells chimed the night away, as the sparrows and thrushes started to sing on the gingko tree outside, note by note and line by line, a song arrived, a song so perfectly formed, so fluently phrased and finely honed that when he climbed out of bed and played it softly, so softly on the piano, it sounded as if it had been in the air for ever just waiting to be played.

The next morning the sky was a deep, infinite blue. The trees outside were turning and their leaves were blowing golden and amber all over the pavement. Monroe walked to Borough Hall as usual, bought a five-cent ticket and took an express train to Forty-Second Street and Broadway. From there he walked three blocks to the Exchange Building on West Forty-Fifth Street where the Universal Music Corporation was located on the second floor.

Although the rest of New York had been awake for hours – the cobbles swept, the milk delivered, the bagels boiled and baked, the billboards at the newspaper kiosks already pasted with stories of distant tragedies and war – at 10 a.m. West Forty-Fifth Street was only just beginning to come to life. Doors and windows were propped open to let the previous night's tobacco fumes escape; empty bottles clanked and smashed as they were thrown down rubbish chutes and cleaners launched arcs of soapy water into the gutters where they fizzed briefly before rolling down the drain.

Even though they had only just woken up, however, the streets above Times Square were already busy: men in tightly buttoned suits and colourful ties, the ropers-in, tried to entice people into their respective publishing houses; secretaries gossiped with each other outside the drugstore; delivery boys, their arms laden with parcels wrapped in brown paper, staggered up stoops or waited for lifts; and trails of young women in too much make-up and dresses maybe a size too small walked purposefully towards appointments or stood silently mouthing the titles of the songs displayed in the publishers' windows.

'I heard they were hiring in Chicago,' the girls told each other. 'You'll love Phoenix. The theatre manager is a darling.'

Every time Monroe turned the corner on to Forty-Fifth Street, he always paused for an instant and just listened, really listened. Above the splutter of motor cars left to idle on the corner, above the chitter and blurt of chorus girls and the bragging of promoters, above the roar, even, of the printing presses that churned out fifty pages of sheet music a minute, was the unmistakable, unforgettable sound of the piano, not just one, but ten, twenty, thirty, all playing different tunes at the same time.

Monroe was too young to remember the early days but the old-timers, the doormen and the veteran printers, talked about the first music publishers in the 1890s with reverence. They'd opened offices in Lower Manhattan, on the Bowery, before moving to Union Square and then up to the West Forties. Firms like Shapiro's and Remick's followed the path of the entertainment industry uptown until they were settled in a triangle of high rises and brownstones called Upper Longacre Square, a triangle that was now surrounded by agents, bookers, theatres, music halls and vaudeville houses.

Although the whole industry was known collectively as Tin Pan Alley, only a handful of publishers still had their offices on West Twenty-Eighth Street, the street that had originally been given the name. If you went down to the 'Alley' now there would be little more than tourists and hustlers, ten-cent stores and sheet music wholesalers. But if you tried to describe it, and many had, you would eventually come to the conclusion that Tin Pan Alley was much more than a location. It was a flutter in the belly, the float of a crescendo followed by the crash of a minor seventh chord. It was the buzz of adrenalin or the first draw of a cigarette. Something new mixed with something old, it was a cocktail of melancholy mixed with a generous shot of pandemonium.

With a coffee from the diner on the corner in his hand, Monroe headed up two flights of stairs, through the swing doors of the Universal Music Corporation and past the receptionist to a row of cubicles. His was third on the left, number 3, which like all the rest was fitted out with a piano and two chairs.

A new song had been propped up on his stand, a song called 'My Little Girl'. He hung up his jacket on a coat rack, placed his coffee on the floor beside him and played the first few bars. The lyrics were sentimental and the tune was a dirge, but he had to admit that it was irritatingly catchy. Von Hofe had been on at them all for the last couple of days to push this song as hard as they could. Only one in about two hundred published songs actually caught on. And this one, or so his boss guessed, had to be a sure-fire.

From the next cubicle along, Billy Gold broke into a rousing rendition of the song, shifting into classical until he had the song sounding like a hymn. From the cubicle on his other side, Abe Groblensky started playing the song at twice its normal speed. Monroe played a single note, a middle C. The music from the pianos on either side of him slipped in and out of synch, their notes clashing and jarring and then unexpectedly harmonizing. He played the C again, and listened as the note reverberated and then slowly dissolved. The truth was, however, that nobody knew why some songs took off and some didn't; it was in the colour of the air, the direction of the wind, the random scatter of the stars.

Monroe had been a song-plugger for the Universal Music Corporation ever since he had graduated from the Brooklyn Boys' High School in 1910. He had not become a classical pianist, as his teacher had once hoped he would, and instead, at his mother's insistence, had taken a fifteen-dollar-a-week job with the song publisher. It was a good job. Most of the boys in his class at school had gone on to work in the Navy Yard for less than forty dollars a month.

Universal was one of the smaller music publishers; it had ten demonstration cubicles, plus a general office, a stockroom and an advertising department. Monroe's boss, the Professional Manager of the firm, was a middle-aged ex-plugger called Hubert Von Hofe. It was rumoured that he had single-handedly sold more than a million copies of a song called 'A Garland of Tears' by playing it in every whorehouse and saloon within a day's train journey of New York. He was the man who showed Monroe how to sell a song: how to shift the key or change the tempo, how to flag up the chorus and simplify the verse, how to flatter and coax, to encourage and congratulate, anything, in fact, that would convince a singer or a vaudevillian to buy the rights to perform a new song.

For Monroe, even with Von Hofe's strategy, it was rarely easy. Most of the songs he had to plug, although written by a team of in-house composers and lyricists, were pale copies of other more successful songs around. And when he complained, politely, he was always told the same thing: you want to sell a better song, you write a better song!

Monroe had written plenty of songs; they filled three boxes at his feet and several manila folders on the piano lid. Half a dozen had been published; in 1914 a song called 'Friday Moon' had been picked up by the star performer in a vaudeville house in Chicago. Unfortunately, the show had flopped and closed after only five weeks. He had framed his royalty cheque; he had earned a total of fifty-six cents. And now Von Hofe was unconvinced, he was wary, he was not taking any chances.

'Listen to this one,' Monroe would still insist. 'It's got the best verse I've ever writtten.'

Von Hofe would smile and try, unsuccessfully, to hide the disappointment in his face. Had the kid learned nothing? Verses didn't matter; no one cared about the verses. A good song, he had told him more than once, was all about the chorus, a chorus that people could sing along to, a chorus they could hum on the trolleycar, a perfect alchemy of phrase and melody that you only needed to hear once or twice before you remembered it for ever.

'It's very pretty, Simonov,' Von Hofe would always tell him. 'But is it the kind of song they'll be singing round the parlour piano in Poughkeepsie? Could you imagine the lady in the post office humming your tune in Pittsburgh? What about factory workers on their lunch break in Portland? I'm sorry, I just don't see it. You got to lighten up a bit. Relax.'

That morning as his coffee cooled and he sorted through Universal's back catalogue, there was a knock on the glass door of his cubicle. A dark shape, a blot, had appeared in the dimpled surface.

'Come in,' he shouted.

'Don't mind if I do!'

Rolly Tipple, according to just about anyone you asked, was a second-generation Russian immigrant and third-rate vaudeville performer. He invariably played a Blackface or a Bowery Tough but could fill in as an Irish or Jew when he felt his act was getting stale. He had just come back from the 'Death Trail,' a tour of small Midwestern towns, and stage make-up, a shimmering of pearl powder and a lick of burned cork were still visible in the wrinkles around his eyes and the deep lines that framed his mouth like a pair of brackets.

'Good to see you, Rolly,' Monroe said. 'You're looking well.'

'Can't say the same for you, Monroe, my boy,' he yelled. 'What's the matter? You lovesick or what!'

Rolly laughed, a big hollow laugh, which came from his throat and stopped as abruptly as it began. Monroe smiled politely. Rolly Tipple always said this. To everyone he met. It had never been funny.

'This a new song?' he said and grabbed the copy of 'My Little Girl' that lay on top of the piano.

'Sure,' said Monroe. 'By all means. Take a look at it.'

Rolly started to read.

> *My little girl you know I love you,*
> *And I long for you each day,*
> *My little girl I'm dreaming of you,*
> *Tho' you're many miles away.*

'I like it,' he said. 'Let's hear it.'

Rolly Tipple had been Monroe's neighbour for a short time on Joralemon Street before he had found brief and fleeting fame in a Big Time review in Flatbush and moved with his wife and five children up the street to Brooklyn Heights proper, to Pierrepont Street. The success didn't last, the show was axed, and he had to move again, this time to a rooming house near the Gowanus Canal. 'Snakes and ladders,' he used to say. 'Flippin' snakes and ladders.'

Monroe started to play the song. He knew he was no singer but he interpreted the music in front of him with what Von Hofe called 'a unique sense of musicality'. His voice was soft but melodic; he didn't have the projection of some of those who came to see him but he could carry a tune. Rolly tried to follow the melody but his voice cracked and broke. He was a belter; he could yell a song, as long as it was simple, but this one was way beyond his range.

'How about something else?' Monroe suggested when the last chord had faded. 'Something a little—'

'You want to give me last year's hits?' Tipple interjected. 'Nah, nobody wants to hear that stuff any more.'

Tipple sank into the only other chair. He seemed to have suddenly lost about a third of his body weight. The long days on the Death Trail had clearly aged him.

'I can learn it at home,' he said. 'Say, Monroe, ma boy. Can I have a copy on the house? I'm a little short at the moment.'

'I'm sorry, Rolly,' Monroe said. 'If it was up to me . . . but I can't. Company policy.'

New songs, at least those that were expected to be hits, were only offered for free to big Broadway names. If Fanny Brice wanted to sing your song, in a matter of weeks the whole of the city, the whole of the state, the whole of America would be singing it and the company would sell a million copies. Everyone else had to pay.

Rolly sighed and cracked his knuckles. And then his face suddenly illuminated; an idea had occurred to him.

'Last time you said you had written a couple of tunes that I could have for free,' he said. 'You got anything new I could use?'

Monroe's fingers were already resting on the piano keys. In his head he could hear the opening chord of the song he had written that morning.

'Sure,' he said.

'Let's hear it then,' said Rolly and rubbed his eyes with his fists.

Monroe's pulse began to race. His palms grew damp. His fingers flexed. The melody was already visible in the smallest twitch of his fingers; all he had to do was play that opening G. This is for you, Suzette, he thought, wherever you are.

'You're right,' said Rolly. 'Forget it.'

The vaudeville performer had taken his hesitation as reluctance and before he had even played a single note, Rolly Tipple had risen to his feet and had started to pace back and forth between the window and his chair.

'I'm getting desperate,' he said. 'Been doing the same act for two years now. I need a break, I need a sure-fire hit. Or else I might as well get the wife to pull the trigger and put me out of my misery.'

Monroe dropped his hands into his lap. 'How is the wife?' he asked. 'And the kids?'

Tipple blinked. 'Thinking of trying them out on amateur night at Keeney's,' he said. 'Make a little loose change. Heck knows we need it.' Rolly leaned back against the radiator and rubbed his face with both hands. 'You sure you couldn't spare a copy of that song?' he asked.

Monroe glanced towards the door instinctively. And then he pulled out a copy of 'My Little Girl' from a manila envelope and handed it to him. 'You didn't get it from me,' he said softly. 'Understand?'

'My lips are sealed. Much appreciated,' Rolly replied as he folded it up and put it in his pocket. 'Been down to the Russian Club recently?'

'No,' Monroe answered. 'Not for months. You?'

The Russian Club was a two-storey brownstone on Hester Street on the Lower East Side. It was a place where Russian was spoken and tea with jam was served. Monroe usually avoided it.

'Actually,' Rolly said, 'I've taken on a few shifts, just until I get another break. Come down and let me buy you a drink. But you better make it quick because with this I'll be back on my feet in no time.'

'I'm sure you will,' Monroe said. 'They still have that piano down there?'

'Still there,' Rolly said. 'But I don't think they like our kind of music. It's way too happy.' And he laughed, a big round laugh that left no room for dissent, for clarification, for comment. 'You'll be seeing me, buddy,' he said. 'But not if I see you first. Time to shuffle off to Buffalo.'

A master of the quick exit, with one step he was away, slamming the door so hard behind him that the glass shivered in its frame and almost shattered.

'See you later, Rolly,' said Monroe. But he was already gone.

That morning, Monroe played twenty or thirty different songs, mainly to chorus ladies and amateurs. And while his fingers mashed out major chords and his voice crooned its way through a series of clichés, there was another melody, another song, that he could not get out of his head.

2

While hair can be dyed, eyes blackened and noses powdered, a woman's mouth, thought Inez Kennedy, a woman's mouth always betrays the truth eventually. She sat on the bottom deck of a tramcar as it stop-started its way down Madison Avenue, and examined the faces of the women who sat on the opposite bench. The first, a woman of about fifty, had pretty blue eyes and a hat with a red ribbon on it, but her mouth was narrow and set into a permanent curve of disapproval. Philandering husband, Inez considered, or gallivanting son, both of them womanizers or gamblers or opium smokers. The woman beside her filled out the crossword, and while the rest of her face was in a small way triumphant, her mouth spoke of a life of disappointment. Jilted lover, thought Inez, abandoned wife, or, worse, the never-noticed wallflower. Inez ran her finger over her own mouth. What would hers say in thirty years' time? What secrets would it inadvertently share with the world? And then she noticed that the disapproving woman's gaze was now fixed on her. She glanced down. There was a large hole in her silk stocking just above the ankle.

'Thirty-Seventh Street,' shouted the conductor.

'Lordy,' Inez said under her breath. 'Almost missed it!'

She stepped off the tramcar on to the wide pavement and hurried through the main doors of the Lord and Taylor Department Store.

'Good morning,' said the doorman.

'Morning,' echoed Inez as she ran across the shop floor, turning right at the handbag counter, heading past kid gloves and French cosmetics to a waiting lift whose doors were just about to close.

'Going up?' she asked the lift attendant.

'Going down to the stockrooms,' he replied. 'Won't be more than a minute or two.'

'Then I'll take the stairs,' she said. 'I'm running a little late.'

Inez ran up the wide shallow carpeted stairs two at a time, only pausing to catch her breath once. On the sixth floor, right next to the stairs, was a pneumatic postal system terminal. Fashioned out of solid brass and covered in decorative scrolling, it had two openings, one for sending and one for receiving canisters. Every sale in the department store was dealt with by the cashiers in the basement. Cash and sales receipts were sent back and forth in canisters through a vast set of pipes using compressed air. This terminal, however, had never been connected to the circuit; when you held your hand underneath one of the openings there was no faint breath of cold air on your palm. And yet the foot pump seemed to work. Inez pressed it and a canister fell out. Inside was a spare stocking that she kept there for emergencies.

A row of outfits was waiting for her in the staff room of Ladies' Ready-Made Suits and Occasional Wear: hobble skirts and dinner dresses, tailored suits and fitted coats, fur hats and felt bonnets in sombre shades of blue and brown and grey. There were layers and layers, however, to be put on first: corset, camisole, underslip, dress and over-dress. Marion, the other part-time model, had hung her street clothes on a hanger and was already dressed in her first outfit. She was sitting on a chair right next to the radiator engrossed in a movie magazine.

'Good morning?' she said without looking up.

'Not really, at least not so far,' Inez replied. 'My, how can you see to read? It's so dark in here!'

A huge American flag, a hundred feet wide, had been hung from the roof a few weeks earlier and covered an entire side of the department store. The window of the staff room was now behind a white star on its blue background.

'You get used to it,' said Marion. 'Just like you get used to this place, this job, eventually.'

'But I don't intend . . .' Inez started to say. But her words were drowned out by the rush and whistle of compressed air, as a canister sped through the pipes on the roof above their heads to the finance office.

'To stay beyond summer . . .' said Marion, completing her sentence. 'That's what you always say. And it's already November.'

'I was going to say Christmas.'

Marion raised her eyebrows and flicked rapidly through the magazine before slapping it on the floor.

'If only Douglas Fairbanks would come and take us away from all this,' she sighed.

'It could happen,' Inez remarked as she changed her stocking. 'You never know.'

'Sure it will,' said Marion. 'You'd better hurry. There's a full house this morning.'

Hidden from the shop floor by a heavy velvet curtain was the Salon, a spacious room lit with three electric chandeliers. It was decorated, supposedly, to look like the Palace of Versailles in France. As well as a dozen pale blue velvet-upholstered chairs, there were a couple of chaises-longues and several ornate occasional tables all liberally gilded. Inez guessed that a dozen ladies already sat waiting. Most of them were thick-set wives from Long Island or New Jersey or trussed-up spinsters who lived in the new apartment blocks on the Upper West Side. Did they have nothing else to do, she always wondered, nowhere else to go, nothing else to think about than what they would wear to lunch?

'Here you are, at last,' the manageress said as she came through the curtain. 'We were about to send out a search party.'

'My alarm,' Inez explained. 'Didn't ring.'

'Didn't ring?' she echoed.

But it was more of a chastisement than a question. Hortense was from Paris, and every clipped word that came out of her mouth was tinged with dismay, even when she might have been intending to convey the opposite. Inez had almost finished buttoning up her undergarments and so Hortense helped her slip on the first outfit, a dinner dress of pale pink silk crepe with five detachable bows.

'Late night, Inez?'

'No,' she said. 'I've been as good as gold all week.'

It wasn't a lie. She had been in bed at ten. But although the lights were off and the window opened, she had been unable to fall asleep, unable to slow and calm the whirr and buzz inside her head, and when her alarm clock rang she had already been wide awake for several hours. Of course it was then that she finally fell into a deep sleep, and when she woke with a start half an hour later she felt even more tired, more worn out, more tearful than when she hadn't slept at all. She checked her face in the full-length mirror as Hortense fussed with her hem; there were dark circles beneath her eyes and a single red bloom on her left cheek. She tried to smooth down her hair but even though she had already spent ten minutes pinning it back, it still looked as if she had just climbed out of bed.

'Maybe I should wear something on my head?'

The manageress nodded but didn't even glance up. 'I think that would be advisable on this occasion.' Hortense produced a huge hat with a feather from a box and handed it to her. 'That should do it,' she said.

Inez pulled it on and stared at herself in the mirror. Apart from looking tired, her face looked the same as usual, didn't it? Now she wasn't so sure. Her mouth, was there something different about the line of her mouth? If she looked hard enough she was sure she could see the tiny creases of misfortune beginning to form. She blinked twice and her eyes began to fill. He had seemed so decent, so kind, so trustworthy. How could she have been so wrong about him? And now she was in a predicament that was worse than awful: it was catastrophic.

'Are you all right, Inez?' asked Hortense.

'I'm fine!' she replied. 'Absolutely!'

Hortense made her entrance into the Salon with the least amount of elegant fuss. The show was about to begin. Just don't, Inez told herself as she dabbed her eyes with a handkerchief, just don't think about him, not here, not now. After she had applied some fresh powder and a little rouge, she took a deep breath, closed her eyes and tried to compose herself.

'In Paris, despite the conflict,' Hortense was saying, 'the look for autumn and winter is a little fuller than last year. Hems are rising

21

and, of course, the hobble skirt and the war crinoline are still with us. But this season we have something quite new, the dropped shoulder. And so, without further ado, Inez, Marion, do come through and meet our guests.'

Inez pulled back the curtain and smiled her closed-mouth smile. Then she began to walk back and forth on the thick carpet, turning this way and that, as Hortense had taught her, to show the flare of the dress and the slip of ivory lining. The ladies' eyes, however, were impassive. They ran down her length from the hat to the shoes without actually seeming to see her. To them, she was nothing more than a jar of pickles or a slice of shop-bought pound cake.

The streets of New York City were not unlike the carpeted interior of the Salon. No matter what was happening in the rest of the world, the ladies who strolled down Fifth Avenue or around Lexington on the Upper East Side changed their outfits depending on the weather, the season or the time of day. And so Inez modelled outfits for every occasion: day dresses, evening ensembles, walking suits, afternoon jackets, opera coats, tango shoes and elaborate headdresses, in serge and satin, with ostrich-feather, ribbon or beaded trim. They all had one thing in common, however: they were clothes to be noticed in, with huge feathers or massive bows, or multiple pleats and complicated drapes.

Despite the fact that they were fussy and rigidly tailored, Inez knew that the clothes she modelled looked good on her. She carried them off because she wore them so carelessly. The customers, the ladies spending their husbands' salaries or their huge family inheritance, were rarely so lucky; the clothes, the frills, the bows and the ribbons, when they finally tried them on, made them look not so much dressed-up as gift-wrapped.

'What do you think?' they would ask tentatively, aware that they were not as young or as pretty as the girl who had modelled them.

'Perfect,' Hortense would usually respond. 'So uniquely you.'

That was all they needed: the suggestion of originality rather than beauty, the measured reassurance and the tactful – but extremely necessary – flattery, and out would come the soft leather wallets, a sale would be recorded and a not inconsiderable amount of money would shoot off in a canister never to be seen again. It was almost too easy.

Even if she could afford them, Inez would never wear any of those clothes, not with their ruffles and flowers and buckles, their hobbles and wires. Although she bought her generously staff-discounted clothes from a cheaper range at Lord and Taylor's, she took up her dress hems until they were a good eight inches shorter.

'Immodest,' observed Hortense.

'Patriotic,' she would retort. 'Less cloth, you see.'

'Plus ça change,' Hortense replied with a small shrug.

That morning, Inez had glanced through a side window and noticed a single red leaf dancing in the air above Thirty-Eighth Street. It might be, she considered, the last one of the year. The trees on Bryant Park that had worn their autumn colours so gloriously had become skeletal. Time was passing. It had been almost two months since she had last seen him. How quickly, she considered, how rapidly his face had become blurred in her memory.

'A pure beaver collar,' Hortense was saying. 'Lined with moiré silk from Paris. Luxurious but not overstated, and very reasonable, considering. Thank you, Inez.'

Before she bowed her head and slipped behind the curtain, Inez glanced up from beneath the brim of her hat and inadvertently caught the eye of a woman in the front row. The woman had small hands and wore a dark green dress and over-jacket that were simple yet artfully cut from expensive cloth: she had not bought her clothes from Lord and Taylor's, that was obvious. In the overheated, over-dressed confines of the Salon, the woman looked as out of place as Inez always felt.

'We hope to see you again soon, Madame Denisova,' Inez heard Hortense call out. She glanced through a gap in the curtain; the woman from the front row was heading for the lift. She turned, inclined her head, but she did not answer.

Hortense talked about the new customer as they sipped a cup of mid-morning tea in the staff room. She had read about her in the newspaper; she was a Russian on a tour of America preaching women's rights.

'She obviously believes in a woman's right to shop,' Marion quipped.

Hortense ignored the remark. Later that day, the Russian would send a single order by courier, for Inez' first outfit, without the detachable bows.

'Still seeing your Russian?' Marion asked.

Inez started. She had forgotten she had told Marion about him. And she had forgotten too that that was what she had called him at first, *the Russian*, as if he were a brand of cigarettes.

'That's all ancient history,' she said. 'Long gone . . .'

'Shame,' Marion said. 'He sounded like a bit of fun. Didn't you find him on Tin Pan Alley playing songs on a clapped-out piano?'

'Did I?' she said vaguely. 'I can't honestly remember.'

'I remember,' Marion said. 'You went with your friend Meg and pretended that you were both vaudeville performers from out of town. Didn't you both put on ridiculous accents? Didn't you say you came from . . . where was it?'

'Halifax,' replied Inez. 'Halifax, Nova Scotia.'

'That's it,' she said. 'That was it.'

And then it all came back, just as vividly as if it had happened only yesterday.

Mr Simonov, as he had introduced himself, had invited her to sit down, told her he had a song that would be perfect for her and had started to play. Inez had been expecting someone middle-aged, someone who used too much pomade, someone slightly shabby. Her eyes fell on his hands, however, and the way they moved and she had to admit that he was none of those things. Apart from the fact that he was around her own age, he had the high, wide cheekbones and plump lips, the clear eyes and open expression of a Greek statue she had once seen in the Metropolitan Museum.

'Well?' he had asked. 'What do you think?'

And she had simply nodded because she knew that if she opened her mouth just a fraction of an inch her voice might betray her.

'I'll play it again,' he suggested. 'Just so you can familiarize yourself.'

And so he had played it once, twice, three times while she had tried to sing it until his boss had come in and told him he had a 'real important' client waiting and he had been obliged to stop. But although she tried to ignore it, it was clear that she was as reluctant to leave as he was to let her, and when he had touched her sleeve and asked if she would care to meet him for an egg-flip that evening, her heart jumped in her chest and her face began to blush.

'Why shuu-er, Mr Simonov,' she answered before she could stop herself.

He held out his hand for her to shake. 'You can call me Monroe,' he said.

She was still a little flustered when she met Meg in the foyer.

'Come on,' Inez had said, taking her arm. 'Let's go.'

'But we've still got to go to Remick's,' said Meg.

'Not today,' she replied. 'I've got a headache.'

Inez wasn't going to meet the song-plugger or even tell Meg he'd asked. He must, she decided, invite girls out all the time. He would probably not show up or expect her to buy him a drink or spend the entire evening talking about all the famous people he had met; he'd no doubt be a bore or a flirt or a cheapskate or a flake.

And so she walked all the way home to her residence hotel, on Eighty-Ninth Street, fully resolved to spend the night with a book. But the room was so airless and the book so dull that she suddenly changed her mind. It was only an egg-flip. What harm could an egg-flip do? Maybe he could help her with her career, introduce her to a few of the right people and let her know of some openings.

Without letting herself think it over again, she changed her blouse and fixed her hair and took a downtown train to the diner on Broadway that she had suggested because she knew that no one she knew would ever dream of setting foot in there.

Inez was descended from an Irish trader who'd made his fortune in furs and then lost most of it in gambling dens and whorehouses. On one of his highs, he married a French woman and over the next few increasingly poverty-stricken years he produced seven sons and three daughters. His sons moved into agricultural machinery, which was considered a much more stable profession, but they made all the same mistakes, gambling on new ideas and squandering their capital on 'entertaining'. Although in several generations the family had managed to lose and regain their fortune more than once, by the time Inez was born they had lived on Jefferson Avenue, Detroit, for forty years, and had forged a certain hard-won respectability.

Inez Kennedy – that was her real name; Suzette Kinross slipped out of her mouth from nowhere – was lined up for far greater things than dancing on a shabby vaudeville stage or modelling ladies wear in a department store; she was the sole and only heir of the Kennedy and Son All Purpose Tractor fortune. Her father had always dreamed that one day he would launch his daughter into New York society with a lavish dinner dance at Sherry's Ballroom on East Forty-Fourth and Fifth. That was until he had found out what they charged. Her mother had more realistic expectations and suggested an education at an eastern college might introduce her to the right sort of people and coach her in the etiquette of conversation.

Her mother's family had been schoolteachers whose parents had both emigrated from the same small village in Normandy. They were poor, religious and eternally grateful that their only offspring had married a Detroit Kennedy. It didn't matter that the two families had nothing in common; they read up on horse-drawn harvesters, cream-separators and twine binders and brought them up in conversation long after it was clear that their new in-laws had no interest in them either. And when they died, within a year of each other, they were buried within the Kennedy plot, by the back wall, in the shadow of the large marble angel that was poised for eternal flight above the family tomb.

All through her infancy and childhood, her mother had tried not to 'coddle' Inez. She had lost two sons as infants to diphtheria and measles, illnesses that her husband implied were caught due to over-mothering. The fact that their third and only surviving child, a girl, had shaken off any disease that she had caught with barely a sneeze, and certainly with the minimum of cosseting and bed-rest, only proved his point. Inez, he liked to say, was a true Kennedy: hardy, resilient, her body coursing with the red, red blood of the pioneer.

Inez's childhood, therefore, had been lonely, her mother distant as if unsure whether to risk her affection on a child who might go the same way as the others. And yet Inez had been given everything a child could wish for: boxes of toys, a fully furnished doll's house, a Shetland pony, lessons in piano and horse riding and dancing. But she was soon bored by the dolls and clockwork trains, the pony was a biter, and the piano teacher informed her father that he was wasting his money. The only thing she stuck with was dancing. It was here, in the mirrored studios of a teacher who claimed she had once danced on the stage of the Mariinsky Theatre in St Petersburg, that she could imagine herself as something other than a miserable little rich girl with nothing in front of her but a miserable marriage to a man whose only quality measurable to her father would be the size of his bank balance.

'Why did you marry Daddy?' she once asked her mother when she was too young to know any better.

'Because he asked me,' replied her mother.

'But did you love him?'

'You have to follow the path laid out for you,' her mother had retorted. 'That is what women do. And anyway he gives both you and me everything we could ever want.'

It was only when she reached New York that Inez realized that her mother had been mistaken. Despite the fact that he had a small summerhouse on Lake St Clair and had been granted membership of a number of exclusive country clubs, her father's wealth and status were nothing special in the east. But it wasn't just a matter of money. 'I want it; it's mine,' was one of her father's favourite phrases but Inez soon worked out that it didn't matter how much money he had, he still would never be able to rent a house in August on the beach at Chatham on Cape Cod, or procure an invitation to an open house party in a mansion on Long Island.

These privileges and casual entitlements were still the preserve of people to whom money had no real value: those families whose ancestors had come over in the *Mayflower* or shortly after; who before the war had spent every summer in Europe and the winter season in a Manhattan townhouse; who married each other to make sure none of their wealth was dissipated because they were so wealthy that they could guarantee substantial incomes for their children and their children's children whatever the rest of the world chose to do.

No, although he must have known that the chances of Inez bagging a Vanderbilt were slight, her father still expected her to marry profitably, to get her hands on some old money in the form of a well-bred husband. He was, predictably enough, a snob. The Civil War, in his eyes, had been lost. America was year by year being diluted, polluted, impregnated. He loathed Italians, he detested Greeks, he couldn't stand the Jews and he even disliked his own, the confounded Irish, as he called them. The irony, of course, was that although Inez's great-great-grandfather had arrived in America scrub-poor and physically stunted by malnutrition, over the generations the Kennedys had started to look like aristocrats. Inez was elegant and narrow-boned, long-necked and wasp-waisted; she looked genetically refined. All apart from her hair, of course, which was the colour of Bushmills Irish Whiskey.

He should have known, however, that a girl whose body ran with the red, red blood of the pioneer would put up some resistance to his plans. At fifteen she had a reputation for being 'a little loose'. She was caught in a clinch with a neighbour's boy in the back seat of a sleigh after a Christmas dance and was banned from attending any social event for the entire spring season. She didn't care, she told herself at the time. The boys of Detroit were a measly lot, snub-nosed and mouse-haired with little interest in anything other than threshing machines and sport.

A year later she had attended a charity ball at a local hotel, and after giving her mother, who had come along to act as a chaperone, the slip, was discovered in the lithe and muscular arms of a professional tango-dancer who was touring the large hotels of the Midwest in search of a patron, a wealthy mistress or both.

With the family's reputation in jeopardy, drastic action was decided upon. As soon as they could, her parents had enrolled Inez in a small private women's college in New Jersey that was known for the strictness of its regime and its emphasis on teaching the importance of chastity before marriage. To their dismay, however, Inez quit after only six months, citing the seemingly implausible reason that far from being educated, most of the girls were being groomed for a possible position as bride of one the headmistress's three as yet unmarried sons.

The college denied it; Inez was never under serious consideration. The headmistress explained that she was made 'of the wrong mettle'. Her parents should have swallowed their outrage, they should have given up their demands for a refund and realized that even though it was possibly true, for Inez it was just an excuse. She wanted to be a dancer not a wife, at least not a wife just yet. And so with her parents' reluctant permission, she moved to Manhattan to improve her 'mettle'.

Her father, scared of losing her but unwilling to encourage her, displayed another characteristic of the Midwestern wealthy: he could be extremely extravagant but usually he was judiciously parsimonious. Wary of subsidizing his precious daughter's descent into disgrace, he gave her the minimum to live on, enough to pay the rent and eat but that was all. Everything else – clothes, trips, jewellery, spending money for socializing – she had to ask for. Although he would deny it, it was an attempt to keep her close, to keep her under his influence, to keep an eye on her.

'You want to go to another ball?' he would shout down the telephone from Detroit. 'Once you get some young gentleman to take you, just give me his name, occupation and birthplace and I'll send you a cheque for a new frock.'

No wonder Inez stopped asking. No wonder she stopped calling long-distance. She would rather, she decided, wear last season's dress for the next twenty seasons to come than provide the information her father asked her for. Her silence puzzled and worried her parents – was she really so unsuccessful with men? – but her father would not concede a penny, not if she didn't ask for it. And so, faced with the prospect of never going out, or dressing up, or eating out again, Inez found a job. She was just one of a number of reasonably well-off young girls who lacked sufficient funds from their families to support them in New York and who had taken up modelling to earn a little extra pocket money while they waited for their adult lives to begin. Modelling ready-to-wear fashion was preferable to having to take a real job, as some of the less attractive girls had to, such as tutoring spoilt children or acting as companions to elderly heiresses.

And so Inez took the subway, she wore clothes that had been made in a factory, she worked, she went to auditions, she lived in a slightly tattered residence hotel for women; she was as independent as you could be without a husband, a decent income or a vote. It was to be, however, her last year in New York. After she had dropped out of school, she had taken one year, then a second and then a third year out. But despite unlimited enthusiasm, she had had no luck whatsoever in finding a position as a dancer. She had once been called back for a second audition at a small theatre in Queens but had such bad insomnia the night before that she had bottled out of it. The truth was that she found it hard to stand in a line with five other girls and perform the same moves; she baulked, she sulked, she went left when they went right. As her physical education mistress had put it more than once, she wasn't what you would call a team player. But what else could she do? She couldn't sing with any real conviction, she couldn't act; all she wanted to do was dance, preferably by herself.

In fact she'd met dozens of men that her father would have bowed down before and placed lips on boot, if only he had known, but none of them, in her opinion, was worth the effort. They were too dull, too stuck-up, too ugly. The feeling was mutual; for most of them she was too tall, too Irish, too independent. And when she danced, the older married set watched her with disdain. She was from the Midwest, they whispered, as if that explained everything.

But it wasn't so easy to hook the right kind of husband even if she'd wanted to. New York was still the place where everything happened but the war had changed the nature of that everything. With so many rumours flying around that America might be about to join the Allies, all parties, balls and extravagant weddings were deemed to be in bad taste and had been replaced by charity dances, informal teas and knitting bees. Inez had resigned herself to the fact that it was over for her in New York. She would go back to Detroit and live a life of eccentric spinsterhood, maybe starting up a children's dance school. In the time she had left she wanted to have fun, to feel free, to go to Tin Pan Alley and pretend to be someone else.

She had spotted Monroe Simonov through the window of the diner almost as soon as she had surfaced from the subway. He was sitting at the bar with an egg-flip in front of him. Did anyone actually drink that stuff? she had asked herself. As she watched he lifted his glass towards his mouth, but his hand trembled so much he placed it back on the counter again without taking a single sip. Then he ran his hand through his hair, straightened his tie and checked his watch. She was fifteen minutes late but she still hesitated at the smeared glass door of the downtown diner. Look at him again, she instructed herself. He's probably a Russian Jew. And a song-plugger for God's sake. He was bound to live in Brooklyn. A taxicab was approaching slowly down Broadway towards her, bumping over the potholes and exhaling grey exhaust. It was fifty cents a mile, it was far too expensive, but she knew she should probably hail it. My father, she told herself, wouldn't even let him through the door. She was going back to Detroit in a matter of months. Why waste her time?

'Go home, Inez,' she had accidentally said out loud.

He must have heard her voice, because he turned, he looked round and when he saw her his face broke out into such a smile that her own hands began to tremble. Then again, she had thought, my father can go to hell. She took a deep breath and pushed open the diner's stiff glass door.

'I thought you'd changed your mind,' Monroe had said.

'I did,' she replied, 'and then I changed it back again.'

He frowned at her. Her hand flew to her face and she traced the line of her mouth. What was she saying? Did that sound rude?

'Well, anyway, here I am,' she continued. 'How's the egg-flip?'

'I'm so sorry,' he said. 'Would you like one?'

'Yes. No . . .,' she answered. 'Actually I think I'm in need of something stronger.'

He was still looking at her with that questioning expression. She was suddenly nervous. What was wrong? She smoothed down her hair. She checked that her dress was still buttoned demurely. And then she remembered. She was supposed to be from Nova Scotia.

'I shhuuuar am,' she added.

'That's the first thing I noticed about you, Suzette,' he said. 'I just love the way you talk.'

'You love it?' she said.

'I do, I love it,' he whispered back.

That was how it had started, in the early summer when everyone was leaving town, when dark-skinned boys dived into the river from the piers of the Lower East Side and the girls who worked in the factories in the Garment District sat out their tea break on the fire escapes, their dresses as bright as flags.

'Let's go somewhere else,' he had said.

'What about your drink?' she had asked.

'Actually,' he whispered, 'I don't know how anyone can drink the stuff.'

The evening was warm and the heat shimmered off the city streets like lengths of silk. And when he had leaned over and some-what audaciously kissed her cheek as they walked to another little place he knew, she had let him. It was, she had thought then, without guile, without consequence, a kiss as weightless and light as the breeze that blew up in gusts from the Buttermilk Channel.

It grew dark just before Inez's lunch break. The sky closed in and then the rain started, falling so heavily that the great glass dome above the restaurant on the eleventh floor reverberated with the barrage of a million drops. In the staff room, the American flag slapped the window as it strained on its ropes. A draught ruffled the feathers and blinked the sequins of a rack of evening dresses that Hortense had chosen for the afternoon.

'Thirty minutes, girls,' she told them. 'And try to keep out of the rain.'

'You coming to the staff canteeen?' Marion asked.

'I need some air,' Inez answered. 'I think I'll go out and grab something from the deli round the corner.'

A newspaper boy was standing beneath a dripping umbrella. He took her nickel and handed her the *New York Times*. The British had won the Battle of the Somme, one headline read, but there had been more than one million casualties. How many? The number was unimaginable. She turned the page. Thanksgiving plans take their usual course, read another headline. Turkey and fixings will be served in spite of rising prices. Even though Woodrow Wilson had been re-elected in the recent presidential election with the slogan, 'He kept us out of war', the conflict on the other side of the Atlantic was making everybody nervous. Although the population tried to carry on as normal, it was always there, that element of something outside your control, that sense of jeopardy just below the surface. And it manifested itself in a kind of universal madness, a voluntary blindness to the presentation of what looked like insanity on a huge scale. No wonder she had been impulsive, no wonder she had let herself be swept away, no wonder she had let everything grow until it was out of hand; nothing felt real any more.

As another deluge began and Inez sheltered under a shop canopy, she remembered the time they had taken the train out to Amagansett on Long Island. As the sun beat down on the sea and the salty air baked, they had lain out together on a blanket and eaten bagels and drunk beer until the sea wind and the scorching heat and the cold beer had flushed their cheeks and made them reckless. And so they dived in and swam out as far as they dared and then they looked back at the distant lip of beach and the great blue sky above.

'Would you keep swimming with me,' she said, 'would you keep going further and further?'

'If you wanted me to,' he replied.

'Kiss me,' she had said.

Treading water and swallowing sea, he had kissed the breath out of her. His skin was firm and smooth; his mouth was warm and charged. And round and round they span in each other's arms, oblivious to the dark inky depths that slowly engulfed them. It was he who pulled away, it was he who dragged her up for air, and it was he who pointed out that the strength of the undertow had taken them much further out than was safe.

'Race you back, then,' she had said.

Later, when he had spread out on the hot sand, she had danced herself dry, with grand jetés and pirouettes and entrechats.

'Bravo,' he had called out. 'Bravo.'

On the beach that day she had danced until she felt her body bend and stretch to its absolute limit, until she felt the current of the tide flow through her like a breath. And at that moment, as she had danced and he had watched, she felt so present in herself, so perfectly alive that she knew she had him; at that particular moment he couldn't help but love her.

From further along the beach a whistle blew, once, twice, three times. A policeman fully dressed in uniform and cap, came running along the beach towards them. 'Stop, stop dancing,' he shouted at Inez. 'Stop in the name of the law.'

At first Monroe assured her that the policeman was a vaudeville actor out to drum up an audience for a local show.

'He doesn't look as if he's fooling around,' said Inez as he approached.

'You forgot your flyers?' Monroe called out with a smile.

'You find this amusing?' the policeman said as he approached. 'Very interesting. I'll have to record that as part of the evidence.'

'I don't think he's a performer,' whispered Inez.

The policeman pulled out a notebook and demanded to know Monroe's full name, occupation and the name of his immediate superior.

'Universal Music Corporation,' the policeman repeated. 'Von Hofe sounds like a German name?'

Monroe agreed that his boss did have a German name.

'Just as I thought. Headquarters will have to know about this. And about what I caught your girlfriend here doing.'

'About what I was doing?' she said. 'What was I doing? I was only dancing.'

'It's all right,' Monroe had said. 'I'll deal with this.'

'Since when was dancing a crime?' she interjected.

'Signalling, more like.'

The policeman started to write. He was red-faced underneath cap. A trickle of sweat dripped from his forehead and splashed on to his notebook, blurring the words he had just written.

Inez felt the laughter welling up inside her. She bit her lip and cleared her throat as she struggled to keep a straight face. 'To whom would I be signalling?' she asked.

'To German U-boats,' he replied. 'You know what they did to the *Lusitania*. For all I know, you both might be German spies.'

'I'm not a spy,' Monroe had replied. 'I'm a song-plugger.'

Inez had loved him at that moment, as the wind whipped his dark hair into his grey eyes and the salt began to crystallize on his skin. Before he lost his temper.

'For a German,' the policeman muttered.

'Just what are you trying to say?' Monroe retaliated, his voice rising in pitch.

'And the young lady?' the policeman went on. 'Is she German?'

'My girlfriend hails from Nova Scotia,' Monroe replied. 'She's a speciality dancer at Ziegfeld Follies. Her name is Suzette Kinross.'

'That's what she told you,' the policeman replied. 'For all you know not a single word of it might actually be true.'

Inez's face suddenly blazed up. Monroe, thankfully, didn't notice.

'What are you saying? That my girlfriend is a liar?'

'Monroe,' she said, 'calm down.'

'Well, are you?' he asked Inez.

There was a fraction of a second when she couldn't meet his eye.

'No!' she retaliated.

'I think I'll need to bring you both in for further questioning,' said the policeman.

'Bring us in? What have we done?'

Monroe's voice was louder now. In fact, he was practically shouting. His fist was clenching. His face was growing flushed.

'Let's start with espionage!' the policeman said.

There was a split second when Inez was certain that Monroe was going to punch the policeman. His chest was heaving, his mouth was clamped shut and his knuckles had turned white.

, she said, stepping into the space between
r hand on the policeman's arm. 'I understand
really, I was just dancing. It won't happen again.'
her a look of such contempt that she felt as if he had
instead. The policeman's face, however, softened and
The girl was a pretty little thing, he admitted to himself.
S   n't look like a spy. Besides, he had never met a German with
red hair.

'Well, I suppose . . . this time,' said the policeman. 'In this day
and age, you can't be too careful.'

'Thank you so much. We really appreciate it. And Monroe, we
should be going. We've got a train to catch.'

Inez pulled her clothes over her bathing costume even though it
was still wet. And then she gathered up her things and walked
quickly towards the boardwalk with sand still in her shoes.

'Why did you apologize?' Monroe had said when they reached
the main road. 'Why did you just leave like that? We had the rest
of the day.'

'Because he was going to arrest us,' she replied. 'And really, I'd
rather not have to spend a night in jail.'

Neither of them said a single word while waiting for the train, or
on the long rattle back to Manhattan. As the train crossed the river
and entered the city, the sun flashed between the uneven soar
of glass and brick and the blue sky was obscured by the tangle of
tramwire and the flap of washing. And then just after the conductor
had announced that it was ten minutes to Grand Central, Monroe
shook his head and started to laugh.

'Dancing German spies,' he said. 'Hard to believe. What an
imagination. Come here.'

When he pulled her into his arms and tried to kiss her again, she
let him. His skin, his mouth, his lips all still tasted of the sea.

'Come away with me?' she whispered. 'Leave all this? Let's start
again like two new people with different names and different jobs
and things.'

'You'd like that?' he whispered back.

'Let's leave now. Let's keep going, west maybe? We can get our bags and catch a night train somewhere. Who knows where we'd be tomorrow.'

Monroe gently kissed her forehead. 'I can't go anywhere today, honey,' he had said. 'I got a job; I have to work.'

She pulled back and examined his face. 'Is that all you want? Surely you want more, more than that?' He let her go and stared hard back at her.

'Give a guy a chance, why don't you? What are you running away from anyway? Look at you, you're Suzette Kinross, a speciality dancer at Ziegfeld's, all the way from Nova Scotia. Why on earth would you want to give all that up?'

And she had shrugged and said, 'S'pose so,' because he was looking at her in that way, a way that suggested that he was in love with a girl, even though he didn't know that it was a girl who didn't actually exist.

At first he had asked her for tickets, then he had begged to come to rehearsals and then he had raved and ranted and threatened just to turn up at Ziegfeld's regardless, goddam it. Why, he whispered as he held her in his arms much later, didn't she want to let him watch her dance? Was she ashamed of him? Didn't she love him?

And so she had told him another lie, a white lie, a lie to cover up the first one, a lie that slipped out of her mouth so easily that she almost believed it too. The fact that when she had told him, he had turned his back on her and played Mozart, made her even more certain, at the time, that it was the right thing to do. But as she had walked back along Joralemon Street towards the subway, she began to sob so hard and so breathlessly despite herself, that a passer-by made her sit down on the wide shallow steps of the Church of the Pilgrim until she recovered her composure.

It took three weeks before her first thoughts every morning weren't of him. It took a month before she could stop mapping out her day in line with his. It took five weeks before she could safely say that the weight of it all, the sadness that had settled in her chest like a cold, had finally begun to lift. It took her six weeks before she realized that she hadn't bled for over a month. She was late, so late that she immediately suspected the worst. A doctor to whom she had given another name confirmed it. Instead of feeling devastated, however, she felt a rush of relief. She would see him again, she would come clean about who she was. Her father would be furious. But the world was changing, she would tell him, and they would all just have to change with it.

At her insistence her friend Meg had gone down to the music publisher's and given Monroe her note.

'My plans changed. I must see you on a matter of some urgency,' it read. 'Meet me at the diner tonight at 6 p.m. sharp, Suzette.'

Maybe he had guessed what the 'matter of some urgency' was. Or maybe he'd met someone else. Or maybe she'd just worn off him, like scent on a wrist. Had he even, she asked herself, received the message at all? She'd waited for an hour but he hadn't shown up. And when she had asked Meg later that night how he reacted when she'd handed over the note, Meg had snapped back that he had taken it, read it and then thrown it in the bin without a word. Inez was astounded.

'He did that?' she had said. 'Are you sure you gave it to the right man? To Monroe Simonov? The song-plugger?'

'Sure I'm sure,' Meg had answered. 'The Russian Jew from Brooklyn. Good-looking, if you like that sort of thing. You had your fun and now it's over. He's doing you a favour, believe me.'

And they'd fought and fallen out and stopped speaking. But Meg didn't know. No one knew.

In Lord and Taylor's at closing time, Inez pulled on her hat and took the lift down to the ground floor. White sheets had been pulled across the glass cases that contained the gloves, the cravats and the gentlemen's hats. All the jewellery had been taken out of the display cabinets and locked up in safety deposit boxes. A couple of customers dawdled their way to the exit clutching parcels but the tills had all been counted and they couldn't have actually bought anything even if they had wanted to. The main door was propped open to let air from the cooling evening circulate and a row of taxicabs was lined up on the kerb.

As she headed through the wide swing doors, the doorman started to whistle a song as he polished the brass finger plates. Inez knew the tune but couldn't place it.

'What is that?' she asked him.

He smiled. 'You like it? 'My little girl I'm dreaming of you,' he sang. 'Tho' you're many miles away . . .' You must know that song, everybody's been singing it.'

'Yes,' she admitted. She did know the song, after all.

3

The meeting-house of the Women's Institute was a dilapidated brick building in a back street to the west of Greenwich Village. Anna Denisova stepped out of a cab and felt her heels sink into several inches of mud. Half a dozen streets away, on Fifth Avenue, the city looked as if it had been built to last for ever, but here it seemed that only the churches and seminaries had been built with any optimism that they would still be standing in ten years' time. Apart from the lack of street lighting, cobblestones were missing and had not been replaced, leaving gaping holes, the gutters were choked with fallen leaves, and most of the wooden-framed houses that faced the meeting-house were on the lean to one side or the other.

It was growing dark but the door of the meeting-house had been blown open and the lights from inside streamed down the steps. No matter, whatever the city in America, Anna had come to realize, the halls all smelled the same, of charitable acts and commiseration, of undrinkable coffee and stale cake. This one was no different. Two women, one of about nineteen and another of fifty, were sitting at a piano in the corner, peering at a piece of sheet music. The elder one placed her hands on the keys and started to play. The younger one began to sing, 'I know a millionnaire . . .'

The meeting-house door swung shut with a bang and they both turned. By the look in their eyes Anna could tell immediately that she was not quite what they were expecting.

'Am I too early?' she asked. 'You are expecting me?'

'Of course! You must be Madame Denisova,' said the older woman. 'Come in and take off your things.' She stood up, closed the piano lid and wiped her hands on her shapeless dress of muted grey.

'Please, call me Anna,' she replied, taking off her hat. 'Don't stop playing. What is the song?'

'You like it?' said the younger woman. 'It's called 'When I Leave the World Behind'.'

'A sad song then . . .'

'I suppose.' The younger woman blushed.

'So, how many are you expecting?'

'Well,' she said, 'I must have given out over a hundred leaflets. It's our last big event before the Christmas Fair.'

'I expect it will be standing room only,' the older woman clarified. 'We're all very excited to host something of this calibre.'

Anna bowed her head and then politely turned down an offer of coffee and home-made fruitcake.

Although it was clear that she didn't need to watch her weight, Anna Denisova's age was less easy to define. She had a youthful figure that could have fairly been judged as somewhere between twenty and thirty. And yet her pale grey eyes were loaded with the acumen of an older woman. In fact, she was thirty-seven. Six years earlier, she had divorced her husband, an adviser to the tsar, and moved from the provinces back to the capital. She had taken her only child, a boy named Kima, with her, and joined the Social Revolutionaries.

St Petersburg in 1910 was a city full of radicals and intellectuals, anarchists and revolutionaries. In the years following the revolution of 1905, in parks and municipal gardens, in shady doorways beside the Fontanka Canal or in the café at the Finland Station, ideas were sounded and plots hatched. There were dozens of factions all with slightly different aims, objectives and methods. As well as Social Revolutionaries, there were the Social Democrats, the Bolsheviks, the Mensheviks, the Ultimatists, and the Maximalists. Some openly proposed the murder of the tsar, or, if that proved to be too difficult, government ministers, the heads of prisons, the police force or directors of large industries. Others organized strikes and peaceful demonstrations demanding democracy, better working conditions and the protection and emancipation of women. All agreed on one thing, however: that the Imperial Age in Russia had to end.

Anna lived in an apartment on Zagorodny Street, near the Church of St Vladimir. It had two doors, a main entrance and a secret exit to the back stairs that was hidden behind a curtain. At night, well after the inns, the theatres and the large hotels on the Nevksy Prospekt had closed their doors, the rooms would be full of people talking, arguing, smoking and drinking. Although there were rumoured to be dozens of police informers operating in the city, they all felt safe, they told each other at the time, among friends. Until, that is, they heard the ominous sound of confident footfalls in the darkened street outside, and one by one the guests downed their vodka and fled through the curtain.

It was here that Anna met a young man called Pokolitov. Ten years her junior and straight from the rye fields of Georgia, Tadeus Pokolitov had a blazing temper and small, intense eyes. Such was his outrage at the unfairness of the human experience in his country, at the obscene wealth of the rich and the heartbreaking poverty of the poor, that he had a premature crease, a horizontal exclamation mark scored right across his forehead.

In their group he was tolerated, he was humoured, he was sometimes teased. He was bright but uneducated, able to speak Russian as well as his native Georgian, but without a basic knowledge of the French they all spoke fluently. And when he brought his own rough country bread and beer to drink instead of the French wine and caviar that was offered, he earned the name 'Le Brouillon'.

'Why do you call me this?' he complained to Anna.

'It's a compliment,' Anna replied. 'Today, a *brouillon*, a rough draft, tomorrow, *terminé*, finished, a polished manuscript.'

'You think of me like a book?'

'Of course,' she said. 'To open your pages is to be taken to another world.'

It was one evening while she was reading to him from one of the many banned books that had been smuggled into Russia – it was in German – that she was literally taken from behind.

'Kiss me,' he said. 'Tomorrow, I may be caught.'

What he had done, however, he would not say.

A few months later, the apartment was raided by secret police and as well as the banned books, a revolver was found in Anna's wardrobe. Although she insisted it wasn't hers, she wouldn't say who it belonged to. The judge had no sympathy for heroic deeds by women who should have known better and even though she appealed for clemency, citing the care of her son as one factor to be taken into consideration, she was imprisoned for six months and then exiled to a penal colony near the Arctic Circle. Kima was sent back to live with his father. No one knew what had happened to Pokolitov; it was rumoured that he was dead, murdered while in police custody.

After two long years in Siberia, Anna had escaped with nothing but a clutch of smudged letters and a notebook of ideas and writing that she intended to publish. The journey south took several weeks and involved changing trains nine times to make sure that her trail wasn't followed. When she arrived at the apartment in Zagorodny Street, however, she had found that in her long absence her former husband had sold it.

Although Dmitri Denisov supposed that he had lost the mother of his son, not only geographically but also emotionally, he had loved her throughout her radicalization. Anna still loved her former husband too, in her own fashion. And so when she appeared at his provincial estate exhausted, malnourished but still undefeated, they embraced each other with a tenderness that neither had felt since the early days of their marriage.

Kima wept when he saw her. 'I need you,' he had said over and over. 'Stay with us.'

Anna had stayed for a week and slept, ate and played the piano. She knew that news of her escape would soon be widespread. And when it was, her former husband's estate would be the first place that the Okhranka, the secret police, would look. If they caught her, not only would Dmitri be imprisoned, but she would be taken into custody and tortured. It was far too dangerous, she told her son, to stay; she had no choice but to leave Russia and go abroad. And so Denisov bought her an international train ticket and arranged to send money every month to a Swiss bank account. She would come back, she told them both, when Russia was emancipated, and that, she assured them, would be only a matter of time. Until then she

43

would travel to Paris, to Geneva, to London, to New York, writing, lecturing, waiting.

In the flesh there was something a little too defiant in Anna Denisova's face to be labelled beautiful. But in photographs, when her features were tamed and frozen by the photographic process and you could examine the clarity of her eyes and the bloom of her cheek without fear of reprisal, it was clear she was quite lovely.

Also, Madame Denisova, as she was called on her extended lecture tour of America, was always impeccably dressed. That day she was wearing a coat of crimson-coloured Italian wool that had been made for her in Paris, and a matching hat with a large peacock feather in the brim. Her boots, although caked with the mud of a poorly maintained Manhattan street, were of the softest Italian leather; her gloves were stitched from the finest white kid. And if she cut a strange and vaguely unsettling stance among her scruffily dressed and badly turned-out peers, she was unapologetic. After she had escaped from Siberia, she had peeled off and ceremoniously burned the clothes she had been wearing for so long. Dressed in the beautiful, now ill-fitting, made-to-measure clothes that she had left behind in her former home, she had decided that she would never again compromise that sense of herself, the sense that demanded nothing less than the finest fabric, the most intricate cut and the most elegant design.

Inside the meeting hall in the East Village it was even chillier than on the street outside. The damp and cold, however, were caused by neglect rather than by climate. The paint on the walls was peeling and the bathroom tap could be heard dripping through a door that didn't quite close.

'Is there somewhere I can prepare?' Anna asked the elder of the two women.

A shaft of grimy light from a single window positioned too high in the wall to see out lit the small side room she was shown into. Pamphlets had been piled in the corners and mounds of yellowing newspapers threatened to slide all over the floor. She shivered as she sorted out her papers. The title of the talk was 'Free Love?'. Was love ever free? Although her speech attacked traditional marriage and preached in favour of relationships freely chosen and based on mutual sexual attraction, she didn't think she could ever give that much of herself again. Of course she had searched for Pokolitov, written letters, asked everyone she met for news of him but no one knew anything. He had simply disappeared. It must be true, she had decided eventually, he must be dead, murdered while under interrogation.

Since then, the only love she allowed herself to give freely and unconditionally was to Kima. She could still remember the firmness of his embrace and the sweet smell of him as he slept; she could still summon up the fullness of his lips and the silk stroke of his hair. When she had left he had been a boy. Now he was sixteen; he was almost a man. How could she have missed so much of his life? How could she have let it happen? And the ache she worked so hard to suppress, an ache of regret and sorrow and of things broken that could not be fixed, suddenly engulfed her.

When Rosa Sacchi, the younger of the two event organizers, was sent to ask the guest speaker to come through to the main hall, she found the small Russian woman sitting motionless, her brow furrowed, her fists clenched, her eyes staring through the window at the telegraph pole outside. There were tearstains, she said later, on the woman's face. And she looked smaller than before, as small, almost, as a child.

Rosa Sacchi knew the bitter taste of loss herself. Three sisters and most of her friends had perished in the Triangle Shirtwaist Factory fire five years earlier. If she hadn't been in bed with a head cold on 25 March 1911, she too would have had to jump from the ninth floor along with the other female textile workers to escape the inferno. The fire exits had been locked by the owners to prevent theft or the girls from taking breaks, and one hundred and forty-six young women and teenagers burned to death or hit the pavement on Washington Place, 'like rain', as one bystander had described it.

'Take your time,' Rosa told the Russian. 'They can wait.'

'Thank you,' said Anna Denisova. 'Maybe I will take a little coffee after all.'

It was dark when the organizers and the invited speaker left the hall and made their way towards the Village, as it was known. Rosa was going to meet her fiancé in a saloon on Bleecker Street. The older woman was heading uptown so they split up when they reached Broadway. 'Do come again,' the older woman insisted. Although she suggested otherwise, Anna thought it unlikely. The audience seemed visibly unmoved by her arguments.

'You should be preaching birth control,' one woman had shouted. 'Not free love.'

A man at the back had laughed out loud. He had walked in late, taken a seat in the back row and spent the whole talk with his chin in his hands. And then at the end he had sauntered to the front, written a cheque with a flourish and handed it to Anna.

'For the cause,' he said softly. 'Whatever it may be.'

'The Women's Institute.' she replied. 'To whom shall they pass on their thanks?'

The gentleman pulled out his card and handed it to her. 'I'd be happy to hear from them,' he said. 'Or you, for that matter.'

And then he left the hall and climbed into a large white car that was idling on the kerb.

'Do you know that man?' Anna asked Rosa.

'No. But it happens sometimes,' she replied. 'They pass by or they find a leaflet. He probably found the sound of your talk titillating. Anyway, he was far too well dressed to work for the American Protective League.'

When Anna had first arrived in America, she had spoken every night to packed houses. In every town and city people had gathered in halls and meeting-houses to discuss the end of government and how to improve working conditions for the lower classes. But the war had split the new immigrant population from the older more established communities. Agitators and radicals were now watched and their movements recorded by voluntary organizations such as the American Protective League.

There was no radical feeling on display on the streets of the Village that evening in November. Instead it was thronged with people out for the evening, with so-called 'Bohemians', who wore their hair loose, their clothes covered in paint and their index fingers stained black with ink and yellow with tobacco. Here, Anna suspected, the conflicts in other parts of the world had about the same importance as a bluebottle caught in a jam jar in the corner of their studio, faintly distracting but wholly without consequence.

Usually, Anna Denisova would have headed straight back to her faceless Midtown hotel. She would have closed the door to her room, run a deep bath and then dedicated what was left of the evening to reading. But she liked Greenwich Village – it was so unlike the rest of New York. And so they strolled down to Washington Square together and Rosa pointed out famous cafés and restaurants: the Black Cat, the Brevoort and Bertolotti's.

'All the places were Italian a few years ago,' Rosa said. 'My mother used to work in Baroni's before she was sent to the insane asylum.'

Anna frowned and wondered for a moment if she had understood the girl correctly.

'She's not mad,' Rosa explained. 'She was arrested for giving out leaflets with Margaret Sanger, the woman who opened the birth control clinic in Brooklyn. She's now in Snake Hill Asylum in New Jersey.'

'How long for?' Anna asked.

'That's a question you should put to the governor,' Rosa replied.

She led Anna to a basement bar. Here, the air was thick with smoke and laughter as Italian men joked and lit up cheroots. In a booth at the back, a meeting was taking place. In contrast to the rest of the bar, thirty men sat in silence and listened to an intense-looking man of about thirty-five, as he spelled out his discourse with an equal emphasis on every word.

'That's Faccini,' Rosa whispered. 'He's an anarchist.'

As she couldn't understand him, Anna watched him; she noticed the way his thick arms were encased in freshly laundered cotton, she took in the blue in his oiled black hair and thick moustache that shone in the lamplight, she noted the colour of his skin burned maple by the sun. And then her eyes were drawn to his hands. They were long-fingered but coarse, the skin calloused and

47

rough – manual labourer's hands. At that moment, he looked up and caught her eye. She did not look away.

Dante Faccini's hands smelled of metal, cigarettes and the eau de cologne he had splashed on his face that morning. Later, as they lay side by side in her hotel room, she held them to her face and inhaled both in turn. Outside, the blackness of the night had given way to dawn. In the hours earlier, as they had talked and walked and finally ended up in bed, she had discovered that despite so many hours holding a pickaxe or shovel, Faccini's hands had held hundreds of books. He had written dozens of articles and had even published a book, a bomb manual. And when they had run out of polemics, of histories, of compliments, they reached for each other and tried to make love as democratically as they were able.

'You awake?' he had asked her afterwards. 'Or are you still dreaming?'

She opened her eyes. His voice had startled her. She had been away from that room with its stiff white sheets and its view of a ventilation shaft, away from the naked Italian anarchist, away from the present, and back in the far north, back in Siberia, in Mezen. She had been imagining herself in the back room of the general store again, the store where she had been allowed to play the penal colony's only piano, and where she would sit and play Bach and Mozart until her fingers grew clumsy with cold.

As the music had filled the air, the notes seemed to soak into the sacks of rye flour and the fish that had been hung up to dry, drowning out the noise of the men playing cards in the room above and the scritch of the mice in the corners, and she felt sure that she would not lose herself, as one other woman had done, a writer from the suburbs of Moscow, going insane and walking out into the snow and never returning. And Anna hadn't. She had escaped that frozen place, that place of wolves and polar bears, of snow and the ice that locked the harbour in all winter. She had survived. But something of her time there had seeped into her almost invisibly, like the music into the rye, and her heart still seemed to strain, as if still listening for the first crack in the endlessly frozen sea, despite herself.

'I'm awake,' she answered. 'Where were you?'

'Mexico,' he replied.

'Mexico?' she repeated. 'Why on earth Mexico?'

'If your tsar falls,' he said slowly, staring up at the ceiling, 'and revolution comes to Russia, the Eastern Front will crumble. The Allies will be overwhelmed and the Germans will win. Therefore, America will join the war. But they only have 300,000 troops. They will have to begin drafting. The only way to avoid conscription is to leave the country. Canada is too cold for me. I will go south.'

'Do you think he will?' she asked. 'Do you think the tsar will ever fall?'

'Most certainly,' Faccini replied. 'And when he does, Mexico!'

There was a soft knock on the door.

'Are you expecting anyone?' he whispered.

Without waiting for an answer, he jumped out of bed and darted behind the curtain where his bulky figure was still perfectly visible behind the drapes. Anna pulled on her robe and answered the door. It was the bellboy holding a vast box wrapped up in pale blue tissue paper.

'You can come out now,' she said when she had closed the door. 'It's just a delivery.'

Faccini stuck his head out, his lower body still swathed in curtain. Anna was on the brink of laughter – he looked like a character from a French farce – but something in his expression as he eyed the Lord and Taylor wrapping paper made her pause.

'You like to shop?' he said.

'Yes,' she replied. 'I like to shop.'

'And you call yourself a revolutionary?'

A rush of heat came to her face. 'You think elegance a barrier to revolution?' she asked. 'Must every radical wear moth-eaten rags and worn-out boots?'

He shrugged and dropped the curtain. But his nudity, rather than being a sign of contrition, as he might have supposed, seemed to her a statement of active hostility. She suddenly decided that she would never see him again like this; if their paths ever crossed accidentally, she would avert her eyes and find an excuse to remove herself immediately from his company.

'I think you better leave now,' she said. 'I have work to do.' She turned and did not look at him. Behind, she heard him gather up his clothes in his arms and dress quickly.

'Anna?' he said softly, touching her gently on the shoulder. 'I didn't mean anything. I'm going to Boston today. Maybe I could see you when I return?'

But when she did not answer, he left without another word.

Dante Faccini would eventually go to Mexico, but only after he had spent three months in prison. Arrested when anti-war demonstrators clashed with police in Boston the next day, he was charged with incitement to riot. On the morning he was released he hoped beyond any rationality that she would be waiting for him at the gates. With a brown paper parcel that contained his pipe and a couple of books in his hand, he had stepped out on to the street. But there was no one on the street outside to greet him, just the blind cripple with the dog on a rope whose slow daily shuffle to the liquor store and back he'd watched every day from his cell.

Anna made the bed, smoothing down the sheets and plumping up the pillows until all trace of the Italian's recent presence was gone, until the only hint that he had been there at all was the faint, but lingering, smell of stale sweat and Turkish tobacco.

4

Hubert Von Hofe marched into Monroe's cubicle at 10 a.m. without the customary knock, with a sheaf of paper in his hands.

'I got news for you, kid,' he said, 'so don't stand up.'

The first thought that occurred to Monroe was that he had been chosen to play on a new Pianola roll that was being cut that week.

'News?' he replied. 'Well, I had been kind of hoping . . .'

When Monroe looked up, however, his eyes locked with Von Hofe's and it was immediately clear that his initial response had been wrong; the news was going to be of the very bad kind.

'How many songs you think you sold last week?'

'I couldn't say exactly,' he replied. 'Thirty, forty?'

Von Hofe sighed. Then he produced a piece of paper from his pocket and adjusted his spectacles. 'My figures say you sold seventeen,' he said. 'What's got into you? You forgotten everything I taught you?'

Monroe stared out of the window. It had been snowing hard all morning and one side of the cylindrical water tank on the building opposite was completely frosted white. It looked the way he sometimes felt recently: numb, inert, frozen.

'It's just . . .' started Monroe. 'Maybe it's the songs. They sound, I don't know, a little, you know.'

'You don't like the songs.' Von Hofe sighed. 'You got anything better?'

'I've been working on a new one,' he said and motioned to his piano, 'but it still needs a little polish.'

'Let's hear it,' said Von Hofe, 'polished or not.'

Monroe started to play but his hands stumbled, his voice grew thick. The words tumbled out all wrong.

'Stop, stop, stop!' said Von Hofe. 'We don't need any more ballads. We already got too many. And, I have to be honest, you think it tops 'There's Someone More Lonesome Than You'?'

Monroe sat back. The cubicles on either side of him were silent. Everybody on the floor was listening. 'I have a new rag,' he said and pulled out a much corrected piece of music and opened with a major chord.

'Rag, schmag, you know what I'm saying?' said Von Hofe. 'Everybody's going crazy for those South Sea Island tunes. What d'ya call them? Hawaiian. You got any of them?'

'Well . . . not at the moment. No.'

'Take a look at this, kid.'

Von Hofe produced a sheet of much folded music out of his pocket and handed it to him. It was a song called 'On the Hoko Moko Isle'. Monroe read it over quickly.

'You don't have to like it,' said Von Hofe. 'You just have to sell it.'

'Well. It's quite . . . I mean, I suppose—'

'Business is tough,' Von Hofe interrupted. 'What with the war in Europe, people just ain't buying songs like they used to, even for Christmas. We need to work harder, make sure our songs get heard. I want you to get out of this place and to play this song where people congregate. Go to dime stores, public taverns, department stores, amusement parks, anywhere where people get together. Anywhere where they'll have you.'

Outside the wind picked up and a flurry of snow was driven against the window.

'Excuse me? Am I being fired?'

'On the contrary,' said Von Hofe. 'Think of it as a step up. That tyke Irving Berlin used to sing on street corners for nickels and now, between you and me, he has the best ear for a tune in the city.'

'And what if I write you a hit?' Monroe said softly.

Von Hofe suddenly looked tired, his pale blue eyes watery and his face a mask of sags and tucks.

'You still got to get out there and sell it,' Von Hofe said. 'It won't sell itself. And anyway, kid, you look like you need to get out at least once in a while.' Von Hofe let his hand rest on Monroe's shoulder.

'I'm not a kid,' he replied, pushing the hand off.

The music publisher laughed. 'You are to me,' he said. 'But then everyone looks like a pup when you're my age.'

'Can I have a little time to think about it?'

'Sure! You due any holidays before the New Year?'

'I have a day, I think.'

'Well then, take it. And let's see a smile on that youthful face of yours once in while. Good for you and good for business.'

The trouble was that Monroe still caught sight of Suzette Kinross regularly. Even though she was in California, he saw her climbing up the stairs to the elevated trains on the Myrtle Avenue Line, he saw her walking through Washington Square, her hair bright beneath the Hanging Tree, he was even sure he spotted her ankle among all the other ankles of the Christmas shoppers on Fifth Avenue. But she was always just a little too far away, a little too quick, a little too elusive, as she disappeared up metal stairs, down badly lit streets and into the maelstrom of a crowd.

Outside, the snow was being blown horizontally all the way from the East River to the Hudson. As soon as he stepped into the street it blew into his eyes, his mouth, his ears, until he could barely see where he was going. And so he turned right on Broadway and walked north to evade the worst of it. At Columbus Circus, he turned and looked back. It was snowing so hard that all but the most recent imprints of his best brown leather brogues had been covered over. I leave no trace, he told himself. Not on the pavement, not on Tin Pan Alley, not on her heart. It's as if I had never been there at all.

December was his least favourite month. He tried not to think of his family, of the impoverished Hanukkahs of his childhood where his mother would light the menorah and weep inconsolably for the village and the family she had left behind, until the rabbi would be called and they would all be sent to bed without any supper. And so he let the tune that Van Hofe had given him play out in his head. 'On the Hoko Moko Isle'. It was a ridiculous song with stupid lyrics.

But everybody was writing Hawaiian songs with titles like 'Hula Boola Boo' and 'I Can Hear the Ukuleles Calling Me'. He didn't believe he would ever be able to sell a song like that, not from his cubicle at the Broadway Music Corporation, not from a theatre foyer and never from a dime store. He would have to quit. He would have to get a job in the Navy Yard like all the other boys he'd known at school. He would have to move out of his boarding house in the Heights and into some ramshackle room in Red Hook. He turned west and headed into the driving snow.

By the time he had walked three more blocks, he no longer felt his toes, his fingers or the tips of his ears. His head ached and he could tell by the slide of his socks inside his shoes that his soles weren't holding up too well and were letting in water. He was dressed for a day in the office, in a suit, tie and a starched cotton collar, not a walk in the snow. His coat was made of heavy brown wool but had become encrusted with white; he was icing up all over. Now I feel the same on the outside as I do on the inside, he said to himself, now I hurt all over. And with the hurt came a rush of anger. He was angry with Von Hofe, with Suzette Kinross, but most of all with himself. He was a fool. A failure, an inconsequential. No wonder she had dumped him.

He walked on, stamping out his fury with every step until it gradually subsided and was replaced by a sudden and unexpected sense of clarity. The snow had stopped and everything looked pin-sharp, the streets, the tenements, the spiky winter trees, the strings of Christmas lights. He had walked further than he had intended, to a street west of Amsterdam Avenue, to an area he hardly knew. He could hear the blast and bellow of a trumpet played somewhere high up in an apartment block before it was drowned out by a stream of passing traffic. He inhaled: pork belly and fresh coffee. I'm still here, he told himself. I'm still here; the only crime I committed was to love her.

A coloured boy of about fourteen was standing in a doorway dressed only in an orange scarf, dungarees and a thin cotton shirt. On his feet were a pair of boots without laces or socks. He was shaking uncontrollably.

'You're even worse dressed for the weather than me,' Monroe said. 'You just arrived?'

The boy nodded. Monroe had heard that the streets west of Columbus were changing fast. While the neighbourhood directly to the south was predominantly Irish and the one to the north was Italian, the apartments and brownstones here were rented out to coloureds from the south, from New Orleans and the Carolinas. The war had partly put a stop to emigration from Europe, but the north still needed men to work in the docks and dig in the mines. And so when rumours that New York was hiring reached the southern states, men came in their thousands, straight from the cotton fields and the fishing grounds, with nothing but an address in Harlem or here, in San Juan Hill.

The boy's lips were blue. His hair was full of snowflakes and his eyelashes blinked with melting ice.

'Let me buy you a coffee' Monroe suggested. 'Before you freeze to death. Hell, you look like you could do with it.'

'My brother . . .' the boy said, his accent thick with the burr of the Carolinas. 'He told me not to move from this spot.'

On the other side of the road was a drugstore with a soda fountain. Monroe nodded to it.

'We can go in there,' he said. 'Keep an eye on this spot. And as soon as he comes back you'll see him.'

But the boy wouldn't be persuaded. And so Monroe brought him a coffee in a paper cup and then, on a whim, pulled off his coat and handed it to him.

'Take it,' he said. 'You're going to need it in this city. And good luck.'

Monroe had just reached the subway steps when he felt a hand on his shoulder. He stopped and turned round.

'We ain't beggars sir.' A young man of his own age, wearing a crushed felt hat and a suit a little too big for him, held out the coat in front of him. The boy with the orange scarf stood beside him, his eyes fixed on his boots. The fallen snow illuminated the black man's face, lighting up the white of his eyes and the cracks of his lips.

'Your brother looked half dead with cold,' Monroe said. 'Keep it. It's a gift. Happy Hanukkah!'

'Take it back!'

'Thank you, but no thank you.'

'Just take it!'

'I will not! '

The black man's arm shot out with the coat. Monroe refused it. The black man grabbed Monroe's hand and tried to force him to take it. Monroe tried to pull his hand away but found he was held fast. For a second or two both men were fused together, wrist in fist, thigh to thigh, eyeball to eyeball. Suddenly the black man shook his head and relaxed his grip. But the force with which they were locked meant that the rebound was more violent than either of them expected; as the coat fell to the ground, both men's hands flew back and hit Monroe smack in the face. Spots of blood began to rain down on the snow.

'My hand, dammit, my hand,' the young black man yelled.

'My nose! I think you broke my nose!'

A policeman's whistle rang out through the cold air.

'Now what?' said Monroe.

The cop grabbed both men by the shoulder and held them with more constraint than was strictly necessary. But when it was clear that neither was about to run away or throw another punch, he stamped the snow off his boots and pulled out his note-book. First he licked his pencil and then he checked his pocket watch.

'Eleven-twenty two exactly,' he announced. 'The 14th of December, 1916.'

With extreme slow-handed care, he noted down their names, addresses, occupations and the full name of their employer.

'Monroe Simonov, 32 Joralemon Street, Brooklyn. Piano player,' said Monroe. 'Universal Music Corporation. Boss's name – Hubert Von Hofe.'

'You work for a German. I should have guessed it. You?'

The black man paused, still nursing his hand, and when he spoke, he looked straight at Monroe.

'Edward Mackenzie, 1157 Tenth Avenue. Piano player. Currently looking for a position.'

'Unemployed,' the policeman corrected. 'I see any more brawling and I'll have you both locked up before you can whistle 'Yankie Doodle Dandy'. This was once a respectable neighbourhood. We don't tolerate bad behaviour from Negroes, or from Jews. Or from folks who work for Germans. You hear me? Now who does this coat belong to?'

'It's the boy's,' replied Monroe and held the black man's gaze.

Finally the other man conceded, finally he shrugged. 'Put it on, Little Joe,' he said. 'Quick before you die of cold.'

The boy pulled on the coat. It fell to his ankles. The policeman snapped his book shut and warned them that next time he'd slam them both in a cell.

'You really a piano player?' Monroe asked when the policeman was out of earshot.

'I was yesterday,' he said. 'But I think your nose broke my hand.'

'Yeah well, you shouldn't go chasing folk when they're just trying to be decent.'

'You should have taken the coat back, what's wrong with you?'

Monroe sighed. 'Where do you want me to begin?'

'Is it a girl?'

'Hell, yes.'

The black piano player's face broke into a smile. 'Then let me buy you a beer. You and I got a lot in common.'

The narrow streets of San Juan Hill stretched from Amsterdam Avenue to the Eleventh Avenue railway tracks and from West Fifty-Ninth Street to West Sixty-Fifth Street. The tenements and brownstones were so overcrowded up here that despite the snow and the freezing temperature, each stoop had a dozen people or more sitting on it, playing cards or dozing in their coats, waiting for their date to show, or for the shift in the bed they rented to come up. Children's faces filled the windows above as they watched the day go by from behind the relative shelter of a piece of cracked and filthy glass. In every basement there was a nightclub or a bordello, a poolroom or a saloon, and on every street corner a stall served jerk chicken and corn bread for a dime a pop.

As they walked down West Sixtieth Street, Monroe was suddenly nervous; he remembered hearing something about gang warfare between the blacks and the Italians on one side and the blacks and the Irish on the other. Since they had left Amsterdam Avenue, he hadn't seen a single other white face. People stared as they passed and he realized he must look a state: coat-less with his shirt covered in blood. He stopped mid-block.

'Is it far?' he said.

'It's right in here.'

Edward Mackenzie led the way down some stone steps to a door that had once been painted dark blue. There were no signs outside to show that it was a drinking establishment. Monroe hesitated at the top of the stairs. Was he going to be mugged and left for dead in an area that few policemen ever dared to enter? The boy in his coat was waiting at the bottom of the stairs, holding the door open for him. What did he have, he asked himself, to lose?

Monroe's eyes slowly adjusted to the lack of light inside the saloon; he saw a pool table and a bar made out of empty beer crates. He picked up one of the two bottles of beer that stood waiting on the makeshift counter and took a long draw.

'That'll be twenty cents,' the barman said.

A single dollar bill was slammed down on the bar. By the look on the piano player's younger brother's face, Monroe guessed it was, if not the last they had, then maybe the second last.

'I'll get the beers,' Monroe said and pulled a roll of notes from his inside pocket.

The black piano player turned to him, his face suddenly serious. 'I said I'd buy you a beer, didn't I? Let me buy the beer.'

Monroe wasn't used to drinking before lunch and he felt the alcohol slowly spreading through him. It was rough stuff, stronger than he was used to. He liked it. For a moment they both drank in silence.

'Say, you want to hear my sorry tale of lost love and self-pity?' said Monroe.

Edward didn't answer. His eyes were fixed on a beat-up piano in the corner.

'You got someone to play that thing?' he asked the barman.

'Just about the whole neighbourhood,' the barman replied.

'Do you mind?' Edward asked.

'Be my guest.'

He sat down at the keys and quickly examined his hands.

'Edward,' pleaded his younger brother, 'haven't we got plans for today? We got to go wait for Uncle Will.'

'Just need to assess the damage,' he said to everyone and no one in particular.

And then he laid his fingers on the keys and started to play.

Later, when Monroe tried to recall the exact collision of notes and melody, he was unable to. He recognized the music – it was a piano sonata by Mozart – but as the left hand tapped out a rhythm, at first in the lower register but then shifting up to middle C and beyond, the right shifted in and out of the pattern of the tune, spinning new threads out of the old.

'They seem to be still working,' Edward said and examined his hands again.

'Where did you learn to do that?'

'Do what?' Edward said.

'It's called stride, isn't it,' Monroe continued. 'The way you let your fingers stride all over the keys. I've heard about it but I've never seen it done.'

Edward shrugged. 'That's just the way I play,' he replied.

Over another beer, Edward Mackenzie told him he had lost a girl too. She had gone to Charleston to marry a man who sold soap powder door to door.

'Her mother had it all arranged,' he said. 'Used to make her hang around the train station so she'd meet the right kind of men; she told me she never got to go anywhere, ever. And this was her chance.' He shook his head and laughed. 'So Joe and I here, we decided to go further away than her. Just to show her that the world's bigger than South Carolina.'

'I'm sorry,' said Monroe.

'You don't need to be sorry. Once I make some money, I'm going down there and I'm going to get her back. How'd you lose your girl?'

Monroe let out a deep breath. And then he told them about Suzette, how she had danced, how they'd fallen in love, how she'd gone off to California and how he was beginning to suspect that he would never see her again.

'You could buy a ticket to her movie,' said Edward.

'Yeah, but the thing is,' Monroe said, 'the thing is, I forgot to ask her the title.'

Edward's laugh burst out of his mouth, a huge bubble of hilarity. He slapped his knee and threw back his head until Monroe, despite himself, found he was smiling too. Little Joe sat and stared at his boots.

'You homesick already?' Monroe asked.

The boy looked up, and his eyes watered. 'No,' he said. 'Well, only a little.'

'You play in a theatre or what?' Edward asked Monroe.

He explained that he worked at a music publisher's, that he sold songs.

'Or I did, anyway.'

'Play one.'

'I really couldn't,' Monroe began. 'In fact, I really ought to be going . . . well, one, I suppose.' Monroe sat down at the piano and started to play.

'What is that?' Edward asked.

'It's just something I wrote,' Monroe explained.

Edward took his place at the piano and played it the way Monroe had.

'I like it,' said Edward. 'You really write that?'

'It's just something . . .' he began. 'Yeah, I wrote it.'

'What's it called?' Edward asked.

'The Sweetest Time,' Monroe replied and cleared his throat.

Edward turned and gave him a wide white smile and played the song again.

'Don't you need the music?' Monroe asked.

'I think I got it.'

And Edward started to play the song once more. But then he began to change it: the beat loosened up, the melody moved around but always returned eventually to the original phrase. Monroe's face began to redden, his hands to clench. Apart from the fact that the boy was good – no, better than good, he was gifted – the way he played the piano was like nothing he'd ever heard before. It was exciting, it was liberating, it was modern. But most shocking of all was that he seemed to be making it up as he went along.

'That,' said the barman from behind his empty beer crates when he had finished, 'is jazz, pure jazz.'

'Jazz?' Monroe asked. 'What is that?'

'You know, ' said the barman. 'Jazz . . . sex.'

5

From the window of the sixth-floor apartment you could look right across Central Park as far north as North Meadow. The whole park lay underneath a layer of fine snow that had turned pale blue in the last light of the afternoon. On the frozen pond, next to the Menagerie, a couple of skaters in red and purple hats twirled round in the dusk. A single pony and trap, its oil lamp flickering as it passed through the trees, looped around the Ball Ground and headed up towards the Casino. But at this time in the evening there were few people on the paths or strolling through the Ramble to the Belvedere. Central Park grew dark and darker still as, light by light and window by window, the towers and brand-new apartment blocks of the Upper West Side were illuminated.

Inez placed her empty glass on the tray that was passing and took another. Like the last one, the drink was purple, flat and extremely sweet.

'What is this stuff?' she whispered to her friend Maud. 'Is it even alcoholic?'

'Sssh,' Maud said. 'It's called Phez. It's going to be more popular than Coca-Cola. Apparently. Made of loganberries.'

'It's practically undrinkable.'

'Please, Inez,' Maud hissed. 'He's standing right behind you.'

'Who?'

'The man whose company makes the stuff. Do you want to get us both thrown out of here?'

Maud was the one girl from the college in New Jersey whose number Inez had kept. She too was considered to be of the wrong mettle even though she was a distant cousin of the Guggenheims. In New York, she was regularly invited to cocktail parties and soirées, as even she conceded, to 'make up numbers.' Before October, when Inez had called her out of the blue and suggested they hook up, she had only gone at her parents' insistence. Why else would she go to sit alone and unnoticed, a dowdy wallflower in overheated rooms full of exotic and elegant blooms?

With Inez at her side, however, Inez dressed in something diaphanous and cut daringly short, Maud suddenly found that men began to notice her. They engaged her in conversation and laughed when she told them that she was a whizz at gin rummy, as long as there was more gin than rummy. Although everyone always talked about these functions in terms of what they could offer – the standard of the French chef, the hot-shot cocktails or the expenditure on flowers – the truth was that most of the young women who dressed up and perfumed their cleavages did so for one sole reason: to bag themselves a wealthy husband. Surely, Maud believed, it would only be a matter of time before one of them succumbed to her ample charms. As for Inez, she could pull men to her but something in her manner pushed them away again.

'Haven't seen you at one of these things before,' they might whisper conspiratorially.

'They carried me out in a box last time,' she might reply.

'I'm sorry?' they would say, thinking that they hadn't heard her correctly.

'I died. Of boredom.'

Without a smile to suggest that she was joking, the men would examine her face in detail, taking in its beauty but also the glassy note of sheer indifference in her eyes. And then they would shift from one leg to the other, gaze into the distance and suddenly remember that they had to put through a call to their office.

'Too old, ' Inez would say in the taxi ride home that they always shared and for which Maud always paid. 'Too fat. Too dull. Too rich.'

But now as the darkening park began to smudge behind the window and her breath blurred the reflection of her face in the glass, she knew that time was running out for her.

Maud wandered off to find something to eat, leaving Inez alone at the window. She turned and casually scanned the room, taking in the groups of people who stood next to the lavishly decorated Christmas tree or who hovered beside the door. The most easily identifiable were the newly-weds, husbands in dress suits, wives in brocade and loosely knotted chignons, who were uniformly inseparable and predictably smug. Elsewhere the sexes were clearly divided; the men talking sport and downing Scotch and the women discussing nannies and holidays and school recommendations. The girls, for some were no more than sixteen, sat on the strategically placed occasional chairs in pairs or alone, with a look of what could only be described as pert expectation on their faces.

Inez knew a few of them by sight: the Cheswick heiress who always dressed in the same yellow satin gown and who was said to prefer women to men; the unfortunate Woodbury girl, whose last two fiancés had both died in car accidents; and Freda Hilden, whose father made millions in shipping but who was said to have the occasional 'funny turn.' Inez momentarily wondered if anyone ever recognized her from Lord and Taylor's. But it was unlikely that any of these guests would ever have considered buying clothes from a department store. Their clothes, she could tell just by looking, were made to measure by personal seamstresses who had probably been making the family's clothes for decades. There was not a loose thread or a squint seam to be seen.

A couple of middle-aged women were talking about her on the other side of the room. The taller one was shaking her head and the smaller one throwing tiny intense glances. Inez smiled in their direction. As a tactic it was unbeatable: they both quickly looked away and sipped their loganberry juice.

The apartment was handsomely but blandly furnished. A vast crystal chandelier hung from the ceiling, and on the walls were paintings of racehorses and landscapes of rolling country. This was clearly a man's room, but what kind of man? There were no books, no treasures picked up from foreign trips, nothing that might endear the casual observer to the owner of this house. It could have been owned by a large corporation – it probably was.

A black waiter relieved her of her glass, still filled with Phez, with a small nod. She watched him pick up glasses and empty the ashtrays. Like all the waiters here, he wore a white jacket, bow tie and dress shirt, and passed through the party like a ghost; no one acknowledged his presence, no one uttered a word of thanks, and if anyone should collide with him in the corridor or on the stairs accidentally, they would exclaim in surprise as if they had walked into an unexpected pillar or a poorly placed pot plant, and then they would glide on as if nothing had happened.

A gramophone in the corner was playing a phonograph. 'There's someone more lonesome than you,' the singer crooned. Well I'd like to meet them, she said to herself. In an alcove stood a grand piano. It had been covered with a paisley-pattern cloth held down by a vase of winter roses, but another guest had been playing earlier, badly as Inez recalled, and the cloth lay over the stool. A waiter polished an ashtray nearby, and as she watched he glanced round surreptitiously, lifted the piano lid and very gently played a couple of notes. The hammers hit the strings making a perfect chord that rose up into the air and made the chandelier tinkle.

'What do you think you're doing?' A voice roared from across the room, making everyone jump. It was Mr Phez, the soft drink man, a balding forty-year-old with a pince-nez around his neck. The waiter dropped the lid and raised both palms as if it were a gun he was reacting to rather than a verbal blasting. The room had fallen so silent that the clamour of the kitchen and the high register of a woman's laugh in the next room were suddenly clearly audible.

'You people! When are you going to get it into your thick skulls that you keep your hands off our pianos?' And with a shake of his head, he continued his conversation. 'Where was I? Oh yes, what is your opinion of the PhiAna New Town Car?'

Maud came back a few moments later with some triangles of Gentleman's Relish on toast in a napkin. 'There's salmon,' she said in a hushed voice, 'potato salad, asparagus vinaigrette, plus chocolate pudding and peaches in chartreuse jelly for dessert. You should have some quick before it's all gone.' Maud popped a slice of hot salty toast into her mouth and ate it quickly.

'I'm really not hungry,' Inez said.

'What? But it's such an impressive spread. Are you sure?'

'Actually, I'm watching my weight.'

Maud, a small, plump girl who curled her hair in paper every night and whose daily battle with a mid-morning English muffin was usually lost, sighed loudly. 'Oh, stop it. You're as skinny as a pin and you know it.'

'It's the corset,' she replied. 'Honestly, if you could see my stomach, you'd be horrified.'

'Let me get you a gin martini then. If you're not going to take advantage of the food, you might as well get sloshed. Anyway, I've had a look around and there are no men here at all. No men worth speaking of anyway. We'd have better luck picking someone up in a bank.' Maud raised her eyebrows conspiratorially. Inez knew what she was referring to. A month earlier, they had gone to visit a second cousin of Maud's twice removed, who had met and fallen in love with a teller in J.P. Morgan's after dropping in to cash a cheque. When the cousin had discovered that she was expecting, she had married the teller hastily and in secret, was subsequently cut off from her inheritance and now lived with him and their baby in a brownstone just off First Avenue. Inez was not expecting it all to be quite so squalid: the single room and a couple of cupboards filled with bedding, the lines of washing hung from the ceiling, the view of a water tower and the noise, from the street outside, from the floor below and from the baby himself.

When the second cousin brought them tea, however, it was in a fine china teapot and poured into porcelain cups and saucers. That made it all worse, somehow. Maud hid an envelope with twenty dollars inside under a saucer, and they quickly drank the tea and made their excuses. They caught a cab just outside the Cooper Institute and drove to Delmonico's for a glass of something sparkly, just, so they told each other, just so they could get the taste out of their mouths.

But later, when her mouth was sour with the taste of champagne, Inez wondered if the second cousin was someone to be pitied after all.

'Money isn't everything,' the second cousin had proclaimed. And when she smiled and kissed her baby on the top of its little head, it seemed impossible not to believe that she was right.

At the party, a hush fell momentarily. The waiters had put down their trays and, with stools in one hand and guitars, ukuleles or banjos in the other, they arranged themselves into a semicircle in the far corner and began to play.

Inez had seen this arrangement before, hired staff who served drinks first and then became the musical entertainment. Almost every black man, or so it seemed, played an instrument with varying degrees of competence, so why not hire them to do both jobs? The novelty, however, had long since worn off; conversations were rapidly resumed, drinks were sipped and nobody paid the band the slightest bit of attention. The Phez man simply raised his voice. 'But what about the horsepower?' he shouted. The band played on, slipping in and out of rhythm at first but gradually gelling as they played rags and foxtrots and South Sea shanties. The waiter who'd played the piano earlier glanced around the room and caught Inez watching him. Almost imperceptibly, he winked.

'Let's dance,' said Inez.

'What? With whom?' Maud replied.

'With no one. With each other.'

'Oh, no. I couldn't possibly do that.'

'Why not?'

'Well, it's . . . it's just not right.'

'Oh, Maud,' breathed Inez. 'You're such an old stick.'

And with that Inez put down her glass, moved into the centre of the room and started to dance. At first her body seemed to jar; it was too bright, she was too sober, the space was too small. But then the syncopation of the music began to reverberate within her chest and she felt her head, her shoulders, her arms, her hips, relax. As the band slipped into another Hawaiian tune, she imagined she was a palm tree swaying beside a warm southern sea. And so without a man to hold her, she danced alone, alone with the baby, now the size of a Christmas satsuma, that she knew was growing inside her.

It was dark outside and the soft lights inside the rooms made them appear suspended like Chinese lanterns in the ink-black night. At first nobody noticed the copper-haired girl as she danced to the Negro band. Or if they did, they pretended they didn't. Most of the guests had only recently, regretfully, given up dance cards and the idea of a woman dancing without a partner, without prior invitation, was frankly abhorrent. And so they carried on talking about British casualties and Woodrow Wilson's peace initiative until they realized, as one, that their host, Ivory Price, the aeronautical magnate who had made a million, or so it was said, out of a ten-dollar investment, was not listening to a single word they were saying.

'Who is she?' they had asked each other as she danced alone in the flickering light of the crystal chandelier.

'Who are you?' a man's voice had whispered in her ear. When Inez opened her eyes at the end of the song, she found she was staring into the round and flaccid face of a man she hadn't noticed before.

'Why don't you arrange an introduction?' she replied.

'That would take too long. Just tell me.'

'My, what insolence. Someone ought to throw you out.'

He burst out laughing, his round face softened even further by amusement. 'But I live here,' he replied.

Later, when his hands felt compelled to stroke the kinks out of her hair as she hovered on the doorstep with her coat on, her blasted fat friend tugging at her sleeve and begging her to come, he admitted to himself that he was smitten. Inez knew it, but just in case, as an insurance policy, she had left a paste hair clasp on the mantelpiece.

'Do come again,' he said.

'If I'm not otherwise engaged,' she had replied.

The lift bell rang, the doors opened, closed and Maud descended alone.

'It was awfully nice to meet you,' he whispered, his mouth inches from hers. 'I'm Ivory.'

'Ever so pleased,' she replied. 'Ivory.'

'Tell me, are you in town for the holidays?'

'Where else would one want to spend them?'

'You know,' he replied, 'I've been thinking exactly the same myself.'

Inez inclined her head, gave him one last smile and then ran down the wide, shallow carpeted stairs, two by two, round and round, from floor to lower floor, from the lobby to the street outside, to Central Park West and finally to the idling taxicab where Maud was waiting with her handbag filled with pastries and her face in a tizz.

'What kept you?' she was saying. 'I said I wouldn't wait.'

Inez happened to glance up just before she stepped inside. And there he was again, Ivory Price, standing at the window of his sixth-floor apartment, watching her leave.

Since she had been moving in the right circles in Manhattan for only a couple of months, Ivory Price was a name that Inez barely knew. To anyone who had been resident in Manhattan for longer, however, he was one of a growing number of newly minted young men who had appeared from nowhere with too much money and not enough taste. To those who remembered the bitter spring of 1912, he was also known as the Man Who Survived the *Titanic* Disaster.

He had never talked about it, not to reporters, not to his friends, not to his business acquaintances, but there were various rumours about how it had happened, one of which he may have started himself: he had helped to load the women and children on the first-class deck into a lifeboat, and then, when no extra crew could be found and the women pointed out that they were unable to row, he had climbed aboard to quite literally 'man' the boat. When they were picked up hours later by the *Carpathia*, and the crew found a single man rowing the full weight of more than thirty women and a dozen children, it was reported that both of his hands were bleeding and he was faint with exhaustion. But this story just didn't bear up. There were more crew than passengers on the *Titanic*, and there were almost as many men as women in the half-empty lifeboats. Other theories, however, had him swimming away from the sinking ship dressed only in a fur coat before being plucked out of the ocean, already half dead, by a passing lifeboat, or pushing aside pregnant women in his haste to climb aboard any available lifeboat and leave hundreds of more honourable men, women and children to drown. Whatever the truth, he was regarded as a man who still wore a certain air of melancholy drama about him; dark, impenetrable and either vaguely heroic or unforgivably cowardly, depending on whom you talked to.

Snow was falling heavily on the day Inez received the first bunch of white roses. The tightly closed buds, the leaves and thorns were covered with tiny ice crystals, making them look frosted, frozen, each one a rare confectionery almost entirely without colour. The flowers were tied with a length of white silk ribbon, through which the envelope of a tiny card had been threaded.

That Ivory Price had found her so quickly didn't surprise her. Maud had been formally invited and his secretary had all her details on file. With a little flattery, a little coaxing, a little gentle prodding, she knew her friend would have blurted out Inez's full name and address without a thought. As the snow melted and formed tiny pools on her dresser, Inez ripped open the envelope. Inside was a card with a telephone number written with a flourish in Indian ink and the initials I.P. She would never call him up. It just wasn't the done thing. But he would surely know that. Or was it a test? A way of sifting out the wheat from the chaff?

Roses arrived on the next day and the next and the next, each bunch bigger than the last. She ran out of vases pretty quickly and so she had to let the roses lie on her dresser still in their wrapping where they quickly parched, the tightly closed petals never opening and turning to paper, the dark green leaves curling in on themselves like tiny hands before they crumbled and broke. She would wait a fortnight, she had decided, until after the year turned. No more, no less, and then she would send him a card and ask him to return her clasp.

A week later when she woke up, however, her breasts ached, her mouth was dry and her head spun. The room was too hot – the cast-iron radiators in her room pumped out heat day and night and there was no way to adjust them. She could not get up: her body was too heavy; her stomach was too swollen; her head was too hot. But she could not lie in bed any more either; she was sick of the sight of the ceiling; she was trapped by the tight wrap of the starched cotton sheets. The cast of the snow outside threw light up into every corner of her room. Three feet had fallen on the city the day before and more was expected. Inez suddenly longed to be out there, to feel the cold air in her lungs and the icy wind on her face. And so she decided she would drag herself out of bed and call Lord and Taylor's from the phone on the landing. It was much easier to get out of bed once the decision had been made. Hortense would be given the message, the switchboard operator told her. Food poisoning again? She should be more careful what she ate.

Outside, the snow from the roads had been shovelled into huge piles, while narrow paths had been dug on the pavements just wide enough for a single person to walk along. At every intersection, however, was a quagmire of ice water and mud that had to be jumped over or waded through. The air was freezing, much colder than she expected, and she immediately regretted not wearing a hat. But she strode on anyway, her hands stuck down deep in her pockets, her coat buttoned tightly right down to her boots. And as she walked, briskly, purposely, she began to warm up a little. She passed a street vendor and his smoking drum of roasting chestnuts, and remembered that she had skipped breakfast. And so she bought a ten-cent bag and walked towards Riverside Park where she found a bench and sat down.

'You shouldn't eat those things. You don't know how long they have been lying around.'

Inez opened her eyes. Ivory Price stood in front of her, a brown cap pulled down low over his eyes, a pale grey cashmere scarf wrapped around his neck and a pair of brown leather driving gloves in his hands. He wore chequered plus-fours and a pair of thick Argyle socks. Parked on the street behind, a long white car stood with its motor running. Inez bit into a chestnut and chewed slowly before she spoke.

'Thanks for the tip.'

'Sorry to disturb you,' he said. 'But I was just passing by and

71

I saw you sitting here and so I thought I'd come over and say hello.'

She nodded but didn't reply. It was obviously a lie. How long had he been following her for? She squinted up at him again. He had a small moustache. Had he always had one? She couldn't remember. It was combed out over his top lip, dark brown flecked with grey. He started to clap his hands together and shift from foot to foot. His face was radiant in the cold winter sun; his skin was tanned, his eyes screwed up in the light. A couple of pink spots had appeared on each cheek. He was dressed for driving, not standing around in a city park when it was four below.

'Well,' he said.

'Well?' she echoed. It was a moment she returned to many times; the way he slowly seemed to capitulate in front of her. With Monroe, she had been the one who had been nervous, she had been pulled along unbidden by her feelings, scared that he might not feel the same way as she had. But as she sat on that cold cast-iron bench in that park she seemed to watch the whole scene from afar, aware that his strings were clearly visible to her, strings that she could pull almost without risk, without effort.

'Did you get the roses?' he asked.

'Were they the white ones?' she said.

'White? Yes,' he replied.

She nodded and took another tiny bite of chestnut.

'Jolly good,' he said.

'You English?' she asked.

'No. I went to college there . . . a place called Cambridge, those words just kind of stuck – jolly good, bottoms up, crikey!'

'Right,' she said.

'Miss Kennedy, Inez – may I call you Inez? You didn't tell me your name so I had to do a little detective work of my own,' he said a little too quickly.

'I was going to write to you,' she said before he could go any further.

'Oh,' he said. 'Were you? You've got my address? Of course you have.'

She nodded and for a fraction of a second she held his gaze.

'Because you left . . .'

' . . . my clip,' she finished.

He smiled at his shoes. They were, unlike her boots, still dry. A delivery truck had parked behind his car and the irate driver inside was honking the horn. He caught her gaze and followed it. But he seemed unconcerned.

'Ivory, you better go,' she said.

With a sudden lunge forward he grabbed her hand, knocking the bag of chestnuts out of her lap and all over the ground. As they rolled across the wide path and bounced their way down towards the river, he held her palm to his mouth and placed his lips upon it.

'If you knew how much it means to me to hear you say my name,' he whispered.

His moustache was surprisingly soft, his mouth shockingly warm. And then he looked up and she caught his gaze again for a fraction of a second. His eyes were the colour of glass washed up on a beach: pale opaque blue. And in a flash she decided. She could try to love him; it wasn't impossible. A small boy and his nanny walked past and the child sniggered. Inez retracted her hand and glanced away at the distant shores of New Jersey, at the blackened quays and landing bays all picked out stark against the snow. Aware of the change in her, he immediately rose and cleared his throat.

'So you'll write,' he stuttered.

'That's what I said,' she replied.

Ivory Price gave a formal bow and took a step back. A roasted chestnut crunched underneath his shoe. A look of surprise crossed his face; his moustache twitched above his upper lip, his eyes lost focus. Inez waited for his reaction with an almost anthropological fascination. Would he acknowledge it? Crack a joke? Offer to buy her another bag? No, he chose to pretend it hadn't happened, turned on his heel and walked quickly back to his car where a chauffeur in full livery had suddenly appeared and was holding the door open for him.

New Year's Eve fell on a Sunday that year and 1917 was welcomed at watch night services rather than with confetti and tin horns on Fifth Avenue. A small crowd did assemble on Broadway and Forty-Second Street to watch the great ball of lights descend the pole on the Times Building, but most of the restaurants and cabarets were half empty and had to close at 1 a.m. anyway to comply with the new Sunday licensing laws. Inez lay in her bed and listened to the occasional whoop and burst of laughter on the street beneath her window, but by 2 a.m. the city was quiet, even quieter in fact than a normal Sunday night. It was the earth's birthday, the clocking of time, of history, of her life, but what was there to celebrate?

The year before she had spent 31 December backstage at the Century on Broadway. Her old friend Meg had a friend who was in the back line of the chorus. Despite bad reviews, the show was about to go on tour and they were a few girls short, so she had heard. As the bells chimed and everyone kissed, as a dozen girls twirled on their heels and threw their arms around men they would usually, of a day, ignore, Inez Kennedy found herself on a sofa next to the producer.

'We need a girl like you,' he had told her as he laid his hand on her knee. 'Ever been to Atlantic City? You'll love it. Give me a call on Monday.'

But he hadn't given her his number and she was too proud to ask. There's plenty of time, she had told herself. Let him come and find me. Only there wasn't and he hadn't. And now she ached with what could have been, what should have been and with what she couldn't change.

The next time she pulled back the curtains in the women's ready-to-wear section's Salon, she saw Ivory Price squashed in to the front row between two middle-aged ladies. They looked decidedly disgruntled by his presence, the pheasant's feathers on their hats twitching in displeasure. Of course, she didn't acknowledge him; as she paraded back and forth dressed in fine cotton lawn, in almost weightless silk chiffon and starched pleated linen, her eyes glided across his oiled hair, his wide face, the pull of his stare as if she did not see him.

He must have spent an hour or more lingering in the perfume department on the ground floor, feigning interest, she supposed, in scents and creams and fine French soaps. He was waiting at the entrance when she tried to leave for her lunch break.

'We meet again,' he said.

'Now there's a surprise!' she said as coolly as she could. But her face was flushed and she was already too hot in her coat.

'Look at you,' he said, oblivious of her anger. 'You're glowing.'

'Do you know everything about me?' she asked him. 'You know where I live, where I work?'

He produced a bag of chestnuts from his pocket. 'I bought you some of these. I know you like them.'

She made her way through the wide entranceway, turned and walked up Fifth Avenue. He followed, the chestnuts still in his hand.

'You going for lunch?' he asked.

'Yes. I expect you know where I'm going too?'

'The Polish deli on the corner,' he admitted. 'You always have the same thing. Swiss cheese on rye. Inez . . . Inez, let me take you . . . let me take you out . . .'

Out of where? Of what? Out of her overheated rooms in the residence hotel, perhaps, out of the job that she would have to leave soon anyway, as the zips were sticking and the seams puckering; out of the life that was on the cusp of tipping into the horribly wrong, the disastrously desperate, the shunned and disgraced, the unwed with child, the fallen.

She stopped abruptly at one of Lord and Taylor's huge glass display windows and gazed up at the wax mannequins dressed for spring. Everything was reflected in the polished glass: the blur of cars, taxis and trams speeding along the street behind, the bustle of men in heavy wool coats and women in fur collars as they hurried to lunch appointments or to buy a sandwich; only Ivory Price was static. He took off his hat and approached her tentatively. She had no time, she told herself later, she had no time to think, no time to consider. Could she have done things differently? No. There was no choice. Inadvertently, she had made her choices the previous summer.

'All right,' she said without letting him finish.

75

Within a month of their first meeting, Inez had resigned from her job. Ivory himself had handed in her notice at the women-only residence hotel on East Eighty-Ninth Street and had her moved to the much nicer confines of the Imperial on West Seventy-Second Street. Inez Kennedy had formally agreed to be Mrs Ivory Price in the padded leather back seat of his car some time in the middle of January. He had parked on the sand on Rockaway Beach, and as hailstones bombarded the car roof and the wind whipped the sea into dark cliffs and grasps of froth, the aeronautical millionaire had pulled out a ring and proposed, punctuating each word with a kiss. The whole world outside seemed so white, so unblemished, so perfectly clean that for a moment Inez believed that her future was indeed a blank page: unwritten, empty, immaculate. But as if to contradict her, she felt an unfamiliar tug, a jolt inside: her baby had started to kick.

The French dressmaker took Inez's body measurements but made no comment. The girl was tall and slim enough to hide her condition for another month, or at least until after the wedding. She did suggest, however, that the dress be cut to fall beneath the bust and that she set off her outfit with an over-large bouquet. The bride readily agreed.

The wedding was lavish despite the haste of its arrangement and the given political situation. Everyone agreed that the bride looked ravishing with her copper hair tamed by garlands of oleander and her body swathed in the finest white satin, but they confessed in private that they found it all a trifle distasteful.

Ivory Price, he told her on the first night of their honeymoon, was a man who was used to getting what he wanted. He had got her, hadn't he, the elusive Inez Kennedy, the girl who had shunned him and toyed with him and teased him before finally allowing him to ask for her hand.

'Not yet,' she had whispered as he began to kiss the lace at the neckline of her nightdress. 'Give a girl a little rope.'

He had laughed then. He told her he loved her Irish ways. He claimed he adored the fact that she had worked in a department store as a model and he thought her family were just swell. The reason for his tempered libido, however, was that he had visited Consuela, his Argentine mistress, the night before and had urged her into a particularly vigorous session.

Inez rolled away from her new husband, away from the bedside light so he wouldn't see the rise of shame that slowly spread from the base of her throat right up to her hairline. Two days before, her parents had arrived from Detroit and immediately invited them both out for a pre-wedding dinner. Ivory had booked a table at the Waldorf-Astoria.

'I'd like to announce,' her father had said, 'that as soon as you are legally married, I shall transfer two thousand shares in Kennedy and Son All Purpose Tractors into an account in your name, Inez. At current market prices, these are worth in the region of five hundred thousand dollars.'

'Thank you, Daddy.'

'Just don't spend it all at once, sweetie.'

Her father had blanched when he saw the prices but still he had ordered French wine and oysters. And that was just for starters. But then came the potato incident. It was the last remaining piece of his food on his plate and as he ceremoniously cut into it, he remarked that the food had been excellent. The potato fell open under his knife to reveal a rotten black interior. The waiter was summoned who in turn summoned the head waiter, who summoned the manager, who summoned the head chef. The offending vegetable was examined and prodded several times, while her father became increasingly outraged and Inez's fiancé increasingly amused. When the manager begged him to accept their most humble apology and then announced the whole meal, naturally, would be on the house, Inez's father beamed with self-righteousness, thinking it had been the power of his argument that had resolved the problem so cost-effectively and not the fact that they were dining with the venerable Ivory Price.

Of course, being of Irish stock and easily offended by a potato, he had left no tip, and only Inez saw the hundred-dollar note that her husband-to-be slipped beneath the sugar bowl. But what was worse was the fact that Inez had seen the whole potato charade before.

And as she lay there in the honeymoon suite of the Plaza Hotel, she was certain of two things only: that in less than five months she would have a child and that the rotten potato had come from her father's own pocket, smuggled on to his plate when no one was looking.

'Ivory,' she whispered.

'Yes,' he whispered back, his lips on her shoulder, the brush of his moustache on her skin.

'Do you promise you'd love me whatever?' she asked.

'I'd love you whatever,' he replied.

And so she turned round and gazed into those opaque blue eyes. It wasn't love that she felt flooding through her, not love but such a rush of affection, such a tide of pure relief that she let it sweep her away, she let him gather her up, she let him unbutton, undress and caress her.

'Good God,' he gasped as he finally breached all her resistance, a conquistador in heathen lands. '*Me voy . . .*'

6

At first the rumble sounded like a slow train passing, a deep melodious boom that seemed to reverberate right through the masonry, the polished floors and the light fittings of the Snake Hill Asylum. Instead of fading, however, instead of heading off along imagined tracks until it was a hardly audible hum, the rumble became louder. Anna had been waiting on a bench in the main corridor of the asylum for twenty minutes. The governor had asked her to sit there while he considered her request to visit Maura Sacchi. She had also asked for a reassessment of her mental state. Rosa had convinced Anna that she was the right person to do it; she was respectable, she was educated, she was articulate. Unlike Rosa, Anna was sceptical that it would do any good; she was also a foreigner and a woman.

That morning, however, she had received a letter from Russia. In his familiar curling hand her former husband had written the words that she suspected might come. Kima had been drafted into the Russian Army. In the time it had taken for the letter to reach her, Kima had been kitted out and despatched to the Eastern Front, the front where General Brusilov had lost the land he had fought so hard to gain the previous summer, the front where conditions were so bad that it was said there weren't enough rifles or boots to go round, the front where more men were dying of typhus than from German bullets. And since she had opened the letter she could think of nothing else but her son.

'No passenger steamers sailing at the moment,' she was told at the shipping offices on Chelsea Piers. 'There's a war going on over there, you know. Every ship is needed to transport supplies.'

As she walked away, the streets of Manhattan began to blur until she was only aware of the occasional flash of a polished window or the ripple and plunge of a passing car. But she could not shut out the city for long: the air churned with noise – the shrill blast of a conductor's whistle, the clatter of horses' hooves and, below it all, the dull boom of the pile driver. And it gradually dawned on her that even if she could manage to return to Russia, she could still do nothing, nothing but live in the restless limbo of her imagination. She hoped he wasn't cold. She hoped he wasn't sick. She hoped he wasn't in pain.

And as if she had summoned him out of her imagination, there he was. In the flickering shadow of a passing tramcar, a young boy in a sailor suit was standing next to a lamppost. Under his breath he was singing a song that Anna recognized, a Russian song. Anna closed her eyes and looked again. He was still there. But now she saw of course that he was far too young to be Kima; he was only about six.

She took a couple of steps towards him and looked around. First Avenue streamed with traffic. A nurse pushing a pram bumped it over the kerb and then walked hastily uptown. A couple of men swaggered by and then hailed a cab. But there was no one else, no one who looked as if the child belonged to them.

'Are you lost?' she asked in Russian.

The boy nodded his head.

'Do you know where you live?'

The boy nodded once more.

Together they took an uptown train to the Bronx. The address he had memorized was in a row of workers' houses. Anna rang a bell and three storeys above a window flew open. A woman's head poked out followed by a man's. A few minutes later they were both standing at the door with the boy in their arms.

'I found him on First Avenue and Eleventh Street,' she said.

'Did you really walk that far?' the mother asked the boy.

'Thank you so much,' said his father. 'Who knows what might have happened to him if you hadn't brought him home. I'm Leon,' he added by way of introduction, 'Leon Trotsky.'

'I heard that you were coming to America,' Anna replied. 'I'm Anna. Anna Denisova.'

'Madame Denisova. What an unexpected pleasure,' he said. 'I hear you are a terrific speaker. Would you like to come in for a cup of tea?'

'No thank you,' she answered. 'I have an appointment.'

As she stood in the asylum corridor several hours later, she remembered the thrill of meeting Leon Trotsky and the way it was followed by the stab of envy. As he put his arms around his son, the absence of her own son became unbearable. She had decided then and there that she would have to do something, go somewhere to occupy her mind.

'I've brought her some food and some books,' she had told the governor. 'I'm a friend of her daughter.'

'Ah,' he had replied.

'Is there anything the matter?'

'She's on hunger strike. Won't do her no good.'

'Maybe if you let me talk to her?'

'Talk to her, eh? What about exactly?'

The governor of the asylum didn't like foreigners. He was perpetually on the lookout for spies, for saboteurs, for turncoats. America, in his opinion, was crawling with enemy agents hatching murderous plots.

The Sacchi woman was an Italian; her visitor was a Russian. They were the enemy, weren't they? His grasp of world geography was rudimentary, his knowledge of international politics poor. In November, however, he had taken part in a 'Preparedness March', where he had paced the length of Manhattan along with financiers and factory owners carrying a banner that read, 'Fight God's Fight'. The marchers were all white, they were respectable, they were uniformly patriotic and they were all too old to go to war.

And now, despite the fact that the Russian woman was impeccably dressed, despite the fact that she was probably the most elegant creature he had ever entertained in his office, he couldn't afford, he told himself, to be too careful. And so he directed her out to the corridor while he drank his coffee and thought it over.

Anna considered that maybe her demands hadn't been clear enough; she should have been stronger, she should have threatened him with exposure or with ridicule. But as she sat in the corridor she felt cold, she felt numb, she was a pale copy of the woman she wanted to be. A window had been left open at the far end of the corridor and let in a damp, late afternoon air. She stood up and walked towards it, hoping to reach the window latch and close it.

It was mid-January and the temperature had been falling steadily for days. On her way, as she walked up from the train at Kingsland Station to the low cluster of buildings on the Palisades – the penitentiary, the almshouse, the sanatorium and the asylum – she had noticed that the river below was frozen solid and the mud of the New Jersey Meadowlands was glassy with ice. And then she remembered the many times she had taken Kima skating from the embankment at the Hermitage right over to the St Peter and Paul Fortress, and she had to pause to collect herself.

The noise came from the other side of the marshes. Just beyond the raised line of the Lackawann Railway, there was a crimson glow rising from behind a high brick wall. As she watched, smoke billowed up into the air from the compound beyond, thick and black and viscous. Suddenly there was a low boom that felled the telegraph poles immediately to the right of the wall. The blast ripped across the marsh up to the Palisades and with one breath blew in some of the windows of the asylum. The governor suddenly appeared behind her. His eyes were bright with outrage mixed with glee.

'Come away from the window, madam,' he yelled.

'What is that place?' she shouted.

'It's the foundry,' he bellowed. 'The Canadian Car and Foundry Company. They make shells, munitions for export.'

A twist of red-hot metal suddenly shot up into the air. As it arced through the sky it showered golden sparks and white-hot embers, then fell with a hiss into the frozen marshes of New Jersey. It was followed by another that exploded and rained down molten metal on the Hackensack River. The noise was terrifying, but it was also wonderful, exhilarating, spectacular.

'Holy Cow, I think the whole place is going to go up. It's like the Black Tom Island explosion all over again.'

'You think someone did this deliberately?' she asked. He glanced down at the woman. Maybe she had something to do with it? Her eyes shone bright in the fire's glare. 'Enemy sabotage,' he said. 'Clear as the light of day.'

Another shell shot up, and another, and another: explosions of red and amber and brilliant yellow against the cool blues and greens of the approaching dusk. The sky was raining smuts of ash now, some still glowing as they danced and swirled like the very opposite of snow. And beneath the screams of metal cases bursting and the screech of soaring iron came another equally disturbing sound, the high-pitched hysterical cries of the inmates of the asylum.

'Madam,' he said, taking her elbow. 'Once again I implore you. For your own safety you should come into my office.'

'Wait,' Anna said. 'Look.'

She was staring straight into the explosion's heart. He followed the line of her gaze; coming out of the smoke and the haze of the compound were dozens of tiny figures, quivering in stark silhouette in the heat. In twos and threes, workers were walking across the frozen marshes to safety, towards the Palisades, towards the train station or the railway track. They looked like walking shadows; their clothes, their hair, their faces were black, dirty, soiled. From head to toe they were all covered in mud.

'This is the final straw,' said the governor. 'We'll be at war by summer, you mark my words. We're Americans. We don't take this kind of thing lightly. And you, madam? You're one of those damnable pacifists, I suppose?'

As Anna watched another missile light up the sky, her eyes started to water. How many Germans would each shell have killed? How many bullets and bombs had been wasted? Kima would have nothing to defend himself with but his bare hands, hands that she had once taught to play the piano, hands that she could still picture so vividly: the palm, the fingernails, the wrist, the white skin veined with blue.

'My son,' Anna replied. 'My son is a soldier. He is fighting the Germans on the Eastern Front.'

The governor looked at the woman more closely. She might be a foreigner, he would tell his wife of thirty-seven years later, but she was also somebody's mother. The fact that they had failed to produce any children only made his point seem more poignant.

'Most impressive,' the governor replied softly. 'May I salute you?'

For four hours the sky exploded as half a million shells went off. Trains on the Boonton Line were cancelled and thousands of commuters were held up for hours at Hoboken; all the telegraph wires in the area went down and a hundred thousand gallons of milk on its way to Manhattan spoilt. Miraculously no one was hurt, but by morning all that was left of the Canadian Car and Foundry was a single brick chimneystack. Maura Sacchi never met Anna Denisova. She was, however, reassessed a week later and found to be of sound mind. She would be released within the month.

Anna didn't reach Manhattan until after dark. She had had to wait for hours in a freezing station waiting room in Jersey City for a train and so, even though it was extravagant, she took a taxi from Penn Station.

The concierge of the Buckingham Hotel blushed when he saw her. Blotches of mottled red spread from his high-necked collar all the way to his forehead. Anna pulled off her gloves and placed them on the counter.

'Room 233, please,' she asked.

'The manager would like a word, madam.'

'Really?' she said. 'In half an hour I come.'

Anna knew that she should have rephrased her words; her grasp of English always fell apart when she was tired.

'I'm sorry, madam,' the concierge said turning a deeper shade of red. 'But he specifically expressed that you see him before I give you your key.'

This was strange, Anna thought. She had been staying at the Buckingham for three months and although the restaurant was poor and the maid service erratic, she had learned to tolerate it. She stepped behind the counter and from the corner of her eye caught sight of her cases. She inhaled sharply. They had been stacked in a cupboard not visible from the lobby. What were they doing there? They must, she realized with a start, already be packed.

Someone had been through her things. A chambermaid, perhaps, had packed all her dresses, her shoes, her hats, her books, her soaps and her perfumes. They had rifled through her soiled underwear and private notebooks. A boundary had been broken. This would never have happened in Paris, in Berlin, in Rome. She glanced up at the concierge. But his eyes resolutely avoided hers.

'This way,' the concierge said.

The manager looked like every hotel manager she had ever met, as colourless as a raw crayfish, able to handle any occasion with the same transparent deference. He invited her to take a seat but remained standing. And then he informed her that her last two cheques had bounced.

'Europe is at war. The postal service is not what it was,' she replied. 'My bank in Switzerland is still waiting for a banker's draft from my husband. I apologize.'

'Ah yes,' he said. 'Well, you see, that's not the only problem. I am not sure how to phrase this, so I'll just have to speak plainly. We are a family hotel, as I'm sure you appreciate. It has been noted that you have had occasional overnight visitors, male visitors.'

Anna didn't argue. What could she say? It wasn't their business. In Europe nobody would have dared to mention it. In Europe if you paid for a room in a hotel, what you did in it and with whom was up to you. And she wondered if they would have reacted in this way if she had been a man.

'I see,' she said.

The manager of the Buckingham Hotel sighed and glanced out of the window. He hoped she wasn't going to be difficult. 'It puts us in an awkward position,' he continued with emphasis on the last word. 'I'm sure you understand.'

The Russian woman sighed but seemed unmoved.

'Well . . . if there's any way we can help? Forward your mail for example?'

'No, I have a box at the General Post Office,' she answered. 'I will settle my final bill as soon as I am able.'

He looked her in the eye at last. Maybe he had been wrong about her. 'Of course,' the manager said with a bow. 'Of course we don't expect you to . . . the room is yours for another night, if you'd like it. I'll have your cases taken back up.'

'Thank you.'

'No, it's the least . . .' he started to say but the words clearly didn't seem appropriate and he switched tack, '. . . in these difficult times.'

The manager smiled and his face revealed just the faintest trace of relief, that she had not protested, or denied anything, or threatened him with violence or a letter to the papers.

The next morning, Anna Denisova barely glanced at the concierge as she headed for the swing doors of the entrance. The taste of panic filled her mouth. In his recent letter, her former husband had not mentioned that his finances were tight. Had he simply forgotten? His personal fortune was large and he knew she had no other income. Maybe there had been a problem of logistics. But she couldn't believe that the banks in Russia were no longer operative. She walked to the telegraph office and sent him a telegram. Then she bought a paper from the news-stand. On page eight was a report about Russia: more food shortages, prices rising sixfold, transport services at a standstill, mobs on the streets demanding food.

She had one hundred and fifty dollars in her purse. She would have to take a room somewhere much less expensive. Who knew when her former husband would be able to send any more money? And so she took the L train north, to an area called Washington Heights that was known for being inexpensive and anonymous.

As she stepped out on to the street from the station, Anna had to cover her face with a handkerchief. Apart from two or three motor cars and a couple of electric trains, all the traffic up here was still horse-drawn. The smell was overpowering. The pavements were uneven and cracked. Weeds grew in the gutter and empty milk crates were piled up in doorways. Children without shoes begged for spare change or sugar lumps. As she picked up her skirt and headed west towards the river, this, she told herself, is the real New York. This is America.

Seventeen dollars a month, the janitor of the building told her, in advance. The rooms were sparsely furnished with gas for cooking and a shared bath. None of it was comfortable, none of it had been cared for; the stains and the scuffs, the dents and the cigarette burns spoke of previous tenants with unhappy lives and violent tempers. But here she could close the door and feel that nobody was watching her. Nobody cared who she was. Nobody cared what she wrote. Nobody cared who she entertained. Not that she did that any more. Every day she dressed, drank her coffee and then she walked one hundred blocks to the library to save a dime. She always worked at the same desk, third from the door on the left-hand side, working on articles that she intended to send to any one of a number of American-based Russian-language magazines and periodicals. It wasn't easy. She would reach the third paragraph and then dry up, the words on the page sounding dry and meaningless. And then she would put the article aside and write the words that she had written so many times before: 'My dearest Kima'.

Sometimes she was invited to give lectures, to join labour rallies and speak to women's groups in Pennsylvania, or Saratoga or Boston. But they didn't offer expenses and she just didn't have the money to spend on fares. And every day she checked at the bank and every day she was told that nothing had been deposited in her account.

In early March Anna dropped into the offices of *Novy Mir*, a Russian émigré magazine run by Nikolai Bukharin, to suggest an idea for an article. They had just heard the latest news from St Petersburg. There had been a revolution; the tsar had abdicated in favour of his brother. He in turn had been replaced by a provisional government. Imperial Russia was crumbling. Millions of workers were out on strike. The banks were all closed in case of looting. It was chaos, beautiful, liberating chaos. The revolution that she had longed for had finally happened. Bukharin had opened a bottle of wine and was sloshing it into a dozen coffee cups.

'What's the matter?' Bukharin asked Anna as he handed one to her. 'Aren't you happy?'

'My son is at the front,' she replied.

'The war will soon be over for Russia,' he told her. 'Already the soldiers and sailors are mutinying. He is probably on his way back to the capital already. You should drink his good health.'

'Very well. To Kima,' she proposed. 'And to going home.'

'To going home,' Bukharin echoed.

7

Only the cocktail bar of the Beach Palace Hotel on Coney Island was open. A raw wind blew off the Atlantic and scuffed the sand across the tracks of the Marine Railway and into the ornate swirls that decorated the wide, sagging steps of the main entrance. Monroe paused on the bottom step and glanced up. The hotel was huge, with castellated turrets and drooping verandas; ragged flags snapped on poles held fast by rusted metal wire. Most of the rooms with a sea view had a private balcony but the bright red cloth of their awnings had long since faded in stripes to a washed-out pink. Next to the main entrance, a large *For Sale* sign swung on a wooden stake.

Monroe had vague memories of the Palm Court inside and its resident harp player, a woman with an ample figure upholstered in taut blue silk. He had come here once or twice as a child and remembered the time he ordered a plate of littleneck clams and how his father had deducted the astronomical price from his pocket money for weeks afterwards. But although many of the details were hazy, he vividly recalled the sheer scale of the place: five hundred bedrooms and a dining room that could seat two thousand at one sitting, miles of corridor and acres of formal garden.

Only twenty miles from Manhattan, the resort had been built for wealthy New Yorkers over thirty years earlier. They had once strolled on the manicured lawns of the Oriental, the Manhattan and the Brighton Beach, bathed in the bracing sea and watched lavish nightly firework displays. But then the middle classes started coming for the day on a range of new public transport – steamer, electric car or elevated railway – and within a couple of years, more than two hundred thousand people crammed on to the same stretch of sand. The beach became so eroded that one of the hotels threatened to fall into the sea. Coney Island had become dirty, cheap, overcrowded. Now the resort's big luxury hotels were being boarded up one by one. Who wanted two-dollar clams when you could buy a hot-dog at Nathan's for five cents?

Clutching the battered briefcase that held his music and a sandwich wrapped in greased paper, Monroe walked up the steps. A seagull cried overhead, drifting on a current towards Jamaica Bay. Further along the boardwalk were the piers, the Luna Park, 'fine illuminations at night, 600,000 electric lights', the amusement park and the observatory. All of them were locked up for the season and they seemed to huddle, hunch-shouldered, against the cold sea wind, their iron structures skeletal against the ashen March sky.

Beside the main doors, a printed poster encased in glass advertised the Beach Palace Saloon's year-round entertainment. 'Oscar Black,' it read. 'Vaudeville-On-Sea.' Rainwater, however, had seeped inside the case and the paper of the poster had the appearance of tidal sand, ridged and sun-bleached. Monroe pushed open the main door and stepped inside. The door crashed shut behind him as if it were rarely used and furthermore needed a damn good oiling. Inside, the hotel smelled of floor polish and damp deckchairs. He breathed in deeply, straightened his tie and sauntered up to the main desk.

'I'm here to see Mr Black,' Monroe told the receptionist. 'He isn't expecting me but if you'd be so kind as to give him this.'

He held out one of the cards that Von Hofe gave out to all the pluggers, cards that he had carefully inscribed with his own name in black ink below the company logo. The man behind the counter examined the card and then looked back at him with slightly narrowed, puzzled eyes. He's a recent immigrant, Monroe decided, he doesn't speak English, and so he repeated himself at half his usual speed.

'Heard you the first time,' the receptionist snapped back in a broad Brooklyn accent. 'He ain't here today. Off sick. If you'd come by last week . . .'

'Oh,' he said. 'That's too bad.'

'You a song-plugger?' the receptionist asked. 'We don't get many round this time of year.'

'You don't say,' Monroe replied.

'Usually they drop by just before the season starts, around Memorial Day.'

Monroe loosened his tie. Coney Island hadn't been his idea. The place was practically deserted in March – everyone knew that. It had been a long, unsuccessful morning – he'd sold the grand total of three songs to an oyster restaurant in Fulton Street after waiting for an hour at another place for a manager who didn't show – and now he was tired and hungry.

'In that case,' Monroe said, 'I'll take this opportunity to partake of a beverage.'

He didn't know why he sometimes started talking like the travelling brush salesman who used to come to his parents' door three times a year. It was something to do with the briefcase and with the feeling of being overdressed and overqualified for the lowliness of cold-calling.

'You do root beer?' he clarified.

The receptionist nodded towards the cocktail bar. 'In there,' he said. 'Shuts in half an hour.'

The wind had risen outside and it blew the rain in hard, salty hurls against the picture windows. The distant crash and rush of the Atlantic was drowned out by the low rumble of a vacuum cleaner in the rooms above. Half a dozen men sat in the bar of the Beach Palace Hotel. A clerk in a bowler hat sat pondering the colour of his beer. Three coastguards, their glasses empty, stared out at the weather from a table in the far corner. A couple of older men leaned on the bar and drank three shots of bourbon in quick succession.

'Took them one hundred and twenty railroad cars,' one of the old men pronounced out loud to no one in particular. 'Moved the whole hotel six hundred yards inland. And even though it weighed six thousand tons, not a single pane of glass got broke.'

'Not a single one broke,' echoed the other man.

The air in the bar stank of mildew and spilt beer. The windows were draughty, the panes streaked with sea salt. The white wicker furniture, the bath chairs and the occasional tables, once sprayed white, were now worn brown in patches and looked decidedly rickety. And yet the place retained a certain charm, Monroe decided. It had class, albeit faded. Monroe bought a drink, sat down at a table facing the sea and ate his sandwich furtively without enjoying it. It was chopped meat again, made by Nonna Maria no doubt with more love than he deserved.

He examined the list of places in Queens, his next destination. More theatres, pavilions and hotels. He had spent three months on the road, pounding out Universal's songs on a range of pianos, some out of tune, others with keys missing, without much success. He glanced across the room and noticed a piano on a small curtained stage at the far end of the bar. It was a baby grand, a Bechstein. Nice, for a change.

'Do you mind?' he asked the barman, motioning towards the piano.

'Be my guest,' he replied. 'But we close in ten minutes.'

Monroe lifted the lid, pulled out the stool and sat down. He picked out a couple of chords. The keys were tarnished and the tuning was a little out but the action was warm and mellow. The piano must have originally stood in the ballroom and been played at weddings, galas and recitals. It wouldn't last long in here, he thought, not with the damp and the penetrating salt air. He started to play, racing through his usual repertoire, first those hateful Hawaiian tunes, as he privately called them, and then the ballads and the rags. Without a pause, he began to diversify, just as Edward had; he let his mind wander and his hands follow, he circled the melody, he traced it, he toyed with it, he let it go and then found it again until what he was playing bore no resemblance to the music on the stand, until it was jazz.

Edward breaking his nose, Monroe had decided in retrospect, had been a stroke of luck. Once Edward had found their Uncle Will, his uncle had secured Edward a job as a caretaker in a apartment block, put Joe in school and installed them both in his fourth-storey walk-up that looked on to the railway.

'The sound of the trains is in my dreams,' Edward told him. 'All night I'm going chugachugchugachug. No wonder my fingers can't keep still. No wonder I can't stop making music.'

They had met regularly in the basement saloon in San Juan Hill, and while Monroe had played Edward all the songs he knew and he had learned them by ear, Edward had tried to teach Monroe how to play the way he could, shifting from up-tempo stride to down-tempo blues.

'Can't you write it out?' Monroe had asked him. 'Tell me what notes to play.'

'It's not on the page,' Edward had explained. 'It's in your fingers, it's in your feet, it's in the air. You just take it wherever you feel like.'

Jazz was suddenly in the air all over Manhattan. It came pounding out of the pianos of the saloons in Harlem and San Juan Hill. It was in the slow slide of the singers and musicians of the Clef Club on West Fifty-Third Street. It was in the toes and feet of the dancers on stage at the brand-new Apollo Theater on West 125th Street.

The Original Dixieland Jass Band, from New Orleans, had been booked to play at the launch of the 400 Club Room in Reisenweber's Restaurant on Columbus Circle and West Fifty-Eighth Street and Monroe had tickets.

'But ain't they white?' Edward had asked.

Monroe sat back and looked at Edward. 'What has that got to do with it?' he asked. 'Black, white, what's the difference? I got the tickets.'

'What has that got to do with it?' Edward repeated. 'Why, it's got everything to do with it.'

Edward stared back at Monroe, at the stubborn set of his jaw and the rock-hard grey of his eyes. Sometimes he momentarily forgot he was white. But now he felt it keenly. Did he really have no idea? Should he tell him about the state he had grown up in, about being barred from the public parks and the libraries, about the signs that read, 'Negroes and dogs not admitted'? Should he tell him about an uncle who had been accused of being disrespectful to a shopkeeper, about how a crowd of men, women and children, all white of course, had poured gasoline over his head and set him alight? Although white men had taken jazz and made it their own, he knew it had come from the deep south, born out of the field-hollers and the work songs of cotton-pickers and plantation workers, released only fifty-five years earlier from slavery.

Monroe was the first white man he'd ever had as a friend. But he was from the north, he told himself. He was an immigrant. He was different.

'Oh, who cares?' Monroe quipped. 'With my first name and your surname, we're both Scottish anyway.'

And they laughed for so long that the barman took away their empty glasses and didn't offer them another.

Reisenweber's Café was a dance palace and restaurant which boasted a sign that read, 'Delicious Frog Dinner. $1.25'. Monroe had always liked that sign; he always imagined a frog with a napkin around his neck sitting down to a large plate of food, rather than the reality, which was, he guessed, a cooked frog on a plate. The café was frequented by Ivy Leaguers and Long Island socialites, by oil magnates and shipping heirs, who dined on lobster, crab cakes and even frog, before dancing all night to a twenty-piece orchestra, direct, or so it said on the poster, from Vienna.

Three of the doormen didn't even look at Edward. Monroe took that as a good sign until the smallest one, an Italian in a black suit, lunged forward with his arm outstretched.

'No coloureds,' he said.

'We have tickets,' Monroe replied and held them up for him to see.

'Not valid today,' the doorman insisted.

'What!' Monroe said. 'This man is one of Manhattan's most talented young musicians.'

The doorman pointed to the sign on the door. 'No coloureds,' he repeated in a heavy Italian accent. 'You no read?'

'He's with me,' Monroe said. 'Come on, Edward.'

They stepped around the doorman and started to make their way towards the entranceway when a second doorman, who was taller, larger and Sicilian, raised his fist. Without much effort, casually even, he planted it squarely in Edward's belly.

'What are you doing?' yelled Monroe. 'You hit him! Come on then. Hit me!'

The manager, on hearing raised voices, came out of the club. He stared at the young black man doubled up in pain, and his companion, a white man with his fists in the air, and sighed. A large black car was drawing up to the kerb; he had booked the band for a residency but business had been decidedly slow. And so he'd handed out hundreds of free invitations to music publishers, vaudeville performers and producers. He didn't want a scene, not then, not there.

'Take them round the back,' he told the doormen.

The Original Dixieland Jass Band went down a storm that night. A few weeks later, they would record a tune called 'Dixie Jass Band One Step' and it would go on to sell over a million copies.

Monroe and Edward stumbled, bloodied and bruised, back across Columbus and nursed their wounds with bourbon in a tiny place on West Sixtieth.

'I still don't agree with you,' Monroe insisted. 'Colour has nothing to do with it. Not with the music, anyway.'

Edward shook his head but didn't reply. But that night had meant something, somehow. And although the bruises faded, the cuts healed and they never mentioned it again, Edward kept inviting Monroe to San Juan Hill and to Harlem, to clubs and cabarets, to poolrooms with pianos and to rent parties where, on the top floor of grubby tenements, hundreds of people would pay a dollar to squash into tiny apartments to drink beer and listen to a band playing in the living room.

In return Monroe would invite Edward to the Marshall Hotel on West Fifty-Third, a place where black baseball players and prize jockeys drank highballs with white singers and bandleaders, and where a different act performed every night. Every time they went out long-lashed girls would sidle up to Edward and give him that glance. But Edward only seemed to have eyes and ears for the music.

'This is it,' Edward would say as they listened to Wilbur Sweatman's clarinet or C. Luckeyeth Roberts' piano. 'This is where it's at.'

And Monroe, without any hesitation, would have to agree.

'You know "Take Me Out to the Ball Game"?' one of the old fellows at the bar of the Beach Palace Hotel shouted out. 'Can you play something that somebody knows the words to?'

Monroe came to with a jolt and realized that he wasn't playing a variation on one of Universal's songs any more but a blues song that Edward had taught him.

'Take me out to the ball game,' sang the old man in blatant discord to the music he had been playing.

Monroe let the chord die and played along with the old man for a chorus. As the wind howled and the rain fell on the deserted boardwalk, he suddenly saw his life stretching before him, playing yesterday's songs off-season to half a dozen old-timers. Gently at first, but then with more confidence, he started to stride, moving his left hand up into the middle register and then down again and letting his right hand wander. This is how he wanted to play. This is what he wanted to do.

'Hey,' the old man called out. 'That's not how it goes.'

Eventually, he shifted back to the song and played it slowly and deliberately so the old guys could sing along.

A long white car had rumbled along the boardwalk and parked just in front of the hotel, blocking the view of the beach. A man climbed out and opened the passenger door. A woman appeared, a woman with a pretty face and wiry auburn hair, that despite the pins that held it down, blew into a fiery halo in the racy ocean breeze. Monroe's hands fumbled and he played a wrong note.

'We only sing with professionals,' one of the old men called out and everybody laughed. Monroe lifted his hands and listened. The main door of the entranceway swung open and then crashed shut again.

'My man. Are you open?' a man's voice asked. It was clipped and had the long-vowelled affectation of the English upper classes. 'Seems like the whole of Coney Island is closed up. My wife and I would like some refreshments.'

'We have a cocktail bar,' Monroe heard the receptionist reply.

'And it's open?'

'For you, sir, it's open.'

'Don't suppose you have any live music? My wife took a notion and I was told you have a resident act.'

The receptionist muttered something Monroe couldn't catch. The man with the English accent laughed mirthlessly.

A heavy swag curtain fell across the small stage, throwing the piano and its stool into shadow. Thankfully, as they came into the bar, the couple didn't notice the song-plugger.

'Can you knock up a couple of drinks?' the man asked the barman.

'Yes, sir,' the barman replied. 'I can make you a mint julep, a champagne cocktail, a whisky sour?'

'Two gin daisies. With cracked ice.'

'Take a seat and I'll be right over.'

The couple chose a table next to the window, and pulled the chairs around so that they both faced out towards the long white car and the beach beyond. Outside, the clouds had closed in and the tide had pulled out leaving nothing but an expanse of monotonous grey.

'It's so drab,' the woman said. 'And the sea. It's so different from how I remember it.'

Suzette Kinross was exactly the same as his memory of her in every aspect except one. Her accent. All trace of Nova Scotia was gone. In all the buzz of their arrival, Monroe, to his relief, had been forgotten.

He waited until she excused herself to the powder room. And then he came out from behind the piano and the curtain and hurriedly gathered up his briefcase, the detritus of his sandwich and his coat. He threw a nickel on the table for his root beer and pulled down his hat. The man Suzette had arrived with, the man who claimed he was her husband, glanced over. He had a soft, flaccid

97

face with small cruel eyes. A feeling welled up in Monroe's chest, not envy exactly but something more antagonistic. But what had he to be angry about? He didn't know her any more. Maybe, he realized with a jolt, he had never really known her at all.

8

Inez stood over the basin in the chilly, rarely used powder room of the large Beach Palace Hotel in Coney Island and threw up. Just the thought of a gin daisy made her retch. Wasn't the nausea supposed to have stopped by now? She was five months pregnant. She would have to tell him. How would she find the words? And her mouth filled with the taste of bile and her body fizzed and trembled as if it ran with tonic water instead of blood. She had been counting the weeks since the wedding: one, two, and then the days, one, two, three, four. Now she could safely say that she was two weeks late. She could make him believe that it was his child inside her belly. And when it came early and large and looking nothing like him, what could he say? By that time it would be way too late.

She washed her face and inspected her reflection in the mirror. Surely something of her duplicity must be visible? She flattened her hair with both hands and ran a finger over her lower lip. It was bitten and chapped. Her skin was pale but a vivid spot of colour had appeared on her left cheek, making her look flushed and feverish. She ran her fingers down over her dress. Her breasts were swollen to the size of grapefruit, the nipples brown. She turned this way and that; although it was still definitely hers, her body was unrecognizable; she was a whale, inflated, gargantuan, vast. If he had known her before, if he had known her willow-thin figure and small, apple-sized breasts, he would have been able to tell. But he hadn't and therefore he didn't.

'Beautiful,' Ivory Price had said as he weighed her breasts in his hands, like a pair of prize sports balls. 'These will do nicely.'

She would keep her coat on, nevertheless. He would be wondering where she was. Quickly, she reapplied her lipstick and dabbed her cheeks with translucent powder. Then she arranged her face into a smile.

'Ivory,' she mouthed out loud. 'I think you better sit down. I think I might. I think I might . . .'

The front door of the hotel slammed, hard. They should get it fixed, she noted as she picked up her handbag. It sounded like it needed a damn good oiling. And then it slammed again.

For a fraction of a second Inez didn't recognize Monroe Simonov. It might have been the harsh sea light in her eyes or the battered briefcase in his hand that threw her. Or it might have been his expression. He was standing in the carpeted lobby, his body turned half away from her but his eyes aimed straight into hers.

'How was California?' he asked.

How could it be, she asked herself, that when she saw him again she seemed to suddenly lose all sense of inner gravity, of time passed, of decisions made, and instead rise up and flip inside like a fish? But what was Monroe Simonov doing in the lobby of a run-down Coney Island hotel? Was he following her? Did he know? Her hand flew to her belly instinctively. The baby kicked. She pulled her coat around her a little tighter. He was waiting for a reply. She had no idea what he was talking about.

'You here for the day?' she asked.

'No, just working. Same old, same old, you know,' he replied. 'When did you get back?'

'What is this?' she answered. 'An interrogation?'

She smiled but he did not return it.

'You make a film, or what?'

Inez felt a sudden, sharp pain and all the breath left her chest. She opened her mouth but couldn't think of anything to say. It was a lie she had forgotten telling and so she had no back-up, no explanation.

He took a step forward into the space between them, into her silence. 'You were never from Nova Scotia, were you, Suzette?' he said so softly it was barely audible.

'Monroe . . .' she began.

'You don't need to explain anything. Good to see you anyway.'

100

She felt the spot of colour in her cheek burn and one in the other cheek begin to appear. She had put the affair behind her, she had told herself that it was past, it was over, it was history. And yet here he was again and despite everything she was so glad to see him. She took a deep breath, let it slowly through her nose and finally looked up.

'You too,' she said, meeting his eye at last.

'And congratulations.'

Congratulations? What was he talking about? And then she remembered. Ivory Price and the rings that still spun so unfamiliarly on her finger. What had she done? As the vacuum cleaner in the rooms above whined and wailed, as a telephone rang, unanswered in an office somewhere nearby, she realized that this wasn't the way she envisaged her life to have turned out. She thought that marriage would herald a change in her. That somehow she would become another person, with new desires and different needs. But it hadn't happened. She was still the same. She still felt the same. Inez glanced away and smiled her department-store smile.

'Thank you,' she replied, before launching into the response that she now offered so often it was almost automatic. 'It was rather sudden. But I, we, are both very . . . very happy.'

From the corner of her eye, however, she noticed Monroe's expression change. Of course, he saw straight through her. He knew her. He saw everything, well, almost everything. Without another word he turned and walked out. The door fell with a crash behind him.

'Monroe?' she called out. But he was gone.

In the bar Ivory Price had finished one gin daisy and was on to his second.

'What took you so long, honey?' he said.

'Can I have a soda?' she asked the barman. 'You know, car sickness.'

'As long as you drink it quick,' Ivory ordered. 'I really need to be back in the office before five.'

It started to pour with rain as they drove back to the city. It veiled the endless warehouses, the brownstones and mean little terraced houses of Brooklyn. As they drew up at a junction, Inez watched a pale young woman drag a battered perambulator with two babies inside across the tram tracks. She struggled and yanked, struggled and yanked, her face streaming with water, her mouth resolutely closed. On a giant billboard above her head an angel reclined on a giant Life Saver mint.

'You're awfully quiet,' Ivory said. 'And your eyes are all red.'

'Don't mind me,' she told him. 'Sometimes I get melancholy.'

'Women.' He laughed. 'More ups and downs than the French Alps.'

There was a telegram waiting on the hall table when they returned home. Ivory ripped it open, read it, screwed it up into a small ball and threw it, hard, into the wastepaper basket.

'What is it?' asked Inez.

Ivory didn't answer. Instead he lit a cigarette and stared out of the window.

'Aren't you going to tell me?' Inez's voice cut in. 'Did somebody die, or what?'

He blew out a mouthful of bitter blue smoke. Sometimes he just wished his new wife would shut up. Her voice annoyed him, the angle of her cheekbone irritated him, the way she looked at him put him on edge. Why? He knew why. Just after his wedding he had decided that he would stop seeing the Argentine. He would break it off, give her a generous financial gift and then never see her again. And he had. But now as Inez stood in the doorway with her coat still buttoned up and her arms folded, he realized that he was weak, he was impulsive, and he was hopelessly unfulfilled. The park below was still almost bare; there were a few early blossoms and some spring flowers but the temperature was too cold to go out without gloves. As he smoked, he suddenly imagined himself down there in the Ramble, lying in a damp, leaf-strewn hollow, a place where you could almost believe you were alone, in the middle of the Catskill Mountains perhaps, but for the clatter of horse-drawn traffic and the occasional angry blast of an car horn. In his head, however, he was not alone: he was down there with Consuela in his arms.

When he had first set eyes on Inez Kennedy, here in this very room at his Christmas party, when she had danced alone to the music of the Negro band, there had been an undeniable fluidity about her. It was in the way she moved her body, it was in the slow, unfathomable glide of her eyes, it was in the way she appeared likely to slip between his fingers like gasoline. But in the weeks after their wedding something in her had changed. He had caught her, he had won her over, he had secured her for his own, and right before his eyes she had stiffened, she had clammed up, she had become brittle. And now he longed for the heady perfume of his mistress's body, for her soft mouth and yielding body. He longed for the kind of fast, hot, uninhibited sex that left him breathless and blissfully alive, the kind of sex that didn't need kind words and compliments to oil the way, the kind of sex that was so wrong it made everything all right again.

'Another ship gone down,' he said at last. 'U-boat attack.'

'That's terrible. Anyone you know?'

Ivory Price paused before he spoke, as if searching for the right tone. 'You know, my darling,' he replied at last, 'there are some things that are my business. I don't expect you to understand or to ask about them. Is that all right?'

But it wasn't a question. Ivory stubbed out his cigarette, turned and made his way towards the open door of his office, patting her on the shoulder as he passed. 'Just you go and arrange some flowers or go shopping or something. Do you need any money?'

The telephone started to ring in his office. Without another word, he closed the door and was gone.

The Price residence took up half an entire floor of the newly con-structed apartment block on Central Park West and boasted a total of seven bedrooms, six bathrooms and a staff annexe. It wasn't even one of the biggest, Ivory informed her. The penthouse apartment was twice the size but, he added, the guest bathrooms were a tad ungenerous.

Inez had her own room with a dressing room and bathroom. Since their marriage she had bought several racks of new clothes, hats and a seven-foot tower of boxed boots and shoes, but there was still an acre of space in the wall-to-wall closets. The thrill of shopping had worn off faster than she could have ever imagined. She didn't care about clothes enough to devote more time to them than was absolutely necessary.

She opened the window and let in a blast of sharp spring air. The phone rang again but was picked up almost immediately. And then she heard the front door slam. Ivory had gone to his office.

'Can I call you a cab, Mrs Price?' the doorman in the lobby asked.

'No, thank you,' she replied. 'I feel like a walk today.'

She could never call the doorman Eddie, the way that Ivory did. In fact he made her feel uneasy; he had the kind of face that seemed to absorb everything but give nothing away. He held the door open for her but let it go too early so that it slammed just behind her heels.

'He hates me,' she had once whispered to Ivory.

'Who?'

'Why him, that doorman.'

'Eddie?' he had responded. 'Don't be ridiculous. He doesn't hate you. He doesn't have any opinions. He's a doorman!'

'But he does. He hates me.'

Ivory Price sighed. He had so much more to think about than his new wife's opinion of the doorman, the doorman he tipped handsomely every month to keep his mouth shut. He knew plenty, that was for sure, but he wouldn't say a word of it to anyone. That was why he had been a doorman for so long.

'Eddie is there to make your life more comfortable. Just let him do his goddam job,' he had announced. And then he waved his hand in a chopping motion to show that the conversation was over.

'Merchant ship downed by U-boat', the headline read.

Inez bought a paper and read it as she walked along West Fifty-Seventh Street. When the Germans had sunk the *Lusitania* and over a thousand civilians died, they had agreed to stop sinking non-military ships. But since the British were still barricading their ports the Germans had decided to resume 'unrestricted' attacks. The ship, she guessed, must have been carrying something important. Not people, they didn't matter to her husband's company, but supplies for his business.

She headed down Fifth Avenue past the clubs and the hotels, past St Patrick's Cathedral and the Collegiate Church. At Forty-Fifth Street, she turned right. On the next block were the music publishers: Chas B. Ward, Shapiro, Bernstein and Co., Jerome Remick and Co. The air reverberated with the pump of a dozen pianos, with songs, with voices, with music. In the windows of the publishers were displays of sheet music: 'My Honolulu Honey', 'Tell it to Me Softly', 'Easter Egg Rag'.

'You a singer?'

Inez jumped so visibly, she had to readjust her hat. The man who had asked her the question was having a smoke on the stoop. His moustache was oiled into two thin black curls and he was wearing a shabby suit with a bright orange tie.

'Dancer,' she replied.

'What, you sing and dance?'

'No, yes, actually neither. I was just . . . I was just . . . looking.'

The man's eyes dropped to her belly and he raised his eyebrows, just a fraction. 'Sorry, ma'am,' he said, and doffed his hat. 'You take it easy now.'

What was she doing here? Inez asked herself. Why did she let herself be drawn back to places like this, places where piano players like Monroe mashed out tunes all day? What did she want? To climb the stairs to the Universal Music Corporation and ask for him? To bump into him accidentally again like she had in Coney Island? And then what? What could she say? What could she do? He, she reminded herself, had been the one who had dropped her. He had been the one who hadn't shown up. And so she kept walking until she reached Broadway where she turned right, and started the long walk back to Central Park West.

They had been discussing the latest news, the Zimmerman telegram, for an hour. The dining table stretched the whole length of the room and at least thirty people were sipping soup and listening to Ivory Price pontificate on the subject.

'Can you imagine,' he was saying, his face reddened with claret, 'Mexicans in Texas, Arizona and New Mexico. To think those

Germans had the nerve to suggest they finance an attack on us if we enter the war.'

'Who's to say it isn't a fake?' said the host, a man with a bald head and monocle, who sat at the other end of the table. 'A fake by the British. I mean they decrypted it. It could be a grocery list for all we know.'

'That's what Hearst thinks,' said his wife, a shrill woman at the other end of the table. 'More consommé anyone?'

'That's where we'll be if we don't take notice of this telegram,' Ivory Price exclaimed. 'In the consommé.'

Inez dropped her spoon with a clatter. Everyone turned to look at her, as if she had just materialized from nowhere, as if they'd never really noticed her before.

'Excuse me,' she whispered.

The dinner was excruciating. She was sitting between two elderly businessmen who began to talk over her about interest rates. She sat back and started to fan her face with her napkin. It was too hot. The candles on the table were burning too brightly, the fire in the grate was blazing too vigorously. The dining room, dark and gloomy with walnut panelling and heavily framed paintings on the walls, was too stuffy.

Earlier, in an attempt at conversation in the parlour, she'd commented on one of the paintings to another wife.

'Oh! Did you major in art history?' the woman had asked her.

'No,' Inez had answered.

'So what did you do?' the wife persisted.

'Oh, you know,' Inez replied eventually. 'This and that.'

The wife had continued to look at her, as if she didn't know and wanted her to explain. Out of the corner of her eye Inez happened to notice three or four other women all glance over at her simultaneously. She was obviously still a topic of conversation: the woman who married Ivory Price. Who was she? Where had she come from? Who were her family? What was she doing in New York?

A waiter passed with a tray of drinks. She took one, smiled vaguely, and left the woman standing there with her mouth slightly open.

'So tell me, what is Wilson going to do about Russia?' Ivory Price was saying to a circle of men. 'If they drop out of the war, and mark my words they will, the Allies are going to lose.'

Inez hovered at his elbow. Ivory didn't introduce her.

'Do you really think so?' she said in a voice that sounded small and insignificant in the huge room. 'I thought they just won the Battle of the Somme.'

Everyone simply ignored her.

'I tell you one thing,' Ivory had said with a wave of his hand. 'I bet you Wilson will be begging Congress to mobilize within the month.'

'Won't do one jot of harm to Price Aero,' another man quipped.

And they had all laughed while he had conceded that yes, it would be rather good for his books.

The soup had been taken away and she was served a slab of some unidentifiable bird covered with globular gravy from a silver platter. As a spoonful of green peas was tipped on to her plate she happened to glance up just as gravy dribbled off the end of another server's platter on the other side of the table and fell down the back of the chair of the man opposite. The waiter, an elderly black man, caught her eye. She opened her mouth and then closed it again. His eyes dropped and he continued serving. The table had fallen silent.

'So what does your new wife think?' The question reverberated in her head but she realized that it had taken her a moment to process it, to realize that it was aimed at her. She looked up to find the whole dinner table staring at her. 'I'm sorry?' she said.

'Do you think America should go to war?' the host asked her. 'Do you agree with your husband?'

'Why . . . of course I do. Absolutely not!'

The table as one started to laugh. Ivory was staring at her with a look of puzzlement on his face. With a bolt of horror she grasped that she had said the wrong thing. Instinctively she touched her hair. The pins had fallen out. It was sticking up all over.

'I don't think my wife is . . .' he started.

'I'm fine!' she retorted. But she was too hot, far too hot. Her head ached. She had to get out of there. And so she pushed back her chair and stood up. Twenty-nine faces all looked up at her. She had to do something, she had to say something.

'No, actually I'm not.' And without pause, without hesitation, she blurted out the words that she had been planning to say to Ivory later, in private. 'I'm . . . I'm expecting.'

Ivory's whole body swayed back on his chair, as if hit by a colossal wave. After only the briefest of silences, the wife seated nearest to Inez started to clap. The rest of the table joined her, palm striking palm, until their appreciation rose and swelled into a deafening round of applause. And then, as one, the whole table pushed back their chairs and got to their feet to give Inez her first and only standing ovation. 'What did I tell you?' said several wives to each other. 'A honeymoon baby, how absolutely divine.'

9

Anna listened to the sound of the rain. It poured from the broken gutters and spattered on to the row of garbage pails below. A peal of thunder unrolled in the air above, bringing another sudden downpour, another cascade of water to ricochet off the metal treads of the fire escape and stream down the walls of the building opposite. Even though it was midday, the sky was grey; the air was yellow. And there was a strange taste in the air, a taste of metal, a taste of earth, but also of the unearthly. Anna stood up and placed the kettle on the stove. She would make tea. It was a normal day, a Tuesday in April in fact. But when the kettle began to boil with its low, menacing rumble, it seemed suddenly as if the domestic elements were calling out to their wild forebears, steam to mist, water to rain, gas flame to lightning: release us, unshackle us, liberate us all.

Slowly the storm passed overhead, heading north towards Albany, the Adirondack Mountains and the border with Canada. Anna pulled open the window and wedged the wooden frame with a brick to let in some cool air. Usually, there was a thin haze of coal dust over the streets of northern Manhattan but after the rain the air seemed clearer than before, the noises of the city sharper, the smells of the drains and gutters, of horse-dung and gasoline, less obtrusive. She sipped her tea and listened; above the trundle of the elevated railway and the distant rumble of the traffic on Amsterdam Avenue, a child's voice was shouting, 'It's mine, it's mine.' A horse and cart trotted towards Spuyten Duyvil Creek, a boat on the Harlem River blew its horn once, twice, three times for good luck.

Although the small apartment was nothing like its equivalent in Russia – no workers' lodgings there had electric lights, a gas range for cooking and a chute for rubbish – the roof leaked. She looked up and noticed the damp patch on the ceiling had started to spread. The caretaker of the building had been dismissive when she had drawn his attention to it. He told her he'd look into it. He told her it was probably just the steam from her kettle or condensation from her cooking. But it bothered her that her rooms were being impregnated with damp, just as it bothered her that her shoes were wearing down at the heel and some of her stockings had laddered so badly she had not been able to repair them.

When she returned to Russia from America, she had always imagined she would do so triumphantly, elegantly, beautifully. She knew it shouldn't matter but somehow she couldn't help the fact that to her it did. And so she sprayed lavender toilet water from France liberally around the room with an atomizer until it ran out and then she prayed for dry weather. It won't be long, she told herself every day; it won't be long until she would see her country, her city, her son again.

According to the Russian newspapers the revolution had begun as a march for International Women's Day. While students and peasants, society women and children marched along the Nevsky Prospekt, on the other side of town Anastasia Deviatkina, a textile worker, organized a strike. After she encouraged her fellow workers to lay down their tools, they left the mill and headed to other factories, to metal plants and chemical works, to demand not only moral support but active participation. The march gathered momentum as it increased in size and soon two hundred thousand protesters were demanding bread, peace and the return of their sons and husbands from the front. Troops and police were sent to contain them but the crowd was so big and the chance of violence so high that they held back. And so the demonstrators headed out of the workers' districts towards the centre of the city, to the so-called 'Tsarist Citadel'.

Anna tried to picture the scene: the crowds of workers from Vyborg district and the south of the city crossing the frozen River Neva, the soldiers lined up on their horses on the other side, on the embankment, ready to shoot. She imagined hundreds of people pouring on to the river's surface, their banners swaying in the icy breeze, the women's skirts whipping around their legs. She wondered if they slowed their pace a little in apprehension as they reached the further side. But none of the soldiers fired a single shot, none of them carried out their orders to fire on the crowd. And so the marchers simply swarmed up on to the embankment and surged towards the gates of the Winter Palace.

Anna had heard other stories that were hard to believe: a young girl had apparently walked up to an armed Cossack on horseback whose battalion had been sent to block the crowd from entering Kazan Cathedral, pulled a bouquet of red roses from under her cloak and held them out to him. Everybody, so it was reported, watched nervously. What would the Cossack do? Beat her, arrest her, shoot her? But instead he smiled, leaned down from his horse and took the flowers. A week later the tsar had abdicated.

'The atmosphere on the streets,' she read in *Novy Mir*, 'is almost like a carnival. Restaurants are giving out free food to revolutionaries; everybody wears red armbands and bonfires have been lit in the streets to warm the striking workers. And yet the boys, the workers and the students, have armed themselves to the teeth. Girls in stolen cars career around the streets and try to shoot police snipers.'

Although it hadn't been a repetition of 1905's Bloody Sunday, elsewhere in the city the police had shot thousands of protesters, the protesters had shot hundreds of police, and countless numbers of people had died or been injured. All the inmates of the city's jails had been liberated. Shops had been looted. Wealthy people's apartments had been broken into, some of the women raped, their valuables stolen.

In a matter of months the whole power structure of Russia, a system that had been in place for almost three hundred years, had been dismantled. A Provisional Government was hastily formed. From America and Europe agitators and orators such as Lenin, Kollontai and Trotsky were returning to Russia as fast as they could. Nobody had predicted that the revolution would happen so unexpectedly.

Anna had spent hours at several ocean steamer offices trying once again to book her passage, but it wasn't straightforward. There was a

111

U-boat-filled sea to cross and a war-torn continent to negotiate. Plus, there was the question of the fare.

The telephone rang and she listened as it was answered by the caretaker.

'Call for you, Miss Denisova,' he shouted from the hallway.

Anna put down her teacup and stood up. Her first thoughts were of Kima. Had something happened to him? Had he been hurt? Please let him not have been killed. Please, no, not that? Just at the thought of it, her breath came quicker and her legs felt weak. And then she came to her senses. Bad news always came by telegram. It was not possible to call by telephone from Russia; it was unlikely to be about Kima. She straightened her hair, swallowed down her anxiety and hurried out into the corridor and along to the main landing where the telephone receiver was hanging by its cord. Cautiously, she picked it up.

'Hello?' she said.

'Madame Denisova?' It was a man's voice, a voice she couldn't immediately place. 'Forgive me for calling,' he said in Russian, 'but I have to see you.'

She took a deep breath. It must be about an article, an engagement, perhaps, an invitation to give a talk.

'I'm sorry,' she said softly in Russian. 'Who is speaking?'

She didn't like talking in the main corridor. She was sure that the whole floor was listening, even if they couldn't understand what she was saying. She had overheard two other tenants talking about her on the stoop; both suspected she was a spy.

'We met,' the caller said in a voice that was barely audible, more of a whisper than a reply. 'Don't you remember? My name is Noah, Noah Serginov.'

Noah Serginov. She searched her memory for any triggers. And then she remembered: young, attractive, arrogant.

'Oh, yes,' she replied. 'I remember.'

'I asked for your number at the newspaper, at *Novy Mir*. They weren't going to give it to me but I begged them . . .'

His voice trailed off. The silence on the line was filled with static. It was as if she were trying to listen through water.

'Can you hear me?' he asked.

'Yes,' she answered. 'I can hear you.'

'I have to see you,' he said with some urgency. 'As soon as possible.'

'If it's about an engagement,' she began, 'I'm afraid—'

'You know that's not what I mean at all,' he interjected. 'When? Where?'

Anna closed the door gently behind her. A fire truck roared past outside, the wail of its sirens blaring into her room through the open window. She pulled out the brick and without its support the window frame crashed shut with a shower of paint and loose dust. She picked up her cup and took a sip even though the tea had cooled.

There were thousands of Russian speakers in New York. They had been emigrating to America for decades. Many had settled, done well for themselves and were now completely assimilated. Others still lived in destitution in the Lower East Side and made a living by peddling or working in sweat shops. But there were hundreds of others who had arrived more recently, émigrés like Anna, who had come for a visit and found themselves staying longer than they intended.

Noah Serginov had just arrived in America. He and Anna had met for the first time at Leon Trotsky's address to a labour meeting in Brooklyn. The huge hall on Atlantic Avenue was half empty; as well as a small group of Russians who had come out of curiosity rather than from any political conviction, there were several dozen workers from the shipyards and the docks. Although the crowd must have eventually numbered only a couple of hundred, some of them had climbed on to the window ledges or on top of tables for a better view. Others waved red flags. Trotsky's English was poor and he spoke in slow and halting sentences. Often he broke down and shouted out a phrase or a word in Russian. Without a prompt, Serginov had yelled out a translation almost simultaneously. Much of Trotsky's speech was inaudible or garbled, but as if to make up for the smallness of the crowd the audience cheered and clapped and stamped at every opportunity.

Afterwards, as she waited with a group of other Russians to be introduced to the guest speaker, the unofficial translator had presented himself to her with a formal bow and had told her that, like Trotsky and his family, he had recently arrived in America after being deported from Norway.

'You speak good English,' she had commented.

Serginov explained that he had been born in St Petersburg, the son of a naval engineer who had married the daughter of a shipbuilder from Liverpool who had moved to Russia.

At that moment, a swell of people moved towards them; Trotsky was approaching. The translator took her by the elbow and steered her towards him.

'Leon, this is Madame Denisova.'

'Hello,' Trotsky replied. 'So good to see you again.'

'We met in different circumstances,' she explained to Serginov.

After only the most fleeting of conversations, however, Trotsky was whisked away to a rally in Philadelphia. The meeting hall was ready to close; the cleaners were hovering at the doors with their buckets and mops.

'How did you know who I was?' she asked Noah Serginov.

'A good guess,' he said with a broad smile. 'How many other beautiful Russian revolutionaries are there in New York?'

Noah Serginov was already waiting outside the Horticultural House in the Botanical Gardens. Although he was wearing the sober dark grey suit of an office worker, he was pacing back and forth, back and forth, as if life in the city was too slow for him, as if he would rather be on the back of a horse at full gallop than taking the subway or waiting aimlessly outside a hothouse.

The reflection of white clouds skimmed along the mottled blue surface of the ornamental lakes. The flower borders were crowded with pale yellow and dark purple tulips that bowed their heads in the intermittent breeze. It was a day of bright sunshine and brief showers, of feeling too hot and removing your hat and then feeling the chill of an approaching shower and having to put up your umbrella. Serginov had neither hat nor umbrella and his fair hair and the shoulders of his jacket were already wet through.

Anna paused at a small ornamental bridge to fix her shoe. Serginov pulled out a newspaper, shook it, sat down on a bench and started to read. He was still at last. Was it true that she was so easily identifiable? Russians usually gravitated to places where there were other Russians, in Paris at the Café des Manilleurs and in New York the offices of *Novy Mir* on St Mark's Place. Maybe they had crossed paths, or been introduced, or attended the same meetings on another occasion. But she was sure she had never seen him before that day at Trotsky's rally; she was sure she would have remembered him.

She stopped a few paces short of Noah Serginov and ran her finger along a branch of bright yellow forsythia that grew in abundance beside the main path, releasing a shower of droplets.

'I wasn't sure you'd come,' he said.

He lowered the newspaper and started to fold it up. Had he been aware of her all along?

'Neither was I,' she replied. 'So what is so important it can't even wait a day?'

He stared into the distance for a fraction of a second before looking up and fixing her with his eyes. In the daylight they were, she noticed with a jolt, a quite astonishing shade of blue.

'Come for a walk with me and I'll tell you,' he said.

As they walked, Anna conceded that Noah Serginov not only had arresting eyes. He had a fine aquiline nose, thick fair hair, a generous mouth and small white teeth. The only flaw in his face was his skin. His cheeks, forehead and chin were pitted with chickenpox scars. And yet he had the easy, relaxed manner of someone who was successful with women; he was clearly a man used to their capitulation without much resistance.

They headed towards the lakes, passing nannies with arms full of children all dressed in white, elderly couples who squinted at them inquisitively in the late afternoon light and young Jewish couples trailing mothers behind them on invisible strings. Narrow paths led off into small forests carpeted with bluebells or clearings where apple trees were covered with blossom. At first they walked in silence, their shadows, elongated by the low sun, stretching out behind them. And then he told her he was twenty-nine and had been a Revolutionary Socialist since 1905 when at the age of sixteen he had witnessed the Bloody Sunday massacre.

'I was on my way to school with some friends,' he said. 'And then I heard the rifles firing. Everyone else ran home. I kept walking; my parents didn't believe me when I told them what I had seen. We argued. I left home and eventually started writing and distributing pamphlets to the workers. Unfortunately I was betrayed.'

'And were you imprisoned? Were you exiled to the north?'

He shivered slightly even though the air was still warm. 'I was,' he replied.

'I was too,' she said.

'I know,' he said softly. 'I like your dress.'

It was such a sudden and unexpected change of subject that she was genuinely taken aback. Most people who had been imprisoned or exiled seemed to feel the need to talk about it. Names, places, dates would be swapped endlessly and the past picked over as if answers could be found in the chaff. Maybe it was better that she wouldn't have to go over those times again, maybe it was better not to be the bearer or the receiver of bad news.

They walked on, around the far corner of the largest of the ornamental lakes. A couple of ducks swam away from them, slicing the surface of the water into deep Vs. It was the end of a beautiful day. He glanced at her suddenly and to her surprise she felt the rush of anticipation. It was true that she had taken some time to choose what she would wear, but did he think she had dressed for him? Did he think they were embarking on a courtship? Did he think he could meet her on the pretext of important business and then try to seduce her in a park? She stopped and faced him.

'I'm not interested in you,' she said. 'Not at all.'

He looked at her with his blue eyes slightly widened. And then he looked away and swallowed.

'That wasn't,' he began. 'Oh dear . . .'

Anna felt the park, the path, the blue sky above start to swim. Her breath came faster. Her stomach began to plummet in the direction of her boots. How could she have forgotten she was no longer young; she was no longer beautiful; she was no longer desirable? Although her clothes were expensive, they were starting to wear out, to thin at the elbow, to fray at the hem, to wear down at the heel. And now she saw that he had patronized her with faint flattery, like one would an elderly aunt or a precocious child, and she had fallen for it. She was more embarrassed than she had thought possible. And she finally let herself admit that the reason she had agreed to meet him in a park at such short notice was that she had been undeniably, immeasurably, shamefully lonely. She gulped down the sour taste of her humiliation and turned away so he would not see her face. But when she spoke, her voice wavered a little despite herself.

'Is there anything important you have to tell me because if not, I have to go. I'm rather busy, you see.'

'Anna,' he said, with a little more familiarity than was respectful. 'You must have some idea why we're here?'

For an instant she was completely lost for words. She glanced up at him quickly and shook her head. He looked around to see if there was anyone else in earshot, and when it was clear that there was not, he started to talk in a low, urgent whisper.

'I have a message,' he said. 'A message for you from Le Brouillon.'

She stepped back and examined his face. Maybe she had misheard him. 'What did you say?'

'Le Brouillon,' he repeated. 'I'm sure you know him by that name but he also goes by the name of Pokolitov, Tadeus Pokolitov.'

Noah Serginov's face immediately lost all its boyish ease. It now looked older, harder, the mouth set, the blue eyes serious. He looked around before he began again, in a low whisper.

'The reason I wanted to meet so urgently,' he continued, 'was that I have been instructed to make contact as soon as possible. He needs you to attend a rendezvous with one of his men.'

'He has men?'

'As far as I know.'

Anna, however, only half heard his reply. Instead she was listening to the sound of birdsong and the gentle trickle of a small stream that flowed from the lake into a series of ornamental ponds. It was so calm, so tranquil, so peaceful. She tried to hold on to the world as it had been just a few minutes previously, where two people, a couple perhaps, walked in the further reaches of a park in the Bronx. Pokolitov was alive. The stream still flowed, the birds still sang and the sun still dropped, but Serginov's message, as Anna Denisova was painfully aware, had already changed everything.

'Madame Denisova, are you all right? Would you like to sit down?'

'No. Yes, I think I might like to,' she replied.

In St Petersburg, life had been so different; she had been so different. Human life was short and harsh, she had agreed. Long live the revolution. And looking back, the sky was brighter, the sun warmer, the snow colder, the wine stronger, Tadeus's kisses more intoxicating than anything she had ever experienced before or since. She had loved him so much that even when she was with him she was sometimes filled with melancholy for the future when they would be parted.

'Don't cry,' he would whisper in his heavy Georgian accent. 'I would do anything for you, remember that.' And he had pressed his hand to her chest and held it there like a promise.

When he had asked her to hide a revolver and a round of bullets one night when he had come in late with a strange light in his eye, she had agreed. Of course she had; she would have done anything Tadeus asked. But the very next morning, the door was broken down by the Okhranka, they were all arrested and she hadn't seen or heard from him since.

'I met him in Norway,' Noah continued. 'He asked me to look for you but he wasn't sure that you were still here. So you can imagine how surprised I was to meet you at Trotsky's rally. If I believed in fate, I would have said that I was led right to you.' He turned to her and smiled, his eyes alight in the pale glow of the setting sun.

'Norway?' she said. 'He is in Norway?'

'I don't know,' he replied. 'I don't think so. Even although Norway has remained neutral in the war, he had plans; none of us stays in the same country for long. You know how it is. . .'

The humiliation she had felt just a few minutes earlier had all but evaporated. He clearly knew nothing. It was obvious to her now that he was a boy, not a man. An affair with him would have been fraught with compromise and difficulty. What had she been thinking of?

'When?' she asked. 'When is the rendezvous?'

'I wrote it down,' he said and pulled out a piece of paper. 'On 24th May at 10 a.m. Grand Central Station on platform 16.'

She took the paper and folded it carefully. Serginov sat back and clasped his hands behind his head. So much had changed so quickly: Trotsky was on his way back to Russia, the war against Germany might be over, but Pokolitov was alive. He was still alive. And her heart was filled with the kind of hope that she had long since abandoned.

A park keeper was walking purposefully towards them holding a rake. He stopped on the far side of the stream.

'I have a public information message,' he shouted over to them. 'The park will close in fifteen minutes. Could you please make your way to the nearest exit?'

They said goodbye at the entrance to the subway station on Third Avenue. An electric tramcar clanked past and the rush of cooler air caught at the back of Anna's throat. She started to cough and found she could not stop; her whole body racked and shook, her knuckles clenched, her skin turned ashen. She pulled a clean fold of handkerchief from her bag and held it to her mouth.

'Are you all right?' asked Noah Serginov. 'Can I do anything?'

Anna shook her head, no, as she was swept up in another bout of coughing. Finally, however, it began to subside, finally her breathing returned to normal.

'I'm all right now, Mr Serginov.'

'Please. Call me Noah,' he said.

'Thank you. Thank you, Noah.'

And then she turned and hurried south along Pelham Avenue as the street lights buzzed and then flickered on, their globes of light a string of beads threaded through the ever darkening park.

10

Only the shallow radiance of candlelight and a dozen mercury vapour lamps lit up the huge cavity of the dance floor. Deep blue velvet upholstery and booths fashioned of American walnut soaked up what little light there was, making the air feel as saturated as blotting paper. There was neither wine nor beer on the drinks list, just bourbon and cocktails. If or when the waiters noticed your presence, Monroe realized, it didn't necessarily mean they would serve you. In fact, although the Velvet Smoke, a brand-new private club for a rich white clientele, had just opened in a basement in Harlem, on 134th and Seventh Avenue, by the way that people slouched on the banquettes and curled themselves around their whisky sours, it felt as if they, and the club, had already been there for decades.

When Monroe arrived, the band was setting up on a small stage, the dull gleam of their instruments catching the candlelight. As well as the other more pungent odours – wax polish and Jamaican rum, expensive perfume and cigar smoke – there was the unmistakable aroma of musical instruments. To Monroe, the inside of a piano or the splay of a horn smelled like nothing else on earth. In that combination of brass and sweat, of damp felt and adrenalin, was a taste that filled your mouth, your throat, your heart, with sweetness.

It was only seven on a Monday night but the nightclub was already almost full. There must have been at least three hundred people crammed around tables and stuffed into the booths. And everyone, it seemed, was talking about America's declaration of war on Germany. Everyone wanted to celebrate.

'To victory over the Huns,' one man toasted. 'America is going to whip them good and proper.'

'Drink as much as you can,' one man was telling his friend. 'Once Wilson starts conscription you won't get the chance.'

But there was another reason why the club was busier than any other week-night: Monday's entertainment was frequented by talent-spotters for recording companies, for publishers, for moving pictures and for shows on Broadway. The crowds prided themselves on being able to discern quality or talent, musicality or whimsy. It was a place where new faces, new songs, new styles of music were tried out and appraised. For that reason the management charged both for admission, one dollar, and for a spot, ten dollars.

The bitter-sweet agony of meeting Suzette Kinross again in the Beach Palace Hotel at Coney Island had not yet worn off. As Monroe had stood face to face with her in the corridor of the run-down seaside hotel, it finally dawned on him: the woman he had yearned for, the woman whom he had loved with both passion and fidelity, had lied to him, had deceived him, had dropped him without bothering to tell him, and then had married another man. And his heart seemed to deflate in his chest. With a jolt, he saw himself as she must see him: poor, shabby, ordinary. He was suddenly acutely aware of all the compromises he had made, of the fact that he had inadvertently become the kind of man he would have despised as a boy: a travelling salesman, a peddler of sheet music. He might as well be selling brooms and brushes. And as those thoughts raced through his head, Suzette had cast him a look in which he could read only pity.

Monroe had slammed the front door of the Beach Palace Hotel behind him, extra hard for good measure. Rain had begun to spot on the polished bonnet of the large white car that Suzette had arrived in and he was tempted to scratch it, to run his key along the perfect finish of its paintwork. But when the momentary thrill of the act had worn off, he knew he would just feel cheap, he would feel guilty, he would feel worse. He turned and as he walked towards the station, into the wind that blew the rain almost maliciously into his face from the Atlantic, he decided that it was time to change everything.

'It's new, its syncopated, it's called jazz,' he told Von Hofe that same afternoon.

'You mean like the Original Dixieland Jass Band?'

'No!' replied Monroe. 'I mean yes! Like that but not as white.'

'Really,' Von Hofe said and looked at him sceptically. 'All right. Let me see the music.'

'There isn't any music,' Monroe explained. 'That's the point.'

'Simonov,' Von Hofe said, 'are you being facetious? I'm a music publisher.' And he laughed, a big deep belly laugh.

'No, but listen,' insisted Monroe, 'it's a whole new way of thinking. It takes a song as a starting point, of course, but then it breaks free of it. Every time the song is played, it sounds different. It's like making love, the act is the same, but every time it feels new, fresh, like it had never happened quite that way before.'

Monroe suddenly had a vivid flashback. Suzette lying in his bed, her eyes half closed, the white curve of her shoulder caught by a glance of evening sun.

'Hey, are you all right?' Von Hofe was staring at him. 'Looks like we lost you for a moment.'

'I'm fine,' Monroe replied.

'Good. As a matter of fact. I was thinking of recording a phonograph.'

'You were?' said Monroe.

'With a full band, just like those original guys from Dixie. If you've got the music, and you think you can pull it off, I'd like to hear it.'

'Now?'

'No, not now,' Von Hofe said. 'You heard of the Velvet Smoke in Harlem? Fix yourself up a spot and let me know.'

Monroe had caught Hubert Von Hofe on a good day. One of Universal's songs, 'Good Mornin' Caroline (you're beautifully mine)' had been picked up by Florence Mills, the 'phenomenal soprano.' With her face on the front of the sheet music and her pledge to sing it at every performance of her sell-out run on Broadway, he had decided to print half a million copies and spend most of the year's advertising budget. It was a bad gamble. A few months later her husband, who was British, would be shot down over France and Florence would unexpectedly decide to retire from show business. But right then, as he congratulated himself on a job well done, he was in the mood for taking chances.

'Harlem,' Monroe repeated. 'The Velvet Smoke.'

'That's right,' he said. 'Just let me know.'

In the dark depths of the back stage, there were already a dozen men, some white, some black, sitting nervously on foldable chairs. Out front, apart from the usual quota of wealthy stockbrokers and businessmen, there were a few well-known faces from the Alley, including Von Hofe sipping a bourbon on the rocks.

This is it, Monroe told himself over and over, this was his moment to show what he was capable of. He took off his jacket and hung it over the back of a chair. Everything would change from this day on. To gain anything in this life, he had told Nonna Maria as the men from the pawnshop humped his piano down the stairs, you have to take a risk now and then.

Spring had come late to Manhattan after an unusually cold winter. Everybody was still wearing too many clothes of the wrong kind of fabric. Monroe had just bought a new suit made of thick grey serge that he wore with a dark blue silk bow tie. It had been fine in the gentlemen's outfitters but now he itched, he sweated, he felt hot and shivery at the same time. He tried to loosen his collar but it seemed to have stuck.

Monroe had booked two spots, one in the first half and one in the second. Two chances, he told himself, two bites at the cherry. In the first spot he would play a song he'd just written called 'In Jazz with You'. With the backing of the band and an audience, how could he fail? Monroe had seen the atmosphere spark and ignite in the black clubs that Edward had taken him to. In the second spot he would play 'The Sweetest Time' first straight through, and then with all the syncopation and improvisation he could muster.

Monroe examined his hands. If he concentrated hard enough, could he make them stop trembling? Out on the stage the band started to play, racing through a medley of recent hits.

'You,' the drummer shouted over to Monroe. 'Boss says you're on.'

'When?'

'Now! You're on first! You got the music for the band?'

'You play jazz?' he asked the bandleader.

He looked at him blankly.

'Just follow my lead,' Monroe explained.

The trouble was that although in the privacy of his own room he could play up a storm, when Monroe buttoned up his jacket, climbed on stage and sat down at the piano, he was shocked to discover that the stool was lower than he expected and the middle D stuck, just a fraction. It wasn't just the piano. A spotlight had been switched on and shone in his face, blinding him to everything but his own reflection in the brass of the music stand. He tried not to let it bother him, he tried to forget about the height of the stool and the heat of the light and the sticky key. And then the band started to play at half the speed he had intended. The chorus, he told himself, surely the chorus will get them. It didn't. It sounded like a dirge, like something you might play at a funeral. It came to the point when his hands should have started to stride, his left wander all over the keys and his right improvise and syncopate, but he froze, he jammed, he could not do it.

Suddenly it was all over; to a smattering of applause and an audible shifting of seats on the wooden floor, Monroe walked off stage as fast as he was able. His face, his ears, his eyes burned while his fingers were white.

'You played it all wrong,' said Edward. He was standing alone, backstage, sucking on a bottle of beer. 'What happened?'

'What are you doing here?' said Monroe.

'I came through the stage door. They see a black man, they figure he's just a musician.'

'That was a disaster,' Monroe said.

Out front there was more polite applause as another man sat down at the piano, spun round on the stool and smiled widely at the audience.

'It's this place,' Edward shouted. 'Don't matter what they say, all these folks want is something familiar, something they heard before.'

As if on cue, the piano player started to pound out 'Hinky Dinky Parlez Vous'. As the dance floor filled up, the resident band joined in and the audience began to sing along. In the fizzing yellow light of the back stage, Edward's face clouded over. He seemed preoccupied, sober, much older than his twenty-two years.

'I'll play one of your songs for you,' Edward offered.

'But you haven't got a spot,' Monroe replied.

'You got another one?'

'Yes,' he admitted. 'But aren't you supposed to be at work?'

'I got let go,' Edward said. 'Kept falling asleep. Too many late nights, I suppose.' He smiled and ran his hand over his oiled black hair.

'So how you going to pay the rent?'

'I got a few ideas; you got to fight the good fight,' Edward answered. 'You know what I mean?'

Edward was wearing a light-coloured jacket. Underneath he wore a white cotton shirt and a plum-coloured neckerchief. He flexed his hands and began to tap his fingers in time with the bass drum.

'Thank you for the offer,' Monroe said. 'I appreciate it but I need to do this myself; though you play way better than anyone.'

'I know how good I am,' Edward said. 'You don't need to tell me.'

When they had first encountered each other, that winter day in December, Edward had nothing more than the tattered felt hat and second-hand suit he was standing up in. But he seemed to have thrived in New York. Even though the wages and tips he had collected from his caretaker's job couldn't have gone very far, he had somehow managed to amass a whole wardrobe of sharply cut suits and silk ties. And he wore them as if he'd always owned them, as if they had been bespoke tailored. Where did Edward get it all from, Monroe wondered as he watched him smooth down his shirt front, all that fathomless self-confidence?

Edward caught him looking at him and shrugged. 'You want anything in this city,' he said, 'you have to act as if you got it already.'

At that point a door swung open up above and in the wash of warm evening light from the street two pairs of legs, a man's and woman's, could be seen descending the stairs from the street into the club. One was wearing dark trousers and a pair of spats, the other a skirt cut above the ankle and a pair of black satin shoes without stockings. The couple paused at the bottom of the steps and blinked in the semi-darkness. It was such an entrance that nobody could fail to stop what they were doing, turn in their direction and take a look. The man wore a top hat and tails, the woman a dress of ivory silk. He was white, she was black. She was in her early twenties; he was in his late forties. A maître d' appeared from nowhere and greeted them both with a supercilious bow before ushering them through the back stage and towards a raised booth on the balcony.

'Hello, Bessie,' Edward said as she breezed past.

'Why, Edward,' she replied. 'You playing tonight?'

He ignored the question but she didn't seem to notice.

'Going to introduce me to your companion?' he asked.

The older man was giving the briefest of nods or flickers of his fingers to people he knew backstage. Either he hadn't heard Edward or had decided to pretend he hadn't. Bessie tried to conceal a smile and failed. She turned and laid a hand on the older man's arm.

'Harold, meet Edward,' she said.

Finally Harold turned round, his gaze opaque, and glanced briefly in Edward's general direction. 'Ever so pleased,' he said. 'Used to come in here and have the place to ourselves. Now they let in any Tom, Dick or Harry.'

'That's right. Even people like me,' said Edward and laughed.

Harold, however, didn't respond. Without another word, he moved up the stairs to the balcony, to the booth that had a huge reserved sign hanging from a hook on the wall.

'And this is Monroe,' said Edward.

'Hello, Monroe,' said Bessie.

'You still at the Variety?' Edward asked her.

'Still there,' she replied.

'Where did you find a man like that?' Edward said. 'They hosting a freak show in there now?'

Bessie laughed. Her hair had been straightened and pulled back from her face. All the gradients of her head, Monroe couldn't help noticing, from the angle of her cheekbones to the curve of her smile, all seemed to lead to her eyes, great dark eyes with copper-coloured irises that hung as if suspended.

'Actually, he's the theatre manager,' she said with a blink.

And then she moved off towards the stairs, throwing a single glance to both of them over her shoulder.

'Who was that?' said Monroe.

'Just a chorus girl,' Edward said. 'But she's also a beautiful singer.'

'You know her well?'

Edward shrugged. 'A little,' he replied. 'She liked you.'

Monroe looked at Edward to see if he was teasing.

'You think so?'

'Uhuh.'

Edward was engrossed in the drinks menu. He had to forget about Suzette. Just like she had forgotten him. She wasn't that special. New York was full of beautiful women. Women like Bessie.

'Let me get you a drink?' Monroe asked his friend.

'Go right ahead,' he answered. 'The barman won't serve coloureds.'

Edward knew Bessie's friend, the theatre manager, even though he pretended he didn't. The manager had offered him a spot at the Variety at the end of the first act. On one condition: he blacked up. That was the way they did it, he said with a shrug, with burned cork and greasepaint. You wanna play like a coon, you have to look like a coon. It was the same story at every place he auditioned. They all wanted him but only if he looked the part.

'You want me to look like a white man pretending to be a Negro?' he had asked. 'Are you out of your mind? My skin is black enough already.'

'You won't get far in this city if that's your attitude,' he was told again and again. 'That's the way we do it here.'

It was after he had turned down his third offer of a job that he had come to a decision. There are other ways, he had told himself, other ways of showing the world what he was made of.

Monroe should never have started on the bourbon. That, he realized later, was his first mistake. By the third shot, the basement club had started to swim with people, with laughter, with dancers. Monroe excused himself to the men's room to throw cold water on his face. Was it so bad to get a little tipsy once in a while? he asked himself. Was it so bad to get drunk when he had to play? The jazz musicians he knew seemed to get better the more they drank.

And then he noticed Bessie's companion standing beside him, brushing his moustache with a tiny comb. Monroe nodded to him in greeting. The look the theatre manager gave him back was one of blatant disgust, as if he had just offered to sell him his body for a couple of bucks. Another man came in to wash his hands. His boots were polished, his clothes looked expensively cut and he wore a gold pocket watch in his waistcoat. The theatre manager's face opened up into a smile as he turned to him.

'I do believe we were once introduced,' he said.

'We were?' the man replied. 'I'm sorry, I don't recall.'

'I manage the Variety,' he explained. 'Didn't we discuss the possibility of a small investment? An associate producer role? I think we did.'

Monroe swayed towards the door that led backstage. Edward wasn't there. On the stage was a ukulele player whose fingers moved so fast Monroe could barely focus on them. The bar was packed now and the floor was writhing with people dancing. Why not? he asked himself. Why the hell not?

'You want to dance?'

Bessie looked down at him with an expression that was closer to surprise than enthusiasm. She glanced over at the theatre manager who had come out of the men's room but was still deep in conversation with the well-dressed man.

'But then again if you'd rather not.'

'Sure,' she said. 'I'd be happy to dance with you. You stay there. I'll come down.'

As soon as they reached the dance floor, Monroe realized that he hadn't taken one crucial element into consideration. He was too drunk to dance, and so he gingerly circled the edge of the floor, hoping she wouldn't notice. Twice Monroe had to steady himself with his hand on her shoulder to stop from falling over.

'Are you all right?' she asked him.

'Yes. No. You're beautiful,' he said.

What was he saying? His heart was thumping in his chest. No, he meant it. She was. He sought out her gaze. She was staring over his shoulder towards the door to the back stage. Monroe glanced round. There was only one man in the line of her gaze. Edward.

'Bessie?'

'It's been a pleasure,' she replied automatically. And then she released him, gave him one languid look and headed back to her booth.

'Where you been?' Monroe asked Edward.

'Had to check on Little Joe.'

'Joe? In your apartment on Sixty-Second?'

'You think I can run that fast? No, he's moved in with my aunt round the corner.'

Edward was out of breath and his skin was covered in a faint gloss, a polish of sweat. He smelled of fresh air and clean cotton. With his large brown eyes and wide shoulders, he was undeniably a good-looking man.

'I danced with Bessie,' Monroe said suddenly.

Edward nodded at him slowly. 'See, I told you. Women like you.'

The ukulele player finished to whoops of applause. Monroe was on next. His hands, when he examined them, seemed too far away. His mouth was so dry he could barely speak, let alone sing.

'Holy moly,' he whispered. 'I'll just have to show 'em, won't I?'

But he was too far gone, too drunk, too conscious of his multiple shortcomings. He sat down and rubbed his face with his hands.

'Looks like I blew it,' he said. He looked up at his friend. Edward was always so calm, so collected. 'You take the spot,' Monroe said. 'You play. What have I got to lose?'

Edward rolled up his sleeves, ran his hand over his hair again, climbed up on to the stage and sat down at the piano. Monroe saw that he had something that he himself did not, an easy kind of confidence; he took his time. First he played a couple of scales to test out the keys; he hit the sticky middle D a couple of times as if making a mental note. And then he lifted his hands and waited for silence. It came almost immediately. Everybody watched him. Even the barman put down his dishcloth and turned off the tap.

At first Edward raced through a series of rags, one shifting into another, the pace so frenetic that the dancers on the floor wiggled and clutched and spun. And then he looked up, caught Bessie's eye and suddenly changed tempo. The rag almost seamlessly shifted into the chorus of the song that Monroe had written. The band joined in and for a while they all played together.

He began to sing the verse clear and slow, with each word hanging before sliding down to the next. It was too slow to foxtrot to and the dancers clung to one another and slowly circled. And then his song sounded as if it had always been sung, it sounded the way he had first heard it in his head. But not for long: Edward's hands started to stride, to open it up, to stretch the melody until it almost snapped. Monroe felt like he was being led blindfold to new places, to new landscapes filled with strange and yet familiar shapes. And in that collision of pattern and colour, of notes and tempo, was something raw and exhilarating that he recognised: emotions that he had never been able to articulate, let alone admit to.

A telephone started to ring somewhere. The theatre manager called over a friend and they started to banter, to joke, to guffaw. Edward's face twitched in annoyance. A murmur of chatter began to rise up, as other people followed the manager's example. Without any warning, Edward suddenly stopped playing mid-phrase and looked out at the audience. And then he slammed the piano lid and rolled down his sleeves. His departure from the stage, however, barely seemed to make any impact on the club at all. The chatter continued. The resident band began to play' K-K-K-Katy,' triggering another burst of conversations about the war and a sudden rush back on to the dance floor.

'Only five thousand men initially,' someone was saying. 'That's what Woodrow Wilson said in his declaration.'

'We didn't have a choice,' a woman in a blue hat was insisting. 'How much longer could we have tolerated those torpedo attacks?'

Outside, the air was cool and clear. It had been a perfect early April day and something of its green limpidity still lingered. Monroe caught up with Edward at the junction of 130th Street.

'What the hell did you think you were doing?' he yelled. 'Are you drunk or what? You just blew it. You totally blew it! For you and for me.'

'What does it matter?' Edward replied softly.

Although it was dark there were lights burning in almost every window on the block. The smell of cooking mingled with the scent of spring drifting across from St Nicholas Park. A little girl on a stoop played trills on a harmonica.

'What does it matter? That was your opportunity and mine,' Monroe said. 'To be heard.'

'How can you be heard,' Edward replied, 'when there ain't nobody listening?'

'They would have. If you'd given them the chance. Don't you know how to plug a song?'

'No,' he said. 'I don't. I'm no song-plugger.'

Monroe was breathing fast and his mouth was clamped shut. And then from the direction of the club came the rapid clip of a woman's heels. Monroe turned around to see a woman approaching, a woman in an ivory dress.

'Hey,' he said. 'It's Bessie.'

Monroe took a few steps forward. She did indeed like him, she had followed him, she had decided that she couldn't let him get away. Maybe the evening hadn't been such a disaster after all. Although he could barely believe it, a whole narrative suddenly began to unfold in his head: he would take her in his arms and they would go to a fancy bar and order more of the cocktails she liked to drink. He saw himself sitting in the front row of the Variety every night as she sang to him, he saw himself in bed with her later, he saw himself in love with her and her with him. He tried out her name in his mouth again. Bessie.

'You were feeling bad. I just said it to make you feel better,' said Edward from behind.

The words, however, didn't immediately register. Bessie's footsteps slowed down as she approached him. It was too dark to read her face until she was almost level. When he did, he saw the way her eyes softened and her high cheekbones caught the lamplight, the way she smiled and bit her lower lip. He saw the way she looked at Edward. And his words registered in Monroe's head at last.

'You bastard,' Monroe yelled at Edward. 'She doesn't like me. She likes you. Why did you tell me that? You made me look like such a fool.'

Monroe punched Edward square in the face. Bessie screamed. The girl with the harmonica stopped playing. Edward clutched his jaw. Monroe clutched his hand. Somewhere in the distance, a train whistle blew.

'Well, I suppose we're even,' Monroe said. 'We've both done something unforgivable. Have a nice night.'

Monroe turned and started to walk away. Edward reached out his arm and tried to stop him. A gilt cufflink glinted in the street light.

'Wait,' said Edward. 'We should say goodbye, at least.'

But Monroe simply shook his head and kept on walking. The streets of Harlem were almost empty apart from the long lines of Pierce-Arrows and Overland cars that chuntered on the kerb outside private clubs. Monroe climbed on the subway at 125th and Lenox and rode all night, to Bowling Green and on to Atlantic Avenue in Brooklyn and then back up again through Forty-Second Street all the way to Bailey Avenue. And with the steady rhythm of the train in his ears, as a Chinese man beside him began to snore and a tramp stretched out full-length on the bench opposite, his mind was filled with the sound of Edward playing his song.

It was eight in the morning when he finally climbed off the subway. He headed up for air through hordes of people going to work, his temple throbbing and a thin film of black subway dirt over his skin.

'I blew it,' he asked Von Hofe, 'didn't I?'

'It was a gamble; you took it,' his boss said. 'And that, my boy, is admirable in my book. Where are you heading today? Atlantic City?'

Monroe nodded. 'New Jersey shore,' he said.

The room was beginning to swim. Monroe's eyes burned. The back of his throat felt clogged up with a constriction that he was loath to identify.

'You got a smoke?' he asked.

'Most of the acts were nothing special,' Von Hofe went on as he shook out a cigarette. 'But there was one. The coloured boy. Second act. No jacket. He was good. Best thing we heard all night. You don't happen to know him?'

'That's Edward,' he replied as he lit up.

'In fact I was thinking of cutting a roll, you know, for a Pianola, of that song he played. I have a friend over at Columbia who was also mighty impressed. You know what it was?'

As the smoke cleared, Monroe examined his boss's face to see if he was serious.

'As a matter of fact,' Monroe answered, 'it's one of mine.'

'Really,' said Von Hofe. 'Get me that piano player, we cut a roll, see how it sells. And you know what, I think we might be able to work something out after all.'

Monroe hammered at the main door of Edward's apartment block for ten minutes. Dozens of windows flew open to tell him to shut up, to go away, to leave them in goddam peace, but not Edward's.

'The Mackenzie boy? He moved out,' said one lady on the second floor. 'Left early this morning.'

'Edward? Are you sure? The one with the brother, Joe.'

She gave him a cool look. 'Joe moved in with some aunt in Harlem,' she said as she began to close her window. 'Edward joined up last week; 15th Regiment, Coloured. He's gone to war.'

11

Inez unlocked the French doors to the terrace and pushed them wide open. She could hear the plane long before she could see it, a mosquito buzz slowly rising in pitch as it came closer. And then with a spluttering strum, it flew low overhead, wings outstretched, propeller blurring into a pale disc, as fragile, almost, as a child's model, thrown.

Ivory Price had learned to fly years earlier, but after a series of intensive private lessons, had just been granted his Military Aviator Certificate. At thirty-two, he was two years too old to be conscripted but was planning to enlist anyway, in the Aviation Section, US Signal Corps. All he talked about was the war now, about the Canadian victory at Vimy Ridge and the Nivelle offensive.

'At least you won't have to clean the mud off my boots,' he had said more than once.

That morning the sun was a cool orb suspended in the sea mist. Temperatures had soared over the last few weeks, with thermometers reading record highs of eighty-two degrees. Out front, beyond the garden, the lyme grass rustled like paper in the dunes. Inez stood, her feet bare, her nightgown flapping, her red hair like a virulent type of amber seaweed, blown up and out and everywhere, and watched the plane get smaller and smaller. The fully staffed summerhouse had been rented for a month over Easter. Inez had told Ivory that it would be better for her to be out of the city, away from the preparations for war, the unseasonal heat, and the charity dinners and fund-raising dances that filled their joint social diary.

'Why the beach?' Ivory had demanded. 'Why not my parents' house in the Berkshires?'

'I just like the sea,' she had replied with a shrug. 'More than I like your parents.'

Ivory had laughed out loud. At that point he still found her audacity charming. Besides, he himself had a strained relationship with his family. He knew they believed him to be a foolish playboy with terrible taste in women. They didn't say it but he knew that Inez merely proved their point. Also, he was busy at work. He had heard about plans for a new type of aeroplane engine, a 'Liberty L-12', whose lightweight design would be based on a car's. It was said that the War Department intended to use this new engine for both planes and tanks. Price Aero was working on a tender for the production of thousands of planes of a new design, all of which would use the new engine. If successful, and he was pretty confident he would be, shares in his company would rocket. He was wealthy before, but the war would make him richer than he ever thought possible. If his new wife wanted the beach, he could afford the beach.

The noise of the plane was barely audible now; it came in snatches above the sound of the surf, and could just as easily, Inez thought, be the sound of a distant motor car or the rotary whirr of a lawn mower. It was eventually drowned out completely by the heady drone of a wasp that circled the breakfast table and landed on the rim of a glass of orange juice, which Ivory had been drinking from only an hour earlier, the two whiskers of its antennae twitching for all the sweetness.

Although the sea was still freezing, a warm wind boomed along the beach and un-pegged the swimming towels that had been hung out on the line that morning. Early lilac in the neighbour's garden waved its wands of blossom before reluctantly letting go handfuls of petals. Inez watched the elderly gardener for a while as he weeded and pruned, mowed and planted, and then she wound up the gramophone, let it blast her brand-new Dixieland Jass Band recording into the clear salty air and danced by herself on the terrace.

The plane had almost reached the line of dark blue where the ocean met the sky but then, in one graceful arc, it wheeled round, levelled its wings and headed back towards the distant glint of Manhattan. On the table, the wasp had fallen into the glass and was slowly drowning.

Since Inez had blurted out her news about the baby, Ivory's behaviour had become increasingly erratic. Some days he would treat her like an invalid, bring her cups of tea and insist she put her feet up on a stool. Some nights, however, she noticed a clear and undeniable note of disgust in his face before he rolled over and claimed he was 'tired out'. But maybe that was just the way he was. Perhaps he simply didn't like women as much as he thought he did, or pregnant women, or the woman he was married to. For all she knew he might have any number of any other women to sleep with. He had plenty of opportunity.

Once, she had picked up the faintest trace of woman's perfume on his sleeve. She recognised it: Narcisse Noire. She glanced up at him in alarm. Ivory swallowed twice and then smiled.

'Do you like it?' he said. 'I wasn't sure. The lady behind the counter said it was all the rage. I was going to buy it for you but, but then they ran out of stock! Can you believe it?'

Inez didn't answer. Even Ivory couldn't have believed his explanation was convincing.

'Aren't I enough for you?' she asked him softly.

'Yes,' he replied. 'Yes, yes, yes. Hell, I married you didn't I? And now what with the baby on the way, I'm a different man.'

'Who was she?'

'No one,' he replied. 'What are you talking about?'

And as she lay awake and his bulky figure heaved with sleep in the bed beside her, she realized that she knew him maybe only a little better than he knew her. And he knew nothing about her. Or the duplicity she was capable of. Now she was at least six months pregnant, but officially only three. Luckily she was slim enough almost to carry it off. But even so, her belly was taut, a swell that was rock-hard beneath her palm, her hair was thicker and more unmanageable than ever and sometimes she could see the contours of an elbow, a foot or a knee protrude and retract as the baby shifted and rolled inside.

Physically, for the time being at least, she could get away with it. Emotionally, however, she was much further gone. When she woke in the morning she was filled with the feeling that something good was about to happen but she would momentarily forget what it was – a present, a meeting with someone special, the promise of the most perfect weather. And then she would remember. The baby. And her heart would feel full to the brim and ready to spill. But how could you be this in love with someone you hadn't met? How could she let herself feel that all was well with the world when it so obviously was not? It must be a trick she played on herself, a mental sleight of hand. But she had saved them both, hadn't she? It had been the only option, for herself, for the baby. No one would ever know. Things like this, she told herself, must happen all the time.

Maud was coming down from the city for lunch. But she wasn't due for at least another hour. And so Inez left the French doors wide open, the curtains billowing, the needle in the phonograph tick, tick, ticking in an empty groove, climbed back into bed and fell asleep again with her arms wrapped tight around her unborn child.

Consuela Romero dabbed the back of her neck with a small clean white handkerchief as the bus from the city pulled in to another small town. Like all the other inconsequential little outposts that were strung out along the length of Long Island, the sides of the houses had been painted with signs that advertised toothpaste or hair oil. A small boy sat in the shade and threw stones at a dog that was tied to a stake. A smart city car was parked outside the general store, which sold both engine oil and Sunday bonnets. Two men were loading up the boot with crates of supplies. She watched as boxes of cereal and cartons of strawberries, bottles of soda water and quarts of gin were carefully stacked.

Consuela had brought nothing to drink and even though she was parched, she could still feel the perspiration gather and moisten under her arms and behind her knees. Closing her eyes, she rested her temple on the cool glass of the window and imagined a strawberry crushed on her tongue or a mouthful of ice laced with lime. She ran her tongue over her lower lip and was instantly reminded of the brackish tang of her lover's skin.

The address of the place she was heading to had been tucked in Ivory's jacket pocket, folded up between receipts for rounds of golf and lunch at his club. Why had she done it, rifled through his pockets while he slept? She must have suspected that he was about to do it again: end the relationship. She could feel it in his fingertips as he ran his hand over her breast, she could see it in his face as she kissed his belly, she could hear it in the arch of his sigh just after he had climaxed. It was a tiny reluctance, a breath taken a little too deeply, a speck of light in his eye in her darkened room, a letting go. And so rather than curl herself around his body, inhale his drowsiness until they rose and fell together with each breath as she would usually have done, she lifted his sleeping arm from where it rested, deadweight, wrapped herself in her Chinese robe and began to search, not even certain, at the time, of what she was looking for.

Consuela Romero had been born in Buenos Aires in the Barrio Norte into a Spanish family who had made their fortune in the 1850s quickly and bloodily by exporting beef. She had moved to New York when she was nineteen after hearing Enrico Caruso sing Donizetti's 'Una Furtiva Lagrima'. Caruso was a regular at the Met and she had decided that if it was his adopted city then it must also be hers. Her parents had been initially sceptical until an uncle in Pennsylvania supported her plan; he told her father that he had once heard her play the piano and thought he could secure her a place at a music conservatory in Philadelphia. It was not ideal and the uncle had also added that she could help pay back her fees by helping out at his meat-packing business, but she had persuaded her family it was what she wanted. She knew the uncle had her in mind as a wife for his not particularly bright second son, but anything was better than staying in Buenos Aires waiting for her two elder sisters to be married off so she could be next.

A man she met on the day she arrived in New York promised her tickets to Caruso's performance of Von Flotow's *Martha* at the Metropolitan Opera that very evening. When he noted her hesitation, he had suggested a personal introduction.

'To Caruso?' she had asked, wide-eyed.

'He's just Enrico to me,' he had replied. 'He's my cousin.'

At that point Consuela had been waiting for her uncle for three hours in the waiting room of the railway station and was tearful and, to be honest, a little scared. New York was bigger and dirtier and much more foreign than she had imagined. She couldn't understand enough English to translate the information boards or she would have understood that all trains from Pennsylvania had been cancelled due to a signal failure. And so when Caruso's cousin, in perfect Spanish, struck up a conversation, and on learning what had brought her to America, offered her those opera tickets and after-show drinks with the great man himself, Consuela, against her better judgement, she told herself later, let herself be led to a nearby restaurant for a refreshment while she thought it over. That the man wasn't particularly well-dressed and seemed to have doused himself in oil of lavender was something she overlooked. And when, over a cup of greasy coffee, he persuaded her that her uncle had probably mixed up the date of her arrival, she accepted that the best plan was to come back the next day and spend the night at the opera with him instead.

Of course, Caruso's cousin was not even related. Pablo Degraw was a pimp who lived in a small run-down apartment on the Bowery with a very large lock on the door. As the days rolled past and he found reasons not to take her back to the railway station as he had originally promised, he also informed her that she owed him a small fortune for food, board and other sundry charges that he suggested she pay back in instalments by dishing out so-called favours to his so-called friends. At first she refused – she was still a virgin, a Catholic, a middle-class girl – but then he raped her and told her that if she didn't do as he asked he would lace her food with rat poison, and she realized that she had little choice but to accept his suggestion after all.

By the time she met Ivory Price the pimp was long gone, overcome by the twin mistresses of alcohol and morphine. Without any other profession, husband or family connection to support her – her own family had unceremoniously disowned her when an Argentine customer searching for a little recreation on a business trip had recognized her and written to her father – Consuela still supported herself the only way she knew how. She had been waiting for a client in the lobby of the San Reno Hotel when Ivory approached her and, under his breath, asked her how much she charged. She looked at him with some dismay. Was it that obvious? She had dressed respectably, and thought she looked like a lady waiting for a friend, perhaps, or a wife meeting her husband. Ivory's face was flushed, he was nervous, he was dressed as if he were entering a driving race. And so the figure she named was astronomical. He took a suite immediately, paid her upfront in cash and her client was forgotten. A month later he moved her into an apartment hotel and gave her an allowance so he could come and see her whenever he liked, 'exclusively'.

When he married Inez, Ivory had been 'visiting' Consuela for almost eight years. Three times she had conceived a child by him. And each time she had come to the decision that keeping the baby would mean losing Ivory and all that he gave her. On her third abortion, she was informed with some relish that her womb was so damaged that she would be unlikely to conceive again. When she wept the abortionist grew angry and threw her out before the bleeding had stopped. She would have bled to death if Ivory had not turned up unexpectedly and taken her straight to a small private hospital that was known for its discretion.

The bus passed a signpost. The house that Ivory had rented was in the next town, now only five miles away. Consuela smoothed down her dark blue damask day dress and tried to arrange her once beautiful hair beneath her wide felt hat. But it was so hot and sticky that her top-knot, although carefully pinned and set that morning, was starting to collapse around her ears in oily tendrils. The bus stopped briefly at another small and isolated homestead. A young girl with a hen in a cage climbed on board and sat down in the seat beside her. As soon as the bus pulled off, the girl turned and began to stare at her, taking her all in as if she were an exhibit at a travelling fairground. Consuela knew she looked out of place; only locals and domestic servants travelled on the bus – everyone else paid a few more cents and took the train – and by the way she was dressed it was clear she was neither. She glanced round and gave the girl a half-smile. The girl didn't even blink. The hen began to flap and squawk, filling the air with feathers and chaff.

'I have to get off now,' Consuela demanded.

The bus driver turned and looked at her with both eyes screwed up. 'But we ain't nowhere,' he said.

'This is where I want,' she insisted.

He shook his head in disbelief and then, with a squeal of brakes and a fogging of dust, he pulled in to the side of the road. 'Here?' he asked, looking out at the scrubland and the sea-marshes.

'Yes. Just here,' she replied. 'Thank you.'

The driver rose out of his seat and opened the doors for her. In the shade of the bus there was a little breeze but as soon as it drove away she felt the sun beat down on the top of her head as hot as molten metal. She didn't look up as the rumble of the bus's engine gradually faded; she knew she would see the girl with the hen, still staring at her from the back seat.

A long featureless road stretched endlessly in both directions. Consuela began to walk, her footsteps making so little impression on the distance ahead that it was almost as if she were walking on the spot. The air was filled with the hum and ratchet of insects and the distant grumble of the surf. A couple of motor cars accelerated past, leaving billowing clouds of dust. Overhead, a biplane dipped, circled and then headed out to sea. She tried to ignore the heat and the scratch of mosquitoes, her dry throat and the trickles of sweat that were running down her back, and went over for the hundredth time what she would say to Ivory. She loved him, she couldn't live without him, he was everything to her, without him she was nothing. She ached, she sweated, she was parched, she was desolate. He couldn't end it now. Yes, he had a wife, but in his soul he was married to her. She knew it. He knew it. The wife must know it too. He was hers and nothing on earth could ever change that. 'I'm coming,' she whispered as she walked. '*Me voy.*'

The woman standing on the porch was dusted from head to toe in grey. It looked, to Inez at least, as if ash had been shaken all over her, the hem of her dress and the brim of her hat catching the worst of it. Her skin, however, was damp and her eyes were of a particularly beautiful liquid brown.

'Oh, my Lordy,' said Maud, 'she looks like a ghost. Where did she come from?'

'I don't know,' Inez whispered.

'She asked to see Mr Price,' said the maid.

'Why is she staring at me?' asked Maud.

She was indeed staring hard at Maud, taking in her hair, newly cut short and styled like the dancer, Irene Castle, her thick white lace dress with the high collar and her heavy brown leather shoes, shoes that Inez had never liked, which Maud had to wear because of her wide feet. Then the woman raised her chin, just a little, and moistened her cracked lips as if she were about to speak.

'Can I help you?' Inez said. 'I'm Mrs Price.'

The woman's face switched round to Inez as if she had only just become visible. Her eyes narrowed as she fixed on her face, her hair, and then, with a slow slide, the woman's eyes dropped to her belly. Inez instinctively covered it with her hand. For a fraction of a second nothing moved. On the terrace beyond, lunch was being laid out and the clatter of china and a rattle of silver cutlery cut through the silence.

'If you go and ask the kitchen, I'm sure they'll give you something to eat,' Inez said. 'Or a glass of water or something.'

The woman raised her face but did not raise her eyes. She seemed to sway slightly on her feet as her nostrils flared, just a little. And then, without a word, she grabbed a handful of skirt, turned and, in a cloud of pale grey, she strode back down the driveway.

A child would find the wide felt hat in the dunes that summer and bring it to its mother who would prop it on a broom to scare the birds from her marrow patch. Blown into the sea, torn to shreds and washed up again, the blue damask dress would fade and fray on a stunted tree on the Carmans River estuary. Consuela's naked body would float south, far south to the Gulf of Mexico as if trying to return home. It wouldn't ever reach Argentina but would be caught in a fishing boat's nets off the coast of Florida in mid-October, be taken to shore and buried in a shallow, unmarked grave just outside the small town of Naples. Caruso would also be buried in Naples, another Naples, more than three thousand miles away, only four years later.

'Must be Ivory's secret lover,' said Maud with a giggle. 'I'm starving. Do you think you could tell them that we're ready for lunch now?'

Inez went to the window but the dust woman had already gone. A bus heading back to the city passed on the roadway beyond, its tyres churning up rocks and stones and fine, fine sand.

12

The four-faced clock on top of the information booth in the middle of Grand Central Station read five minutes to ten. Dusty sunlight fell in long slants from the windows, half moons of glass positioned high above the concourse. The air smelled of scorched coffee and brass polish, of engine grease and pomade. Two huge American flags had been hung on ropes from the vaulted ceiling and they billowed gently in the breeze from the street outside.

Anna looked up at the destination board. Trains were just about to leave for Ithaca, for Chicago, for Boston. She momentarily wondered how it would feel to pick one at random and climb aboard, to be bound for another city without a suitcase, without any money, without a plan. She had grown used to Americans in the months she had lived here, to their insipid coffee and courteous manner, to their optimism and barely disguisable ignorance; to their landscapes of overcrowded cities and breathless emptiness. And now, after so long, after so many years in exile, she could go back, back more than five thousand miles, to a country that had changed almost overnight, to St Petersburg, to her son.

But it wouldn't be straightforward. After a euphoric send-off with thrown flowers and rousing speeches, Trotsky had sailed north only to be removed from the ship and detained for a month in Amherst by the British naval authorities. Anna knew she would have to wait a little longer until a route was established, until the situation in Russia had improved. And she would need the right papers, a large sum of money and a personal invitation from the new government. Without them she wouldn't attempt the journey. At the time of her escape, her name and photograph had been circulated to police offices all over Russia. If she wasn't careful, she could end up in a cell in some provincial Russian town miles from home.

A man carrying a thick woollen coat and a heavy leather suitcase bustled past her. Even though it was May and the temperature in the city was soaring, he smelled of wood smoke and snow. He must have just arrived from the north. Would the snow have melted yet on the banks of the Neva? Would the forests in Siberia be shedding their winter dresses drop by drop; would the ice on the Baltic coast be turning glassy, breaking loose and floating away? She suddenly remembered the brush of lips and the timbre of a voice that she had not thought about for years. Pokolitov had been so young, so angry with the world, so full of words and ideas and plans. And yet he could be silent too. She remembered lying together in bed and listening to the spring arrive; a bird singing, a child singing, the air thinning.

'What are you thinking?' she would ask him.

And his eyes would suddenly fill with tears and he would pull her to him. 'That I'm going to lose you,' he would say.

'You won't,' she'd reply. 'I'll always be yours.'

But he could not look at her; he could not believe her.

'Come here,' she would whisper. 'Let me love you.'

Anna knew that Pokolitov believed his life would be short and violent. And so she loved him the way he lived: with everything she had.

A guard was standing in a small dark booth at the entrance to platform 16. A locomotive and a dozen carriages idled on the track beyond, filling the air with steam and cinders. She adjusted her hat, took such a deep breath that a male passer-by glanced down at her, and then walked quickly past the set of stairs that led down to the lower level, towards the platform.

'This train's for Chicago only. Tickets please?'

At the barrier, Anna opened her mouth but could think of nothing to say. She had no ticket. And even if she had enough money in her purse, the queue at the ticket office was so long it would take at least thirty minutes to go back, queue up and buy a ticket. And then she would be late, much too late.

'I need to get through,' she begged. 'Please let me through.'

'If you're waiting for the 11 a.m. from New Haven,' the guard said, 'I can sell you a platform ticket. It'll only cost you two cents.'

The train to Chicago was ready to depart. Inside, most of the passengers had already settled into their seats and were unpacking picnics or unrolling newspapers. A porter struggled up the metal stairs into a first-class compartment with a huge wooden chest while the owner, an elderly woman in a black coat, fussed and scolded. A guard with a silver whistle in his mouth began to slam every door shut, starting at the front of the train and working his way to the end. Those who had climbed on board to say their goodbyes took the slamming doors as a cue and hurried quickly off. The hands on the platform clock clicked into place and then, with his arms outstretched and his cap pulled down over his eyes, the guard finally blew his whistle, long and loud. With a scream of metal and a sigh of smoke, the train slowly shifted forward and began to pull away from the platform, away from the station, away from the scattering of people left behind who blew kisses and waved until their shoulders ached.

Anna suddenly found herself pushing through a throng of people all heading in the opposite direction, all hurrying back to their lives in the city or to their subway rides to the suburbs. Up ahead, a solitary man was buying chewing gum from a vending machine. As she walked towards him along the now empty expanse of platform 16, he banged it, hard, then harder, with the flat of his hand before cursing, softly, in Russian.

The waiting room had a dozen opaque windows on either side and a door with a polished brass handle at one end. Anna picked a bench in the furthest corner and sat down. Almost ten minutes passed before the man she had seen at the chewing gum machine appeared at the doorway, his dark and bulky figure blurred by the frosted glass. He entered the waiting room, slamming the door behind him, but he did not look at her. Instead he paused for an instant and listened: the arrival of a train on another platform, a whistle blown three times in quick succession, the rapid clop and roll of a horse and cart. And then he pulled out a ball of gum, unwrapped it, placed it in his mouth and started to chew.

'I . . .' Anna began.

But the man raised a single finger in warning. Only when he had tried the handle of a cupboard at the far end of the waiting room – it was locked – did he finally speak. 'Anna Denisova?' he said.

'Yes,' she replied.

'Comrade,' he said with a slight inclination of his head.

For a moment the man simply stood and chewed and stared at her, taking in every inch of her clothes, her face, her body. When she realized that he did this without regard for her modesty, she raised her head and stared back. He was badly dressed in a poorly fitting suit and a hat several sizes too small. His face was flabby and grizzled with a beard; his skin was sallow and beaded with sweat, and he had the hooded, cynical eyes of an elderly tortoise.

'And you are?' she asked eventually.

'No names,' he said. 'You can call me Winter Hare. Safer that way.'

'But you know my name,' she protested.

He simply shrugged. 'That is something that cannot be helped,' he said.

The man who called himself Winter Hare removed his cap and sat down on a bench opposite. Even from a few feet away Anna could smell him; peppermint gum, subway carriages and beneath it all the sour, unmistakable odour of unwashed skin.

'Were you in St Petersburg?' Anna asked. 'Do I know you? Have we met before?'

He shook his head and raised his hand. 'So many questions!' he said.

He spat the gum on to the floor and smiled briefly to reveal a set of blackened and broken teeth.

'Anna Denisova,' he said again. 'You know I didn't believe it when I heard about you. But now I see I was wrong. You are the perfect foil. Who would suspect?'

'Suspect what?' she asked. And then she realized. She sat back and folded her hands. 'I'm a speaker, a writer,' she said. 'I don't know what you've heard but I will not be involved in any activity that is linked to terrorism. Not any more. If you'd like me to write you a pamphlet . . .'

He didn't seem to hear her. Instead he muttered his apologies, pulled out a greasy paper parcel and began to unwrap it. Inside was a large pork salami.

'Please?' he asked and offered it to her with a penknife.

'No, thank you,' she replied.

He began to shave it into slices which he rolled up and placed in his mouth. As he chewed, he continued to speak, showering the air between them with tiny flecks of cured meat and spittle. Anna tried not to breathe, tried not to inhale the rank smell of garlic and pork fat.

'We must increase the pressure,' he was saying. 'Fight conscription. Denounce the government of the United States. We must show them all that this is not a war on democracy, but a war to protect the profits of the ruling classes. America has grown rich on the profits from this war; it must feel what we have felt.'

'As I said,' she responded, 'I would be happy to write something for you although publication at the present time isn't exactly straightforward. A leaflet, maybe?'

He swallowed and then looked at her once more, sidelong.

'What would we do with a leaflet?' he asked. 'Have you heard of the propaganda of the deed?'

'Of course, one violent act becomes a catalyst. But that's an anarchist concept.'

He stopped chewing and swallowed. 'And also a Social Revolutionary concept. One that Pokolitov has always endorsed. I thought you knew him?'

'I do. I did. I mean I'd always hoped . . . no one knew what had happened to him. He just disappeared.'

'He was imprisoned,' Winter Hare said.

'I was, too. And then I was sent to the north. But I escaped,' she replied.

Although his eyes were bloodshot and creased with exhaustion, they blinked with something else, something she suddenly realized was compassion. He knew more than he was saying. Carefully he wrapped up the salami and returned it to his pocket. And then he looked up at her again.

'I know,' he said. 'We arranged it.'

Anna inhaled sharply. Had it been arranged? She remembered the day so clearly: the crisp October morning when a group of prisoners, too ill to last another winter, were being allowed to leave. A couple of sleighs were about to depart for Archangel, their horses stamping restlessly in the freezing air. And then came the knock on her door and the whispered information: there had been a death and there was a space on one of the sleighs. If she came at that very moment she could have it.

And so she simply put on her coat, closed the door of her hut, climbed aboard a sleigh, and they had departed, leaving all her belongings, the squat dark buildings and the wintering forests behind for ever. It was almost, she told herself at the time, too easy. Later, that day, however, she had convinced herself that the local police had been alerted and she was putting the whole party at risk. And so she asked to be let off the sleigh and set out alone to walk ten miles in deep snow to a railway station. As a precaution, she covered up her footprints from the road one by one until she was faint and delirious with cold. It was then that she wondered at the wisdom of her opportunistic escape; she had left without supplies, without suitable clothes, without a proper plan.

Winter Hare stared at the woman he had been ordered to meet, the woman who had once been the lover of the head of his cell. Shock registered on her face, in the line of her mouth and in the creases on her forehead, but then she sat erect, her small hands clasped in her lap and her eyes staring straight ahead as if riveted to a spot in the distance. He looked in that direction and saw nothing, nothing but the wave and dip of a large overgrown weed that was growing out of a crack in a wall on the other side of the tracks.

He was tired, his eyes felt full of sand, his body ached and his feet, after standing all night in borrowed boots, throbbed with blisters. He thought suddenly of his wife, a woman he had not seen for three years. She was nothing like the woman who sat beside him in the station in America; Lida was heavy and warm and pliable, her face more familiar to him than his own. She was a good wife, he was lucky to have her. And when they hadn't been blessed with any children, she had slowly started to take on the role of mother anyway. 'My boy', she called him, 'my darling boy'.

'I didn't know,' Anna Denisova said eventually. 'I didn't know . . .' She took a deep breath and slowly exhaled.

'And now look at you,' he said. 'Celebrated, elegant, revered. Mixing with sophisticated Americans.'

'I won't do anything illegal.'

He smiled ruefully. 'What exactly does it mean, "illegal"?' he asked. 'We have two hundred and eighty-five Social Revolutionaries in the Provisional Government. We are the majority. We are the law.'

'But for how long?' she said softly. 'How long before you are thrown out by the Mensheviks or the Bolsheviks?'

He ignored her comment and leaned forward, resting his forearm on his knee. 'I hear that you are living in more modest lodgings. Are you short of money?'

'Of course not,' she retaliated with a little too much force. 'It's just that my former husband is having some difficulty in transferring money.'

'We would like to help you,' he said. 'We can pay you a small allowance and when the time is right we shall provide you with correct papers and pay for a passage back to Russia.'

'In return for what?'

'In return for your involvement. Don't worry. Your role will be as a gatherer of information only. You will not be expected to carry out any acts, any acts that you might find distasteful.'

'Pokolitov suggested this?' The woman's voice was soft now. The last of her consonants were barely audible.

'He did. So will you?'

Anna didn't reply. Winter Hare sat back and wiped his hands on his trousers. And then he got to his feet.

'Madame Denisova, you have a son, don't you?'

'He's at the front. He was drafted.'

'He deserted. He is now one of us, a Social Revolutionary.'

For Anna, the rush of relief on hearing news of Kima was swiftly followed by a wave of unease.

'He's only sixteen. He doesn't know what he's doing. Are you sure?'

Winter Hare raised his eyebrows. 'Have you heard from him?'

'No, not for a few months. Not since he left for the Eastern Front.'

'Think of this as a mutually beneficial relationship,' he said. 'If you work with us, as well as support to help you return to Russia, we will pass on your letters to your son.'

'And what if I refuse?' asked Anna.

Winter Hare sighed deeply. 'It would be bad for your son. And bad for you. You will hear from us soon. Good day.'

The train from New Haven was due and with the ringing of bells and the dull rolling rumble of porters' trolley wheels, the platform slowly began to come to life again. The chewing gum machine swallowed coins and belched out packets with a dull metallic clank. The waiting room door swung open, an old woman hobbled in with a cat in a basket and sat down in the corner. Two porters hovered on the platform outside, the dark blue of their jackets mottled by the dirty glass of the window.

'I tell you, he didn't even offer a nickel,' one of the porters was saying. 'I said, "Sir, this is America. It is customary to reward those who assist you and make your stay in this fine country a pleasant one."'

'And what did he do? Pay up?'

'Did he? Hell no. He replied, "Eh downt believe in teeping. In Russia we think it demeaning." "Well, demean me," I replied. "I expect it."'

Their laughter overlapped with the long low whistle of the train as it made its slow approach into Grand Central.

'Here she comes,' yelled one of the porters. 'Right on time.'

Anna waited until the train had pulled in, one by one its doors had swung open, some of its passengers had been met and greeted and others had gathered themselves up into a hurry. And then she joined the men with carpet-bags and the women with hat-boxes, the porters balancing stacks of cases and the children wheeling dolls in miniature prams, as they rushed through the station and tumbled out on to East Forty-Second Street where they were quickly swallowed up by the open mouth of the city.

13

It was June already, a month that always began with sweet days of cool shade and luminous skies, but which turned hot and sultry as July approached, the nights made sleepless by the electric buzz of thirsty insects and the lingering heat of trapped midday sun.

Monroe emerged red-eyed and brick-headed from the subway on Fourth Avenue and East Forty-Second Street into blinding morning sunshine; he had slept badly again and then fallen into a deep, dreamless sleep just before dawn. Only when he reached the far side of Madison did he notice that the city was strangely quiet. A dozen horse-drawn cabs were stationed at the kerb, the horses dozing behind their winkers; a Chinese laundry worker had come out of his steamed-up shop and was looking westwards. In fact, most of the other people who were streaming up and out of the subway were heading in that direction, to Fifth Avenue. It seemed that the chasm between Fifty-Eighth and Fourteenth Street was forever being taken over by parades: for holidays, for festivals, for protests, for rallies, for celebrations, each one leaving a swirl of ticker tape and a tangle of torn flyers, a littering of candy wrappers and pretzel crumbs in its wake.

He could have gone back down into the subway and taken a train crosstown to Broadway, but he couldn't face the oppressive heat of the platform again. And so he kept walking, with every intention of keeping his head down until he was through the worst of it.

Even from a block away, however, he could sense that this march was different from the rest; there was an air of nervous expectation, the almost imperceptible scent of exhilaration. Hundreds of men in straw boaters and women with parasols were thronging four-deep on the pavement or had staked out a place on the wide shallow steps of the Public Library. All downtown traffic had been diverted and some of the huge department stores had even closed up for the day. A band on the back of a bus struck up 'Yankee Doodle Dandy'. The crowd politely jostled, gently shoved or stood on their tiptoes. A lull descended, in which errant chatterers were hushed, and children warned. And then the sound of applause could be heard from further up the avenue, as hundreds upon hundreds of volunteers came marching down the centre of the wide city street. Line after line of bank clerks, shop hands and longshoremen, short-order chefs, railway guards and factory foremen, dressed up in their Sunday best, in suits and ties and dark felt hats, and some with walking sticks slung like guns over their right shoulders, marched in an approxima-tion of the quickstep in the direction of the army recruiting office in Union Square.

Against the tide of the inquisitive, the patriotic and the related, who all tried to walk alongside in a vain attempt to keep up with the new recruits, Monroe headed up to the corner of Forty-Third Street, and waited for a gap in the march. As the men traipsed by, the air was redolent with the smell of boot polish and popcorn, with sweat infused with last night's liquor. He glanced at a tobacco shop window where a sign advertised the city's widest selection of Cuban cigars. But instead of seeing the cigars, the pipes and the tins of snuff that were displayed, he watched the reflection of the men's faces as they passed, faces thrown into sharp relief by the harsh cast of the morning sun. Some looked placid, some euphoric, others appeared simply bewildered as if it were all too much: the city, the crowds, the sheer scale of everything.

To Monroe, most of them looked like boys, boys who had grown wispy moustaches in an attempt to look older, but boys nonetheless. The deep cut of the avenue only seemed to make them appear even younger. Dwarfed by the newly constructed high-rise towers of Manhattan, and mirrored into infinity by the acres of window glass, they seemed puffed-up and yet insubstantial, tiny but with too much pep, like over-wound toys set down to walk in a straight line until they ran out of charge.

Should he feel guilty that he wasn't beside them? Should he feel outrage and indignation over the loss of innocent American civilians on the *Lusitania* and be intent on taking steps to reap revenge? Should he drop everything and join up, like Edward? Something began to shift inside him; the noise, the music, the atmosphere were unexpectedly uplifting. Maybe this was just what he needed. Maybe this was the answer he was looking for. Maybe this was his escape route. He imagined himself in uniform; he could simply fall into step with the rest of them, he could forget himself, he could forget that refrain in his head, he could forget the bruise that was his heart.

A gap appeared. He could cross now, cross with the delivery boys and the pretzel sellers, the newspaper vendors and the hotel porters with their small trolley-loads of cases. But instead he took one step out into the street and then he paused.

'You enlisting too? You can join my line.'

An officer had spotted his hesitation, had seen the hint of fervour in the glaze of his eye and the look of longing on his face, and grabbed him firmly by the arm.

'One more over here!' he shouted to everybody and nobody in particular. A boy cheered. Two ladies clapped. He was just about to be launched into another wave of men when Monroe resisted.

'I'm sorry,' Monroe yelled. 'But you're mistaken.'

The officer's grip was painfully tight. The crowds of people made him feel disorientated; the spell was broken. He no longer felt mesmerized by the music and the marching. But the officer was still insistent.

'They crucify Belgian babies,' the officer shouted. 'Their blood is on our hands. Join up, young man.'

'Not today,' he replied quickly. 'But thank you for your offer.'

The officer squinted into his face before he reluctantly let him go. 'You'll get conscripted soon anyway, son,' he said. 'If you volunteer, you'll get a better crack at it. Might get a chance to fight at the front, get your hands on a few of them Huns, get a medal to pin to your chest.'

'Thanks for the tip!' Monroe responded. 'Good luck!'

'We don't need luck,' the officer answered. 'Just the love of Jesus and a few good men.'

The officer hurried to catch up with his line, and immediately fell back into step. Monroe crossed the street and headed north to Forty-Fifth Street.

'Five minutes, Laura,' Monroe insisted to Von Hofe's secretary. 'That's all I ask. I got a couple of new songs I want to play him and these ones, let me tell you, he's going to love these ones.'

The secretary sighed and shook her head again. 'I'm sorry, Monroe,' she said. 'He hasn't even got one minute.'

She smiled and glanced up quickly but Monroe was already elsewhere, his face rigid with disappointment.

'You could come back in a fortnight,' she suggested, 'and try your luck then.'

The fan whirred on the secretary's desk and the light curtains at the window flapped in the breeze. In one of the cubicles in the corridor outside, a woman was bellowing a new song, one that Von Hofe was convinced was going to be a hit, a ballad about a mother's pride on sending her son to war. It was called 'Mommy's Tears (are tears of joy)'.

The secretary looked at the song-plugger with all the sympathy she could muster. He was a nice boy. A little too sensitive for this business, she thought, but nice nonetheless.

'Who knows where I'll be in a fortnight,' he replied. 'In a training camp for the army, probably. And then to the fields of France. Or what's left of them.'

He was already halfway down the stairs when he bumped into a young black woman coming up. At first his eye glanced over her; he had already passed half a dozen young women drinking coffee in the reception area; some young and nervous, others old and cynical. Von Hofe vetted his appointments now. No more amateurs or chorus girls, no up-and-comings or potentially fabulous.

'Excuse me,' she said, 'am I in the right building? Is this the Universal Music Corporation?' When she looked up at him, however, her face settled into a smile. 'Hello there!' she said. 'It's Bessie. We met before. You remember?'

'Of course I remember,' said Monroe. 'How could I forget?'

Bessie was dressed in a fitted white coat with a peacock feather in her hat. In the gloom of the stairwell, however, she looked over-dressed and rather flustered.

'You come to look for a song?' he asked her.

'You got one to sell?'

'Sure!' he said and patted his case. 'I got all sorts.'

'Be serious.'

'I am serious. I got rags and Hawaiian, foxtrots and ballads, patriotic and humorous,' he said. 'What kind are you looking for?'

'The kind that'll get me out of the chorus line,' she replied.

'Oh,' he said. 'That kind of song.'

In one of the cubicles at the top of the stairs, a piano started to play, shifting clumsily from a ballad into stride. A man started to sing, badly. Monroe winced.

'You heard from Edward?' Bessie asked.

'No,' he replied. 'You?'

She shook her head. 'Did he . . . did he tell you what he was planning to do?'

'Not a word,' he answered. 'I guess he thinks he's got something to prove.'

Bessie blinked and her eyes glimmered in the murky light. Then she took a deep breath, adjusted her hat and fixed him with her smile again. 'Well then, let's hear those songs.'

Monroe's cubicle had been stripped of his belongings since he'd been on the road but nobody else had been given the key. He borrowed a spare, opened the door, dusted off the piano and invited her to sit down.

'Where shall we start?' he asked.

'Edward told me you wrote your own songs. What about one of them?'

When Von Hofe heard Bessie Lavigne's voice floating out of cubicle 3, he stopped in his tracks and listened. And when he opened the door and found Monroe Simonov at the piano, he could, he said later, have been knocked over by the singer's peacock feather hat.

158

'It's not one of mine. One of yours, Monroe?' he asked when the song was over.

'As a matter of fact,' he began, 'it is. You heard it at the club.'

'So I did. I want the music on my desk by two. I have a headliner who's just going to love this number.' He pulled out his wallet, slammed five dollars on the top of the piano. 'Forget Atlantic City or wherever you were supposed to be going. I want you back here in Manhattan. Writing more songs like that. Starting tomorrow.'

'Mr Von Hofe?' said Bessie. 'My name is Bessie Lavigne. I'm currently appearing at the Variety.'

Hubert Von Hofe turned and glanced back at her. 'You got a spot?' he asked.

'I've been promised one real soon.'

'You're a chorus girl,' he interrupted.

Bessie carried on regardless. Monroe had to admit it, the girl had guts.

'All I need is a good number,' she said. 'If I had a song like this, I'm sure my manager would give me that spot.' She looked up at him and blinked.

'Miss Lavigne,' he said. 'It's been a pleasure. And now I'm late for an appointment.'

Then he disappeared into his cavernous office with its baby grand and its cocktail cabinet where the disgruntled singer Sophie Tucker was waiting with a highball in her hand.

'I guess that was a no,' Bessie said.

'Let me work on him,' Monroe said softly. 'I'm sure with a bit of persuasion . . .'

'Would you?' Bessie asked. 'Would you really?'

'Sure,' he replied.

'Come and see the show tonight,' she said. 'I'll leave a comp at the desk. But why not come backstage before?'

The show at the Variety was late in starting. It opened with half a dozen chorus girls, including Bessie, all dressed in silver, dancing round a grand piano. After that there were impersonations, comedy songs, contortionists, an escape artist and several singers. After the intermission came the 'big act' where Bessie and three other coloured girls danced to the music of a man playing the spoons. And last up was the headliner, an overweight comedian who wasn't funny. The auditorium was half empty. The applause was lukewarm. The show, the doorman told a cab driver, would be closing in a week or two and would most likely end up on the Death Trail.

Monroe had arrived half an hour before the curtain went up. Bessie's dressing room was a damp space in a corridor in the basement. She shared the cracked sink and the stained mirror with all the other chorus girls and a couple of singers. As they smoothed down their stage make-up and fastened their costumes, as they practised a scale or two or stretched their legs into a high kick, none of them seemed the least bit concerned that Monroe was there.

'Want to join me for a drink?' she asked him.

'Sure,' he replied.

'Here,' she said, passing him a bottle of bourbon and a tin beaker. 'You can do the honours.'

Bessie was twenty-two. She had been on the vaudeville stage since she was fourteen. Although she could potentially earn three times what she could in a factory, and, if she became a headliner, make thousands of dollars, so far she had never earned enough to move out of her sister's tiny apartment. Since the show had flopped in New York, it was destined to go on tour, travelling round a circuit of hundreds of venues in towns all over America that no one had ever heard of or could place on a map. Most of them weren't theatres at all, just the back rooms of dry goods stores with a couple of benches laid out. She didn't want to go. She'd been on tour before and still remembered how much she loathed sleeping on a bed of straw every night and entertaining toothless farm boys.

The night before, she had begged the theatre manager to put her on somewhere else, in a small-time show in Queens or Brooklyn.

'You signed a contract,' he had said. 'If you don't like it, you can quit.'

Bessie couldn't quit. If word got round, and it would, that you were a quitter, you would never work again. Monroe was her last chance. If he could get her that song, then she might be able to

160

change the manager's mind. But what would she have to do? How far would she have to go?

'Bessie,' Monroe called softly. 'Bessie? Seems like we lost you for a moment there.'

She shrugged and adjusted her stockings. What could she say? She felt as if he had seen her naked, not naked on the outside but naked on the inside. With one swallow she drained the tin beaker.

'Any more of that bourbon?' she asked.

Afterwards he had waited for her at the stage door. She had poured out of the theatre with a clutch of other dancers and stage hands.

'Come uptown with us,' she invited.

'Thank you,' he replied. 'But it's late.'

'Oh, come on,' she said. 'It'll be a blast.'

Together they piled into a cab and drove north to Harlem, where the entire cast and orchestra of the vaudeville show had crammed themselves into a tiny third-floor walk-up apartment. Music filled the rooms, muffled only by the crush of bodies and the buzz of laughter. Bessie took Monroe's arm and they squeezed themselves along the hallway. A full band was playing in the kitchen; the trumpet player was sitting in the sink and the drummer had set up in the corner; a double-bass player was standing on the kitchen table and the guitar player was strumming with both feet up on the stove. The music was fast, infectious and loud. A neighbour in a flowered housecoat was telling everyone to quieten down but nobody took any notice. Bessie led Monroe into the parlour, around the crowded dance floor, through an open window and on to the fire escape.

For a moment, as they looked out at the skyline, neither spoke.

'I'm sorry about this afternoon,' he said.

Bessie turned her face towards him. 'It's a beautiful song,' she said softly. 'Who's it about?'

'You,' he replied.

'Liar.'

She was so close that he could smell her skin: cold cream and

161

pepper. He could feel her breath on his neck and the swell of her breast against his side. She placed her hand on his arm. Forget Suzette, Monroe told himself. Forget Edward. Forget everything but this. But he couldn't. There was a seed of doubt in his mind that he couldn't ignore.

'Just keep asking,' she whispered.

'Bessie, you don't have to do that,' he said gently. 'I said I'll do what I can.'

She took her hand away so fast it was as if she had been stung.

'Edward said you were different,' she said. 'He was right.'

Monroe turned around to look out at the rooftops with their water towers and strings of washing and behind them all, the distant thrust of the spires of Midtown.

'Let's dance,' he said. 'Let's dance until we get thrown out of here.'

The floating public swimming pools opened at 6 a.m. on the Hudson, the East River and up at Greenpoint. At eight, you could already hear the shrieks and screams of dozens of children as they swam and splashed and dived into their enclosed rectangles of sparkling river water. Monroe was heading back to Brooklyn across the Manhattan Bridge, pausing only briefly to watch a girl strapped on to the top of a biplane fly towards Staten Island. He had walked all the way from Harlem; the night before he had spent every cent of Von Hofe's five dollars on taxicabs and beer. It didn't matter. He had sold a song, finally he had sold another song.

All the shutters in the house on Joralemon Street had been closed to keep out the heat. The hallway smelled of ripe apples and old metal hinges. It was so dark that Monroe didn't see Nonna Maria hovering at the bottom of the stairs with a single letter addressed to him in her hand; it was her voice that made him start.

'Mr Simonov?'

'Nonna Maria. Good morning.'

'I heard your keys,' she said. 'This came for you. Yesterday.'

He thanked her, took the envelope and ran up the steps to his apartment two by two. He knew what it was as soon as he opened his door and the light flooded out. His name was printed on the front in clumsy capitals. He tore open the brown paper of the envelope and pulled out the letter inside. The officer had been right after all; this was it. He was being instructed to register for the draft.

14

Inez opened her eyes; a tiny yellow moon hung in the air in front of her. In the soft glow of the night lamp, it seemed to flicker: shiny, matt, shiny, matt, until she realized that it was in fact not a moon at all but a small, polished brass button. Something was stamped into its curved metal surface; a bird, no, an eagle, an eagle with widespread wings and a long hooked beak. *Inez?* Her name was called but it was a voice that she couldn't place. The eagle shifted, she blinked twice and refocused. *Inez?* And then without warning, the button grew in size and she knew it would soon all be over; the eagle was coming for her with its talons and sharp beak and cruel hooded eyes. And it knew. It knew everything.

'Get it away from me,' she whispered.

'Don't you want to hold her?' the voice continued.

But before the words registered, her head swam and she was pulled down once more into a brief, deep, morphine-induced sleep.

Ivory Price looked down at the woman he had married and shook his head. 'See, I told you,' he said to the physician. 'Not a drop of maternal blood in her body.'

'She's still in twilight sleep,' the physician explained. 'The effects take a while to wear off. And, of course, when she wakes up all memory of the birth will have gone. As well as the morphine, the dosage included scopolamine, which induces amnesia. I've found it extremely effective. It is a little contentious in medical circles, but for women it means a painless birth – no wonder the suffragettes are campaigning for it.'

Twilight sleep. How Ivory longed for twilight sleep. He hadn't slept properly for weeks. His body ached and his eyes pricked with exhaustion. Every time he laid his head on the pillow, however, no matter how tired he felt, the knot in his belly would start to pull and twist and he knew he would be awake all night again. He walked to the window and looked down at the park. From above, the densely planted trees of the Ramble looked as viscous and liquid as ink spills around the torn paper lake. At this time of night it was possible to believe that the world would stay dark for ever, that the park was just a flattened page in a book whose pages had been stopped from turning.

'Surely those suffragettes could campaign about issues of more importance,' Ivory snapped. 'The war, for example. They could campaign for women to knit socks. Every soldier needs a good pair of socks.'

The doctor didn't reply. His own sister was involved in the fight for women's suffrage and he knew what she would say if anyone suggested she should campaign for sock knitting.

'Has the training begun, Captain Price?' he asked as he packed up his bag.

'Not yet. They're building a boot camp at Yaphank, out on Long Island. I'm advising on the logistics.'

Ivory Price now wore his newly issued uniform in preference to his own clothes. It made him feel sombre, serious, resolute; older men doffed their hats and women gazed at him serenely when they thought he wasn't looking. That night he was wearing army dress kit – a four-button jacket with a standing collar, jodhpurs and brown leather boots. It was his button that Inez had gazed at when she had opened her eyes, a single, polished US Army button firmly stitched on to khaki-green wool.

On the other side of the bed a nurse was rocking a newborn child, a baby who had arrived suddenly and unexpectedly at the start of the sixth month, and whose crumpled red body had now been expertly swaddled. Ivory walked around the bed and peered into the infant's face.

'Isn't it usual . . .' Ivory began. 'In your opinion—?'

'She's a little drowsy but you have a very healthy daughter, Captain Price,' the doctor intervened. 'May I offer my congratulations?'

The physician knew what he was going to be asked. But it was 5 a.m. He had been sound asleep when the telephone rang the previous evening and roused him out of bed. His first response when Mrs Price had told him she thought the baby was on its way was to suggest that she try to go back to sleep and he would come and see her in the morning. Upper-class, first-time mothers, in his experience, were notoriously skittish and usually experienced what they described as 'labour pains' from the third month. But then she had told him in gasps and sobs about the flood between her legs and the ripping pain, and he had decided to telephone his driver, collect the patient's notes and make the journey uptown after all. It was only a precautionary measure; besides, he could bill at double his daytime fee.

He had found Mrs Price curled up among the mounds of unironed sheets and boxes of Borax in the corner of the laundry room. Two maids and the cook stood anxiously at the door offering glasses of water and damp cloths but he could tell by their faces that neither had been accepted. When the physician approached the lady of the house, she threw him a glance, cursed, then grabbed his arm and dug her nails so deep that the marks would remain for several weeks.

'I think I'm going to die,' she whispered.

'Now, now,' he replied. 'You have to be a brave girl. It's nature's way.'

'Well then, damn nature,' she hissed before she was carried away on another wave of pain.

'Help me convey Mrs Price to a suitable room,' the physician ordered the household staff. 'I require plentiful boiled water, clean sheets, blankets, a dozen towels and a nip of Scotch on the rocks immediately. And where is the husband?'

The husband was not at home. At the time that Inez's waters had broken, Ivory had been lying on the bed that used to belong to Consuela Romero in the rooms he had rented for her in Hell's Kitchen. As a small fan on the dressing table beat its way through the humidity, his tears soaked through Consuela's starched cotton pillows, her red silk bedspread and white cotton nightgown that he had never seen before but which was still infused with the sweet smell of Narcisse Noire.

Three months earlier he had arrived unexpectedly at her hotel fresh from soaring high over Manhattan and Brooklyn towards the wide mouth of Jamaica Bay in his biplane. His head was still filled with the rush of speed and the roar of the wind. And if she minded, he thought at the time, then he would promise to take her up there, to see what he had seen, to watch the sun fall on the city, making it glitter like a rough-cut jewel with a million facets.

He had let himself in with his own key and then had paced back and forth as he had waited. And waited – all afternoon, all evening, all night. And in the morning no wonder he had left in a fury, adamant that once and for all it was over. He was, determined not to accept any explanation she could offer. His wife was out of town. The night could have been theirs. He should, he told her in his head, have accepted that offer of a game of poker at his club.

Weeks and weeks had gone by and he had heard nothing from her. And he missed her. He missed her so much that he ached with it, he smarted with it; he throbbed and stung and pinched with the dull pain of this unexpected loss. Yes, he had been on the point of breaking it off, of telling her that their affair was unworkable, of informing her that he had married and probably wouldn't have enough time to see her regularly any more. But he was a bluffer. For his whole life he had been a bluffer and she knew it. He had broken it off before but, unable to stick to his own resolve, had taken her back. And now she had called his bluff and he knew that she had won.

He had tried to stay away. He had tried to forget her. He had tried to look around for another mistress. But he couldn't do it. And so here he was, crying like a boy in a room that, judging by the slow rain of dust in the air and the spiders' trails, the chill between the sheets and the echo in the dripping of the bathroom taps, clearly hadn't been occupied for months.

And because she was gone, he suddenly saw her rooms, her possessions, her life in another light. He had never before noticed how shabby the rooms were; how much noise could be heard from the street outside, how much clamour from the rooms upstairs and down, and how what he had taken for a certain aristocratic opulence was nothing more than a couple of cleverly draped shawls and a multitude of candles. If she thought she deserved more, she had never asked for it. He would have given her better, he told himself, he could have given her so much more, if only she had asked.

As he lay staring up at the ceiling his mind spun; where had she gone? Back to Argentina? To another apartment? To another lover? Not that. He got up quickly and started to ransack the rooms in a frantic search for clues. He rifled through the tallboy, looked under the bed, opened her drawers and threw armfuls of silk petticoats and undergarments, stockings and garters all over the floor, half with a view of ripping them to shreds later. And yet her coat still hung on the back of her door, her suitcase was stowed in the closet, her toothbrush still stood to attention next to his, and lying on the dressing table was an opera programme for the autumn season.

He almost missed the small sheaf of paper held in place under a bottle of scent, he almost hurled it into the wastepaper basket along with a pile of old fashion magazines. But it caught his eye; he picked it up and flicked through it. As well as a rent receipt there were a couple of pieces of much folded and then flattened-out paper, one an address written in his own hand, another a Long Island bus timetable from New York to Montauk. Ivory Price sank on to the rickety wooden chair that stood before the dresser and the reflection of his face in the mirror began to blur.

'Two inches,' said the physician. 'Two already. My, my . . .'

Forty blocks uptown Inez screamed so loudly you could have sworn, the maid said later, that she had been skewered right through the middle with a red-hot poker. Trickles of sweat ran down her face but they did not cool her; damp cloths were laid on her temple but she did not let them lie for long; ice cubes were slipped into her mouth but she spat them out. It was as if her body was not her own any more; as well as being cleaved apart with pain, she had been hauled from her corner against her will, half carried, half dragged out of the laundry room and then laid down on a strange bed, covered with a sheet, and inspected by the physician with cold metal instruments. Two inches. What did that mean? Was the baby only two inches in size? She stared at the ceiling but did not recognize where she was. And she suddenly imagined she had been taken back, back nine months in time, to those heavy dark rooms on Joralemon Street.

'Monroe?' she called out.

'Sshh,' said the maid. 'Hush now.'

Why was everyone talking to her like this, as if she were a child? After the next clutch of pain, the slow rise that she greeted with shallow breaths but which she was sure she would not survive until it had peaked and slowly subsided, she sat up and looked around. No, this was not Joralemon Street. The maid explained that she'd been taken to one of the guest bedrooms at the back of the Price apartment, to a room she had never seen before, let alone slept in.

The day had been blisteringly hot and the air here was stale and sticky. Even though a fan had been fetched and switched on, it merely sliced up the warm air before it served it back up again.

'Get this off me,' she said and pushed the sheet to the floor. 'I can't breathe in here.'

'But, Mrs Price,' said the maid, 'what about your modesty?'

Inez almost laughed. Right here, right now, her modesty didn't mean two figs.

'How long?' she asked the physician. 'How long will it take?'

'Hard to say,' he replied. 'But you're almost fully dilated. Which means the baby's arrival is probably imminent. Depending on size.'

Inez blew a damp strand of hair away from her face. And then she leaned up and spoke softly, so only the doctor could hear.

'You do know it's early. You can see that, can't you?'

The physician smiled to himself and began to polish his forceps. Inez laid her head back on the pillow. It was almost here at last. The baby. Her baby. But now came the time she had been dreading. She hoped it would be healthy, she hoped it would have ten fingers and ten toes, but, most of all, she hoped it would be small.

'I can give you something to take away the pain,' the physician offered after the next contraction.

'Why didn't you say so before?' Inez gasped.

After carefully emptying a phial into a hypodermic needle, the physician swabbed her arm and injected. 'This will make you feel much better,' he soothed. 'It will put you into a state called twilight sleep.'

Inez looked up at him in alarm. She knew what twilight sleep was. She had decided never to take it. She grabbed the physician's sleeve. 'You should have told me. Doesn't it make you forget?'

'The trauma? Yes.'

'But I don't want to forget! I want to remember! I want to remember everything!'

'Now, now. Just relax, Mrs Price.'

Inez's grip weakened. Her eyelids began to drop. A cool cloth was placed on her brow and this time it was not removed.

'Right,' said the physician. 'Let's get to work. This baby won't wait another minute.'

At the precise moment that Luella Edith Price took her first, tentative breath, Ivory Price, her father in name only, arrived at his club, the Metropolitan on Fifth Avenue and Sixtieth Street. The night porter started when he saw him. He had just spent the last ten minutes insisting to one of Captain Price's staff that he was not there. In fact, contrary to what she told him, he had not been seen for several weeks.

'Good evening,' he said, even though it had already gone 3 a.m. 'We had a call from your residence. It seems that your wife has had some kind of medical emergency, although not life-threatening. The physician is in attendance.'

Ivory Price looked dishevelled. Even though his uniform was pressed, his forehead was creased and his eyes were red-rimmed.

'Thank you,' he replied. 'I'll go shortly. But first, bring me a cognac. She's in good hands, I'm sure.'

The night porter poured him a large measure of brandy. Ivory Price sat down on one of the large leather armchairs and slowly sipped it. His hands trembled and his mouth was dry. Had Consuela travelled to Long Island? Had she actually gone to the summerhouse he had rented? Who or what had she seen there? Of course he hadn't told her about Inez and her condition. Not after their own history of aborted conception. He thought back over the last few months. And he remembered a day in April, around the time of his final visit to Consuela, when Inez had seemed to look at him strangely, sidelong, before launching into a story about a strange woman covered in dust. He hadn't taken much notice at the time. Inez would talk for hours about how much she loathed the doorman, if you let her. He undid his top button and held the warmed brandy glass to his cheek. Consuela was impulsive, temperamental, passionate. What would she have done if she had seen his pregnant wife? No, he whispered, not that. But as the clock struck three thirty, he suddenly suspected that this was exactly the kind of thing that she might do.

'At last,' said the physician. 'I had the girl call you at your club several times.'

'I was sleeping,' he replied. 'I had told them not to wake me. Is the news very bad? I know that miscarriages aren't uncommon in a first pregnancy.'

It was an obvious conclusion to jump to. It was also one that, if he was honest with himself, he had been inadvertently hoping for.

'The news is very good, actually,' the doctor replied. 'Both mother and baby are doing very well indeed.'

Inez was lying on the bed, her narrow wrists flung wide above her head, a single white foot protruding from beneath the sheet. Ivory looked down at her, at her hair spread out over the pillow and her beautiful face in repose, and felt nothing. Instead he was aware of the poverty of their relationship, the space he had never been able to breach between them, the sense that her unreachable loveliness was something he had bought on impulse but could not return to the store like a pair of shoes.

'Don't you want to see your daughter?' the physician asked. 'She seems quite happy in her cot.'

The baby didn't even cry. It looked at him through the narrow slits of its eyes as if it knew something that he didn't.

'Big,' he said. 'Big, isn't it?'

'She's seven pounds four,' said the maid proudly.

'And the hair. So much thick dark hair.'

'That usually falls out,' said the physician. 'Who knows what colour of hair she will have? Could be fair, like you, or have her mother's glorious auburn locks. Do you want to hold her? Most fathers get the jitters but I can promise you that you're unlikely to drop her.'

'Maybe,' he replied. 'Maybe later. I think we all need to try to get a little sleep before morning. Been very busy what with two jobs.'

'Helping with the war effort as well as your own business. Commendable.'

'Mostly all paperwork,' Ivory commented. 'Nothing commendable about it, I'm afraid.'

The dawn was already seeping into the sky in the east. Inez shifted on the bed and made a small sound in the back of her throat.

'Will she wake?' Ivory asked the physician. 'Maybe you should give her another shot. Just to give her the rest she needs.'

The memory of the tiny moon was still lodged in Inez's mind when she opened her eyes the next morning. A band of pale yellow reflected sunlight shifted across the bedclothes and illuminated a strip of wall, picking out the faded pink peonies and limp green foliage of the paper. She sat up, looked around the empty room and was suddenly aware that something was terribly wrong, something was missing; her belly was flat, her body bruised and bloody, her legs trembled. She climbed out of bed but her legs didn't seem strong enough to support her. For a moment the room grew dark and spun with tiny yellow pinpricks of light, as all the blood rushed from her head. And then, when the light had come back and the pinpricks had gone, she walked, gingerly but quickly, to the door. She found her husband in the parlour, stretched out on the divan in his army uniform.

'Where did you put it?' she asked.

Ivory opened his eyes but did not move. 'Put what?'

'You know. . .' she whispered. And her mouth began to drag at the edges and for a moment she could not speak. 'The body,' she whispered.

'What body?' he replied.

She pushed the hair from her face, wiped her nose with the back of her hand and tried again. 'The . . . the . . .' But she couldn't say the word.

'The baby?' he asked.

Now she could barely keep herself together. She concentrated on her breathing, in, out, in, out.

Ivory Price sighed. 'You don't remember?'

'Of course I don't remember,' she answered. 'He gave me an injection. I just woke up and there was nothing . . . no one . . .'

He let her stand there, swaying, gasping, swallowing for much longer than was necessary.

'She's in the nursery,' he conceded at last.

'A girl? And is she . . .'

'She's perfectly normal.'

With a sharp intake of breath Inez turned. But before she left the room she looked back at her husband. His eyes were closed again.

'She's been fed,' said the nurse who had been hired that morning from an agency. 'So it's best not to wake her.'

'Thank you, but I'd like to feed her myself. Why didn't you bring her to me?'

The nurse didn't even bother to answer the question and tried to bundle the new mother back to bed.

'Don't fret. We have a supply of milk, sterilized. Now come along. Doctor's orders.'

Inez, however, wouldn't be bundled. 'I want my baby,' she insisted.

'All in good time,' the nurse replied. 'And please keep your voice down. You don't want to wake your husband. It's been a long night for him and he needs his rest.'

Ivory Price had, in fact, had his first proper sleep for many months. When the doctor had gone and the baby been taken away, he had locked the door to the spare room and pulled off his leather boots. And then he had taken what was rightfully his; he had pulled the sheet from his sleeping wife and pounded her with his fury until it was spent.

As if to contradict the nurse, the front door slammed, a set of metal doors ricketed shut and the lift began its slow descent to the lobby. For the next fortnight Ivory would visit fifteen morgues and inspect the bodies of eleven women, none of whom would be Consuela. The baby was eventually handed over to Inez but only after a stern lecture on the boundaries of motherhood. But once Inez had her, she would not let her go. She sat with her, she slept with her, she carried her in her arms until she was unable to carry her any more.

'Puerperal fever,' said the physician two days later. 'Her temperature is one hundred and four.'

'Pass me the baby,' Inez insisted. 'I need to feed her.'

'No breastfeeding. No contact. No indigestible foods.'

The physician's words didn't seem to be making any sense. What was he talking about? Why were they all being so cruel?

'Please? Just give her to me,' she whispered.

'Mrs Price,' said the physician. 'Do you hear me? You have childbed fever. You need bed-rest and complete isolation. It is a serious complication.'

The physician stroked his chin and glanced down quickly at the young mother's flushed face as she stared up at him uncomprehendingly. Had he washed his hands before he had attended to the birth? It had been the middle of the night but had he? Yes, he told himself, he had washed thoroughly. The infection could have come from anywhere or anyone. If she died it was unfortunate, but it was not his fault.

'Can you do anything for her?' asked the nurse.

'Not really. You could try giving her warm milk,' he replied. 'Or beef tea, but I doubt that she'll be able to keep them down.'

The first time that Inez had looked into her baby's eyes, she found she could not stop looking. Although the tiny face was screwed up tight and the head was as misshapen as a cobnut, her gaze ran over and over; eyes, ears, lips, nose, eyes, ears, lips, nose, top of the head. Inez had supposed she would feel some tug of familiarity, some thread of herself woven in, but her daughter was nothing like the baby she had imagined.

'Who are you?' she whispered into the warm milky folds of her neck. But the baby just looked back at her, her eyes latched on to hers, her tiny hand wound around her finger like a clamp. And now a great big hook had grown inside her. It yanked her out of sleep; it scored every thought, it dredged through her mind, her dreams, her body, until all she could do was sit and weep and beg, anyone, everyone.

'Give her to me,' she said. 'She needs me.'

But no one did.

Sometimes she thought she heard the baby cry through half a dozen closed doors. And she would try to rise up and go to her and would be found an hour or two later, curled up and shivering in the corridor, delirious with grief.

'I just wanted to feed her,' she told the nurse.

The nurse, who had had enough, sat her down on the edge of her bed and pulled the nightgown from her breast. The girl's tears had been shed so often that they failed to affect her any more.

'Look,' she said. 'Look at your breasts. You haven't got any milk, Mrs Price. And if you don't get back into bed and stay there, you'll die! What kind of mother will you be then? Now do you understand me?'

'But where is she?' she said.

'Luella is not here,' the nurse snapped. 'She's being cared for; that's all you need to know.'

Inez collapsed into bed and cried until her eyes were as dried-up as her breasts. But later, as she lay and listened to the distant stamp and whistle of another military parade, she gritted her teeth and closed her eyes. So there was no choice in the matter; she would just have to get better, wouldn't she?

15

That year Hoboken was colder in October than Archangel. An icy wind raced off the Hudson towards Newark Bay, frosting up the windows of Stevens Technical Institute and jamming the mechanism of the clock dial on the Colgate soap factory in Jersey City. Anna wiped her face with a small cotton handkerchief. The ride from Manhattan, from West Nineteenth Street and Sixth Avenue, to Hoboken in an electric car didn't take long, but it was by way of a deep underground tunnel, which always filled her chest with panic and left smuts of black on her face and clothes.

Four huge ocean-going steamships were moored at the piers and they towered over the single-storey warehouses that lined the wharves. Boxes of military supplies – tins of corned beef, crates of newly stitched boots, reels of barbed wire, as well as boxes and boxes of Lee Enfield rifles – were being hoisted into the ship's holds, while lines of horses and mules were being led up ramps and into makeshift stables below deck.

Another ship was pulling out into the bay leaving behind a cluster of women and children who, given up waving but still reluctant to leave, watched as the boat slipped by degrees into the freezing mist before letting out a single, mournful blast from its funnel.

Anna walked quickly along the waterfront, past cheap boarding houses, run-down restaurants and grimy saloons, already crowded out with soldiers about to be shipped overseas, longshoremen, prostitutes and drunks. Billposters on the wall encouraged people to buy Liberty Bonds to raise money for the war; American flags were draped from windows, displayed in restaurants and flapped on their poles above government buildings.

But despite the ships and the propaganda and the drunken bravado of the men, it didn't feel concrete; despite the uniforms and the tears, the guns and the sentimental songs that everyone seemed to be singing, the war was all happening on the other side of the world – it was another climate, another time zone, another lifetime away. How soft these American boys are, Anna thought, how clean, how well-fed, how naïve, how quickly the memories of their own parents or grandparents who came with nothing from nothing, have been forgotten.

It was also clear that America wasn't ready to go to war. As well as a lack of trained men, it didn't have enough guns, or planes, or ships. Six months after the declarion of war, only a fraction of what was needed had been manufactured. Production lines all over America were being disrupted by strikes and demonstrations organized by the International Workers of the World, or Wobblies as they were known, making it impossible to guarantee a steady supply of raw materials such as wood, steel or coal.

Anna adjusted her hat and averted her face as she passed groups of sailors or strolling couples. The letters from Winter Hare had been hand-delivered, if you could call it that: an envelope jammed under her door with an address scrawled on the inside flap. At their second meeting, once again at Grand Central Station, Winter Hare had taken her letter for Kima, handed her three twenty-dollar bills and explained that she would be told what to do at the next rendezvous. The money had come just in time. She was already late with her rent and her former husband had written to advise her that his bank account had been frozen. He didn't mention their son. Did he know that he had found Pokolitov again? Did he know that Kima had become a Social Revolutionary?

In her pocket she had another letter for her beloved boy. 'Patience,' she had written, 'it won't be long now before I am home; I am doing absolutely everything I can to make the journey as soon as possible. Write to me today, now, I need to know everything. Pokolitov will pass on your letters to me. And give him my best regards and thank him for what he did for me all those years ago, and for his continued support in these difficult times.'

Tadeus Pokolitov. Anna struggled to recall his face, his hands, his smell, the haziest of details; and some came back, images and sensations long buried, such as the crease on his forehead and the lingering taste of earth and beeswax on his skin. But it was his voice that came back most vividly, soft but low-pitched, melodic. And his laughter, a bluster of happiness, as fresh and acute still as if he had only just left the room.

'Did you hear what happened to Pokolitov?' she had asked her former husband on the day that she arrived from Siberia all those years earlier.

Denisov, usually so mild-mannered, became angry and accused Pokolitov of being a police informer, of being a liar, a fake, a plant. 'I hope he's dead,' he had shouted. 'For all our sakes.'

A soldier doffed his hat as she hurried past and offered his hand in marriage. When Tadeus had proposed to her one evening all those years ago in St Petersburg, she had stared at him in horror. 'Haven't you listened to a word I have said?' she scolded him. 'You don't know me at all.' And he had pulled her to him and whispered that, on the contrary, he knew the secrets of her heart.

Yes, at that point, he had understood her, he had known every inch of her body, every flush of pleasure that he gave her, every thought that occurred to her. And she was filled with a sudden longing to see him, to hold him, to feel his arms around her again. But it had been seven years. Seven years. She had changed, grown older, taken other lovers. And so, she did not doubt, had he.

While she had been in exile, where had he been? What had happened to him in all those years? How many of them had he spent in prison? To be part of the new establishment was a big achievement: he was no longer a *brouillon*, that was obvious. Russia, however, was still in chaos. Kerensky had lost all credibility after he had dismissed the military commander-in-chief, Kornilov. Dozens of Russians had already left America and returned to Russia. Lenin and Trotsky were both back in St Petersburg and membership of the Bolshevik Party had almost doubled in size. Pokolitov might be in a position of power now, but for how long would it last? And if her association with him was widely known, what effect would it have on her reputation?

She would have to act fast, carry out whatever task Tadeus had in mind for her and then, she imagined, follow many of her comrades' footsteps, and sail from San Francisco, by way of Japan to Vladivostok and return home. Without the money for the fare or the correct papers, Winter Hare's offer seemed the only viable option.

She walked briskly along River Street and then turned left on to Sixth Street. Number 14 was a run-down tenement with no names on the doorbells. It was a safe-house, she supposed with a sympathetic landlord and a week-to-week lease. At ground level the windows had been shrouded by filthy lace curtains. She rang bell number 2, as she had been instructed, and waited.

Winter Hare opened the door, checked the street outside to make sure that she wasn't being followed and then ushered her quickly inside. He looked hot and agitated, and cursed when the key jammed in the lock of the interior door and he had to shoulder his way back in.

'In this country, they say they copy keys but they never copy exactly,' he complained.

The room on the ground floor was small and overheated. As well as a single bed, unmade, a dented silver samovar on a stool and a washbasin still filled with soapsuds, there was a tattered suitcase on the floor and a pair of boots stuffed with a pair of socks. A couple of young men with cloth caps and long beards sat despondently in the corner and played cards.

'Good morning,' Anna said to the men in Russian. They nodded in response but did not answer.

And then she noticed two tables pushed up against the far-side wall and covered in debris: metal tools, half-filled paper sacks of washing soda, empty cardboard cylinders, wine bottles, spools of wire and boxes of nails. The air smelled of singed wool and damp newspaper. Anna knew the rudiments of bomb-making; she could recognize the pale yellow oily spill and acidic whiff of nitroglycerine;

she could identify the sweet almond smell of dynamite. She had never made or used a bomb herself but she knew people who had. Some of them had taken a life or two, some had lost a part of themselves, accidentally.

'I won't make bombs,' she said.

'Very well,' Winter Hare replied. 'You won't make bombs.'

She closed her eyes and felt a previously unacknowledged stiffness in her shoulders start to relax. She unbuttoned the cuffs and pulled off her gloves one by one. Then she opened her handbag, pulled out an envelope and handed it to Winter Hare. He took it without a word and shoved it deep in his pocket.

'Do you have a letter for me?' she asked.

'No letter,' he replied.

She swallowed down her disappointment. Kima's letters were among her most precious possessions; she had carried them with her from Siberia to Stockholm and halfway across the world to America.

'And are you going to tell me what it is exactly that you want me to do?'

'Yes,' he replied. 'But first, tea?'

As a cup was filled from the samovar, she wandered across to the table and picked up a puff of cotton wool. Unlike everything else in this filthy room, unlike the whole of Hoboken, it was a pure snowy white, it was clean. Only that morning she had gone to see a physician, or an internist, as they called them in America. She had lain down on a cot covered in a starched white sheet and as he had listened to her chest she had closed her eyes and inhaled the smell of starch and soap, of antiseptic and chlorine. When he had diagnosed chronic bronchitis and recommended isotonic sea-water treatment, she had been more relieved than she could reveal. It was not tuberculosis. How could it be? TB was a disease of the poor, of the malnourished. She had a cough, that was all.

She was suddenly aware of the man who called himself Winter Hare standing very close behind her.

'Put it down,' he whispered. 'Here, let me help you.'

Winter Hare's arms slipped around her waist and encircled her

arms. For the smallest moment she inhaled his proximity, his mascu-
linity, his strength, and she felt a little wave of desire break inside
her. But it was not her he wanted; slowly, so slowly, with hands
shaking, he took the puff of cotton wool out of her fingertips and
laid it very gently back on the table. And then with more force than
was necessary, he released her.

'You want to kill us all?' he said. 'That cotton wool was soaked
in nitroglycerine. The smallest movement and it goes off. Explodes.
Boom.'

He took a long swig from a bottle of wine but didn't offer it to her.
Anna looked at her hands; right before her eyes they started to
tremble, as if she were cold, as if she were freezing. She was suddenly
aware of everything in the room: the rustle of the lace curtain, the
curse and stamp of the one of the card players, the rumble of a
distant train.

'I didn't know,' she said simply.

'Bourgeois cunt,' he said below his breath.

'I didn't know,' she repeated.

She looked at him until he glanced away. But he did not
apologize.

Anna had a sudden memory of Kima as a boy, dressed in a grubby
white sailor suit, his blond hair cut by his own hand, so short at the
front that she had wept when she saw what he had done. She
remembered now that he had always loved explosions. One New
Year's Day after a lavish firework display, he had trawled the garden
and collected up the tattered and burned cases of the spent ones,
which he scraped out for the remains of the gunpowder inside. And
then after hours and hours of work, he had created one single rocket,
a cardboard tube tied on to a lollipop stick, that in a secret ceremony
he lit and sent up into the dark Russian night where it exploded in
a small shower of spitting sparks.

'All that work,' she had said to him afterwards. 'For that?'

'What do you mean?' he had replied, his face serious with
outrage. 'It was worth every second!'

She had bought him a boxful of fireworks as a present the very
next day, but he had stowed them away in his room and would not

use them. And when they were found a few years later, they were damp and the paper casing was crumbling, and not a single one would light.

Outside the tenement in Hoboken, a group of newly enlisted men staggered past singing.

'Tell me,' she asked Winter Hare. 'How does he get messages out to you?'

'There are ways,' he replied. 'We have a network all over the world.'

'Men like Noah?'

He nodded. 'Men like Noah.'

A key opened the main door and it slammed shut with a bang. For a second Winter Hare and the two men stopped talking and listened. And then, when they heard the gallop of footsteps up the stairs, they relaxed.

'And all this,' she went on. 'What is all this?'

'Where do you think our finance comes from?' he said softly. 'I do what I do. You do what you can. Each to his own.'

'And you condone it? You don't mind taking money for this?'

Her voice had inadvertently risen in pitch. One of the bearded men looked up and examined her. His leg dropped and her eye was drawn immediately to a lump of metal in his trouser pocket. It was a pistol.

'Bandits,' she said. 'You're nothing but a bunch of bandits.'

The man with the gun laughed, revealing a mouth with a missing front tooth. '*Si*,' he said in a thick Italian accent. '*Bandito*.'

'Our friends here have the same beliefs. Roughly,' Winter Hare said. 'Have you heard the news?'

He held out a copy of *Novy Mir*. 'There is a new act. The Espionage Act,' he explained. 'It is now a crime to urge resistance to the draft. All over America, our people are being raided, arrested and prosecuted by the Bureau of Investigation. In the last few weeks they have also closed down dozens of our newspapers and have put the editors in jail. The rest can keep publishing as long as they print nothing about the war. Of course they will refuse.'

'But that's ridiculous,' Anna said. 'Why would they do that? Surely we're not a serious threat?'

'They turn on us,' he replied. 'It looks as if they are fighting. They make a declaration, a half-hearted gesture, send over a few shiploads of troops, round up a few so-called enemy aliens but they don't want peace. America is making millions from this war.'

Anna sighed. The closure of the newspapers was a blow. She had been hoping to sell some more articles.

'So tell me,' Anna said. 'What on earth do you think I could do?'

Winter Hare's mouth pouted and formed itself into a small regretful smile but he did not answer. Instead he suddenly cocked his head and listened. Outside came the overlapping slap of someone running. The Italians stopped playing cards and stood up. The bell rang and someone pounded at the front door.

'Help me,' a man's voice yelled. 'Let me in.'

Only a few seconds later came the approaching footfalls of a large crowd. The man at the door took off again. Anna and Winter Hare went to the window and pulled back the curtain an inch or two. The man had lost his advantage. They craned their necks and watched as he was caught at the end of the street and held down.

'He was on our streetcar and he called a soldier in uniform a 'rag',' a woman shouted out in explanation. 'He's a Bolshi. . .'

The man's head was pulled back as if an answer was expected. He didn't get an opportunity to reply. The woman's face reddened and her hat had tipped sideways. And then she took aim and kicked him twice in the face. The man on the ground yelled out something in a language that wasn't English.

'How dare you insult an American soldier? How dare you insult America?'

'Don't watch,' said Winter Hare and dropped the curtain.

When Anna left ten minutes later, the man lay lifeless and bloody on the cobbles. She paused and took a few tentative steps towards him.

'We should call a doctor,' she said out loud. 'Or the police. Can't somebody help him?'

'Friend of yours, was he?' A woman was leaning out of a third-floor window on the opposite side of the street. 'Say, Bill,' she yelled over her shoulder. 'We got ourselves another one.'

16

The Memorial Hall on Atlantic Avenue smelled of unwashed socks, stale sweat and hair oil. Monroe was standing in a row of thirty young men, dressed only in their underwear, all facing the same direction. Some men were swarthy, others fair; several were carrying a pound or two extra on their bellies, while a few were so thin you could count the ribs in their chest. Although many spoke English, the rest chattered in other languages such as Italian, Arabic or Swedish. As they waited to be told what to do next, the draft board – two doctors, a couple of military men and a man in civilian clothes – filed in and sat down at a desk at the far end of the hall beneath a window.

'Run,' shouted one of the military men. 'Run round the hall. Get a move on now, men . . .'

There was a moment's confusion as the men started to run in all directions, but then they shoaled together, like fish, and settled into a relaxed jog around the perimeter of the scuffed wooden floor.

'What are we doing this for?' asked a young man running beside him. 'They want to know if we can run as fast as the French. They sure know how to run away.'

'They're looking for flat feet,' someone else called over his shoulder. 'Or two left feet, or athlete's feet.'

'I got them all,' shouted someone up front.

'Me too,' yelled someone from behind. 'None of us is no good.'

When America declared war on Germany, every man between twenty-one and thirty-one, and there were twenty-four million of them, had to register for the draft. Each registrant had been issued with a number from 1 to 10,500. In the Senate Office in Washington DC, the numbers had been put inside a capsule and drawn one by one. Monroe was number 412. His number was drawn fifth.

'Bad luck,' Abe Groblensky had said the day they had found out. 'My number was 7,335 so it looks like it might be a while. If ever.'

Along with coal miners and construction workers, painters and hot-dog vendors, all who had been given the number 412, Monroe was instructed to report for inspection before the draft board at 9 a.m. sharp on 1 November. Failure to attend would result in arrest and imprisonment.

Earlier that morning Monroe's height and weight had been recorded, his chest had been tapped, his abdomen poked, his tongue pressed down with a wooden spatula and his head examined for lice. His eyes had been gazed into, his ears poked, his teeth checked and then, after the run, he had been ordered to get dressed and wait in line to be interviewed. Progress was slow. Monroe closed his eyes and tried to summon up the melody of a song he had been working on. But the hall was filled with the energy, the static, the trepidation of thirty men who might or might not be about to go to war.

Eventually it was his turn; he took off his hat, sat down before one of the examiners and gave his name and date of birth. The examiner frowned, found his notes and began transferring them into a huge ledger. It was all so calm, almost like high school matriculation.

'You married?' the examiner asked without looking up.

'Not yet,' Monroe replied.

The examiner ticked three boxes and placed a cross in a fourth.

'But . . .'

The examiner's pen rose off the ledger and stayed there. A drop of ink fell on to the page.

'Planning on it? You got a girl in the family way?'

'No, no! Not at all. But can you make a note that I'm a pacifist?'

The examiner looked up and raised his eyebrows. 'What, you a member of any religious sect?'

Monroe leaned forward. He didn't immediately make the connection. 'What do you mean? Exactly?'

'How clear can I make it? Mormon? Amish? Jehovah's Witness?'

'No,' he admitted. 'Just a regular Jew.'

'Then what you got against the war effort?'

Monroe cleared his throat and sat back. 'I'm against it on human-itarian grounds,' he replied.

The man behind the desk sighed, put down his pen, placed both hands over his face and rubbed his eyes. 'I'm sorry, Mr Simonov,' he said, 'but you're an American citizen. You aren't a member of a nut society, you seem to be in good health and you have no provable dependants. No matter what you think, you're still eligible to be drafted into the US Army.'

'Can't I appeal?'

'You have seven days to do so in writing, but I wouldn't bet on your chances. What do you do, anyway?'

'I'm a songwriter.'

'Oh, yeah, what do you write? Anything I'd know? Sing something to me.'

Monroe shifted in his seat. Did he really expect him to sing? In here? The man to the left of him was claiming he was blind, the man to the right was shaking his examiner's hand and telling him that he couldn't wait to stick his bayonet into a Hun. To burst into song would make the whole scene even more surreal.

'I don't think you'd know any of them,' Monroe replied softly. 'I mainly just demonstrate.'

His examiner seemed to lose interest instantly and picked up his pen again. 'Oh, so you're a song-plugger,' he said, then, looking down, he found his place and signed the form with a flourish. 'Thank you, Mr Simonov. Your report will be submitted to New York's 77th Division.'

'Did I pass?'

'That, I'm afraid, is confidential information.'

'When?' he asked. 'When do I hear?'

The examiner sighed. 'Wait for the letter,' he answered. 'That's all I can tell you. Next!'

On the steps of the Memorial Hall a group of women huddled into their coats against the cold. As the door swung open and he stepped out, they examined his face briefly and dispassionately; he wasn't their boy or their beau or their brother.

Monroe walked up Atlantic Avenue and tried not to think about what might happen. He wasn't a soldier; as a boy he had fought and scrapped and wrestled like all the others, but the thought of using a gun terrified him. He looked at his hands. They were soft and unlined; piano player's hands, hands that had never laboured or sweated or killed. But he had come up with nothing decent since he had been given his old job back. Ever since Von Hofe had told him that jazz was nothing more than a flash in the pan, he had dried up. Keep it light, his boss kept telling him. But how, he asked himself, could he keep it light when the future looked so dark?

He had always liked this stretch of Brooklyn, the store awnings advertising upholstery services or clocks or millinery or pecan pie, the nannies with babies in prams and old ladies with small dogs swaddled in tartan who lingered in front of the store windows, inspecting scarves or hats or lavish plaster of Paris cakes.

It was well below freezing but the sky was clear and the midday sun was tart and bright. He turned left along Clinton Street, crossing Amity Street and then Union Street. In some of the handsome apartment blocks and brownstones, the basement rooms had been turned into beer cellars and saloons. They were busy even during the day, filled with longshoremen and sailors, salesmen and shopkeepers, and as he passed Monroe glimpsed log fires and breathed in the smell of hops and cigarette smoke. At a bar on Carroll Street, someone was playing a Pianola. 'There's someone more lonesome than you,' a man's voice sang. He was out of tune, but then so was the Pianola.

The further Monroe walked, the emptier the streets became. Although Clinton Street was a busy promenade in the summer, nobody else that day was willing to brave the inclement temperatures and walk into the teeth of the icy winds that raced off the Gowanus Bay beyond.

At the Henry Street Slip, Monroe sat down on a packing crate, lit a cigarette and looked out over the water towards the docks. A barge was heading into the canal and he watched as it slowly edged its way into the narrow black channel of water that ran all the way up to Degraw Street.

As his breath fogged up the air and his eyes began to sting from the salt wind, he tried to tell himself that the odds were in his favour. Why would they choose him? He was a songwriter. And yet he had only ever had a few songs published, none of them a hit. And if he did go to war, who would miss him? The only girl he had ever fallen in love with, the girl he still wanted more than any other, was married. You've blown it, Simonov, he told himself. You're bullet fodder.

On the Gowanus Canal, he watched as the barge tied up below a winch and began to unload. A woman came out on to the deck singing. And what he had taken for a short brown mast suddenly moved. It had ears and a face. As he watched, the hold was opened, the animal was strapped up and winched out of the hold.

'Holy smoke,' Monroe whispered.

It was a giraffe. A real giraffe, all legs and neck, brown and golden against a brilliant blue sky. It was pulled up and over and then gently placed on the quay where a man was waiting with a bale of straw. Then came a cage of parrots, three white horses and a donkey; the barge was carrying a travelling circus. Life is a series of beautiful unexpected moments. If this were music, he told himself, it would be jazz.

Monroe looked around, for someone, anyone to share it with. But there was no one else there, no one but the singing lady and the man operating the winch, and the lonely sound of the north wind being blown up the Narrows.

The envelope had been hand-delivered to Universal and was lying on the lid of his piano when he arrived later that afternoon. Inside was an invitation to a rehearsal of a new vaudeville show that was just about to open in a theatre in Flatbush, and a note.

'Hope you can make it,' the note read. 'I got my break at last. Come backstage after. Love, Bessie.'

Bessie had been given a spot at the end of the first act, the space for rising stars. Dressed up in an elegant yellow gown with a white parasol, first she danced and then, in the wash of the spotlight she let her voice ring out warm and sweet.

'How did you do it?' Monroe asked afterwards. 'One minute you were a hoofer and the next a singer?'

Bessie smiled but did not look at him. 'A stroke of luck,' she said. 'Now I got a couple of writers who want me to sing their songs.'

'Mine not good enough for you any more?'

She laughed. 'You're too late,' she said. 'How's it doing anyway?'

Monroe shrugged. 'They printed up a thousand copies,' he replied. 'But no one can sing it like you did. So how did you do it, Bessie?'

'Maybe I just got friendly with the right people at last,' she suggested.

Two weeks before, Bessie had been packing up her costumes in the basement of the Variety. The show had closed but she had been booked to play on a circuit of flea-pit theatres in the south in the spring. It was a long time to wait, however, a long time to live on her meagre savings when she knew that the money she would be paid on the tour would barely keep her in stockings. A break, she had told herself at the time, all she needed was a break.

'Girls, I got a guy up here that's looking for information on a songwriter,' the doorman yelled down the stairs. 'Goes by the name of Monroe. Anyone know him?'

The dancers and singers, comedians and acrobats joked and laughed.

'What's he wanted for?' somebody yelled. 'Crimes against music?'

'Anybody?' the doorman yelled again.

'I might,' said Bessie. 'Who wants to know?'

Bessie had struck a hard bargain, but she had been asked for more than just information. Eventually they had come up with a deal that would be beneficial for both parties. A huge vase filled with lilies now sat on her dressing table and a rack of new dresses hung on a rail. Although Bessie still didn't have her own dressing room, now she had her own spot, hopefully it would only be a matter of time.

Monroe was looking at her in that way again and she couldn't bear it. She turned and began to fiddle with the fastening at the back of her dress.

'Could you?' she asked.

'Sure,' he replied.

'And . . . and I have a little favour to ask?'

At first he said he didn't want to do it. He said that his tuxedo was at the laundry, he was coming down with a cold, he was tired and hung-over and he had a frog in his throat. Here, he coughed for effect.

'Oh, stop it,' she said. 'Everyone coughs in here. It's the manager's Turkish cigarettes.'

'It is?'

'So you think you could do it?' she asked Monroe. 'Since the show opens next month, they scheduled in a couple of extra rehearsals.'

Monroe didn't answer. Bessie bit her lip. What would happen if he refused? Would all this be taken away from her?

'Please? I'm begging you,' she said.

He sighed deeply. He shook his head. He was going to say no again. How could she not have foreseen this happening?

'I had to report to the examination board today,' he said softly. 'Being examined for the draft.'

'You were?'

'Now all I got to do is wait for the letter. So what the hell? Why the hell not?'

'You'll do it?'

'For you, I'll do it,' he agreed.

'Thank you,' said Bessie. She blinked back what looked like tears. And it occurred to Monroe that she had never looked more beautiful.

'So where do I go?'

Bessie picked up her handbag, copied out an address and handed it to him. 'It's just some party for rich folk on the Upper West Side. They won't listen to you anyway. You could play any old thing and they wouldn't notice.'

'"Deutschland über alles"?' he suggested.

'Maybe not that,' she replied. 'And I'll try to get there by eleven.'

He gazed down at the white lilies on her dressing table, at the stamens laden with bright orange pollen.

'Don't touch,' Bessie warned. 'They're so pretty but they stain something awful.'

Monroe showed her his hand. It already had an amber streak, a burnish of colour, across his palm. 'Too late,' he said.

There was a knock on the door. 'Miss Lavigne?' a voice yelled. 'Rehearsal.'

Bessie made her way to the stage, up a steep set of stairs and through the darkened backstage with its racks of costumes and random props – a pot filled with yellow paper roses and a suit of armour made of cardboard – to the wings. She paused and listened until she heard the stage door slam closed. And then she smoothed down her hair and pulled out a business card from her handbag. The deal, she told herself, had been strictly business. That was all. What happened next had nothing to do with her.

There was a telephone on the wall just beside the lighting desk.

'Miss Lavigne?' shouted the assistant director. 'We need you now!'

'Give me two minutes,' she called back.

'What number was that?' said the operator. 'Could you repeat it?'

'It's 561,' said Bessie. 'It's the office of a company called Price Aero.'

The party that night was in a sizable apartment overlooking Central Park. The main room was wood-panelled with a polished parquet floor and a couple of uncomfortable-looking chairs. A grand piano was covered in a woven cloth and looked as if it hadn't been played for years, its lid used as a surface to display polo trophies. Monroe removed the cloth and the trophies, placed his music on the stand and looked for somewhere to hang up his coat. There was a rack beside the door on the other side of the room. He realized too late, however, that it was the kind of room where every footstep felt like a statement. Tread too hard and it was like shouting. He found himself on tiptoe, a whisper. Nobody else, though, seemed to notice; the maids and hired helps were rushing around, their feet a chorus of shouts and yells, their hands laden with vases of flowers and trays of glasses and plates of canapés.

'What's all this in aid of?' he asked.

'Belgian children,' the maid replied. 'Fund-raising.'

Monroe had read in the newspapers about what the Germans had done to the Belgians. After they had invaded their country, they had billeted their armies in their houses and then eaten all their food, leaving the former inhabitants to starve in one of the worst winters anyone could remember. Some of the reports were of atrocities, of rapes and hard-labour camps; others, like the *New York Post*, had far worse stories, claiming that the Germans were melting down corpses for soap and crucifying babies. Belgian children were the charity of the moment, evoking strong emotions and prompting generous donations. That morning Monroe himself had posted a couple of quarters into a collecting box outside the post office.

He wandered over to the window and looked out across the park. From up here, from the sixth floor, you could hardly hear the roar and clatter of the traffic below as it raced all the way down from Harlem. Not that there was much traffic at that particular moment; a mounted cop walked in front of a small huddle of banner-waving women: suffragettes, demanding votes and equality. Behind them, a long white car blew its horn. One of the women turned round and banged her fist on the bonnet.

The car pulled up right in front of the lobby below and a man in driving clothes climbed out. As Monroe watched he tipped the doorman a rolled-up bunch of notes. What exactly had he been doing, Monroe wondered, to warrant that? Something he wasn't supposed to, that much was evident.

On tiptoe Monroe returned to the piano, sat down and started to play. But as his mind filled with the memory of the giraffe on the barge and the woman singing, the songs shifted away from the way they had been written on the page and became something else entirely.

Suddenly the man Monroe had seen climb out of the car strode into the room and threw his driving gloves and car keys into a copper dish.

'And who,' he asked as he took off his hat and flung it on a chair, 'are you?'

'I'm the piano player,' he replied.

'Are you indeed?'

'Monroe Simonov. Pleased to meet you.'

Monroe came out from behind the piano with his hand outstretched. But the man looked down at his hand as if Monroe had just offered him something unpleasant. He did not take it. Monroe rubbed his hands together and then shoved both deep into his pockets.

'I'm here in substitute for Miss Bessie Lavigne. She has an extra rehearsal tonight, I'm afraid. But she'll be here later.'

'Very good,' the man said. 'Can you play juju?'

'Juju? I think you mean jazz?'

'Never mind what it's called,' he interjected. 'Never mind that. Let's hear you play something.'

'Yes, sir.'

Close up the man looked vaguely familiar. But then Bessie seemed to be acquainted with a string of men like this one, men who had too much money and a taste for what they thought was exotic. He'd probably seen him in the audience at her show. As Monroe sat down again and started to play, the man lit a cigar and inhaled deeply.

'Like the piano?' he asked, through a haze of violet smoke.

'Well, yes,' Monroe replied. 'Nice tone. Had it long?'

'Not too long,' he said. 'You think it's good then? Because if, you see, there was the slightest doubt that it wasn't any good, that it had, perhaps, a fault, something not immediately visible but fundamentally structural, that affected the tone or the tuning, then I would have no hesitation in dumping it.'

'I wouldn't do that,' Monroe said.

'Wouldn't you?' the host said.

'A piano,' Monroe pointed out, 'like any musical instrument, has to be played. Regularly. They get better the more you play them, you know.' And he began to play a little faster. 'You play?' he asked the host.

'No,' he answered.

Somewhere deep within the apartment a buzzer rang. The front door opened and Monroe heard the sound of women's voices. The host, however, didn't seem too concerned; he was staring straight at him. Monroe lifted his hands.

'If this is not the right kind of thing . . .'

'Keep playing,' the man instructed.

Monroe started to play again. The piano was warming up, the keys firm beneath his fingertips, the pedals amplifying or dampening, the melodies he played rising up from beneath the lid in curves and curls as if they were printed on the air like Braille. It was, Monroe realized, one of the most beautiful pianos he had ever played. It must have cost hundreds of dollars.

'Captain Price?' A couple of women were approaching.

'Do come in,' he called out, putting his cigar in an ashtray and placing it on a table at Monroe's right elbow. 'You're early!' he said as he strode over to meet them. 'I still need to change. Has someone taken your coats? Good. Let's go and see where the drinks are.'

The noise of the party guests faded as they moved down the hall. Monroe paused and picked up the cigar. Cautiously, he took the tiniest of puffs. Juju, he said to himself. Let's give them some juju.

Over the next hour, the room gradually filled up with people, old mostly or young but dressed as if they were old in hobbled skirts, silk corsages and hats, in dinner suits and army uniforms, monocles and cravats. Outside, the daylight had gone. The apartment blocks on the other side of the park were all lit up, as if turned inside out in the dark. And then as it began to pour, the rain streaming down the windows and making the night myopic, the distant lights blurred and spangled in the glass.

Bessie was right. No one listened to him. He could have been playing the Prussian national anthem and nobody would have noticed. One woman kept laughing, but it sounded to Monroe more like a ratchet of anxiety than a genuine expression of amusement. He was suddenly aware, however, of a presence behind him. He turned; a small woman dressed in dark green with a sharp, determined chin was standing a few feet behind him, watching him play.

'May I listen?' she asked.

'Be my guest,' he replied.

She stepped up until she was standing beside him. 'Beautiful,' she said in Russian.

'Me or the piano?' he responded in Russian.

'Actually the music,' she said. 'You speak my language.'

'My parents were Russian.'

'And what are you? An American?'

'I'm just the piano player,' he replied.

She smiled and sipped her drink. 'Mysterious,' she said softly. 'Look. We have dancers.'

A couple had taken hold of each other and together they were slowly circling the floor. A woman in a lilac dress was deep in conversation with a man in a uniform, however, and they remained in the middle of what had become the dance floor until, to everyone's amusement, the woman was swept up by an elderly soldier into a languorous two-step.

At first Monroe played waltzes and foxtrots, but then his playing became more syncopated, more rhythmic. The dancing speeded up and one by one the couples retired until only one pair remained, red-faced and out of breath, dutifully circling the room at twice their normal speed.

The Russian woman lit a cigarette and the smoke slowly uncoiled around her face. Few women smoked in public. It was still seen as daringly modern, like wearing ankle-skimming skirts or drinking cocktails. The host, now dressed in an evening suit, saw her and headed over.

'You came. I'm flattered,' he said.

The Russian, with one hand holding a cigarette and the other a cocktail, offered her cheek to be kissed.

'Thank you for inviting me,' she said as he kissed her. 'And giving me the opportunity to return the favour of making a donation.'

The host motioned to a chair. 'Sit down. I hope you'll find it a lot more comfortable than that cold hall in Greenwich Village.'

'Of course.'

The Russian woman didn't move. He glanced over at Monroe, clearly a little annoyed that he was in earshot. Monroe concentrated on playing louder and faster.

'Your call came out of the blue,' the host said softly. 'After, what was it, a year? It was such a surprise, such a pleasant surprise. It's Anna, isn't it?'

'Anna Denisova,' she replied.

'Ivory Price,' he said. 'There now, we've finally been formally introduced. Like the party?'

'Very much,' she said and took another deep drag from her cigarette.

'Still preaching free love?' he asked. 'We should make a date. I want to know more. Fascinating topic.'

'You can telephone me,' she suggested and opened her bag, extracted a pen and wrote down her number. 'Try early in the morning.'

He placed the piece of paper in his breast pocket and nodded. 'I might just do that,' he said. 'I might just.' And then he strode purposefully away towards an overdressed woman with a little dog who had just arrived.

Anna stubbed out her cigarette and took another glass from the waitress. Her hands were trembling.

'Can you sing too?' she asked Monroe.

'If you'd like me to,' he replied.

'Then sing something.'

'I only know sad songs,' he said.

'You're Russian,' she rejoined with a shrug as if that explained everything.

Monroe cleared his throat and then started playing the song that Von Hofe had bought for five dollars, that was now on sale for a dime. Although he closed his eyes, he was dimly aware that the room had gradually hushed. But he kept on playing and thought about the girl with the copper-coloured hair.

'My dear,' somebody said. 'Maybe you should sit down.'

'I'm not your dear,' a woman's voice replied.

Monroe opened his eyes. His hands stumbled. His voice faltered. Suzette Kinross was standing right below the chandelier in the middle of the room.

'My wife hasn't been well,' the host said. 'Inez, please don't make a scene.'

Her hair was unpinned, her coat unbuttoned, her hat was in her hand and she was soaked right through. And among all the pinched and corseted, the suited and the beaded, she looked as if she'd just blown in through the window from the park, like a leaf.

'Mrs Price,' urged a maid. 'Come and take your wet things off.'

'Why have you stopped playing?' yelled the husband in Monroe's direction. 'I pay you to play, so play!'

The girl he knew as Suzette turned, saw him behind the piano and let out a small, barely discernible cry. 'Oh,' she said. 'What on earth are you doing here?'

The party guests all seemed to reply at once: 'So kind of you to invite us. The Belgians! Those poor babies, good heavens!'

But Monroe knew that Suzette, whose name was now Inez, wasn't talking to them at all, but to him.

17

Inez had been out walking again, down Fifth Avenue to Washington Square, through Greenwich Village and back up Broadway. The streets were full of marches and demonstrations now, some in silent protest and others chanting slogans in strung-out unison. But no matter whether they were demanding war, peace, equality, disparity, they all handed out the same grey smudged leaflets and waved the same black-splashed-on-white-sheet hand-painted banners. And she envied them their conviction, their shared belief. Her walks were silent, solitary marches but her cause, she could not deny, was one that was not quite so transparent. Apart from the whole world and everybody in it, who could she blame but herself?

The baby was safe; that was all that mattered, she told herself over and over. The baby was safe; that was all that mattered.

'Most women in your position,' Ivory had pointed out, 'most women of your class or privilege pass their babies over to wet-nurses, to nannies and then to boarding schools. For the time being, Luella will be cared for by a day nurse and a night nurse in the nursery.'

Inez said nothing. Since she had been forcibly removed from outside the locked door of the nursery twice, she had decided on the path of least resistance.

'Nobody expected you actually to look after the child,' he went on. 'Did you?'

And she had to admit that in fact she had.

'Of course you can see her when you're well. Then we can organize a schedule,' Ivory had said. 'Until then the doctor has advised that it would be less disruptive for both of you to put it on hold for a couple of weeks while you recover.'

A couple of weeks. A couple of weeks? At that Inez had lost her resolve and had balked and yelled and cried and begged until the physician had been called. And now just the thought of that little man made her shudder.

'There's nothing wrong with me,' she yelled.

But he begged to differ. 'Post-partum psychosis,' he pronounced. 'A danger to herself and the child.'

He had given her those injections again and she had woken up stiff and sore, groggy and confused, hours, sometimes days later. And so she had vowed once more that she would take her medicine and be a good girl. She would get better eventually, the doctor pronounced, with a mixture of fresh air and lithium. But how, she asked herself silently could she get well without her baby? Her absence was a rip inside, a rent in her fabric, a whistle-clean hole through her heart. And she could not bear it. Pretend, she told herself as she paced the pavement. Pretend, act, and you will be rewarded. If only she didn't fluff her lines, miss her cues, freeze to the spot like an amateur with stage fright.

'Have you taken your medicine?' Ivory would ask before he switched off the light.

'I think so,' she would say.

'I think not,' he would reply. 'Let me bring you a glass of fresh water.'

Ivory was still gracious; he brought her cups of tea in bed, made sure she took her medication and still produced the occasional bunch of white roses, but when he kissed her with that small, cold, wet mouth, she wondered how she could ever have believed that she could make herself love him.

And although he still acted like a husband, she had the sense that everything had shifted; it was in the way he moved around her, rarely coming within six inches of her body; it was in the way he touched her things, lifting her hat, her coat, her books, by the smallest corner so that the least possible part of him touched the least possible part of anything that belonged to her. It was in the way that he never talked about the baby, as if she would simply cease to be if her name were never mentioned.

Every morning, she forced herself to eat her breakfast with Ivory although it tasted of ash and stuck in her throat. And after that, after he had gone to the office and she had agreed to rest, she would stand in the corridor outside the nursery, just listening. Sometimes she would hear the baby murmur and cry and then be shushed by the nurse and sometimes she would listen and hear nothing and be filled with the terror that the baby had died and she hadn't even been there.

'Let me in!' she would shout when she turned the door handle and found it locked. 'Let me see her.'

'Mrs Price,' the day nurse would whisper through the door. 'Everything's fine. Why don't you go out for a walk? I think it's for the best. If you go now I won't say anything. Otherwise I shall have to put through a call to your husband. You'll feel better once you're out in the fresh air.'

Once she started walking, however, her ears roared with the blare and clatter of the city, her eyes were blinded by the slant of the sun's reflection on the multiple glass windows, and her nostrils were filled with the sharp, burned tang of the air that rose from the subway and the hot acrid steam of the Chinese laundries. And then she imagined that her real self was dragging behind her like a shadow, loosened but still attached, hauled against its will into the wrong life.

'Nice walk?' Ivory sometimes asked her. 'Feel better? Where did you go?'

'I can't remember,' she would reply.

Sometimes her walks made her feel better, sometimes worse. That day she had watched the sun set through storm clouds over New Jersey as the lights illuminated in their reds and blues, their golds and silvers, on the billboards around Times Square. She had given all her money to beggars and tramps and then left her purse on a bench. And finally when she was so wet that the rain had seeped right through her shoes and given her a cape of moisture, she made her way back to Central Park West where the doorman made her wait and then let her in with a frown.

'The party has already started, ma'am,' he told her.

'I know,' she replied. 'I know that.'

Inez had completely forgotten about the fund-raising party even though Ivory had reminded her only that morning. And when she stepped into the apartment she had a sudden jolt of memory, she was drawn back to the exact time when it had started, back to the day when she had come to that party with Maud and danced all alone under the chandelier. So much had changed but so little. The apartment looked the same, the people at the party were the same, the food, the drinks, the maids were all the same. It was she who had changed. And, as if tracing her own steps, she somehow drifted through the guests and into the drawing room, where the music was coming from and where half a dozen couples were circling underneath the chandelier.

'Hello,' she said to everyone and no one in particular, 'I'm so glad you could come.'

She knew by the way they peered at her, however, that as a hostess she was unconvincing; she looked bedraggled and tattered, bereft and lost. No wonder Ivory's face was fixed into that smile he used in public, the one that was all teeth and no goodwill.

'My wife hasn't been well,' he offered several times.

The fact that he did not offer an actual illness and she wasn't bedridden implied the worst. She had gone crazy, clearly. She could see that conclusion in people's faces, in the way they glanced up at her only briefly, as if they were embarrassed, or as if her mentally deranged state was contagious. And her eyes began to spill despite herself.

But when she wiped the rain and the tears from her face and noticed the piano player and saw that it was Monroe, her Russian, playing, singing, the way he had the day they first met, she was momentarily struck dumb. The whole sodden, ruined world suddenly flipped; time slipped for an instant as if in one great celestial hiccup and she spoke out, saying the first thing that came to her.

Monroe stood up. And she was suddenly cold and hot and deliriously happy and sad all at once. Then Ivory appeared at her elbow, and something in Monroe's face flared up and then died down again.

'Inez,' said Ivory. 'Come with me now to your room and change out of these wet clothes. We don't want to have to call the doctor again, now do we?'

No, she didn't want him to call the doctor again. But she didn't want to leave Monroe either.

'Wait,' she said.

Once more, any acting ability she had deserted her and she could think of nothing to say or do that would look convincing. And so she let herself be led from the room without a word. As they reached the front door, however, a coloured girl in a long fur coat was being shown in.

'You must be the entertainment,' Ivory said.

'That's right,' she replied. 'And you must be the new associate producer. Thank you so much for that.'

'A pleasure.' He bowed. 'I think we both got what we wanted.'

Bessie shifted from foot to foot and glanced up at the woman at the host's side; his wife. Her hair was wild and her clothes were wet right through.

'Now where is that piano player I sent you?' she said brightly. 'You can tell him I'm here.'

A maid was despatched to find him.

'This is my wife,' said Ivory. 'This is . . . I'm sorry, I've forgotten your name.'

'It's Bessie,' she said. 'How do you do?'

'Inez?' said Ivory. 'Aren't you going to say "Hello"?'

Inez struggled to stay in focus, to take in what she had been asked. But her mind was spinning. What was Monroe doing here? Maybe he knew everything? But how could he?

'Excuse me,' she said. 'What did you say?'

The maid returned and the conversation was dropped.

'You find him?' Ivory asked.

'I looked everywhere but he's left already,' she said breathlessly. 'He must have taken the back stairs. Do you want me to go down and have a look? He can't have got too far.'

'No, never mind,' said Ivory. 'Now, Bessie dear, let me show you where you can leave your things.'

203

The front door was still open wide. Inez stared at it for a second.

'I think I left my umbrella in the lobby,' she said vaguely. 'Will you please excuse me?'

And then she slipped through the door, ran across the landing, straight into a waiting lift and started to descend.

In the apartment, Bessie pulled off her gloves finger by finger. They both watched as the the the lift dial lights illuminated the passing floors, one by one.

'I hope you know what you're doing,' Bessie said.

He laughed. Bessie did not join him.

'I'm a strategist, my dear,' he replied. 'Nothing more, nothing less.'

Monroe Simonov was halfway around Columbus Circle when Inez finally caught up with him.

'Wait! Please wait!'

He stopped and turned round but she saw immediately that he was furious. And his eyes roamed behind and around her before finally meeting hers.

'Did I forget something?' he asked.

She shook her head.

'Payment has been arranged,' he added. 'Thank you. And although a tip is usually appreciated, in these circumstances I don't think . . . Suzette, I didn't know it was your party. If I had, do you think . . .? Jesus Christ. Did you know about it? Tell me it was pure chance. Tell me you didn't?'

'I didn't. I just came home. And there you were.'

A couple with a baby in a perambulator and two small children strolled past. They both were silent until the family was out of earshot.

'I used to go there sometimes,' she said in a rush. 'Back down to West Forty-Fifth Street, to the music publishers, and sometimes I'd stand across the street and try to listen for you, for your playing, I mean, and sometimes I thought I could, I really could hear you, but then again . . . there were so many . . . Shoot, I suddenly don't know what I'm trying to say any more.'

Her hand reached out and she tentatively touched his coat sleeve.

It was wool, rough beneath her fingers but warm. He didn't move away but looked down. And when he spoke at last, he spoke to her hand.

'Suzette, this is crazy,' he said. 'What are you doing?'

What was she doing, he was asking her? What was she doing with a man like Ivory Price? His coat was soft but the edge was slightly frayed. Her fingers ran along the threadbare edge. There were a couple of loose threads where a button had once been. What kind of life would she have had with him? What kind of life would Luella have had? For a moment they stood there as the rain fell and the subway rumbled underfoot.

'You're shivering,' he said. 'You're wet through.'

But as he took the smallest step towards her, her shoulders heaved and she seemed to fold.

'Suzette?' he whispered.

Finally she looked up at him with her face composed. 'Actually, it's Inez. It's always been Inez. I'm sorry,' she said.

He searched her face for an explanation. 'It has, has it?' he said.

'I have to ask you something,' she went on. 'Now you know where I live, don't ever come anywhere near here again. I can't explain why. Just trust me.'

Monroe inhaled sharply and then looked into the distance.

'I don't love him, you know,' she said.

And then she released the sleeve of his coat, turned on her heel and walked quickly away.

Wilson Strutt shouldered the door once, twice, before it flew open and he stepped out on to the roof. Up here, the night air was edged with the smell of damp earth from several pots stuck with dead plants. An empty bird cage that appeared, by the detritus, to have once held white doves stood next to a fraying deckchair. The water-tower stood above, its overflow splashing sharply on to the black pitch below, and just beyond, looming over everything, was the huge girder-stretch of the Manhattan Bridge. Although the roof was littered with empty beer bottles and the stubs of a hundred spent cigarettes, it was clear to Strutt that no one had been up here for months, not since the last days of the previous summer, or even the one before that. And so he made a seat from an upturned seltzer bottle box, pulled out his notebook and began to write.

He had just reached the corner of Delauney Street when Monroe Simonov had disappeared into a residential brownstone. The doorway on the brownstone opposite, however, was locked. And so he had waited, smoking, lingering, fiddling with his shoelace, until someone had come out. Quickly he had noted the door's mechanism, a slow closure with the lock clicking shut after approximately twenty seconds. Ten minutes after that, on the tail of a man who had both arms laden with grocery bags, he was in and no one, he told himself, was any the wiser.

This roof was a couple of feet higher than the roof across the street and it was possible to observe the entire block without being seen. And now all he had to do was to wait for part two of the puzzle, the adulteress. He knew quite a lot about each of them already. A woman named Maud, who said she had been a friend of Mrs Price, before she was dumped 'like a sack of logs', claimed that when she knew her, Inez Kennedy had been looking for a suitable husband for quite some time.

'Like every other girl in New York City,' she added, giving him the smallest hint of a wink.

They had been drinking tea at one of the smaller tables in Delmonico's Restaurant. The woman, who was a good deal larger than those he thought of as his type but attractive nonetheless, opened up under scrutiny like a clam in hot water.

'Has she done something wrong?' she asked, her eyes wide and her body leaning forward.

But Wilson Strutt merely smiled serenely and offered her another piece of French brioche.

'There was a man, I think, someone she used to pal around with. He had a job down on Tin Pan Alley. A piano player. He just wasn't in her class at all. It was me who helped her meet the right kind of people, wear the right kind of clothes, act the right kind of way. She hadn't a clue, she was . . . how can I say this in polite company? Inez was too . . . *Midwestern*.'

'Midwestern,' repeated Wilson Strutt, stirring a third spoonful of sugar into a vastly overpriced cup of lukewarm tea. 'I see. What was his name, this pal?'

'Oh, I couldn't possibly remember that.' Maud pouted. 'I can barely remember what I did last Saturday night. But let's see. Robert? Quincy? Reuben? No, wait a minute. I think it began with an M. Michael? No. Mitchell? No, I got it. Monroe. He was called Monroe. And no, I've no idea how one would track him down.'

Wilson Strutt sighed and sat back in his woven wicker chair. It was in the bag, he told himself. He'd be off this case in a week; he'd negotiated payment in full on completion, and when he was finished he'd pack up a case and spend a fortnight in the sun in Florida. Tea at Delmonico's was worth every cent. Maud was beaming at him, as if she was a child who'd just come top of the class.

'I must congratulate you on your memory,' he said. 'An engaging quality in a young lady.'

'Why thank you,' she replied and ordered another pot of Earl Grey.

It hadn't been easy to find him, however. None of the music publishers would give him the time of day and so he had visited more than two dozen theatres before he found a young black dancer who claimed that she knew him. The relief must have been visible on his face because she drove a hard bargain.

'Let me meet your client,' she had told him. 'I'll deal with him directly.'

Wilson Strutt waited on the roof until midnight. But although dozens of young women traipsed up the stairs to a party on the third floor, none of them was Inez Price. Monroe Simonov, song-plugger, left the building with a short, white woman. When the couple split at the subway station, Strutt decided to call it a day. It had started to rain again and he was cold, hungry and all the confidence he had felt earlier had begun to evaporate.

Earlier that night, Inez had wept in the bathroom as she had flushed the doctor's pills down the lavatory. And then she had changed out of her wet clothes and into a pale yellow silk dress. She had brushed her hair, washed her face and drunk a glass of punch laced with gin in one swallow. Mrs Price, she had told herself. My name is Mrs Ivory Price. And she had sprayed the air with cologne and walked through the heavy scented mist towards the drawing room where the fund-raising party was at the exact point in its trajectory where it was in dire need of the sort of charm that Inez would do everything she possibly could to provide.

'As a new mother,' almost every sentence she uttered began, 'my heart goes out to those poor Belgian parents.'

'Boy or girl?' they would ask. 'I didn't know! How old? What did you call her?'

'You must come and visit,' she would say. 'I'd be thrilled to introduce you. And her name's Luella, Luella Price.'

The door to the nursery was unlocked the following day.

Over the next few weeks the weather turned for the worse; deep snow fell on New York and temperatures plummeted all over the United States. It was one of the worst winters in living memory and it was so cold that it was possible to walk on thick ice all the way from the Jersey shore to Staten Island. Once the novelty of the weather had worn off, however, people began to realize that they were in danger of freezing to death. What little coal there was arrived in the coal ports frozen solid. Trains carrying food and fuel supplies had to be dug out of the drifts.

Ivory's factory had already fallen behind on the War Department's order for two thousand planes. As well as the strikes and walk-outs that afflicted the sawmills and the smelting works of the Midwest, his factory had been targeted by freezing workers who broke in at night to steal coal. But the war effort was in disarray anyway. Nine months after they had declared war on Germany, most of America's newly recruited army were still living in training camps in America, practising manoeuvres with sticks instead of rifles and living in half-built shacks without coats, boots or suitable sanitation. Thousands of draftees had been diagnosed with TB or measles or mumps and since most of the medical facilities at the camps were basic, if they had been built at all, hundreds of soldiers were dying.

Ivory was also beginning to suspect that Wilson Strutt was a con artist; so far he had produced nothing on the piano player and his wife. And Inez, he couldn't help but notice, seemed to have changed. When she wasn't with the baby, she spent her time on war relief work, organizing rummage sales to raise money for Uncle Sam's boys, or collecting donated supplies of food and surgical dressings. If the war, as some people said it did, acted as a curtain to the past, she seemed to have drawn it, swiftly, precisely and with absolute finality. She wasn't alone; some of her new friends had husbands who had been sent to France. Others were in officer training camp in New Jersey. Charitable acts and self-sacrifice had become the new barometer of fashionable society. And nobody worked as hard or gave more of her time than Mrs Ivory Price.

'The Price Effect,' read the newspaper headline. And there, in grainy black and white, was Inez handing over a cheque towards the purchase of chloroform for the Allies, perhaps, or for the Red Cross War Fund.

Maybe it was just a ruse, Ivory considered, to throw him off the scent. Maybe she had foreseen the situation and was trying to make it as potentially difficult as she could for him. But he had the weight of the law on his side. He had watched her face change when she had seen the piano player and knew that he was the one. He had made it easy for her; he had virtually thrust the man underneath her nose. It was only a matter of time. Once he had proof, he could drop her and her child; he could cast off the mantle of cuckold with a clear conscience.

By the middle of December most of the department stores and large hotels on Fifth Avenue had been decorated with Christmas trees and mistletoe, their windows displaying intricate winter tableaux made of plaster of Paris: tiny figures ground their way around glass ponds or went round and round or up and down on motorized trains and ski-lifts. Elsewhere, shop windows, churches and synagogues were hung with spruce branches and painted glass baubles or were illuminated with menorahs. But the festivities were sober and the gifts were modest this year. Even the lights on Times Square were switched off on weekdays.

The Hotel St Regis had been taken over by one of Inez's charities to provide a holiday lunch to soldiers. But although the doors were open and the invitations issued, few soldiers came. They were all out in camps on Long Island or New Jersey or Brooklyn. A couple of cowboys from Wyoming who had joined up only two days before were waited upon by no fewer than fifteen young women. A lieutenant on leave who had been coaxed inside by a pretty face drank a glass of camouflage punch and then made his excuses and left. And their seating for thirty began to look woefully ambitious. As the turkeys began to cool and the gravy congealed, the women took to the streets to lure in any military man they could.

'Soldier,' Inez called as she raced along Fifth Avenue in the falling snow. 'Happy Holidays. Would you like to come and join us for lunch?'

The soldier turned and Inez's smile froze.

'Oh,' she said. 'It's you.'

For a moment they just looked at each other, Inez in her demure wool cape and hat and Monroe in his uniform.

'You're . . . you got drafted,' she said.

'Yup,' he said.

'You look . . .' she started. 'You look different.'

'Do I?' he answered.

'So you think . . . you think you'll go to France?' she asked.

'That's what they're training us for.'

'Good luck.'

'Thank you.'

'We're doing a lunch . . . for soldiers,' she said softly. 'We've got turkey and camouflage punch . . . You see the thing is, what I meant to say was, you never came. I waited for you but you never came. You just ignored my note.' Inez's face began to crease.

'Wait a minute. What are you talking about?' he asked. 'What note?'

'Meg,' she said. 'My friend Meg went down to Universal and gave you my note.'

'No,' he replied. 'She didn't.'

Inez looked away. All at once another narrative unfolded, one

210

quite different from the one that she had been telling herself for so long.

'She didn't?' she said. 'She didn't.'

And then without another word Monroe reached over, took her hand and led her along Forty-Ninth Street until they reached the narrow stairs to a basement.

'I can't,' she said. 'I'll be missed. Someone might see.'

Down below the stoop was an alcove that was hidden from the street.

'No one will see us down here,' he said.

Wilson Strutt, who had a cold and was nursing a dime-store coffee between his freezing hands, walked past the stoop several times just to make sure. But there they were, two sets of footprints in the freshly fallen snow, one of which, he knew for a fact, belonged to Mrs Ivory Price.

18

'My little girl,' sang the man softly in the top bunk, 'I'm dreaming of you'.

Monroe lay in the bunk below and watched the ascent of a tiny red spider up an invisible gossamer thread. The early morning sun broke through the mist and it was suddenly caught in the light, a tiny bead of dark red, floating.

The air on Long Island was a different colour from Manhattan. It was the dry bone white of a sand dollar. And out here in the training camp at Yaphank, the air was full of grains of fine sand which blew up from the wide empty beaches of Fire Island. His breath froze in clouds in the air above his mouth. A crust of frost covered his thin grey blanket. Monroe pulled a silk scarf from his inner pocket and held it to his face. It smelled of Suzette, or Inez, as he knew her now, of her scent, of her hair, of her skin. He closed his eyes and brushed it over his lips. It was 7 a.m. and he had been awake since four, just waiting for the day to lighten.

Monroe had arranged to meet Inez on his next day of leave, on Saturday. It was only Wednesday. And each day, each hour, each minute stretched until it seemed to drag to twice its normal length; he couldn't sleep, he couldn't eat, he couldn't read. How could he bear to wait another three days, another three nights?

'Say you won't go,' she had whispered to him the last time.

'I can't do that,' he had replied. 'They'll lock me up. Say you'll leave him?'

But she had simply stared up at the ceiling and then closed her eyes.

On that evening on Columbus Circle, he had given up on her just as she had asked him to. It was for the best, he told himself, it just wasn't meant to happen. He had been drafted into the

American Army and would probably never see her again. But when they had met by chance on Fifth Avenue a few months later and she had asked him about a note, a note he had never received, all his convictions ceased to mean anything. Down below the stoop where they stood so they couldn't be seen from the street, he held her again and everything flooded back. She hadn't changed, she hadn't changed at all. But then she had started to cry and pulled away and it was clear that he had been mistaken.

'I have a baby,' she said simply.

He had taken a long deep breath, a lungful of ice-cold air. And although he tried to smile when she examined his face for his reaction, his mouth was pulled southwards in disappointment.

'Boy?' he asked.

'A little girl,' she replied. 'She's called Luella.'

And he had let her go, stamped his feet in the melting snow and looked upwards towards the small strip of grey sky above.

'Pretty name,' he said.

'Monroe,' she said softly and reached over to him.

'Maybe you were right,' he said taking the smallest step back. 'The time you followed me down to Columbus.'

But when she took his hand, he let her.

'No,' she had said, 'no, no, no.'

And despite everything he felt: regret, rage, jealousy and remorse, he had enveloped her in his arms and breathed her in, her hair, her warmth, her scent.

Someone was walking up the stoop above them. Inez shivered and pulled her collar around her neck.

'I've got to go,' she said. 'They'll be wondering . . .'

'Be here in a fortnight,' he had said. 'Meet me same time, same place. By then I'll have figured out a place we can go.'

Inez paused before she ran back up the snow-covered stone steps. And she reached out and ran her index finger along the curl of his lower lip.

'Promise me?' he had said. 'Two weeks?'

And she had nodded, her head framed by that burning halo of amber hair. 'Two weeks,' she had repeated.

213

19

Anna lifted her skirt as she walked to avoid the kitchen refuse, the cheroot butts, the piles of horse dung and the pools of bright yellow dog urine that stained the melting snow. The rendezvous was in a nondescript hotel in Hell's Kitchen. Down here, in the streets just south of Times Square, cheap vaudeville theatres still advertised six shows a day, Italian bakeries left their back doors wide open and bakers, their overalls covered in flour and their faces pink from the heat of flickering wood fires inside, drank coffee on the pavement as their bread baked. Further west, towards Tenth Avenue, old women swept their doorways free of tramps and stray cats, and children, too cold to play, watched the world go by from their stoops with a steady unselfconscious gaze. Anna gave one of them, a small boy of about six, a half-smile, but received nothing in return. She wondered who they thought she was dressed up in her fine winter clothes: a philanthropist or a whore?

It was already getting dark and the lights were growing increasingly sporadic. Anna had brought a splaying Baedeker travel guide and paused to consult a wafer-thin map. And then she moved on, glancing here and there and nowhere in particular, until she reached the heavy glass doors of the Ideal Hotel.

The lobby was deserted except for a single middle-aged man who sat on a leather chesterfield, perfectly upright but fast asleep, with a box on his knees that read: *Freedom for ladies with the Andrews patented Rust-Proof Corset*. He didn't wake as she passed him. And that day as the temperature began to plummet, as electric lights began to be illuminated in rooms in which it was now too dark to read a newspaper headline, she was fairly sure that no one had seen her enter the hotel on Thirtieth Street; she was confident that no one had followed her. The lift would be too noisy and so, with only the tiniest tick of her heel, she started to ascend the stairs, stepping up and up and round and round the narrow stairwell to the third floor, her bag heavy in her hand, to the room number that she had scratched out in Indian ink on the inside of her wrist.

Ivory Price listened for the grind and clank of her imminent arrival. He was by nature impatient; in fact he didn't feel relaxed unless he was supposed to be in two places at once. That day he had an appointment with his factory foreman in Keyport to discuss the War Department's order. But his foreman was used to waiting hours for him. That, Ivory told himself, was part of his job. He always turned up eventually.

The lift door slammed far below. He stood up, ran his hand over his hair and checked his face in the over-mantel mirror as the lift slowly ascended. But when the metal doors clanked open and rammed shut again, he could tell that the person who alighted, with much coughing and stamping of feet, was a man.

Ivory sat down again. And then he stood up. Maybe, he considered, she wouldn't come after all. Maybe she had changed her mind. Maybe he should leave now and pretend it was he who hadn't shown up, it was he who had had a change of heart. It was fifteen minutes after five. Did she think he had nothing better to do than this? Nothing better to do than pace back and forth and try to ignore the rattle of air bubbles in the cast-iron radiators and the whisper of the wind in the curtains?

He hadn't been down here for many months, not since the night that Luella had been born. Consuela was a story he told himself now, with a predictable narrative arc and an inevitable end. He had continued to pay the rent regardless. The finality of giving it up was too much of an admission, although of what, he couldn't quite bring himself to define. And if he could have been honest, if he could have let himself remember the suddenness of her departure and all the unanswered questions it raised, he would have admitted that it pained him, it spooked him, it sapped him to be in these familiar rooms again without her, even though he had swept most of her

215

belongings into a box and shoved them in a closet, even though he had lit a fresh fire and changed the sheets on the bed.

No, he was a man, as he had once told Inez, who always got what he wanted. The harder it was to obtain, the more he craved it. Anna Denisova – he rolled her name silently in his mouth – Anna Denisova, richer, much richer than he could ever be, her money old and foreign, her refinement passed down from generation to generation until it hung around her like an expensive scent. While his grandparents had been shopkeepers and salesmen, Anna Denisova gave the impression that she was descended from an ancient line of blue-blooded aristocrats.

He remembered the first time he had seen her, at the lectern of that dingy hall in Greenwich Village. He had been expecting someone quite different, someone hirsute and hoary, someone red-faced with militant fervour. He wanted to see, close up, the nature of what he perceived was the enemy and had found her.

And he remembered the phone call that came quite out of the blue, and that night she had come to his apartment for that fund-raising party. He remembered the brush of her fur collar and the flush of her cheek. He imagined that Anna had grown up in palaces with servants and governesses to be almost classless, nearly stateless, speaking five languages and moving between the south of France and the Russian plains to residencies where the pianos were always in tune and the discussions over the dinner table were always philosophical, political or cultural. No wonder she had become as opinionated as a man, no wonder she had strong ideas and could argue a point; no wonder she was liberated and articulate and ideal-istic. No matter that he thought her wrong. Just the sound of her voice made him begin to swell.

Of all the women he had ever met, she, he decided, was the jewel, the diamond, pure and beautiful, making every other woman, women like Inez, for example, look vulgar and trashy, their energy and their verve nothing more than a little too much voltage in the blood. Anna Denisova: a name with the rhythm of a call to battle. Her body, compact, her energy palpable, but her face as firmly locked to him as the palace gates. He imagined undressing her, he imagined opening those gates, he imagined her face in stillness, in capitulation. He would win her over, the new world against the old, the right against the left, man against woman. Yes, he was sure he would win, if only she gave him the chance to try.

Captain Ivory Price needed a triumph of some sort more than ever. Potentially victorious hands in poker or holes in one at golf just didn't satisfy him any more. He had learned only a few months before that he was not being posted to France. Even though his age had been overlooked because of a shortage of decent pilots, even though his factory built the planes they would fly, even though he begged and pleaded. You have dependants, it was pointed out. You have a family. You are ineligible. Besides that, you have a factory to run, he was told, you are a symbol to the American people of the success of capitalist values, of the importance of the family. If only they knew the truth.

Also, Price Aero was in crisis. He had promised too much too fast. And now he was planning on suffering the indignity of asking his father-in-law, the man with the rotten potato in his pocket, for a loan.

As he paced from the window and threw himself on to the bed, he felt like a boy again, a boy left on the bench while everybody else played out the game in the bright lights of the world stage. It isn't fair, he found himself thinking in his long-lost seven-year-old voice. It just isn't fair.

Wilson Strutt, he had been informed by his lawyer, was the best there was. He had also started, he reported, to get some results. A dossier was being prepared. And once justice had been done, privately, discreetly, away from the glare of the newspapers, and he could unshackle himself from Inez and the child, off he would go to the clear blue skies above La Manche, to Alsace-Lorraine, to the Normandy coast, to fight for America, to fight for Anna Denisova.

It was as he lay sprawled out, his mind filled with gossamer clouds, the spluttering surge of the engines and the euphoric lift of the wind beneath the wings, that he heard a small tap at the door.

Anna Denisova stood on the threshold. Her cheeks were pink with cold and her eyes had lost their colour and were dark and deep as two small wells. She was smaller than he remembered, slight, fragile, and there was something more foreign about her, something untranslatable, a formality maybe, he had not been expecting.

'Did you get lost?' he asked. 'You should have taken a taxicab in this weather.'

'I walked,' she replied succinctly. 'And your directions were very clear.'

Anna Denisova's heart was beating wildly. And she had an almost unnoticeable tremor, which gave her presence a blurred edge, an aura, like the wings of a hummingbird.

'Let me take your things,' he said.

'That would be very kind,' she responded.

The rooms were narrow and dark but furnished in rich warm colours, pinks and reds and oranges. A fire was burning in the grate. As she removed her hat, scarf and gloves, she looked out of the window. A desolate back yard stretched out behind, hung with lines and lines of half-frozen washing.

'I can offer you cider or a glass of wine,' he said.

'Do you have tea?' she asked.

'I'll take a look,' he answered.

As he opened cupboards and rifled through boxes in the tiny kitchen, she glanced through an open door and into a bedroom beyond. A large bed looked as if it had been freshly made.

'Cider,' she called out, 'would be perfectly lovely.'

'No, there is tea . . . is China the thing?'

'Yes,' she replied. 'China is the thing.'

Ivory clattered around for a moment or two with cups and saucers and sugar bowls. A vast brown radiator beneath the window clanked, moaned and then started to tap; a smell rose up of dust and absence. The rooms were warm but the air was slightly damp. Nobody, Anna guessed, had lived here for months.

'So what are you?' Ivory Price asked from the kitchen. 'An anarchist, a socialist or a Bolshevik?'

'That question,' she replied, 'requires a longer answer than I am prepared to offer at this moment. Maybe you would like to read one of my articles.'

'It would be a pleasure,' he said. 'Are they in English?'

A kettle started to whistle on the stove.

'Alas, no.'

'Listen, I'm sorry for having to meet down here,' he said as he came in with a tray which he placed on a small low table. 'It's just, under the circumstances it might appear . . . please, Miss Denisova?' He motioned to the tray where two cups and saucers sat in pools of spilt tea, and then to a small dark red velvet love-seat.

'Please don't call me that,' she said. 'It's Anna.'

'Anna,' he repeated. 'Why don't you take a seat?'

But she did not sit down or pick up a teacup. Instead she started to examine the objects that lay on a dresser beside the door and that Ivory had missed: a small blue ceramic cat, a bronze thimble and a tiny photograph of a man.

'Caruso!' she exclaimed suddenly.

Ivory Price looked puzzled.

'This is your apartment?' she asked.

He picked up his cup and drank it all in one swallow before he spoke.

'Yes, no,' he said. 'I mean, I rent it but I'm rarely here . . . any more.'

She nodded. It was an apartment for a former mistress. Of course. The picture must have belonged to her. She put it down again.

'Caruso is here, in New York City,' she said. 'The queue is so long outside the Metropolitan Opera House that they have to open the doors two hours early. Can you imagine!'

Anna stared out of the window. It had started to snow again, the heavy flakes swirling and racing down from the darkened winter sky. Ivory Price put down his empty cup. And then he came and stood beside her. A ginger cat ran across the back yard, stopped, turned and stared up at them. Its eyes, like the children in the street, were chinked with numbed suspicion. A gust of wind blew in from the rooftops, showering snow and soot into a huge swirl, a dirty cloud. The cat pulled back its ears and ran on, its brilliant orange coat fading to a dirty brown. Ivory pulled the curtain closed.

'I didn't think you'd come,' he said softly. 'Tell me more, tell me more about free love.'

'Love is never free,' she replied. 'It always comes with a price. Sometimes you may still be paying for it many months or even years later.'

Ivory Price shoved both hands deep in his pockets and turned away. It was a movement at once middle-aged and childlike. He was wearing a white cotton shirt, with braces, a pair of driving breeches and dark grey and black Argyle socks. It was clearly his off-duty, weekend leisure outfit, but he wore it stiffly, as if he were wearing someone else's clothes, a younger man's, perhaps.

'Your tea is getting cold,' he said.

She knew that he would telephone her after the party. She had seen the way he had folded up the piece of paper with her telephone number written on it, she had observed the way he placed it in his pocket, as if it were something too valuable to lose.

'Meet you?' she had whispered into the telephone when he called a week later. 'Of course. My pleasure. No, not this week. The week after, perhaps.'

They had met twice already, both times in public places where they both knew it was unlikely they would have been spotted: a cheap restaurant in Midtown; on a bench on a ferry to New Jersey. Finally, after cancelling several times, Anna had agreed to meet him in private. She knew instinctively that she would get the best results if she played him slowly. No woman, it was clear, had made him wait so long before. No woman had made him want her so much. Now he would do anything. Now he would tell her anything. Ivory was clearly nervous, unsure of his plan, or of her response to him. She was older than him: she was educated, she was someone whose name appeared at the bottom of articles in newspapers. Did he know he was so easy to read? Anna wondered. Like a billboard, a sign lit up by a connected circuit of incandescent lights. And she suddenly thought of the blood coursing around his body, to his head, his heart; bright electric red in the warm, wet dark.

In the next room but one, a male voice could suddenly be heard.

'Don't you tell me . . . liar! You must have boiled the whole batch!'

As they listened, the sounds of the city seemed to cut through the static air of the room they were in: motor cars and ships' horns and the distant clatter of pots and pans. And they both felt the parameters shift. They might be surrounded by millions of other people but the door was still closed; they were still a man and a woman alone in a room together.

'Rusty, by God,' shouted the voice. 'Of course they're rusty, goddammit!'

'The corset man,' Anna whispered.

'Friend of yours?' he whispered back.

'No,' she replied. 'I saw him in the lobby. He was fast asleep . . .'

'And so you tiptoed past . . .'

She nodded. 'Of course; we don't want witnesses. Do we?'

And she looked up at him with a glance that said more, much more than her words. Ivory's face broke into a wide, concertina smile. The ice was broken. And all the doubt he had felt suddenly lifted. She had come, hadn't she? She was here for the same purpose and with the same intentions as his own. He was, he told himself, on home territory. He moved towards her again and placed his hands on her waist.

'You wear a corset?' he said. 'Even though your mind is liberated?'

She smiled and rested her head to one side. 'My waistline, sadly, is not.'

He shifted even closer until the line of his body ran down the line of hers. And then he ran his hands from her breast to her hips, so that he could savour the perfect whalebone curve of her. When she didn't turn away or protest, slowly, as slowly as he was able, he kissed her full on the lips. She tasted of snow.

'No one knows we're here?' she whispered.

'No one,' he replied.

'There is no risk of us . . . getting caught?'

'None at all,' he assured her.

Ivory Price had been caught many times for minor misdemeanours

221

but never by any forces that could have changed the direction of his life: not by the father of his best friend at school when he had seduced his younger sister and then abandoned her; not in the motor car he was driving after drinking two bottles of claret that had spun out of control and slammed into an oak tree only the year before; and not by the cold black Atlantic Ocean, awash with corpses, which lapped at the bows of lifeboat number 5 in 1912. No, he had a knack of escaping anything that could possibly harm him, from the wrath of fathers to random acts of God, from the impact of icebergs to the virile wriggle of his sperm. And even Inez – he had begun to regard her now as a trap – could be escaped too if he kept his wits about him. Although he would never admit it to anyone, he had come to believe that his life was charmed, that he would not die, not in a plane high above the battlegrounds of France, not in one of his cars as he drove it as fast as its engine would go, and certainly not in a tryst with a beautiful Russian revolutionary. And so he always made a point of pushing the pedals down harder, of flying higher, of chasing the unobtainable; he took risks as they presented themselves. He had escaped alive from the *Titanic*. Nothing could touch him.

'I have to go to . . ' Anna said. 'Where is the water closet?'

She sat on the edge of the chipped enamel bath and held her handbag in both hands. You could tell by the hang of the fabric and the strain of the strap that it was too clearly heavy to be holding the usual things that women carry, such as a paperback novel, a wallet and a small tub of rouge. Through the soft velvet, Anna could feel the weight of the cold metal inside. It was a small pistol that Winter Hare had bought from the Italians. You must protect yourself, Winter Hare had said. If he suspects anything you never know what he might do. Although it was not a size or make she was familiar with, she knew how to use it. As a girl she had gone hunting duck and rabbit with her father; she was a better shot, her father had laughed, than the gamekeeper.

In the last few months, as the American war effort had been slowed down and sabotaged by strikes and walk-outs, dozens of union leaders and Russian activists had been arrested and plots uncovered. There was someone who knew what was going on, someone on the inside. Anna's mission was simple: to infiltrate the world of an industrialist and find out where the information was coming from.

'If you ask, he won't tell you,' Winter Hare had told her. 'It needs to be pillow talk.' Winter Hare had looked at her sympathetically and raised his eyebrows. 'Your work might save many lives,' he had said. 'Just remember that.'

My son, Anna told herself. This is for my Kima. It won't be long now, it won't be long at all. But even though she took several deep breaths and washed her face in cold water, her mouth was still filled with the taste of panic.

'Anna?' Ivory Price called softly from the other side of the door. 'Are you all right?'

The corset dealer ranted and raved and slammed the door, twice. It still wasn't clear to whom he was talking. Perhaps, Anna suggested, he was shouting at himself. The night was dark and dense and flat as paint. Ivory didn't turn on the lights.

'Kiss me,' he said. And so she closed her eyes and let what had to happen, happen.

Ivory was stretched out below her, his skin as pale as paper, his hands demanding more of her, always more, his grip hard and then even harder. She moved slowly, shifting, pressing, positioning. He gasped with pleasure. Her body moved of its own accord on top of him, as if it were divorced from her head, following its own currents, pulling the rest of her along. Here, now, this, is all that matters, it told her. Here, now, this; was it so wrong? If all that mattered was the moment, this moment, then they were free to love one another, without guilt, without consequence, without history, without a future.

As she grew breathless, however, she found her mind could not disengage, it could not forget. How much would this cost her? How much? His face was in shadow, his eyes were closed. His grip was so tight that it would leave marks. He was a stranger. They were undeniably connected and yet still existed in two different, parallel universes.

But despite the distance between them, despite the pain, despite the fact that she felt nothing for him, she couldn't deny that he was warm, he was alive, he was a body with a beating heart and a head full of memories. He was a man with a corn on his toe and a shaving cut just below his left ear. And he was alive in the same moment, desiring the same end, as close to her as any man could or would ever be. And suddenly, without intending to, she started to cry.

'What? What is it? Oh, no!' said Ivory Price. As he sat up and held her in his arms, all notions of victory, of triumph, of conquest suddenly dissipated. 'I'm so sorry,' he said. 'I'm so sorry, Anna.'

'I can't,' she sobbed.

'We don't have to do anything,' he whispered into her hair. 'We can talk instead. I'll make some more tea. Would you like that?'

And when she nodded he saw in the dim light of the room that she was still a girl really, a naked girl with her hair unpinned and her arms wrapped around her knees because she was cold. And his heart swelled with something he had never felt before.

It was when he brought her her things, however, that he felt it. He dropped her clothes and lifted her bag.

'What's this?' he said and pulled the gun out of its velvet pouch.

'No, don't touch . . . it is . . . . how you say?'

Silence rang in the air between them, as loud and deafening as fire sirens.

'I . . . I don't remember the English word,' she whispered eventually.

'It's a revolver,' said Ivory Price. 'A Colt .38 calibre. His face blushed red but he remained calm. 'What are you? An assassin? A terrorist?'

'No,' she sobbed. 'I am not!'

'Were you going to shoot me, Anna? When? Later, when I was asleep.'

She shook her head.

'But you do . . . like me, don't you?' he said.

As he stared at her, the balance of Ivory's world tipped from one side to the other. He suddenly realized that he might, for the first time, be dizzily, intoxicatingly in love. And rather than it being a feeling of elation, as he had always imagined, he was shocked to discover that the most overwhelming sensations were of anxiety. Of fear. Surely he couldn't have been so wrong, could he? Surely she must feel something of what he was feeling. Surely she didn't want to harm him?

Almost imperceptibly, Anna nodded. Ivory exhaled with relief. She did feel it too. He sat down beside her, held her tightly and just breathed her in. It was going to be all right. Everything was going to be fine.

'You know,' he said, 'I bet it's not even loaded.'

And Ivory jumped up, still naked, placed the gun on his right temple, just behind the eye, and pulled the trigger.

The corset salesman had just fallen asleep and was dreaming of digging sand on the Long Island beach where he had been taken on holiday as a child. He awoke with a start and let out a curse. The reverberation of the gunshot died away so fast that for a moment, he almost thought he had imagined it. But just in case, he tentatively climbed out of bed, pulled on his trousers, waited a minute or maybe three, opened his door an inch and looked along the corridor just in time to see the swish of a woman's skirt jerk hastily down the stairs.

20

'My little girl,' the soldier still sang in his bunk. 'I'm dreaming of you.'

'Is that the only song you know?' asked the soldier in the next bunk. 'How about "Over There"?'

The men started to sing softly.

Outside, the wind threaded its way through the hastily erected wooden huts, its voice rising in pitch from a low moan to shrill hysteria. It was hard to get used to all the noise, to the unhindered quality of it: wind unbroken by tall buildings, gusts unchannelled by the grid of the city, free to run and roll, to whisper and shout, deafening one minute and dying down, just long enough to hear sounds previously unheard, the next.

'Be quiet a minute,' said Monroe, 'and listen.'

The men stopped singing, the wind howled and then quelled, howled and then dropped. And there, underneath it, was the sound of voices, rising and falling, rising and falling in the distance, unearthly in the sudden silence.

'Do you hear it?' Monroe asked.

'That's just the Negroes,' came a voice from the other side of the hut. 'They shipped in last night from the south.'

'Here? To Camp Upton?'

'Hell, no. Got to be stationed a mile away. Regulations. And I heard if we got it bad, they got it worse. Some don't even have a tent to sleep in. Others don't have no uniform, no boots, hardly any blankets. Have to light a fire just to keep warm at night.'

'Where they from?' Monroe asked. 'The Carolinas?'

'I heard they're all from New York. Just got sent south for training.'

Monroe sat up. 'Anyone want to come over and say hello?' he asked.

'You out of your mind?' said the soldier in the bunk above. 'The reason they got sent back here is that there was so much trouble in the south that the whole lot of them're being shipped to France.'

'Ain't they lucky,' said a voice from the corner.

'Too right they are. They won't be fighting,' said the man above. 'Just labourin'.'

Monroe pulled on his boots and buttoned up his uniform. Breakfast was in half an hour. At least a walk would help him warm up a little. He glanced out of the window as he tied his laces, at the track churned up into mud by days of freezing rain and marching boots, and then further, much further, to the pine trees and potato fields of Yaphank. Although Camp Upton was only a two-hour train journey from Penn Station, it was still practically a wilderness, wild but for the U-shaped encampment that had been carved into the soft soil in a clumsy, inelegant curve. He stepped outside and his boots crunched on the frozen mud. The sky in the east was as pale as a rose petal. On the other side of the railway slip, to the north, it was still dark but for a curl of white smoke rising up into the air like a semi-clef.

Camp Upton had only just been finished, and although it was eventually expected to accommodate and train forty thousand troops, when Monroe had arrived with the first couple of thousand men two months before, there had been nothing there, nothing but a forest of scrub oak and a mosquito-infested swamp. At first he had worked on the land, digging foundations and felling trees. And then he helped the large team of carpenters who had been hired and together they threw up hundreds of huts in rows in only a couple of weeks. At the end of December, even though it wasn't finished, thousands more men arrived at the camp on trains on a newly completed rail spur which connected up with the main line of the Long Island Railroad.

Monroe lit a cigarette and shoved both hands into his pockets. His palms were all blistered and he had lost a fingernail to the smash of a hammer. But he had enjoyed it; it had been just what he needed, to work hard all day without time to think or to regret or to wonder how things could have turned out differently. But sooner or later, he knew he would have to come back, to the person he had been before, to what lay ahead, to the mess that was his life. Another soldier ran past on his way to the latrine.

'Hey there, Simonov,' he said. 'You playing tonight?'

'Sure,' Monroe replied. 'The Liberty Theater. After eight.'

'Swell,' the soldier said. 'I'll be there.'

Here, it didn't matter if you were Russian, or Jewish, or both, if you were Italian or Swedish or Scottish; no one cared if you were a baker or a banker. Everyone was the same once they had a uniform on. And the one thing that helped unite them all further was music; to sing together was to accept that you were a soldier, that you were an American, that you were about to take a bit-part in history itself.

Training, ideally, lasted sixteen weeks and covered all areas of combat including marksmanship, gas warfare, tank driving and first aid. Weary-eyed French and English officers had been brought across the Atlantic to train them, instructing the draftees how to dig a series of trenches in the hard winter ground, and demonstrating going 'over the top.' They also taught them how to use a hand grenade and how to crawl through barbed wire. Professional boxers gave lessons on how to fight, hand to hand, although the British officers were openly sceptical that anyone would ever get close enough to a German actually to swing a punch.

Even when Monroe had been measured up for a uniform, however, even when he had been given a pair of boots, a rifle, allocated a tin plate and cup and been signed up to the 20th Infantry Division, 152nd Depot Brigade, the war still seemed a very long way off, a whole ocean away. But just the spectre of it, the possibility of it, was enough to make him reckless.

A fortnight after their first meeting, he had taken the Long Island Railroad to Manhattan to meet Inez with a set of borrowed keys in his pocket. He was early but she was there already, below the stoop, waiting.

'I can't be seen with you,' she had said.

'Then follow me,' he had told her. 'I'll lead you.'

And so they had walked, he in front, she half a block behind, as if connected together by an invisible thread. At one point, he had stopped and turned and waited and found her gone.

He ran back the way he had come and found her again at the other side of a busy intersection. Trams, hansom cabs, cars, carriages, bicyles raced by, a grey blur against the glare of the shovelled snow. He caught her gaze and held it, he on one side of the street, she on the other, and if he had been in any doubt at all, he knew now that he had been mistaken. Suddenly the traffic cleared, she started to cross, he turned around and kept on walking.

And then when finally they had closed the door to that tiny, sparsely furnished room in Chelsea, he had loved her without reservation, without modesty, without hesitation. Although it was not long enough, not nearly long enough, and before he knew it, he had to dress again and would need to run all the way to the station to catch his train, the resonance he felt inside was of a major chord, with all the pieces in place, the root, the major third, the perfect fifth.

'Monroe,' Inez had said before he left.

'No,' he said, 'we shouldn't talk about anything. Not now.'

'There's something I have to tell you.'

'I know everything that I need to know,' he had said.

'No,' Inez had replied, as she pulled back the tangle of her hair and her face flushed. 'You don't.'

'Tell me next time,' he had whispered as he had pulled on his coat, pocketed the silk scarf she had given him and kissed her for a final time. 'Keep the keys. Two weeks' time? You'll be here?'

And she had simply nodded her head and held his gaze until it was broken off by the swing of the closing door.

The day was lightening and the sky was streaked with pale red when he set off across the sandy scrubland to the Negro encampment. It was true what had been said. The Negroes didn't have many tents. Thirty men with blankets around their shoulders were crouched around a smouldering fire. When they saw him approach, some of them stood up.

'Beautiful morning.' he said.

None of them replied. He shifted his weight from leg to leg and stuck his hands in his pockets.

'Any of you happen to know an Edward MacKenzie?' he asked.

Although he was thinner, Edward's smile was as wide as it had ever been. His handshake was long and loose and his eyes were bright. And he wore his uniform as if he owned it, even though it was a size too small, with all the buttons polished and the hat worn at an angle.

'When they said you boys were from New York,' said Monroe, 'I just had a feeling you'd be here.'

They stood and drank thick black coffee beside the fire as it spat sparks into the air.

'So you volunteered,' said Edward. 'Thought you said it would be the last thing you'd ever do.'

'I got drafted. It was this or jail,' Monroe replied.

'Figures. Still writing songs?' said Edward.

'Not really,' said Monroe. 'Still playing?'

'There aren't ever no pianos,' he replied. 'I'm in the wrong division. Been asking for a transfer to the Buffaloes, the 369ths. James Reese Europe's got an infantry band called the Hellfighters.'

'I've heard of them. Aren't they a brass band?'

'If they gave me a clarinet or a trombone, I'd learn it just as fast as I could. I can't stand not being able to play. It's too damn quiet in my head.' Edward flexed his fingers, cupped them to his mouth and blew on them.

'Come and play with me then,' said Monroe. 'Tonight. I got a spot at the Liberty Theater. At eight.'

Edward smiled. He glanced round at Monroe; he could walk into the Negro encampment just because he felt like it. But would it be the same for him if he entered Camp Upton, a black soldier in the white soldiers' camp? He didn't think so. Hadn't Monroe read about what had happened in Houston? When the 24th Infantry, a regular all-black army division, took a walk around the city they had just been posted to, they found that they'd tightened up the Jim Crow laws and newly hung signs informed them that they had to sit

230

in certain sections of the tramcars and the theatres. And so they took down all the signs and wore them round their necks at a dance. A few days later, one soldier was pistol-whipped and arrested when he tried to stop a policeman beating up a black woman and, according to the newspaper, this led to a clash between the soldiers and the police which left two black soldiers and seventeen white men dead. The trial had been held in December. Thirteen black soldiers had been condemned to death and forty-one sentenced to life imprisonment.

'I don't know . . .' said Edward.

'Come on,' said Monroe. 'I'll meet you at the main gate! It'll be a blast.'

When Edward had joined up, he had no idea that it would be like this, that the regiments would be segregated by colour, that when he was shipped to France the only position he would have in the American Army would be Kitchen Engineer or as part of a 'labour' battalion. He had joined up to make a difference, to fight the Germans, to protect the free world. Instead all he would be doing would be peeling potatoes and felling trees. His hands curled into fists. Just the thought of playing again made his fingers ache. It had been so long, months since he had felt the tap of ivory beneath the tip of his finger and the reverberation of the hammer on the string. Houston, he told himself, was not the same as Long Island, was it? He'd have to get written permission from his commanding officer and, even with that, they might not let him in.

'It's a nice piano,' Monroe was saying. 'Good tone even though it's pretty bashed up. So, will you play?'

Edward looked out at the thin strip of dark blue sea that seemed to underline the sky. 'Hell, yes,' he said. 'I'll do it!'

Monroe arrived back at his hut at the same time as the camp postman. There was a letter from Manhattan and one from Egypt; one envelope was made of thick white paper, his name bang in the middle, spelled out in capital letters punched out on a typewriter. The other was made of paper so fine that the ink of the handwritten script inside showed through, the palest of blue, like veins on a wrist.

Von Hofe had written to tell him that after a slow start, his song had started to sell. He enclosed a royalty cheque for forty dollars and an invitation to an event that would introduce him to all the leading Broadway theatre managers and vaudeville producers and give him an opportunity to play them some of his songs. The letter was typewritten apart from the PS, which read: 'This is not optional, kid, just so you know. No show means no show, literally.'

He folded the cheque and posted it into his breast pocket. It was more money than he had ever imagined a song could make. It must have sold, he deduced, several thousand copies. Forty dollars was enough to put down a deposit on a new place for him, Inez and the child when he got out of the army, and pay the rent for a couple of months.

The other letter was from his mother. Together with his three sisters and their families, she had been evacuated to Alexandria when the fighting between the Allies and the Turks had reached the outskirts of Jerusalem. Although the British had finally defeated the Ottoman Empire, won Jerusalem and were planning to make Palestine an independent Jewish state, she had lost everything; she had heard that her home had been looted and her lemon trees destroyed. But at least, she concluded, we have been lucky. Of the people who remained in Palestine, hundreds had starved to death or had been murdered by the Turks. Her dream of a shared life beneath the lemon trees, however, was gone.

For the rest of the day Monroe marched in formation, charged into old potato sacks holding a wooden stick instead of a bayonet and practised target shooting. But he was distracted, he missed, he turned on the wrong foot, the sack swung back and hit him so hard in the chest that he was winded.

'Simonov,' shouted his officer. 'If this was a war situation, you'd have a bullet in your head by now. What's eating you?'

The rest of his infantry company laughed. He smiled but didn't reply. He would wire the money to his mother. If Von Hofe wanted more songs, he would give him more songs, songs that would be even more successful than the first. And for the rest of the day, the rhythm of the parade became the rhythm of the big bass drum, and in his head he heard melodies, refrains and the wandering cadenza of a trumpet.

The Liberty Theater was full by half past seven. Thirty rows of soldiers sat with bottles of army-issue beer in their hands and cigarettes in their mouths. Edward cracked his knuckles and flexed his fingers. His hair was oiled and his cap was in his pocket.

'Thank you for this,' he said to Monroe.

Monroe felt himself sink inside. He had seen the way that Edward had taken in the difference between this encampment and his own: the smoke rising from inside the huts, the mess tent, the hospital hut, the theatre. It was hardly comfortable but compared to his camp it was luxurious. But he hadn't said a word. And now he was thanking him for being offered the chance to entertain an all-white audience. Monroe was ashamed, of the segregation, of the army, of himself.

'You want to go on first?' Monroe asked.

'Sure,' said Edward.

At first the soldiers shouted out for songs they knew, and then, when it was clear that the Negro piano player wasn't taking any notice, half got up and left and the other half settled down and listened. And even though Edward said he hadn't played for months, the songs, the melodies, the rhythms came back thick and fast. Most of the audience looked as if they didn't know what had hit them; cigarettes fizzled out, beer went flat, the air grew warmer and warmer still but nobody left their seat to open a window.

Edward seemed oblivious to everyone else in the theatre. There seemed to be an electric current between his eyes, his hands and his feet. Monroe watched and was amazed all over again. And when Edward finally removed his hands from the keys, wiped his face and said simply, 'That's it,' the audience cheered for so long that there didn't seem to be any point in going on after.

'Your turn,' said Edward.

Monroe rolled up his sleeves, sat down and started to play. He started with one of his old songs and then he launched into a tune he had written in his head earlier that week, a tune that he had been confident would be glorious, melodic; sure to bring the house down.

He began slowly with an extended verse before launching into a chorus. How many successful songs would he need, he asked himself as he played, how many hits would he need to build a life together? This song wasn't particularly original, the sentiments weren't in the least bit sincere but he had written one hit, he had told himself again and again, he could do it again.

A cold feeling began to spread from the top of his head right down into his fingertips and he knew that he had been mistaken. No matter how he played – fast, slow, with swing, without – it still sounded weak and insubstantial, turgid and sentimental. He didn't need an audience to tell him it wasn't any good. Without a pause he shifted straight into 'Over Here.' What was left of the audience sighed with collective relief and started to clap along in time.

'You got a girl?' asked Edward afterwards as they stood in the doorway of the theatre and smoked.

Monroe winced and swallowed before he spoke.

'Yes, no,' he said. 'It's complicated. You seen Bessie?'

'We got married.'

'No kidding!' said Monroe.

'She wrote to me,' Edward said. 'Found out my division and where I was stationed. It seems she got out of some tour and managed to get a spot – I always said she was one hell of a singer. Anyway, I got some leave so we spent a few days together and then we just decided. Top secret. No one knows. Not even her theatre manager.'

'Congratulations.'

Edward smiled and then he started to cough; he coughed until he couldn't catch his breath, until he couldn't breathe. Monroe hurried back into the theatre and poured him a glass of water.

'Now all I got to do,' Edward said once he had drunk the water and his breathing had returned to normal again, 'is to stay alive until I can get back to her.'

'You should see the camp doctor.'

Edward raised one eyebrow but didn't answer. When he had

reported sick a couple of weeks earlier, he had been given a dose of castor oil and dismissed as fit to work.

'Any more of that water?' he asked.

The jug was on a table beside the main door. Before he could refill Edward's glass, however, a group of soldiers surrounded him and one of them grabbed the jug from his hands.

'Coloureds don't drink from the same jug as whites,' one said. 'And what's he still doing here?'

Edward must have heard the raised voices because he suddenly appeared, framed by the doorway. 'I'm a musician,' said Edward. 'Enjoy the show tonight?'

'Edward,' said Monroe. 'I'll deal with this.'

'I'm just trying to be friendly,' Edward said. 'Let's not fall out.' He put out his hand and offered it to the nearest soldier. Instead of shaking it, however, the soldier looked down at it in disgust. And then he spat. 'That's what I thought of your music, nigger.'

Monroe tried to keep his temper. He tried to hold back. But the sense of his own many failures, as a songwriter, as a lover, as a friend and as a man, overwhelmed him. He slammed his fist into the face of a former farmhand from Saratoga and then, when he was down, he slammed his boot into his belly. Retaliation came almost instantly with more force than he thought he could bear. The taste of blood filled his mouth, tears spilled from his eyes, the breath had left his chest and had to be slowly and painfully inhaled. Finally the blows stopped coming. He opened his eyes: three white soldiers were holding Edward down while two more stamped on his hands.

'Welcome to America,' one of them said before walking away.

21

Inez lay naked under the white sheet. Time had slipped past, minute by minute and then hour by hour. The day had slowly dwindled but still she hadn't reached over and switched on the lamp. Outside, snow had started to fall again, blurring the acute angles of the rusting fire escape on the brownstone opposite. The city was saturated with shadow, submerged in darkness, with only the briefest radiance of the falling snow to illuminate the approaching night.

Her eyes took in the blacks and greys of the room, the fall of the walls and the great loom of the wardrobe, and she tried to see colours there, maybe the palest wash of purple or the hint of blue. But there was none. Monroe hadn't come. There it was. She said it again out loud this time: Monroe hadn't come. And in the dark swim of the evening she had watched their time together drain away until it was all gone.

A lamp was switched on in the brownstone opposite, its wan light diffused behind brown curtains. Inez climbed out of bed and started to pull on her clothes again, smoothing out the wrinkles that had been caused by the haste in which she had removed them. That sense of release, of shedding layers of clothes so tight and restrictive that she could barely breathe, now seemed ridiculous. These were her clothes; this was her life. Her corset had left two red lines along the top of her hips that had only just faded. As she snapped the fastenings up the front, she tried to tell herself that something must have happened at the training camp. Maybe they had been shipped out early? But they wouldn't send them to France with no warning, would they?

She buttoned up her dress and laced up her boots, then paused before she tied the double knot. He had changed his mind, that was it. And why shouldn't he? She was married, she was a mother, she was an adulteress. He had changed his mind just as she had once changed hers. And she had a sudden memory of the last time they had met, of being stuck at the junction of Seventh Avenue and watching Monroe recede into the crowds on the other side until he was gone. Standing there as the traffic had rushed past, as hundreds of wheels and hooves had streamed by like the rapids of an uncrossable river, a thought had suddenly occurred to her: walk away, turn round and walk away now. But then she had found her eyes drawn to the other side of the road into the only pair of eyes that mattered, and as a gap in the traffic appeared, the thought vanished. And now she had come to tell him that yes, she would leave Ivory, she would leave Ivory just as soon as she could, no matter what.

In the sepia-toned light, she pinned down her hair in the mirror on the back of the door until the lamp in the brownstone suddenly went out. She walked to the window and looked across. The whole building was dark again, the windows, two to each floor, were black, like eyes, closed. A tiny flare of red suddenly appeared on the roof up above. The dense, unmistakable figure of a middle-aged man was standing at the edge of the snow-covered parapet. As she watched, the red glow flared up again as the man took a long drag from the cigarette; he seemed to be staring straight down at the window, at the room, at her. He pulled out a notebook and wrote something down. Inez quickly pulled on her coat, tried to ignore the pressure in her throat and the burning in her eyes, opened the door, locked it behind her and, after a moment's hesitation, pushed the key under the door.

As usual, the doorman to her building made her wait. Even though the snow was coming down thick and fast and the wind was rising, he made her wait. Why had Ivory never given her a key? Why did she have to rely on a doorman who never came? She stood there trying to stamp the cold out of her feet but her toes were already numb. Although she had caught a tramcar on Fifth Avenue almost immediately, she was chilled right through. Ivory used to laugh at her insistence on using tramcars and the subway. Take my car, he had told her. That's what it's there for. But Inez had spent four years without car and driver and was insistent that she didn't want them now. Too restrictive, she would say, too slow. I like to slip from here to there without any fuss. The only downside was this, the implication that it was somehow wrong, somehow a sign of inferiority to arrive without the announcement of an engine. Finally the doorman appeared, and with a loud sniff he unlocked the door, pulled it open and stood back to let her through.

'Is my husband home yet?' she asked.

'No, ma'am,' he replied. 'Didn't he say he was going up to Connecticut?'

As she stepped inside, the doorman's eyes slid past her own and fixed on the polished brass door handle. Inez started to pull off her gloves.

'Did he?' she said. 'Yes, you're right, maybe he did.'

A glove dropped on the floor between them.

'Oops,' she mumbled.

The doorman's eyes flickered downwards but he did not move; he wasn't going to pick it up for her. Inez's face coloured. She shouldn't have acknowledged the glove. Now he knew she had seen it. Otherwise she could have walked away without it and pretended she hadn't noticed. She looked into his face, she tried to meet his gaze, but his eyes were still cast down and wouldn't budge.

'My glove,' she said, as she dipped down and picked it up. 'Essential in this weather.'

'Yes, Mrs Price,' he replied.

The door to the apartment was always open but she was met by the maid who, in contrast to the doorman, seemed to hover in the lobby and wait for her return. And once the maid had padded back to her quarters after hanging Inez's coat and storing her hat, the apartment fell silent. Inez inspected her mail: nothing but invitations to patriotic rallies and fund-raising dinners. Dear Mrs Ivory Price, they were all inscribed, or, more often, just Mrs Price. A lump rose in her throat. She leaned her head against the cool plaster of the wall and closed her eyes.

The hall smelled of floor wax and leather, Pears soap and the lingering note of cigars. It was the smell of Sunday afternoons, of the inside of books, safe, solid, unchanging. I am a fool, she told herself, I am a fool. This is my life. This is the life I chose. But what were the alternatives? To live in penury like Maud's cousin? To make a commitment to a man who could not make a commitment in return? She had been selfish, she had been irrational, she had been about to undo all the securities she had worked so hard to put in place. Luella was a Price now, and she was safe, she was rich, and her future was as secure as the wrought-iron girders on the Manhattan Bridge.

Inez found the nanny in the back kitchen. Luella was in bed and asleep already, she was told: 'Heavy cold, I wouldn't disturb her.' Inez crept into the nursery. The little girl's face was lit with pale yellow from the hall light. In, out, she breathed, in and out, each breath a tiny miracle. Inez leaned over the edge of the cot and kissed her on the forehead.

'It's you I love the most,' she whispered, 'my little Lou.'

A door slammed in the apartment upstairs and there was the sudden smatter of voices in the street outside. Luella woke with a start, looked up into Inez's face and burst into tears.

'It's all right, I'm here,' Inez said as she picked her up.

The nanny switched on all the lights and took the screaming infant from her mother's arms. 'Didn't I say . . .' said the nanny. 'Now, now, little miss, did someone come in here and wake you? Look at you, not even a blanket.'

'I didn't mean to,' said Inez. 'Has she been cranky all evening?'

'She'll be fine once she's settled again, Mrs Price,' said the nanny. 'We'd both be happy to see you at the usual time tomorrow morning. I'm sure by then she'll be feeling better.'

'Nanny,' said Inez, 'let me try to settle her.'

'I don't think—'

'But I do, you see,' Inez interrupted.

'Mrs Price . . .'

Inez took the screaming child back and held her tight. 'I think she's hungry. Could you bring me some milk?'

The nanny's head tipped back so that even though she was small, she could look down at Inez. 'Milk?'

'To my room,' Inez added. 'Thank you, Nanny.'

239

Later, much later, there was a small knock on the door. Inez had been lying on her bed with her arms around her sleeping daughter for hours. She wished she was able to show her to him, to Monroe, to say: look, look what we made, isn't she perfect? Her hair was dark and her eyelashes were long and fine. Her eyes had faded from blue to the same slate grey as Monroe's. She was as much his as she was hers. And contrition burned in her belly with a hot black ache.

'Mrs Price,' said the maid, 'There're some gentlemen to see you.'

The policemen had taken off their hats and were standing in the parlour. She could see it in their faces immediately, bad news so bitter in their mouths that they rolled it around on their tongues and couldn't wait to spit it out.

'Mrs Price,' said one, 'maybe you should give someone the baby.'

'No,' she replied. 'I don't want to wake her.'

'Very well,' he said. 'Mrs Price, you better sit down. I'm afraid her father has fallen victim of a felony.'

A wave of pure terror rolled up and washed over her. 'At the camp?' she gasped. 'I knew something must have happened.'

Everyone, the policemen, the maid and the nanny who had come to see what all the fuss was about, stared at her.

'What camp?' he said. 'It happened here, in Manhattan. I'm afraid Captain Price has sustained a bullet wound to the head.'

Inez let out a tiny sigh of relief. It was not, however, noted. Then she turned and stared out of the window.

'He said . . . I mean . . . I thought Ivory was in Connecticut. Is he . . . is he going to be all right?'

'We can take you immediately to the Polyclinic Hospital where he is being treated. It's too early to say at the moment.'

'So, you're saying that somebody . . somebody shot him?' she asked.

'Looks like it,' the policeman replied. 'At close range.'

'I'll get my things,' she said and handed the still sleeping baby to the nanny.

The streets were almost deserted, many of them strips of pure untrodden white. On Broadway, however, outside the Metropolitan Opera House, dozens of men in black and women in brightly coloured opera cloaks were swarming on to the pavement and into lines of waiting cabs or city cars.

'Caruso's in town,' the policeman said.

Inez didn't reply.

'I see that your husband likes Caruso,' the policeman said. 'While we were waiting, I took the liberty . . . he has several phonographs.'

'My husband has never played Caruso,' she whispered.

The bullet had entered the skull at an angle just behind the eye. Due to the corset salesman's quick intervention, blood loss had been minimal. The eye, however, could not be saved. As for the damage to the brain, it was impossible to know until he regained consciousness, if, the doctor clarified, he regained consciousness.

Inez sat beside the hospital bed all night. A policeman was on duty in the hospital corridor. The newspapers, she had been told, would know nothing, not until they could determine what had happened. Ivory's head was swathed in clean white bandages. Only one eye, his nose and his mouth were still visible. His face looked as if it were made of wax, the wax of a candle, recently blown out. Who had done this to him? And why? She had no idea. They had barely spoken, she realized, for weeks. It was the swaddled face of a stranger. And before she could stop it, the thought that had been sparking in the back of her mind suddenly caught light: If he dies, she thought, if he dies, then I am free.

'Can you drive me home?' she asked the officer on duty at 9. a.m. the next morning. 'I have to see to my daughter.'

Luella wasn't in her cot. The nanny's room was empty. The kitchen too. Inez ran from room to room until she reached the parlour. And there she was, fast asleep in her grandmother's arms.

'We had expected you to send a car,' her mother said. 'We had to wait for thirty minutes for a cab. And that doorman of yours almost refused to let us in! It was hardly the welcome we had been expecting.'

'I didn't know you were coming,' she replied. 'What are you doing here?'

Her father, who had been examining Ivory's polo trophies, turned round quickly. 'Your husband invited us,' he announced. 'He must have told you?'

'No,' she whispered. 'He didn't tell me.'

'Maybe he meant it to be a surprise. Anyway, we finally get to meet Luella,' said her mother. 'Adorable little thing. Not sure who she takes after, though. Even though he's fair, Ivory must have some Spanish blood in that body of his. I hope you don't mind, but I gave that nanny the rest of the day off. What's wrong, Inez? Has something happened?'

Marjorie Kennedy examined her daughter, the daughter they had half expected to end up on some godforsaken vaudeville stage, penniless and pregnant, the daughter who had surprised them all and married above herself, the daughter whose child she had allowed herself to coddle, indeed the baby she had waited for most of her life to coddle. Inez didn't look well, she now noticed; her face was pale and her unruly red hair was flat and lifeless.

'I'm so pleased you're here,' Inez said quite truthfully. 'And yes, something's happened.'

'He was found,' the policeman told her later that day, 'in a room in a downtown establishment called the Ideal Hotel at around 7 p.m. Does the name mean anything to you?'

'No,' said Inez. 'As I said, I thought he'd gone to Connecticut.'

'And where exactly were you last night?'

Inez suddenly remembered the room, the dark, the snow, the ache of waiting.

'I was waiting for a friend,' she replied.

'I'm sorry to have to ask you this. It's just procedure. Which friend would that be?'

The policeman licked his pencil and waited. Inez rose from the divan, walked over to the grand piano and shut the lid.

'My husband has been shot. Does it really matter which friend?' she responded.

The telephone was ringing in Ivory's office. All morning Inez had ignored it but finally she couldn't stand it any longer, opened the door, paced across the room and picked it up.

'Hello?' she said.

The caller hung up.

She looked around the office, at the room where her husband spent most of his time. The thought occurred to her that she shouldn't be in there, that Ivory might walk through the door any minute and give her that look he always gave now, the look that said, What the hell do you think you're doing here, in my room, in my apartment, in my life?

A framed photograph of his aeroplane hung on the wall next to a mounted copy of his pilot's licence. The drawers in his desk weren't locked. The first contained cigars and fountain pens, the second a book, no, not a book but a diary. She flicked through it at random; there was nothing in it but names and times. Who was Wilson Strutt? She flicked through the year, the whole of 1917. And there, just a few days before the date of the party for Belgian children was a name, his name. Monroe Simonov. Ivory knew, Ivory had known about Monroe for months. Had he arranged for him to play at that party? And if so, she asked herself, why? To see what she would do? To test her? To hurt her? Why? And how long had the man on the rooftop been watching her? What did he know?

The phone rang once more and startled her. At first she let it ring until it stopped. And then, when it began to ring again, she picked it up immediately.

'Ivory?' a man demanded.

'This is his . . .' She paused and swallowed. 'This is his wife. Can I help?'

It was the manager of the aviation factory. Ivory had not turned up to a meeting the day before.

'We waited,' the manager said. 'Ivory has a habit of being several hours late. But this time he didn't show at all. Can you ask him to come out immediately? We have a problem.'

'I'm afraid that won't be possible,' she said. 'My husband . . . my husband has had an accident.'

'Too bad,' he said. 'If he's laid up, maybe I could arrange a meeting at his bedside, that is if he's up to it. It is very urgent. We need some signatures out here. It's been tough trying to meet our orders for the US War Department. Some of our best men have been drafted. And then, of course, there are the coal shortages. But unless we pay all the invoices for our raw materials, they're going to stop the supply.'

'I'm sorry,' she replied. 'He's not seeing anyone.'

'Just five minutes?'

'Is it really that urgent?' Inez asked. 'I mean, there must be someone there who can sort it out?'

Ivory had never taken her to any of his factories before. They were in New Jersey, that was all she knew. He once told her that he considered his factories in the same way as a sea captain considered his ship: it was bad luck to invite his wife on board.

The next day, Ivory's car and his driver waited outside for her, as arranged, at 2 p.m. They took the ferry across the Hudson, drove out over the salt marshes of Newark Bay, through the town of Elizabeth and across the Raritan River, to Keyport on the coast. A pair of wrought iron gates, with the words *Price Aero* in a scroll, were opened by the guard. Five hangars and six low buildings were grouped around a small paved road. At the end of the road, where gravel gave way to sand, just before the bluff of the beach, was a runway.

The office was nothing like Inez had imagined. It was a small desk in a draughty hut with a telephone, a filing cabinet and a stack of unpaid bills. The manager, a large man with screwed-up blue eyes, as if he had spent too long facing into the wind, apologized profusely for everything including the rain, when it came, rapping against the window like a handful of rice.

'Would you like a beverage?' he asked. 'All we got is coffee.'

'Coffee,' she replied with a smile, 'would be just perfect.'

He paused just before he opened the door and headed out into the wind. 'And, Mrs Price, if there's anything I can do. . .'

Inez swallowed and picked up a pile of invoices. 'He's in good hands,' she said. 'The best in Manhattan.'

After he had gone, she stared out of the small glazed window, at the clouds that scudded across the sky, the scuffed winter sea and the curve of a sandbank across a narrow sound. A small bird clung on to a telephone wire. The wind blew so hard it seemed in danger of being blown off one way or another until it suddenly leaned into the wind, opened its wings and took off.

There was a knock at the door, and without waiting for an answer a young woman stepped inside. She was about Inez's own age and dressed in a stained apron.

'I've come for my husband's wages,' she said. 'The name's Joe Panzinetti.'

'I think you need to speak to the accounts department,' Inez replied. 'This is the director's office.'

'Been there and they told me to come back in a week. That was a week ago. Went there this morning and they told me to come back in a week just like before. And just like I told my sister, that's no way to treat the wife of a man that's been drafted. So, I ain't leaving, see, I ain't leaving until I got what's due.'

The woman rubbed her nose with the back of her hand. The door behind her swung open and a little boy of about four peeked round the jamb.

'Johnny, I told you once,' the woman yelled. 'Stay there.'

Inez pulled out her handbag and extracted her cheque book. 'How much were you expecting?'

'Three weeks,' she said. 'That's forty-five dollars, sixty cents.'

'So that's what in total? About one hundred and thirty-five dollars?'

'No, forty-five dollars, sixty cents, is the total. Three dollars a day, six days a week, makes eighteen dollars. But then there's tax to pay.'

Inez wrote out the cheque and handed it to her.

'Tell your boss that if you need more staff, I'll do it,' said the worker's wife. 'I heard about the women taking over their husbands' jobs in New York City. While the men are training to go to war, the wives are delivering the mail and selling tickets on the trams. I could do what my Joe did and it won't even cost you the same.'

'And why not?'

The woman looked at her as if she were crazy. 'Because that's the way it is. Women never get paid the same as men.'

The woman paused and looked her up and down.

'You tell your boss. I'm Rose, Rose Panzinetti. I'll work for two dollars a day. There ain't nothing else out here. And like lots of folks around here, I depend on this place.'

'Very well, Rose. Thank you.'

A large filing cabinet stood in the corner. Inez pulled open the top drawer and extracted bank statements, order books and outgoings. For the next hour she examined the figures.

In Manhattan the phone rang a dozen times before her father answered it.

'Daddy,' she said, 'I need to sell those company shares that you gave me. How many? All of them.'

Inez had signed twenty, maybe thirty cheques when the manager finally reappeared with her coffee.

'I had a visitor,' she said without looking up. 'The wife of one of the men who works here. I paid her the wages he was due but didn't know where you kept the receipt book for chits. She said she'd be willing to take on her husband's job. Is it true she would be paid less, because surely if she does the same job she should be paid the same? Is that coffee?'

'Sorry it took so long,' the manager said as he placed the cup on her desk. 'We were clean out of milk. And, Mrs Price, these gentlemen would like a word.'

Inez looked up. Behind him in the narrow frame of the door were two policemen. She stood up. 'Is there news?'

They glanced quickly at each other before they spoke.

'I'm afraid . . . can we speak to you in private?'

So this was it. This was how you were told. The hats were off, the manner deferential. She sat back on the hard wooden chair and nursed the cup of coffee in her hands.

'There's no need. When did it happen?'

'He's not . . . I'm so sorry but we need you to come with us to the station,' one of the policemen said. 'Your husband's condition hasn't changed.'

'So why do you need me now?'

'We need to ask you some more questions,' he went on.

'But I've already told you everything I know.'

246

The policeman sighed, his eyes resting on the curls of steam that rose from the cup of coffee.

'A woman,' he said. 'A woman was seen leaving the scene of the crime.'

'Really? A woman?' Inez waited for the fact to register, to feel something, anything. She felt absolutely nothing.

'We just need to ascertain . . . .'

They wouldn't look at her. Neither of the policemen would look her in the eye. And all the implications of what they had just revealed suddenly hit home.

'It wasn't me,' she whispered. 'If that's what you think.'

22

The ice was melting on the Hudson now and floating down from Indian Head and Tappan Zee towards the wide mouth of Upper Bay in large grey slabs; a dirty marble floor broken by successive blows of a giant hammer. The winter was gradually lessening its grip, the ache of it subsiding, just a little, in the small of the back and the fingers and toes.

Anna's bags were packed. Her train ticket west, to San Francisco, was on her dresser along with details of her passage on a ship heading to Vladivostok, via Japan. And from there she would head west, to St Petersburg. Only three more days, she told herself, three more days to wait. And then she would say goodbye to New York, to its cliffs of steel and stone, to its vast metal bridges and tangle of elevated railways, to its filthy, overcrowded tenements and its newly constructed penthouses with their views of the stars, and she would head home.

In February, she had received a letter from Russia. It was from an official representing Trotsky. He wrote to inform her that in November Kerensky's government and the Mensheviks had been overthrown by the Bolsheviks. Trotksy was one of the five Bolsheviks appointed to serve on the newly created Politburo Committee. He had also been given the position of Commissar of Foreign Affairs by Lenin. The committee, the letter stated, was negotiating a peace treaty with Gemany but the fear was that socialism could not be attained in a single country, that for it to work it had to be global. And so, as an accomplished writer, linguist, speaker and agitator, Trotsky was inviting Anna to return immediately, to help run the new government propaganda bureau and to write pamphlets, leaflets and newspaper articles that would be distributed to German troops.

These would encourage them to stop fighting, to overthrow the kaiser, to follow Russia's example and stage a revolution. All the visas required for the trip back, it concluded, and the cost of travel would be provided. All she had to do was to accept.

The Bolsheviks' seizure of power had split Russian opinion in America. Some were supportive and some were vehemently opposed, claiming it wasn't another revolution at all but a coup. Anna had never been a member of the Bolshevik party but the promise of peace, of ending the war was all she longed for. Political allegiances, she told herself, could change. She was a well-respected speaker, a writer and a woman: that Trotsky could need her just as much as she, at that particular, moment, needed him, wasn't an outrageous proposition. But what had happened to Pokolitov? Was he part of the new government or had he been part of the former one? And where was Kima? And why hadn't he written? She accepted Trotsky's proposition by return of post.

The Social Revolutionaries' fall from power was the reason, Anna supposed. She hadn't heard another word from Winter Hare. Even though she would wake up most nights at 3 a.m., her body bathed in sweat, her hair a tangle of static, no more messages, to her relief, had been pushed through her door giving details of another rendezvous. Maybe no one would ever know what she had done. Maybe her name would never be associated with Winter Hare, with terrorism, with murder.

She put the kettle on the stove and watched the blue heat of the burning gas turn the silver black. As for Ivory Price, she had convinced herself, it was unfortunate but it wasn't her fault. Although she could never prove it, she hadn't killed him. It would be his fingerprints that would be found on the trigger, not hers. And yet there had been nothing in the newspapers, she had checked; no reports of his death by a gunshot wound to the head.

It was the absence of anything solid, in print, or in words or even uttered in conversation, that she found so hard to deal with. And sometimes she wondered if had it happened at all. Maybe she had only dreamed that night, in that hotel apartment alone with Ivory Price. But then she remembered the metallic taste of blood on her lips and the ringing in her ears and she knew that she had, in fact, been there.

Anna had seen men die before, she had seen trails of fresh blood on the snow and the empty eyes of corpses, but nothing had prepared her for the violence of this particular act, for the volume of the shot, for the sheer amount of blood and bone that she had so quickly wiped from her face, from her hair, from her naked body before she had pulled on her dress, her boots, her coat and stuffed the rest of her clothes, her corset, her stockings, into her handbag just as fast as she could and left the rooms before anyone had come.

Anna clenched her fists and blinked back the tears that in recent weeks seemed to well up and fall of their own accord. What had he done? Despite herself, the rent inside, the rent that she had so patiently patched and stitched with facts and certainties, began to tear again. She had discovered nothing. She had no idea who was passing information to the Bureau of Investigation. In the last couple of months the Bureau, together with the self-appointed American Protective League, had arrested dozens of radicals, public speakers and dissidents. Most were given long jail sentences and some had even been publicly lynched. In reaction, a series of bombs, or 'poofs' as they were known, had been found in Chicago, New England and Milwaukee. Some didn't explode; some did, killing policemen, federal agents and a couple of innocent bystanders.

Looking back, she wondered if she had succumbed to some kind of madness. What had she been thinking of? How had she let herself become involved with terrorists, with assassins, with criminals, with bomb factories? She once thought of herself as an intellectual, a socialist, a revolutionary, a pacifist. What was she now? A hypocrite.

And so she could not rest, she could not sit still. She could not relax. Every police car that passed, she imagined, was coming for her; every man in a felt hat, a detective who she then had to lose in the crowd. It had been five years since she had left Russia. Now, as the date for her departure approached, she was too restless to read, too impatient to write, too anxious to sleep. Although she still longed for St Petersburg, for its gilded palaces and wide open spaces, for its uniforms and parades, for its clean streets and city parks braced with cool wind from the Gulf of Finland, she found it hard to believe that she would soon be gone. Leaving New York was like leaving a slovenly but still beloved lover. Dressed up in brash shiny clothes with dirt beneath its fingertips and with shoes kicked off to make it easier to dance, the city's hold was at once passionate and indifferent. Go? it seemed to say. You'll never let me go.

The day she received Trotsky's letter she had cut her hair short, just below the ears. It made her head instantly feel lighter and her face look younger, more fashionable, maybe less recognizable. Then she swept the mass of thick dark hair into a pile and placed it in the dustbin. Leave America and what happened here behind, she told herself, break it up and let it float away like the ice on the Hudson. It is almost in the past already.

There was a knock on the door, a phone call for her. Rosa Sacchi was on the line. Two of the main speakers at a fund-raising ball for Russia that was being held the next night in Harlem were ill. Would she be able to speak in their place? The change would be well advertised. Anna politely turned her down, once, twice, three times.

'But Anna,' Rosa said, 'just one last speech. One final appearance before you leave.'

Anna had glanced at her packed suitcases, at her pile of papers and visas and tickets that were all correctly signed and stamped and paid for and wondered how she would be able to stand another three days in this room, on her own, waiting.

'Artillery Red is the colour this season,' the woman in the Ladies Department of Lord and Taylor's announced. 'And, of course, the ribbon hat. Come in and meet our guests, Marion.'

Although there was only one model instead of two and the clothes were made in America rather than in Paris, the Salon in Lord and Taylor's was just as busy as it had been before America had joined the war. Now the emphasis, however, was on dresses that were narrow to save on fabric. 'Think of it as dressing "patrioti-cally",' the saleswoman suggested.

Anna spent twenty-five dollars, money she had hoarded so care-fully for months, and bought a red dress and a wide-brimmed felt

251

hat. She would wear them both on the day she arrived home, the day she would find Kima, the day she would take her place beside Trotsky in the Revolutionary Socialist Party of the new Russian state. But first she would wear them to the ball in Harlem.

Taking up the entire block between East 126th and East 127th on Second Avenue, Sulzer's River Casino was a huge beer hall opposite Randall's Island in the Harlem River. In summer its outdoor area, a riverside park, was always packed with picnickers and strollers, and in winter its low windows were usually fogged up with condensation and its dance floor spilled out into the street. By the time Anna arrived, there must already have been over five hundred people inside. A band played in the corner and two dozen couples danced the foxtrot or the Castle Walk. Anna wandered around the perimeter of the hall and overheard half a dozen different languages: Italian, Russian, German, Finnish, Yiddish, plus several more she couldn't place. There were also dozens of different political groups and factions; the International Workers of the World, the American Socialist Party, the Union of Russian Workers, plus several clusters of Italian anarchists.

How would she find anyone she knew with this many people? How would she find Rosa? At last she saw the new editor of *Novy Mir*, Gregory Weinstein, who had taken over from Bukharin when he had returned to Russia. But when she reached him, she found him deep in conversation. And so she kept going, as if it were someone else she was aiming for, someone else who was awaiting her company.

The air smelled of pipe smoke and spilt beer, of feverishness and revolutionary ardour. Those few women present wore the same sombre colours as men: brown and black and grey serge. But their eyes were shiny and their lips were soft. And as those couples on the dance floor moved together back and forth, to and fro, it was clear by the way they looked at each other that, primed as they were for dissent, for action and even for violence, their bodies still ached for release, for distraction, for the thrill that could only be found in somebody else's arms. Although nobody believed in God, in government or in law, somehow the sanctity of love still held.

252

'There's a collection,' she overheard one man telling his entourage. 'For Big Bill Haywood.'

'Isn't he in prison?' someone else asked.

'Been in there since September. But the rumour is he's about to be let out on bail.'

'I heard he wants to go to Russia. Sick of this damned country. Keeps getting arrested. I tell you, you can't have a game of cards in this country without someone showing up and telling you it's un-American.'

'Cards are monarchist anyway,' someone else pointed out. 'We should get rid of the kings and queens and knaves and replace them.'

'With who? With Charlie Chaplin?'

'Mary Pickford!'

'Joe Jackson!'

'Nah, we need real people. Our people: Lenin. Galleani . . .'

'And for a queen?'

The group turned and as one, or so it seemed, saw Anna Denisova.

'Ma'am,' said the man nearest. 'I saw you speak in Pittsburgh. You were very . . . very passionate. You look a little lost?'

'No, not at all,' she replied. 'I'm speaking tonight, actually.'

'I'm sure you will be the evening's highlight.'

Anna inclined her head in thanks and moved on. But the lights were so dim and the room so warm that she suddenly felt faint. She found a chair, sat down and began to fan her face with her hand.

'Miss Denisova? How nice to see you again.'

A figure was looming above her. Anna shaded her eyes and looked up into the face of Noah Serginov.

'Noah!' she said and stood up to greet him. 'How are you?'

'I'm very well, very well indeed. You've changed your hair. I like it.'

'I'm so pleased to see you,' she said ' I came alone. I'm supposed to be meeting friends but I can't find anyone.'

'This place is cavernous, enormous. Well, at least you found me.'

'I'm going back to Russia,' she told him. 'In two days' time.'

'Congratulations!' he said. 'That's wonderful news! Which route are you taking?'

After she had told him all the details and bemoaned the problems of crossing the Atlantic, she realized that he had said very little.

'And you,' she said. 'Surely you will go back.'

'Of course,' he replied. 'Just as soon as I can.'

He smiled at her but there was something closed about his face that she hadn't noticed the last time. And a sudden thought occurred despite herself. What did he know about what she had done?

'Noah?' she said. 'Have you heard news from . . . Winter Hare?'

He looked at her with unmasked irritation. 'I'm not sure this is the right time,' he began and turned around so that he could not be overheard. 'Anna, the last thing I heard was a rumour that he'd blown himself up. Wasn't he one of yours?'

'One of mine?' she repeated. 'No. I wouldn't say he was one of mine.'

'I thought he was. My mistake.'

A chill ran through her and she pricked with sweat. She remembered that day in Hoboken, the sweet smell of glycerine, the softness of the cotton wool and the moment it had been taken out of her hand. Poor Winter Hare.

In the corner, the band stopped playing, the dancers came to a halt and a cheer rose up as the first speaker took the stage. Anna felt the light touch of a hand on her arm.

'Anna? I've been looking for you everywhere,' said Rosa Sacchi. 'If you come this way, I can show you the room I've put aside for you so you can prepare.'

The crowd had thinned at the back as everyone surged forward to listen. Rosa led her quickly to a small door at the side of the hall. On the way they passed Dante Faccini, the Italian anarchist. He inclined his head when he saw her; she inclined her own head back, the merest of movements invisible to all but him. Near him was a younger man who looked familiar. He had a thick black beard and clear grey eyes. He stared at her briefly before looking away.

'Who is he?' Anna asked Rosa. 'That young man?'

'That's Andrei Dreslov. At least that's what he says his name is. Just come back from Mexico.'

'He's a Russian?'

'Yes. But dodging the draft like a true Italian,' she clarified. 'You're on second. Is that all right?'

Later that night, after she had given her speech, after the lights had been turned up and the crowds had tumbled out into the midnight streets to head towards the subway station, or the elevated railway, Anna had been swept along by Rosa's enthusiasm, and walked south with her to East 116th Street and Third Avenue, to a restaurant called the Vesuvio in the Italian section of East Harlem.

Dozens of people had already crammed inside by the time they arrived, and were listening to Dante Faccini speak, in Italian, about the search for a man called Valdinoci by Federal agents in Cleveland. Anna broke away – she could understand very little – and wandered past the rest rooms, up the back stairs and out on to the roof. It was clear and cold; out on the river a passing boat blew its siren, the moon shone full and liquid. Although it was almost midnight an ambulance clanked and hooted as it made its way down Lexington Avenue, a drunk man yelled up at an open window on the next block, '*Letmein, damnyutahell*,' a baby cried and could not be comforted, and below it all was the low roar and dull clunk of the subway trains.

The evening had been a success. Her speech on free love, which had always gone down without much comment at women's meetings, had received a standing ovation. 'Free love is not about sex but about liberation,' she had pronounced. 'It is about self-ownership. What it requires is a revolution in thinking. What has begun in Russia will spread from country to country and from continent to continent.' And right there on the stage at Sulzers, in front of more than a thousand people, she believed it.

'Vive la révolution,' she said to herself.

She was suddenly aware of a presence and turned. The Russian she had recognized earlier was standing on the parapet and staring due south towards Harlem Meer. Had he been there all the time? She couldn't be sure.

'It's Andrei, isn't it?' she said softly.

At the sound of his name, however, the man did not turn. Rosa was right. It was not his real name.

Initially, she could not place him, could not place the beard or the delicate fine-boned face in *Novy Mir*'s office or in the audience at any of her recent talks. A bluff of wind whistled around the chimney stacks. It was cold up there. She decided to go inside again, to head back downstairs to the restaurant, when a piano started to play inside and someone began to sing 'The International'. He turned just as she was about to step through the door.

'Wait,' called the man who wasn't Andrei. 'Wait. Can we talk? We have met before . . . maybe you don't remember. I didn't have a beard then.' His mouth flickered with the merest hint of a smile, which nevertheless seemed to illuminate his face like a lamp.

And then she suddenly remembered. 'Of course,' she said. 'The piano player?'

He lit a cigarette. His hands, she noticed, were trembling.

'Not any more,' he replied in Russian. 'I'm a labourer from Kiev. My name is Andrei. Have a cigarette.'

'No thank you,' she said.

'Take one,' he urged. 'Keep me company at least.'

He lit a second cigarette, exhaled and filled the night air with the fog of his breath. As he passed it to her, he accidentally brushed her hand with his. Apart from a damaged nail and a calloused palm, it was soft and smooth.

'You may have spent some time digging holes in Mexico,' she said, 'but you'll never pass as a labourer.'

He smiled and then he turned to her, his face suddenly serious. 'Anna, may I call you Anna?' he said. 'I need to ask you a favour.'

She placed the cigarette between her lips. The tobacco was sweet and peppery; she inhaled quickly and immediately felt her throat begin to burn and her head lighten.

'You want to go back to Russia?' she said. 'Like everybody else? I'm sorry, I cannot be of any help.'

'Oh, no,' he said. 'That's not it at all. I need to get a message to someone. And you're the only person I can think of.'

The wind howled around the roof, rattling the rusty metal hooks that held the washing lines. The door back down to the restaurant swung open on its hinges.

'I'm very busy,' she said, turning away. 'I'm leaving in two days' time. But who exactly are you talking about?'

'The host of that party,' he said. 'I need to get in touch with . . . with his wife, with Inez. You were there that night, and when I heard that you were speaking.'

He still didn't make any sense to Anna. 'I'm sorry,' she said. 'I don't know who you mean.'

'You may know her by her married name. Mrs Price, Mrs Ivory Price.'

There was a moment when it seemed that the world slipped, just a little, on its axis. Or more likely, Anna realized, it was she who lost her grasp of where she was, of the tarnished metal sky and the black scuff of the pitch-covered roof. There was a time; a breath, a second, a heartbeat only, when she was aware of a membrane between the husk of her body and the world around her, as it turned flat and flimsy as a painted theatrical backdrop. Reality, time, the prospect of returning to Russia were all constructs in her head, unreal and insubstantial. And she was suddenly sure that she could be stuck in this moment for ever, that the future she so hoped for might expire like a match blown out; she would never leave this city, this country, the long dark shadow of a man called Ivory Price.

A train rang its bell at a station on 114th Street. A bottle smashed.

'It's not possible,' she whispered. 'I'm sorry.'

The piano player sighed and his jaw clenched.

'There must be ways,' she offered. 'Other ways.'

'Sure,' he said. 'Just haven't thought of them yet.'

Downstairs someone started to play an aria from *La Traviata* on the piano. Anna Denisova shivered and pulled her scarf more tightly around her shoulders.

'As I said,' she repeated, 'I cannot help you. I am leaving so soon, you see. I am going home.'

'Ah' he replied. 'Now there's the thing. There's another reason I need to talk to you.'

'I would have liked to hear Caruso sing,' she went on. 'But I heard that the tickets were hard to come by and rather expensive.'

He fumbled in another pocket, found a folded piece of paper and handed it to her. She opened it out – it was a note written in Russian. In the flickering light of an elevated train heading north, to Pelham, she read her own name.

'It looks rather official,' she said. 'What is it?'

'It's a sentence,' he replied softly. 'A death sentence.'

Anna's mouth went dry and she felt a cough rise up in her chest. 'Where did you get this?' she cried. 'Where?'

23

Monroe Simonov was not a good soldier; he was too slow, too untidy, too easily distracted. Half the time he looked as if he wished he was somewhere else entirely rather than lying flat on his belly dressed in khaki with a steel helmet on his head. He was, however, a good piano player. Captain Amos of the 20th Infantry Division, 152nd Depot Brigade was more than a little disappointed to find him locked in the slammer after what was officially recorded as a bar-room brawl. Simonov's playing was good for the morale of the division and indeed for the whole camp; real music was so much better, so much less expensive, so much more versatile, in his experience, than a gramophone and a stack of discs. The men could sing along, they could dance with each other, they could forget what the hell they were doing there in the first place and where they were about to be sent.

The captain peered into the murk of the cell where at least half a dozen men had sat out the night on a dirt floor and quickly picked out Simonov. While the other men, a motley bunch of Italians from another division, were playing cards, the piano player was scribbling with a pencil on a piece of paper.

'Simonov,' he yelled through the bars, a little louder than was necessary.

The soldier stood up stiffly and shoved the paper in his pocket.

'You cooled off yet?' the captain asked him.

'Yes, sir,' Simonov answered.

The door was unlocked as the soldier pulled on his jacket. In the daylight, his face looked far worse than the night before. It was grazed and bruised, the left side mottled purple, his lower lip split and swollen.

'Wait outside my office,' the captain instructed. 'First door on the left.'

The captain left him in the corridor for a good fifteen minutes before he called him through.

'We've decided to be lenient in your case,' he said. 'We're letting you out.'

'Thank you, sir.'

'Someone said you're a songwriter. Is that true?'

'I've written a couple,' Simonov replied.

'You think you could write a couple more? Songs to entertain the troops, keep up morale?'

'I've never really thought about it,' Simonov said.

'Well, think about it now. There's a chance, and I'm not promising anything, an outside chance, that you could stay on at the camp, put on a show every night, become a sort of regular fixture. What would you say to that?'

'You mean I wouldn't get shipped to France?'

'That's right. Of course there has to be some punishment but I think in your case no leave for a month would suffice. You don't need to thank me.'

The captain smiled in anticipation of his reaction. Simonov, however, did not look in the least bit grateful. It was not what the captain had expected. He had, in fact, argued for his entire tea break and half of lunch that this soldier was of good character and no troublemaker. He had even offered to vouch for his behaviour one hundred per cent. What was more, there had been an urgent wire from the War Department. Another couple of thousand draftees were due to arrive in a week's time: 20th Infantry Division, 152nd Depot Brigade were about to be shipped to France.

'And where's my friend?' Simonov demanded. 'Edward Mackenzie from the Labour Division.'

'If you mean that Negro,' the captain retorted, 'he was disciplined by his own division commander. I think he got a fortnight's solitary.'

The piano player wiped his forehead with the back of his hand. And then he shook his head in disbelief.

The captain felt his temper rise but he kept his voice steady. 'These people bring it on themselves,' he continued. 'And you needn't look so sore. You could have got the same, but with my intervention all you did, son, is lose your privileges.'

'You should have caught the other ones,' Simonov said, his voice rising in pitch. 'The guys who started it. And I'm not your son.'

The captain sighed. By the time he had arrived there were no other ones, just Simonov and the black man sitting in a shower of broken glass.

'I need to go into Manhattan on Saturday,' Simonov said quietly. 'I've got an appointment with the place I used to work, with the Universal Music Corporation on my day of leave.'

'Excellent,' the captain replied. 'Maybe they could publish a couple of the songs you're going to write. Give us all a boost. I'll talk to them when we get there.'

'You mean you're going to come with me?'

'The terms of your punishment are no leave,' he repeated. 'Either you don't go at all or I accompany you. In fact, now I come to think on it, I could do with a day out in the city.'

Despite his ungrateful behaviour, the captain couldn't help but feel a little sorry for the songwriter; he had a younger brother who had had a similar temperament: artistic, highly strung. If he had not died of TB at fourteen and a half, he might have grown up to behave just the same.

On Saturday, the train rattled along the line at half its usual speed, stop-starting and occasionally groaning, like a beast with belly-ache. By the time it reached Jamaica in Queens it was already an hour late. Monroe's hands bloomed with sweat even though he was freezing cold; the carriages weren't heated. Come on, he urged. The engine seemed to exhale long and slow, before juddering forward with a screech of metal on metal track and then coming to a halt again. Captain Amos snored on the wooden bench opposite. He had spruced himself up: he had shaved and waxed his moustache, he had polished his brown leather boots and spit-rubbed his buttons. And now as he slept, he was blissfully unaware of the time, of the delay.

The sky above was brooding and dark; it looked as if it were full of rain, or even snow. Monroe raised his fist. It would be so easy to punch the captain in the face, to beat the living daylights out of him. But what good would it do? And then he caught sight of his reflection in the glass of the window and was momentarily shocked. How could he think of doing such a thing? As he pulled off his campaign hat and unfastened the top button of his army shirt, he suddenly remembered watching the parade of volunteers down Fifth Avenue. He had become one of them, a man who knew how to inflict the maximum damage using the least possible effort. And now he was supposed to write songs that glorified the experience, that comforted or roused the troops before they went off to kill some German or get killed themselves.

He knew he looked a sight; his left eye was ringed with purple and yellow, his lower lip was puffed. And he longed to take off his uniform, to feel the smooth cool swell of her mouth on his face. Only her kiss would make it better. Only her eyes would make him heal. How long would she wait? One hour, two? How long would she wait before she decided he wasn't coming? And he threaded her silk scarf through his fingers, in and out, in and out.

Stepping inside the Universal Music Corporation was like stepping inside his old life again. Nothing had changed except the season. Von Hofe, with much aplomb, was playing a selection of songs from the back catalogue. He looked a little shocked when he saw Monroe.

'Here he is at last,' Von Hofe said. 'The newest rising star of Universal. But what happened? You meet a Hun out on Long Island?'

Around the room the assembled composers, lyricists and writers laughed politely. Some, like Abe Groblensky, Monroe knew, and some he didn't. The coffee and bagels laid out earlier had been devoured; all that was left by the time they arrived were a few crumbs and a dribble of lukewarm coffee. The vaudeville producers looked bored; they checked their watches, they stared out of the window, they talked about box-office receipts. With their starched white collars, brightly coloured silk ties, distinctive moustaches and handkerchiefs tucked into a peak in their breast pockets, they all wore the same uniform of middle-aged non-conformity. If they looked as though they rarely set foot outside in the daylight, then they probably didn't.

'Looks like it's gonna snow,' one of them told the captain.

'I'd say the chance of precipitation is about sixty-five per cent,' replied the captain.

An awkward silence prevailed.

Abe Groblensky was playing, rattling through his new repertoire. None of the songs was any good and the vaudeville producers' eyes were beginning to glaze over. Only the captain clapped enthusiastically at the end.

As everyone waited for the next songwriter to begin, a frail-looking man Monroe had never seen before, the room fell silent apart from the faintest knocking on the window; it had started to snow after all, in great white smuts that swirled and seemed to pause a little before they landed on the glass of the music publisher's window. Everything was running hours late. Monroe was on last. Of course.

This was it, he told himself, his golden opportunity, his chance to be heard. He had new songs, he had demonstrable commercial success, he had a captive audience of the most influential producers on Broadway. All he had to do was sit down and play. But what did they want, songs with recognisable structures, with sing-a-long verses and rousing choruses? He couldn't do it. His head, his fingers, his heart yearned for something else, for the space where there were no rules, no instructions, no patterns to follow or paths to tread: for jazz. But most of all, he longed for her.

It was easy enough to slip out. The captain seemed captivated by just about every player and insisted they all sign the back of his train ticket, 'for my wife'. Monroe excused himself to the bathroom and then doubled back, ran quietly down the stairs and out on to the street that was already becoming blurred and muffled with the falling snow. The cars and carriages were bright-eyed in the dark, streaming along the high-sided canyons of Midtown, leaving trails of spilt red light and blotches of black, black oil.

'It has been decided,' said Captain Amos to the assembled group of vaudevillians and music publishers, 'that the boy will stay at Camp Upton and compose songs suitable for soldiers. Suits us both. What do you say? Simonov? Where the hell is he, anyway?'

Monroe was over three hours late for Inez but maybe, he thought, just maybe. He took the stairs two by two, passing a woman with a baby and three small children and an old man with a cat on a lead. He knocked softly but there was no reply. He tried the handle. The door to the apartment was locked. He got down on his hands and knees, and just before the light in the corridor switched itself off he saw the bunched shadow of the keys pushed under. She had come, that he knew for sure, and then she had gone.

The Italian safe house was in a back room of a garment factory just south of Houston Sreet. Within ten minutes of arriving he had changed out of his uniform and thrown on a roughly made suit and a pair of ill-fitting boots. The man in charge had let him in immediately when he had told him he was a friend of Antonio, one of the soldiers he had shared a cell with the night before. They would leave for Mexico at dawn the following day.

'Perhaps,' Monroe had suggested, 'I could hide out here. Just for a week or two at least.'

The man in charge looked at him and shrugged. 'They catch you, you get up to twenty years in prison,' he said. ' Make you into an example. And what about us? We all get locked up too. You want that?'

'No,' he replied. 'I don't want that.'

Together with two Italians, Monroe crossed the border in a delivery truck at midnight and then spent another couple of days driving south. The Italians' camp was on the outskirts of Monterrey in the foothills of the Sierra Madre Oriental. Half a dozen adobe huts faced on to a piece of raw scrubland where an open fire was surrounded by a littering of tin cans and discarded beer bottles. A couple of stray dogs limped around, nosing through the rubbish and scampering off whenever a fist was raised or a boot aimed in their direction. Antonio arrived a week later after skipping out on his last day of leave.

'The regiment were shipping out,' he told Monroe. 'They're going to finish their training in France, the poor bastards.'

All the other men were Italian, men who had left their wives and families, their jobs and routines for this, to squint into the blinding sun, to sit and wait, writing and preparing to return to Italy where, they were convinced, a revolution was just about to begin.

While most of them had found menial jobs in the town – cleaning hats or pounding dough in bakeries – Monroe played the piano in a hotel bar frequented by American 'coyotes', as they were called, men who smuggled people across the border. The piano, which had been brought to Monterrey on the back of a cart by the enterprising Texan who had opened the hotel thirty years before, hadn't been tuned for a decade. The Texan was long gone, north to pan for gold, and the piano was sticky with sand and spilt Mexican beer, but the hotel bar had a wooden floor and a couple of fringed divans that had been made to order in New Orleans. If it wasn't an actual operating brothel, then it certainly felt like one.

Monterrey was a town that was full of impromptu music; everyone seemed to play the accordion, the guitar or the clarinet and in the evening the men joined together to play Mexican music in styles known as *norteño* and *banda*. Monroe often wondered why on earth anyone would want to listen to him play songs on an out-of-tune piano. Nonetheless, on a good night, when the tequila was flowing and the local girls were complicit, he could make up to ten dollars in tips. On a bad night, he played to a few toothless dishwashers who chattered away in Spanish before falling asleep on the bar.

One month had passed, one hot, drawn-out month, when he tried not to reflect on what he had done. He couldn't go back. But he couldn't live here for ever either. And then one evening an American slammed five dollars on the lid of the piano and brought out a piece of torn and crumpled sheet music.

'Can you play this?' he asked. 'You know it?'

The American had his arm around a young Mexican girl in a yellow dress. 'It's my wife's favourite song,' he explained.

Monroe flattened the music on his thigh. 'I know it,' he said.

When he played 'The Sweetest Time' for the first and only time in Mexico, when his fingers ran over the keys and finally ended on a G minor chord, it was as if a veil had suddenly lifted. And there, staring him in the face, was the only option.

'If you must go back,' Antonio told him, 'then become a Russian, a real Russian. There are thousands of them in New York with no papers, no language, nothing. Grow a beard, learn a trade and you could just disappear. But don't play the piano, not if you don't want to give yourself away. And don't trust anyone. Russians are worse than Italians.'

It was far more dangerous crossing the border back into America than it had been leaving. A few months before, an Italian anarchist had been imprisoned for six months for failing to show his draft registration card. But Monroe paid a coyote ten dollars and, with new identity papers, he caught a bus north to queue up at the international crossing point at Reynosa. While the Mexicans ahead of him were forced to strip, hand in their clothes to be steam-sterilized and then be de-loused with kerosene and vinegar, he was allowed to walk through with nothing more than a cursory glance at his papers; he was white, he was literate, he had the eight-dollar-a-head tax. He hitched a ride to Brownsville where he jumped on a freight train north, to Tulsa. From there he calculated he had just enough money left to take the train to Chicago and then back east to New York.

The Russian Club on Hester Street was open late. As soon as he walked in he was immediately enveloped by the smells of his childhood: cabbage and dill, pork fat and cheap tobacco. Rolly Tipple dozed behind the bar, a damp dishcloth flung over his shoulder.

'Hey, Rolly,' Monroe said softly. 'It took me a little longer than I promised but I got here in the end.'

The vaudeville singer's embrace was so solid that it crushed all the breath from his chest.

'I heard you'd skipped town,' he said. 'When did you get back?'

'About an hour ago,' Monroe replied. 'It's so good to see a familiar face.'

'And you don't need to say it, but what a face it is! I'm looking younger than ever! Monroe Simonov. What a turn-up for the books.'

'You know what,' he whispered. 'It's better not to call me by that name. It's Andrei now. Andrei Dreslov.'

Rolly stood back and took him in, his tattered clothes and his weatherbeaten face. 'No problem. And you know what, Rolly Tipple's on an extended sabbatical too, just until he gets another spot. The name's Ivan, Ivan Guerensky. Listen, let me finish up here. And then we can catch up.'

In the meeting room, as well as the old-timers who sat playing chess, hammering out Yiddish songs on the piano in the corner or stirring jam into their tea, the club was now frequented by a new wave of immigrants. Whether they were radicals or socialists, Communists or anarchists, they all had one thing in common: they all liked to talk loudly, at length. Monroe's arrival barely registered. He was another pair of ears, another voice to say, yes, yes, you have a point.

'You look exhausted,' said Ivan. 'You got a place to stay?'

'Not yet.'

While most of the club, the meeting rooms and the dining room, the office and the kitchen, were open to anyone, there was one room on the first floor that was kept locked. The Tsar's Room, as it was known, had been decorated twenty years before by a painter from St Petersburg to resemble the interior of the Winter Palace. The walls were gold with trompe l'oeil windows painted with scenes of the city the painter had left behind, and the room was lit by half a dozen candelabras holding three dozen liturgical candles. A large four-poster bed was offered to distinguished visitors but in recent years most of them, his friend explained, had turned it down for ideological reasons.

'You can have it for as long as I'm here,' he told Monroe. 'I'll get a key cut for you, but keep it quiet.'

'I will,' he said.

'Be great to have you around,' Ivan said. 'You know what? That piano has taken a good pounding since I've been here. Be good to hear some real music for a change. You're welcome to take a meander around those keys any time, my boy.'

'Thanks, Rolly.'

'I like to be of service. Anything else I can help you with?'

'You got any suggestions where I can get a job, a real job, cash in hand no questions asked?'

'Sure,' he replied. 'But I wouldn't exactly recommend it.'

Every morning Monroe would walk to Fulton Street to stand in line with a hundred or so others Russians, Irishmen and Scots, Native Americans and blacks and offer himself as a temporary worker in a chemical factory. He started at seven thirty and knocked off at six in the evening. The conditions were appalling, the factory floor was baking hot and the light was poor, but after tax he earned fifteen dollars a week.

On his day off, after he spent a few hours in the Russian baths on Hester Street, cleaning off the week's grime, he walked north. He would sit on the low wall of the perimeter of Central Park West near Inez's building for hours until one day he noticed the plain-clothes policeman chatting to a coachman. He needn't have worried. In this part of town he was practically invisible. As the large cars purred by, their occupants seemed swathed in the kind of velvet half-dark that made them seem detached from the city they drove through. It seemed clear now to Monroe that Inez belonged to another world, a world that was said to be financed by the spilt blood and bruised hands of the lower classes, the blacks and the immigrants, a world that he could never set foot in again.

Without warning, Ivan, or Rolly Tipple as he was now known once more, announced that he was off on tour until summer.

'Why don't you come along?' he asked Monroe. 'The money ain't good and nobody ever promises you a bed, but it'll be a blast.'

'Not this time,' Monroe replied. 'But thanks for asking.'

'It's your call,' he said. 'Hey, listen, I'm sure you could still use the room. If you kept it quiet.'

Twice in the last week, however, he had been woken in the middle of the night by a club member with a young woman in tow, who also had a spare key to the Tsar's Room.

'I think I need to move on. Get something else sorted.'

'Sure you do. You're a songwriter. And one hell of a fine one. Something'll come up.'

'Be seeing you . . . Ivan,' said Monroe.

'Not,' he replied, 'if I see you first.'

That night there were few people in the meeting rooms of the Russian Club. Monroe sat down at the piano and began to play. After an hour, or maybe two, Monroe became aware of a man applauding. With small, slanted eyes, a large space between his front teeth, a brand-new derby hat and a battered cane, he looked half showman, half tramp.

'Bravo,' he had said. 'What is the English word for that?'

'Jazz,' answered Monroe.

'Oh, so you're an American?' he said in Russian.

Monroe didn't respond.

'American?' he said slowly.

'Yes, but my blood is all Russian,' Monroe replied.

'Ah, yes, you are a Russian who has never been to Russia and who doesn't speak the language. So you are an enigma. A puzzle.'

'I speak Russian,' he said, 'when I have to.'

'You play well,' the man said.

'I'm out of practice.'

'What are you doing in a place like this?'

Monroe glanced quickly around the room but they were the only ones there. 'I was drafted. I skipped out. I went to Mexico. And then I came back.'

'And what next?'

'I'm not altogether sure,' he replied. 'You?'

'Just passing through.'

The Russian pulled out a small sharp pocket knife, unfolded it, and started to pick his teeth with the point, while looking at him, up and down, up and down, as if weighing something up. And then he spat on the floor and snapped the knife shut.

'I think maybe we can help each other,' he said and held out his hand.

Monroe hesitated for a fraction of a second as Antonio's words came back to him.

269

'My name is Tadeus, Tadeus Pokolitov,' said the man.

'Your real name?'

'Of course,' he said.

'Monroe,' he replied as he took the Russian's hand and shook it. 'Monroe Simonov.'

'Your real name?'

Monroe laughed. 'Of course,' he said.

Pokolitov loved jazz. He lived in a rented townhouse on Tenth Street which had a spare room and a piano and he was determined, so he told Monroe, to learn. They agreed to daily lessons in return for board. With his large hands and complete inability to differentiate between the notes however, Pokolitov was a poor student. Mostly he was content to listen to Monroe play. Sometimes he drank so much vodka that he fell asleep after only five minutes. On other nights he wanted Monroe to keep playing until the early hours.

'What are you doing here?' Monroe asked him one night.

'Same question to you, my friend,' he replied.

Monroe laughed. 'I told you already. You know I wasn't going to come back,' he began. 'But this is my home, my city.'

'I know, my friend,' Pokolitov said, 'that you do not tell me the real reason.'

Sometimes Pokolitov drank himself sober and then he would sit with his head in his hands and weep for a woman he once knew.

'When did she die?' Monroe asked.

'She's not dead,' he replied. 'But she might as well be. Her name is Anna. And she is here, in New York.' And he handed him a piece of paper stamped with the insignia of the Politburo.

Monroe saw the cough rise up in Anna Denisova's chest, he noticed the way it racked her throat until she couldn't hold it in any longer. As her shoulders shuddered and her whole body heaved, she pulled out a small white handkerchief and held it to her mouth. In the pale light of the moon, he noticed with shock that it was peppered with dozens of dark spots.

Finally she caught her breath again, finally she could speak.

'Are you all right?' he asked.

'It's only bronchitis,' she replied. 'But I don't understand. They sent me the papers, the tickets, everything. For what? For this? Someone has betrayed me.'

A siren sounded in the street, followed by the slam of several car doors. A lamp was switched on in the neighbouring building, illuminating them both with a rectangle of light.

'You should probably move, cover your tracks,' he said. 'Try to stay out of sight.'

'And why should I trust you?' she asked.

He shrugged. 'You could give me away,' he answered. 'I'm a deserter. I was in Mexico. I came back.'

The Russian woman took a deep breath and then let it out.

'All right. I can tell you what I know about your friend. Her husband was shot. But you probably know that.'

Monroe turned and looked at Anna Denisova. But her eyes were fixed on the distant twinkle of the lights on the George Washington Bridge.

'No! I didn't know,' he replied. 'Is he . . . is he dead?'

'That I do not know.'

'Who did it?' he asked.

Before she could answer, there was the sound of splintering wood. A woman screamed, a whistle blew. As they watched, down in the street below dozens of Italians were frog-marched out of the restaurant, handcuffed and herded into vans.

Half a dozen heavy boots pounded up the stairs towards the door to the roof. A lamp in the neighbouring building was switched off. Without pause, the Russian woman pulled his mouth down to meet her mouth. The door flew open and three policemen appeared. But when they saw nobody trying to escape across the rooftops, nobody but a courting couple indulging in what looked like copulation against the parapet, they cleared their throats, loosened their grip on their batons and turned away.

271

24

It was an especially beautiful sunset: the light, the colour and translucency of a slice of watermelon. The towns and high-rises of Manhattan rose up in silhouette, stark and black against the billowing sky. The sun that had filled the room with burnished copper light slowly slipped away and then was gone.

Inez put down her book and was about to wander over to the window when a hand shot out from under the bedcovers and clasped her lower arm.

'Where are you going?' Ivory's eye, his one good eye, stared at her.

'I was just going to close the drapes,' she said. 'I thought you were asleep.'

'Well, I wasn't asleep,' he said.

Inez glanced down at her arm. He let it go.

'The doctor is coming in ten minutes,' she said softly. 'I'll go and see to your supper.'

'Yes,' he replied. 'You do that.'

Just five months previously everybody had believed that Ivory Price was going to die. The bullet had entered his frontal lobe, severing the main arteries to his right eye and causing a massive haemorrhage in his brain. He was unconscious for a month, in intensive care for two and was not declared out of danger until the middle of March. And yet, despite several setbacks, he had begun to recover at an expeditious rate. After discharging himself from hospital, he came home to recuperate and had taken up residence on a day bed in the parlour.

Even though the description given by the corset salesman did not fit, Inez had been questioned by the police for hours. But still she refused to say who she was waiting for and where. When Ivory had regained consciousness, he had had a few long, private conversations with the police inspector and the file drawn up on Mrs Price, and there had been no doubt that there was one, was shelved. The previous month a press release had been prepared: Ivory Price had been the victim of a radical extremist act perpetrated by an enemy alien. He had been lured under false pretences into a trap, of which the details were not provided, and wounded, almost fatally. As a result, he had announced his decision to stand in the November Congressional elections from his sickbed, and to make his first priority to root out and eradicate 'New York's endemic revolutionary activity.' His recovery, therefore, was also something of a rally. It was also a battle with his body, with the notion that his disability would thwart him.

'I'm just the same fellow I was before,' he announced to his visitors. But just one look at him suggested the opposite. And indeed, he wasn't.

Yet the whole city, the whole country had begun to feel different. In March 1918, the War Industries Board was set up to initiate the conservation of all vital resources. They vetoed rationing but introduced a series of measure to preserve supplies: Heatless Mondays, Meatless Tuesdays, Wheatless Wednesdays and Gasless Sundays. For six days a week, the Lightless Night was rigidly enforced: all the restaurants and cafés, the theatres and cinemas turned off their signs and exterior lighting to save fuel. The city had switched itself off and the nights were longer and darker than anyone had ever known.

Luella was with the new Irish nanny who Inez's mother had hired before she went back to Detroit. Mrs O'Leary was soft but strict, sensible but affectionate and, what was more, she loved the baby and the baby loved her. She took Luella to Mass every morning, for the music, she would say. And although Inez would never admit it, she liked the idea that someone, somewhere, was negotiating regularly for the salvation of her daughter's soul.

Inez often sat by her husband's bedside and read him the newspapers. She read of American battles at Cantigny, at Chateau-Thierry

273

only forty miles from Paris, and at Bouresches and Belleau Wood, of the 'doughboys' – she hated that term – who, fighting under General Pershing, had saved Paris. And then she silently scanned the newspaper casualty list.

'Anyone we know?' he would say.

She would shake her head, turn the page and fix her eyes on advertisements for Mallory Cravenette Hats or Cream of Wheat instead.

As Ivory Price watched his wife read, he took in the way strands of her hair floated down across her face, no matter how often she swept it back, and the way she moved her slender body, all wrist and neck, turning. How, he asked himself, could he have failed to see her before? Of course, he had married her but he had not seen her, or even attempted to; he had not really known her.

'Inez?' he would say. And she would look at him with those clear green eyes, with such a look of absolute puzzlement on her face that any notion that there could ever be anything between them, any hope for reciprocal emotion, would be quickly swallowed down or bitten back.

'Could you bring me some water?' he would say. 'And make sure it's cold this time.'

At first, when Ivory realized that a part of his body, the right side of his face and his right arm, had been rendered useless, when the feeling did not return and they remained numb and dead to him, he had been furious. He had sacked the nurses who had been hired to care for him, one after the other. When Inez had stepped in, to feed him, to change his dressing and to help him exercise the parts of his body that were affected, he had yelled at her, he had insulted her, he had blamed her for every passing emotion, all negative, that had swept through his injured brain. And when, finally, she had put down the pair of scissors she had been holding and called him an arrogant pig, he had been quite taken aback.

'What did you call me?' he said to the back of her head.

'I was going to leave you,' she replied without turning. 'Before this. And when you get better, I will.'

'But what about the girl?' he said.

274

'The girl,' she said and turned round. 'Her name is Luella. And Luella would be better living in a tenement in the Bronx with nothing rather than with two people who despise each other. Don't you agree?'

'I don't despise you, Inez,' he had countered.

'I've never asked you who you were with and what happened. I don't want to know.'

And she had closed her eyes and sighed.

'Shall I hire another nurse to do this?' she said eventually.

Ivory shook his head. Self-pity flooded through him until his one good eye turned red and began to water. Inez handed him her white cotton handkerchief.

'I have a cold,' he said. 'That's all.'

'I know,' she said. 'I know.'

And he could not deny that something in him had begun to soften and fold, and all those notions of invincibility that he had used to protect himself from the world had slowly fallen away.

The first time he asked her to dance, she had looked at him with her face closed. Only her eyes suggested that she thought he was making fun of her. And then she shrugged and put a record on the gramophone and began to move in circles, her arms sculpted around some imaginary, invisible partner. Initially she looked self-conscious, stiff, embarrassed, and twice she had stopped and suggested that she was so bad, so out of practice that she would and should stop. But he had insisted, he had begged, he had pleaded. And so she had no option but to oblige, and soon her arms, her legs, her head, her neck had loosened up and she had danced until she forgot the room, the time, her audience of one.

Ivory watched her circle back and forth at the end of his bed and was reminded of the first time Inez Kennedy had danced in front of him. And he remembered that at the time of the party when they had first met, he had believed himself to be something of a lepidopterist, net raised, in the presence of a rare and covetable specimen. After a dedicated pursuit he had caught her, but, to his disappointment, the colours of her wings had faded almost instantly. She was

275

nothing but a Common Buckeye, he had quickly decided, a Cabbage White.

But now as she danced, alone, or on occasion with baby Luella in her arms, he saw in her a grace that he lacked, a dignity that came from compromise. Ivory Price's marriage to Inez Kennedy, he saw now, rather than being a dreadful mistake, had been a stroke of luck. Not only had she saved his business from insolvency, she was also beautiful, smart and kind. But like everything else that Ivory desired, however, the part of her he wanted more than any other was unavailable to him.

If only, Ivory put it to himself, she knew what he knew. If only she realized that her chances of seeing the piano player again were slim. It had been a calculated risk to put them together to see what they would do. But he had to be sure he had the right man. And once he knew it, he would be able to use the information to his advantage.

Wilson Strutt had earned his fees after all. After the incident in January, as he now referred to the circumstances around his injury, Strutt had been called in to the hospital by the detective assigned to the case. By the bedside in his private room, Strutt had been warned; he could be throughly discreet, but to lie, to cover anything up would be regarded as perjury. And so he had confirmed that he had been hired by Price to carry out a long-term surveillance procedure on Inez, his wife. From what he had observed it was clear that she was romantically involved with a former song-plugger who had been drafted, a soldier called Monroe Simonov.

'You knew this?' the detective asked Ivory.

'Yes,' he replied, 'I did.'

According to Strutt's notes, using information garnered from several sources including an extended interview with Simonov's army superior, at the exact time Ivory had been shot, Monroe Simonov was supposed to have been at the Universal Music Corporation with his captain. Simonov had been reprimanded after a saloon brawl at the training camp and it was decided that his visit to Manhattan would be strictly supervised. But at around 5.30 p.m., under the pretence of needing to relieve himself, he had surreptitiously left the music corporation and disappeared. Although a 'decent fellow,' Simonov had not returned to Camp Upton that night, as his curfew instructed, or the following day. Just before his regiment was shipped to France he was officially listed as a deserter.

Mrs Inez Price had been under Strutt's own observation that afternoon. She had entered a building in Chelsea at 3 p.m. and had left alone at 6.05 p.m. No one else, save a postman and three residents, had been seen entering or leaving. If there had been a rendezvous between his wife and her lover, it had failed. And where, the detective had asked Wilson Strutt, did he think Simonov was now?

'Across the border in Mexico, probably,' he replied. 'Or Canada. Somewhere very hot. Or very cold. Hellish either way.'

Simonov could not return to the United States, Strutt went on. At least not without the risk of arrest. He was, if not dead, then as good as.

'You see him, you call us,' the detective told Ivory. 'We're going to put a plain-clothed on your building. And ask your doorman to intercept any mail addressed to your wife.'

Later that day, Ivory had paid Strutt the entire fee plus a little extra and thanked him for all his hard work. The private detective took the money and pulled a half-smoked cigarette from his pocket. He would have liked to have caught the couple at it. He would have liked to have provided dates and times and exact hotel room numbers. As it was, he knew he had failed. But then again he had never warmed to Ivory Price and his arrogant manner. The man hadn't adequately explained the circumstances of his gunshot wound. Who was the woman the police were looking for and what was he doing in those downtown hotel rooms with her? Maybe, he decided as he relit the stub of his Chesterfield, they both deserved everything they got.

The doctor had come and gone. Her husband was well, he had declared, as well as could be expected. Inez brought him supper on a tray but he waved it away.

'Is there nothing in this house but salad?' he said.

'It is June,' she protested.

'Already?' he replied.

The sky in the west was a pale, pale green, scored with the last breath of several vapour trails and the hard glint of distant stars.

'Where do you think they went, those planes?' Ivory asked Inez.

She shrugged. 'Could be just about anywhere,' she replied.

'Inez?' Ivory said, the good side of his face lit by the last slant of day. 'Am I still unbearable?'

She looked down at him, held his gaze, and shook her head. And yet her mouth, no matter what her eyes said, remained resolute and strong. She would get what she wanted in the end, the curl of her upper lip seemed to say; all she had to do was wait.

It had taken her months, but gradually, tentatively, Inez had gone over and over Monroe's absence that day in January and decided that she might have been wrong to assume it was because he had changed his mind about her. He might have been delayed, he could have been shipped out early, he might have been taken sick. Anything could have happened. Anything. And so with all the courage she could muster, she had phoned Camp Upton from the foyer of a drugstore on Fifty-Seventh Street. Of course they had asked for her name before they put her through to the officer in charge of the camp and she had given one that she had made up beforehand.

'You related?' he had asked.

'No,' she replied. 'Just a friend, a good friend.'

The line sighed and crackled and she lost a dozen or so words of his response.

'I'm sorry, ' was all she caught of the captain's words. 'He's gone.'

Inez gulped a mouthful of air and posted another five cents in the slot. Her fingers wrapped themselves around the telephone cord.

'I can't hear you, the line is bad. Where?' she asked. 'Where in France?'

'France! He never got to France,' the officer replied. 'He absconded in January. Now if you'd like to come by and answer a few questions . . .'

With a small click she cut the line.

The Fourth of July Parade that year was to be the biggest ever seen in New York. Beginning at eight thirty in the morning, over a hundred thousand people would walk from Washington Arch in Greenwich Village to the Stadium of the College of the City of New York on 140th Street. With one hundred and fifty floats, dozens of bands, twenty military aeroplanes scheduled to fly over the city in battle formation, and a dirigible balloon that would drop thousands of copies of 'The Star-Spangled Banner' along the route, the 'patriotic parade' would continue for twelve whole hours.

Almost every immigrant community, from the Jews and the Hungarians to the Italians and the French, had been keen to take their place in the parade and pledge their support to America's war effort. Every church group, every charitable organization, every political party – under the watchful eyes of two thousand policemen who had been briefed by the Censorship Committee – had spent weeks creating spectacular floats. Just in case anyone should forget, in all the tickertape and bunting, just what the whole thing was in aid of, a life-size replica of no-man's-land, complete with electric flashes to represent gunfire, had been constructed by a sculptor on the steps of the Public Library. But the climax of the entire day would be a huge rally where floats would be judged, prizes awarded, and performances given by opera stars and a chamber orchestra.

Mrs Ivory Price's input and presence was requested on half a dozen floats including the Young Women's Christian Association, the People's Institute and the American Defense Society. She agreed to help out with all of them but, she explained, she would only be able to give a little time to each. She had another obligation.

It had rained before dawn but it was still a glorious day. It felt as if the weather, doubting the talent of the city's inhabitants who had been up for hours preparing, had given everything a second polish. Ivory's float was an open-topped car that had been dressed to

279

look like a boat. Red and blue bunting and an American flag flapped from a wooden mast, and a banner read: *Fight the Right Fight with Ivory Price*.

As he instructed his driver to fix the swags of cotton, rehanging and looping them more securely, the right side of Ivory's body seemed to twitch with palpable excitement. It was his first public appearance, his first footstep on to the campaign trail. The patch across his eye, the useless arm, the limping gait – the feeling had returned to his leg but it was not the same – suggested, if you did not know what had happened, that he was a veteran of the war. And his face, half mobile, half frozen, half still image, half moving picture, was not so much disfigured as reconfigured: nothing was hidden, nothing masked. No wonder the bystanders on Greenwich Avenue invested him with a certain hard-won nobility. No wonder when they leaned into the car, shook his hand and wished him good luck, they meant it.

'I'm Ivory Price,' he told them. 'You'll see my name on the ballot paper in November.'

A pile of leaflets had been printed listing his credentials for office: a self-made millionaire, an aviator, a staunch supporter of the war, a vigilant member of the community. He had suggested that Luella be brought along too – a child would give the whole proceedings a more domestic slant – but Inez would not hear of it, and she left the child with Mrs O'Leary. But Ivory still had his wife, the indefatigable, or so it had once been written in the *New York Times*, the inexhaustible Mrs Ivory Price.

Inez wore the pale blue sash of the Young Women's Christian Association, of which she was a board member, and had pulled her hair under a large white hat to protect it from the sun. Her face was in shade as she announced her plans for the day and Ivory could not read it.

'I'll join you at Colombus Circle,' she told him. And then, before he had time to object, she strode off down the street towards Washington Square.

The streets around the square were crowded with people, with colour and noise as bands tuned up and participants put final touches to floats and gave their costumes and hats one last check. The parade organizers, dressed in white, and holding clipboards, marched up and down and shouted orders. It seemed impossible that any kind of parade could materialize from this chaos. But at eight thirty exactly, with the polished glint of brass, a band burst into 'God Bless America' and, as the crowds cheered, began to surge through the arch and head up the wide canyon of Fifth Avenue. Inez skirted the perimeter of the square with her hat pulled low across her face and then headed east along West Fourth Street to Broadway, where she caught a tramcar heading uptown.

Earlier that year, Inez had felt as if the ground she had been standing on had suddenly given way, leaving her treading water in the deepest, darkest sea. Many times she felt as if she were going under, many times she was sure she would drown in the certainty that she would never see Monroe again. The worst thing about it was that she had no idea where to look for him. He would not come to her, not with the plain-clothed cop who stood on the other side of the street all day. And although she picked up the mail every morning half expecting to see his handwriting, nothing ever came. But if he was alive, he would be here, she told herself, in New York. So where should she start? Where should she begin? In a city of a million people where do you find a single man?

Inez could not bear to be in the apartment with Ivory for any longer than was necessary. As well as the smell of medicine and linen starch, his presence was a dull ache in the air, the taste of melancholy, a constant reminder of every bad decision she had ever made. And so she had thrown herself into any world she could find, as long as it was not the one that belonged to her.

Once Ivory was well on the road to recovery, Inez asked to be driven out to Price Aero in New Jersey again. At first the manager humoured her, tolerating her presence but little more. He had no idea that it was her money that was paying his wages. It was soon clear that Ivory had had very little to do with the actual running of the factory and the manager obviously believed that it was only a matter of time before his wife lost interest.

The factory office was always cold and draughty; the sea wind whistled round the hangars all day until it was hard to think straight, let alone work. But the charity work had been useful; Inez had learned how to organize people, how to balance books and how to delegate. By summer, the factory was almost reaching targets and producing twenty planes a week.

'I'm paying the women more,' she told Ivory one evening. 'They work just as hard and produce the same as men. I've checked the records.'

Ivory shook his head in amazement, and looked at her afresh. 'But my dear—' he began.

'And I've sourced a supply of wood from Canada. The savings we make from that alone more than compensates. The company is making money. A lot of money.'

'You didn't have to do it,' he said. 'I didn't ask you to do it. I'll pay you back every nickel, every cent of the money you spent.'

'It's not about the money,' she replied.

'You should buy yourself some new gowns,' he had gone on, 'a mink coat. You would look divine in mink. We can afford it.'

But Inez had simply lowered her gaze and turned away.

Hortense at Lord and Taylor's had remembered Ivory Price. Together they had picked out a dozen outfits that, Hortense assured him, would fit his wife perfectly. Inez, however, had opened the boxes, taken one look at the satin, the lace and the fur inside, and then returned it all to the shop.

One evening when she came home from New Jersey she heard piano music. The grand piano in the parlour had been taken away and in its place a brand-new Concert Grand Apollo, a Pianola, had appeared. Ivory, his good leg pumping, was playing a rag.

'Darling,' he called out, 'I bought us both a present. And the doctor said it's very strengthening for my condition. I bought a dozen rolls and they're going to keep sending me all the latest tunes.'

Inez stood and watched the wide white piano roll turn on its cogs while the pneumatic mechanics inside mashed out the tune.

'I preferred the piano,' she said.

Ivory stopped pedalling and the music came to a sudden halt on a minor chord. 'I thought you'd love it,' he said. 'I can play you the music that you adore so much. Most of the tunes have got the lyrics. I thought that you could sing if you were that way inclined.'

'I appreciate it,' she replied.

But as she turned and started to head back to the door, Ivory stood up and limped towards her.

'No,' he said. 'You don't.'

'I have to see Luella,' she said. 'Mrs O'Leary is expecting me.'

'You can have anything,' he said. 'Anything you want. But nothing seems good enough for you.'

He was panting now, but it was not just the exertion of playing the Pianola. Inez noticed that his brow was damp, his face mottled, his lip bitten.

'Are you feeling all right?' she said.

'How many times and in how many ways can I say I'm sorry,' Ivory said softly. 'I made a mistake. I was fooled, tricked. And I paid it for it dearly, by God!'

Part of the problem was that when Inez thought of Ivory with another woman, she felt nothing. And what could she say when she knew that Ivory knew about Monroe? Their marriage was a sham, a façade. How could he pretend it was otherwise?

'I love you,' Ivory declared and then he took her hand and kissed it. 'You're my wife. Come back to me.'

But Inez could never come back because she was never really there to begin with.

'What other songs are there?' she said softly. 'Can I take a look?'

Most of the songs were tunes she knew, with choruses she had heard sung by the girls in the factory. But there was one she didn't know, a song called 'Dancing with My Girl on the Amagansett Sands'. She picked up the lyrics and began to read, and as she did so her face began to colour.

'Play this one?' she said quickly before Ivory noticed.

'This is a good one,' he said. 'Very popular just now. Makes a change from all those ballads about mothers losing their sons although the lyrics don't make any sense at all. And it's got a smashing melody, too. You want me to try to sing it?'

'No, let me just follow the words,' she said.

> My Suzette's the swellest girl
> Dancing on the beach as the flags unfurl
> Her hair is red, his kiss is kosher.
> I love that girl from Nova Scotia.

Casually, so casually, she glanced at the name of the writer.

The lobby of the Universal Music Corporation was so dark that it took a moment or two for her eyes to adjust to the light. The place seemed deserted. A small woman with a tightly wound grey bun was sweeping the stairs.

'Is there anyone here?' she asked.

The woman shook her head. 'Never until ten,' she said. 'But most of 'em won't be in today. Taking part in the Fourth of July parade.'

'Of course. Actually I'm looking for someone,' Inez said. 'I wanted to leave a message. You may happen to know him? His name is Andrei Dreslov.'

The cleaning woman, however, seemed distracted, her eyes drawn to a presence behind her. Inez turned round. And there, panting at the top of the stairs, was Ivory.

25

Anna Denisova lifted her suitcase as the tramcar approached and climbed aboard. To the passengers already sitting in the lower seating deck, she looked like a teacher of dance, perhaps, or an instructor in watercolour painting. Her small frame and determined chin, her fingers, bare of rings or any other ornamentation, suggested that she was an attractive spinster, a woman whose pride, bad luck or a mixture of both, had left spouse-less. Most of the passengers on the lower deck on that tram in Baltimore were married, they were wives whose own husbands had either been drafted or had taken on extra shifts at the steel works or the canning factory to meet demand, and of whom they now saw very little.

Anna took a seat about halfway down the aisle and immediately consulted the wafer-thin pages of her Baedeker. The other passengers looked away, but not before they had taken in the cut of her coat, and tilt of her hat. Her presence made them all feel undeniably shabby. What was a lady like that doing riding on a tramcar, they asked themselves, when she could clearly afford a cab? It was, however, too hot a day to travel anywhere. Even though it was already late afternoon, the air was humid and stale, making even those who had recently emerged from the cool of the kitchen or the shade of the veranda breathless and prone to perspiration. The sun cut at an angle through the dirty glass, making bare skin itch with heat. Several of the women closed their eyes, dozing as the tram swayed around corners, sped up and slowed down again. An elderly woman in the back seat let her mouth fall slack as she dreamed of the cool Shenandoah Valley streams of her girlhood.

They crossed over Jones Falls, the river that divided the city in two, and then headed down towards the Chesapeake Bay. But just as they were almost at the City Halls, a horse, untethered from a cart or bolted from the barracks paddock, ran straight into the path of the tramcar. The driver braked hard, but not hard enough, the horse was hit and Anna Denisova's suitcase flew off the seat where it had been sitting, bounced twice across the aisle, and opened, throwing its contents up and out and everywhere. As well as clean undergarments and several hefty books, eighteen sticks of bright red dynamite landed on the floor before slowly rolling back and forth, hitting feet and shins and bags of groceries.

The passengers on board seemed slow to take it in; the sudden jolt, the colour of the horse's blood on the windscreen, the contents of the suitcase, had all given the moment the aura, they agreed later, of a nightmare. A crowd had gathered on the pavement to watch the horse in the throes of death try and try once more to get back on its feet. A siren blared as a police car approached. A child started to sob. And in all the confusion, in all that noise, Anna Denisova simply rose out of her seat, knelt down, picked up the suitcase, stuffing all that was close at hand inside, and disembarked.

Nobody, the other passengers a little sheepishly admitted, had tried to apprehend her. Nobody had stopped her. But when questioned as to why not, they all offered a different explanation. I thought she was an actress, one woman said, and they were props from a play. They could have been candles, another suggested. Or candy. And anyway, everyone agreed, she was there one moment and gone the next; she simply disappeared.

Anna walked quickly down Liberty Street towards Camden Station. Although her hands, her knees, her lower lip still trembled, she realized with relief that she had taken the wrong tramcar and rather than heading to an address in the suburbs as she had intended, she had merely circumnavigated the centre of the city and come back to the same place she had started. The station was foggy with dust and the faint taste of soot. On the nearest platform, a train to Philadelphia was just about to depart. She bought a ticket and climbed aboard just as the whistle blew its mournful note.

The train wasn't full; it was too early for commuters and too late for those going up to the city for the day. She found a seat in the parlour car, sat down and, as the train pulled out of the station, buried her face in her hands and tried to catch her breath.

If she was busy, she found the pain was less. If she was planning routes or organizing the delivery of letters and plans, if she was travelling and changing trains or negotiating stations, the yawning hole inside her chest didn't ache quite so badly. But when her hands were idle and the whirr inside her head began to slow, a wave of sorrow overwhelmed her.

Earlier that month, a letter had finally reached her from Kima. Although it was risky, she had picked it up from her postal box at the General Post Office. His father, her former husband, had been shot from a car by a young female revolutionary, a random act of anarchy in a city that was out of control. The revolution had promised so much: equality, peace, the end of an unfair, unjust regime. And yet in under a year, he wrote, it was already proving to be worse. The Okhranka, the secret police of the tsarist regime, had simply reformed and become the Cheka, the secret police of the Bolsheviks.

The war was over on the Eastern Front but the Treaty of Brest-Litovsk had conceded more land and natural resources than Russia could afford; it had lost a third of its population, half of its industry and nine-tenths of its coal mines. In Petrograd, as St Petersburg was now called, there was no bread and the population was beginning to starve to death. Fighting had broken out all over Russia as the newly formed Red Army fought the White Army, who were made up of displaced monarchists. Kima wrote that he had become a Green, one of the growing swell of radicals and students opposed to the Bolsheviks and the Imperialists. Thousands of Social Revolutionaries and anarchists had joined forces. The revolution, they argued, should have made life better for ordinary people, not worse. He didn't, however, mention Pokolitov. Did he know what had happened to her? Did he know her situation?

The train picked up speed. Anna opened her suitcase and carefully checked the contents. Of the eighteen sticks, she had collected seven. The authorities would be alerted. There would be a description. And yet she had almost accomplished what she had agreed to do. This was the last city; for three months, she had travelled as far

287

as Chicago and Milwaukee to leave her packages in station lockers, at faceless addresses in characterless suburbs. Now she would have to dump what she had, just in case she was stopped, just in case she had been spotted getting on to the train.

She looked around. The carriage was almost empty. At the far end, a young woman laughed with a little too much animation at her male companion's joke. The slap of crockery and the smell of soup came from the dining car in the next carriage. She turned the other way and headed down the aisle towards the very back of the train.

When she opened the door and stepped out on to the observation platform, the noise of the wheels on the track was deafening, but the air was cool and tasted of salt. The tracks ran alongside the ragged edge of the bay, past sand dunes spiked with marram grass and the oily wash of the estuary. Although the sun was still shining, the sky in the east was loaded with storm clouds; it would rain heavily before nightfall. The door to the carriage was swathed in a lace curtain to offer some privacy, she supposed, to smokers and lovers. No one would see her hurl the sticks of dynamite, one by one, as far as she could. Their red paper casings were more visible than she would have liked against the washed-out colours of the shore but by tomorrow the casings would have faded, and slowly their contents would seep into the sand, into the earth, into the sea. She would never, she decided then, carry explosives in a bag ever again. It was too risky. There must be another way, a way to conceal them without anyone suspecting.

She jumped, visibly, when the door behind her opened. A man stepped out with a newspaper under his arm. He greeted her courteously and lit a cigarette. Anna Denisova waited until it was polite to leave, until it could not be construed that his presence had ruined any solitude she might have sought, and then turned and opened the door. A newspaper headline caught her eye.

'Do you mind?' she asked the man. 'Could I take a look?'

'Be my guest,' he replied.

'Ex-Tsar of Russia Killed by Order of Ural Soviet,' she read. 'Nicholas shot on 16 July when it was feared that Czechoslovaks might seize him.'

The article went on to state that his murder had been approved by the Bolsheviks. The tsarina and her children, it reported, had been sent to a place of security. An ink portrait of the tsar illustrated the piece.

Anna shivered. She remembered Nicholas as a young man. In 1896 she had been taken to Moscow by her father to watch the coronation parade. He rode a light grey dappled mare and passed through the cheering crowds as if he could not hear them, as if his mind, his eyes, his ears were already focused on higher things. And he looked so gallant, so handsome, so noble, it was impossible not to fall slightly in love with him; it was impossible not to believe that Imperial Russia would last for ever.

It had made her giddy, the gilded carriages, the crowds, the lavishly decorated streets, the gunshots fired from the Tainitskaya Tower, the bells rung in the Assumption Cathedral, and she had asked to be taken home. The celebrations went on for days. A week later, however, tragedy struck when thousands camped out on the Khodynskoye Pole were crushed to death or injured in a stampede.

Imperial Russia and the reign of the tsars were gone for good. And yet what had replaced them? Corruption, bloodshed and murder. And now it had crossed several oceans and had reached her. She had begun to feel safe in America, she had been able to fall asleep at night without the fear that she might be woken by the thump of a fist on her door in the middle of the night. But all that had changed. She had been betrayed.

Since the night of the ball, Anna had become part of an underground, never staying in one place longer than a week, moving from boarding house to furnished room, and from Queens to the Lower East Side, taking a series of short-term lets and becoming a Swede, a Finn, or a German, with a different name each time. New York was a huge city but she could still be found.

Dante Faccini had saved her. At that point he had a large network of safe houses and trusted contacts. Feeling among the Italian community was running high. Dozens of his friends had been arrested and imprisoned. Together with several thousand others, he had gone underground, planning militant action and targeting prominent members of the authorities. It was to these small groups of close-knit radical Italians that she shipped packages, slipping from city to city and from safe house to safe house without detection. She was paid, in cash, on the completion of the job. Maybe, she told herself, if she had the money she would find a way. Maybe someone in the new government would see sense and overturn the Okhranka's sentence.

Out on the bay the lights from fishing boats threw yellow ribbons on to the black surface of the water. A couple of curlews glided effortlessly on a warm thermal above. A gust of cool air blew and large drops of rain began to fall on her face, on her shoulders and on the newspaper, turning the words, the image of the tsar, transparent. She rapidly handed it back to the man with the cigarette.

He glanced down at the story she had been reading.

'Dirty business,' he said. 'Those Reds are a motley lot of murdering barbarians. And what's more, they're over here, thousands of them.'

'Really,' she replied.

'Ship 'em all back,' he went on. 'Deport the lot of them! Where you from? Sweden?'

She nodded.

'I knew it,' he said, taking one last drag of his cigarette. He threw the stub out and over the railing and watched as it hit the tracks in a shower of red sparks.

'Say,' he said. 'May I invite you to the dining car for a cool beverage?'

He turned but the door to the observation platform was already closing. Through the haze of the lace he watched as she made her way back to her seat.

A single policeman was on duty at Broad Street Station in Philadelphia when the train arrived from Baltimore. He saw nobody suspicious climb off the train but then he wasn't really looking. By the time the police department in Baltimore had drawn up a description, Anna Denisova was already on board a commuter train chuntering through New Jersey, the distant darkened towers of Manhattan growing larger by the minute.

26

The suit was made of black serge with a fine white stripe. Like Pokolitov's, it was cut from the finest wool the tailor had in stock, 'wedding cloth,' as he put it. With white dress shirts, starched collars and straw boaters, together they looked like a couple of swells, a pair of gamblers or, at a push, speculators in gold or oil.

'Just have to stitch the left leg trouser hem,' the tailor said. 'Just one more minute.'

His voice was muffled by a white cotton mask. It covered his nose, his mouth, his whiskers and his chin. Only his large bespectacled eyes were visible. Around his sleeve was a black armband.

'My wife,' the tailor said when he noticed Monroe's eyes linger upon it. 'Died last Tuesday.'

'The Spanish flu?' Monroe offered. 'My condolences.'

'Much appreciated,' he replied. 'My daughter and all her children have come down with it too. May God have mercy.'

The Spanish flu epidemic had come, or so it seemed at the time, from nowhere. It was mid-September, and tens of thousands of people in New York had caught the disease and fallen sick. From New York it had spread rapidly from state to state until it was officially recognized as a pandemic. In Manhattan, the morgues couldn't cope, the city's orphanages were full, and, to cut the risk of transmission, theatres, schools, taverns and churches had all been closed. Those who had no choice but to work outside – tramcar conductors and police officers, postmen and newspaper sellers – wore wide cotton face masks made of two layers of gauze folded over and tied behind the head. Spitters, coughers and sneezers could be arrested and fined. The city, usually so noisy and colourful, seemed inhabited by the light step and the white faces of a population of tentative ghosts.

That autumn, a cool dusty wind blew in from the west, covering everything with a fine layer of ash. Despite the cold weather, all the windows on trains or tramcars were permanently wedged open to let fresh air circulate. Everyone buttoned up but sweated inside their heavy winter coats; their eyes blinked with grit and their newspapers flapped and ripped in the draught. The news was always bad. American casualties in Europe were the heaviest yet. The Germans seemed to be on the point of stalling, on the point of surrender, but still they fought on. A mailboat, the RMS *Leinster*, had been torpedoed on the Irish Sea and over five hundred passengers, many of them American servicemen, women and children, had drowned. But popular music, if you wanted to play it in your parlour or buy a roll for your Pianola, was still unflinchingly upbeat. Ballads and patriotic songs such as 'Hunting the Hun' and 'If He Can Fight Like He Can Love' filled every dime store window and were being played in saloons, hotel lobbies and Sunday gatherings all over America, elevating the fervour of those women who waited into an indomitable force, and rousing passions if they were still strong or fit enough to be roused.

Monroe hadn't caught Spanish flu, but Pokolitov had. Overnight his throat had begun to swell, his body ached, his brow burned with fever and his lungs filled with fluid. Monroe had tried to call a doctor but Pokolitov had stopped him. They were all busy or sick, anyway; the hospitals were full and had run out of beds. And so Monroe had nursed the Georgian with wet poultices, cool tea and boiled rice. At one point in the middle of the third night, Pokolitov had called out for him. He was feverish but still lucid, and slowly, with cracked lips, he had spelled something out, word by word.

'I don't speak Georgian,' Monroe had explained. 'I'm sorry.'

In response, Pokolitov took his hand and held it until he fell asleep.

'Don't worry,' Monroe said. 'You're going to get better.'

Unlike so many others, Pokolitov did recover. And a week later, he was more grateful than Monroe believed his help had warranted.

'I owe you my life, little brother,' he had said as he recuperated.

'Anyone in my position would have done the same,' Monroe replied.

'No,' he said. 'They would not. If I have learned anything in my life it is this: I look after myself. No one else is going to. And friends like you are few and far between. Now go downstairs and play me one of your songs.'

The rented townhouse on Tenth Street had been taken furnished. It belonged to a woman who had recently moved to Westchester. The parlour, where the piano had been placed, was decorated in shades of lilac and the bedrooms in purple with red lampshades. Paintings of lush women in large hats decorated with flowers, silk flower arrangements and heavy glass paperweights inlaid with floral designs covered every wall and every surface. Pokolitov, although he had a tendency to catch the corner of his coat or his elbow on anything that wasn't nailed down, loved them. He would pick up a paperweight carefully and trace the lines and loops of the petals inside.

The first time Monroe sat down at the piano and started to play, he raced through the songs he knew, songs that he had once been paid to plug, playing them in chronological order until he reached his own song, 'The Sweetest Time'. And there he stopped.

He was still no closer to seeing Inez. He had written her dozens of letters but hadn't posted a single one. What kind of trouble would they have landed her in? Twice he had gone to her apartment and was on the point of instructing the doorman to tell her he was outside when he changed his mind. Maybe it wasn't such a good idea. There must be another way to reach her, he told himself, he just hadn't found it yet.

But even if he could see her again, he was beginning to wonder what he could offer her. His old life was gone, he could never work again, at least not in his former job on Tin Pan Alley. There were too many people who knew him and what he had done, and although he doubted whether they would report him, it was still a risk he couldn't take. Plus, he had begun to see America and the way it operated in a different light. It was true what the socialists said: the war had not only made the industrialists who traded in weapons, transport and canned goods millions, it had brought a huge amount of money into the American economy. No wonder they had joined the war: to prolong it. And Inez was married to a man who represented everything he had now come to despise. With his foot on the sustain pedal Monroe started to play Beethoven's 'Für Elise'.

'No more!' Pokolitov called out when he had played the piece three times over. 'How about a Georgian song? Or a Russian song? Or an American song?'

Monroe placed his hands on the piano and, for Pokolitov's sake, started to play 'Yome Yome', an old Yiddish folk song. And then he shifted the rhythm, he gave it syncopation, he added another melody which he laid over the original. He remembered another time, a time when everything had seemed deceptively simple. And then without even trying, the words came.

'I like that,' called Pokolitov. 'Where is Amagansett?'

'Long Island,' he replied.

'And why did you never play this before?' Pokolitov asked.

'Because I only just wrote it,' Monroe answered.

Von Hofe was waiting in the basement café of Bertolotti's on Third Street in Greenwich Village with a half-eaten *zabaione* on the table in front of him. Monroe Simonov, a song-plugger who had surprised them all by writing a tune that had sold several hundred thousand copies, was a strange fish. He could have sat out the war in relative comfort, composing songs for the army. And if that wasn't enough, several Broadway producers had been keen to hear anything he might care to write and indeed had come to hear him play that day in January.

And yet he had skipped out, he had deserted, flunking out of a career that was just about to spark and take off. In spring, he had heard was that Simonov was living in squalor in Mexico and, if the reports were correct, playing for tips in a bordello. A week earlier, however, he had received a letter from Monroe himself, with a New York postmark, requesting a meeting. Von Hofe was an American citizen second and a businessman first. He blocked off an hour and informed his secretary that he had a dentist's appointment.

Although it was early summer, Monroe Simonov was dressed like every other young man of modest means in New York City, in a dark suit that had seen better days, a pair of boots that could have done with a polish and a faded black felt derby. But the thick scrub of a beard made him look older, more foreign. And there was something new in his manner, a restlessness, a dart in the movement of his eyes that suggested an inability to relax.

'Don't worry,' Von Hofe said softly, 'no one will see us here. Why would anyone notice us when they can look at them?'

He nodded towards a table to the left where two women and two men, with their hair long and unkempt, their clothes 'artistic,' all large collars and shades of red and yellow, sat in a cloud of their own cigarette smoke and talked about poetry.

A fan circled slowly on the ceiling. The waiter brought them iced water and coffee without breaking off from an argument, in Italian, with the chef. A fly buzzed and settled on a jug of peonies. The light from outside, which filtered through windows above, was the colour of water, blue with pale green shadows.

Von Hofe pushed his cuffs back one by one along each forearm and leaned forward, his large eyes glazed with good humour.

'So,' he said. 'Why did you run out like that?'

Monroe sighed and pulled his face into a smile. 'I should have known that you never did start with the easy questions,' he replied. Like, 'How have you been?'

'Simonov, it's good to see you,' he said. 'But you want to tell me why we're here?'

Monroe laid the page of musical notation on the table and Von Hofe picked it up and read it. As he did so, Monroe watched his face, his eyes, his mouth, taking in every small twitch, every tiny sigh, every blink that he made. Finally the song publisher sat back. He looked about to speak but instead he reached forward and drank the dregs of his cold coffee.

'Of course I'd rather hear it,' he said. 'But even on the page, it's good.' He pulled out his wallet. 'Same deal as before?' he said and slapped five dollars on the table.

'It's not about the money,' replied Monroe.

'It's all about the money,' Von Hofe clarified and then he smiled. 'Look, son, I don't know what happened, although I can take a guess, a bad debt, a girl in trouble, a wife and kids you ran out on.'

'No . . .' began Monroe.

'Just take the money and buy yourself a new hat. Oh, and who'll I say wrote it? I don't suppose you'll want to be advertising the fact you're back in town.'

'Use the name Andrei,' said Monroe. 'Andrei Dreslov.'

'That's no kind of name for a songwriter,' he said and screwed up his face, 'but if you say so, kid, it's your call.' Von Hofe looked at his watch, rolled down his sleeves and called for the bill. 'I don't suppose you got an address?' he asked. 'Never mind. How about I send any correspondence to the Russian Club on Hester?'

'Sure! Send every letter to the Russian Club,' Monroe agreed. 'How long before you publish it?'

'That depends. But things are looking a little sparse in the next couple of weeks. Let me see what I can do.'

'Thank you,' said Monroe. 'I'd appreciate if it could be sooner rather than later.'

In response, Von Hofe simply inclined his head, pushed his own brand-new derby on to his head and headed towards the stairs to the street.

It was a far-fetched idea, he told himself, in fact, it was probably crazy. But it was the only way he could think of to reach her. Only she would know what the words meant, only she would understand the significance. And then, if she still felt anything, she would get in touch with Universal and they would tell her to write to him care of the Russian Club.

But how long would he wait? How long would he stay in New York? Living with Pokolitov was a temporary arrangement, and, although he would never voice it, Monroe sensed that his generosity was not entirely motivated by altruism. He never admitted where his money came from, although Monroe could make a fair guess that it came from Russia.

'I'll pay you back,' Monroe would say. 'Just as soon as I can.'

'No need,' Pokolitov would reply. 'You are my friend.' And he would look deeply into Monroe's eyes with that steel gaze as if it were a bright light, probing.

Monroe hadn't told him about selling the song; he wasn't entirely sure that he could trust him. First there was that business with Anna Denisova. And then there was the maid, who lived upstairs on the upper floors and had been kept on to keep house and prepare meals. Gradually her dresses had changed in colour and quality, from grey cotton to scarlet silk, and then Monroe began to hear her creeping out of Pokolitov's room in the early morning. The townhouse, however, became increasingly untidy and the meals sporadic, until, quite suddenly and without comment, she was gone and another maid, a surly old woman, originally from Minsk, was hired to replace her.

'Can't speak a word of English,' Pokolitov proclaimed in her favour. 'Even worse than me. What do you think? Shall we keep her?'

'It's your call,' replied Monroe.

Pokolitov tipped his head back and inhaled. His eyes slowly roamed over Monroe's face. 'Ah,' he said. 'You leave? When? Tomorrow? Where you go?'

'No,' Monroe said. 'I didn't say that. I'll stay, if that's all right with you.'

Pokolitov let the breath out, raised his eyebrows and gave his large head a little shake, as if there were someone else in the room, someone else who was listening and, what was more, thoroughly agreed with him.

'My friend,' Pokolitov said one day, 'I have a favour to ask you. I have business to do in America and my English is not good enough. I need a translator. Would you do this?'

'What kind of business?' Monroe asked.

'You will find out. Yes or no?'

'Well, Russian was my first language,' he replied. 'I suppose so.'

'Very good.' Pokolitov beamed. 'And I have another smaller request. I need to open some bank accounts, but as I am not a citizen it is difficult to arrange. Would you open them for me and use your name?'

Monroe hesitated.

'It would only be for a very short time,' Pokolitov went on. 'A few months. Who would know? I will pay for a box somewhere. All mail will be delivered there. It is essential for my business.'

'Just a few months?'

'They will be untraceable. You have my word. Just a small request . . .'

'Well,' Monroe replied, 'I guess so.'

'We start as soon as possible. But look at us. To do American business, we have to dress like American businessmen.'

The tailor brushed off a few streaks of chalk from the hem and inspected the lapels for lint. Monroe looked at himself in the glass. That morning he had had a wet shave and his hair had been trimmed and oiled. He wore polished tan-coloured boots that had been made for him by the shoemaker on Hester Street and a brand-new hat. He could hardly recognize himself; he felt transformed.

The outfit, however, didn't seem to have the same effect on Pokolitov. Even though his face was shaved and his shoes were shined, he wouldn't give up the battered carpet-bag that he always carried. Also there was something about him, drawn by the lines on his face, perhaps, or the shrug of his shoulders or the space between his teeth, that didn't change no matter what he wore. He still looked rough around the edges. He still smelled of tobacco and late nights.

'How much?' Pokolitov asked in Russian.

The tailor waved his hand. 'You pay me next time,' he said through a mouthful of pins.

Pokolitov smiled and thanked him. Monroe noticed that his hand had not even reached for his wallet. Although he always seemed to have pockets full of cash, he rarely paid for anything. At first Monroe had assumed it was because people liked him. But one night when his host was playing cards with a group of fellow Georgians he had heard a scream. Monroe rushed into the parlour to see what had happened. Pokolitov was calmly staring out of the window, smoking. A man was gasping for air in the corner, his hand wrapped in a shirt that was staining red. On the card table was a king of hearts. A single finger lay beside it.

'What happened?' Monroe asked.

Pokolitov shrugged. 'He cheated,' he replied.

It was a bright, clear autumn day. After they left the tailor's, they headed downtown. Pokolitov carried the carpet-bag in one hand and an umbrella with a couple of spokes missing in the other.

'So can I trust you?' said Pokolitov as they crossed Canal Street.

'Surely you know by now?' he replied.

'I think I can,' Pokolitov said. 'Excellent.'

'And where are we going?' Monroe asked.

'Wall Street,' he said as it started to rain.

The bank lobby was palatial, with a vaulted ceiling, heavy brass door handles, a pale marble floor and a dozen tellers all wearing face-masks stationed behind panes of engraved glass. Pokolitov carefully deposited his umbrella in the stand at the door and then cleaned his left ear with his little finger.

'Will you be so kind as to ask to see the manager?' he said.

The nearest teller was eyeing them sceptically.

'In a place like this—' Monroe began.

'Just ask!' interrupted Pokolitov. 'Tell them I want to deposit some gold.'

Pokolitov smiled broadly when the assistant manager eventually came out to greet them. Ten minutes later, they were sitting in his superior's office in two large leather armchairs.

'Now what do you want me to say?' asked Monroe. 'It was a great way to get in here but they'll need to see proof. And then they'll chuck us both straight back on the street again.'

Pokolitov laughed. Then he reached into his carpet-bag and pulled out a small gold bar. 'Take a look.' He threw it to Monroe.

It was heavy, much heavier than Monroe had expected, and was stamped with the double-headed eagle of the Russian Imperial Court. 'Where did you get this?' he asked.

But Pokolitov simply smiled and began to bite the hangnails from his fingers and flick them into the fireplace.

By the time they had visited Morgan's, City Bank and the Guaranty Trust, they had opened three new bank accounts in

Monroe's name and had been befriended three times with increasing enthusiasm.

'The pleasure's all mine,' the manager of Guaranty Trust had said. 'And if I can ever be of any assistance? Or if you'd just like to play a round of golf, or see a ball game . . . be my pleasure . . .'

As Monroe translated, he sensed Pokolitov start to blink more rapidly.

'Tell him that there is something,' he said. 'Very soon I shall be putting together a most interesting business proposal. Would he happen to know of any of his clients who are looking for investment possibilities in my home country?'

The bank manager cleared his throat and lowered his voice. 'Indeed I would,' he replied. 'And who exactly are you representing?'

'The new government,' Pokolitov replied. 'The Bolsheviks.'

'Very good,' the bank manager said. 'As soon as you come up with the proposal, I would like to insist that you come here first. It has been a pleasure. Now can I call you a cab?'

As Pokolitov listened to Monroe's translation, his smile grew wide and wider still. He turned down the offer of a cab and motioned that he would rather walk. As he left, he stopped at the umbrella stand and extracted a leather-handled, silk umbrella with silver-plated fittings. Outside, the rain had stopped.

27

On election day, 5 November 1918, the winter sky was heavy with rain clouds. Downtown a thin mist enveloped the upper floors and narrow spires of the Woolworth, the Singer, and the twin domes of the Park Row Buildings. Across the Hudson, New Jersey had dissolved, a blur of black ink on wet paper. Even the frigid air, so often churned and shaken by the friction of a million lives unfolding, seemed to have stilled.

Inez bundled Luella up in a coat, a scarf and a hat, put her in her pram and waited in the lobby for Ivory. In Central Park a couple of horseback riders trotted up the Mall on their way to Cleopatra's Needle. Outside the entrance, half a dozen motorized park carriages idled, their engines clouding the air with thin grey smoke. But there were few people willing to pay twenty-five cents for a tour of the park or take a light refreshment at the Dairy at the foot of the Terrace Steps. Everyone who ventured out on to the streets walked with a purposeful click. And below the buzz of traffic and the rumble of the elevated train came the tinny high-pitched whine of the loudspeaker.

Finally Ivory arrived from his campaign office across town and they walked a couple of blocks to the nearest polling place, a candy store on Amsterdam Avenue. All over the city, barbers and tailors, kindergartens and schools, candy stores and undertakers had been designated as polling places. In twenty-three assembly districts, every New Yorker who had registered could vote for a governor, a secretary of state and could elect forty-three representatives to Congress.

It was impossible to see the jars of peppermint humbugs and preserved fruit in the window of the Crawfurd's Dry Goods and Candy store. A huge queue of people – women with little dogs, matrons with white sashes and large hats, men with their hands in their pockets and pipes in their mouths – patiently waited in line outside. On the kerb a solitary man in a long coat with a velvet collar held up a banner with the words, 'Opposed to Women's Suffrage' written on it.

It seemed, however, that the suffragettes had already won. In the west, state by state, from Utah and Colorado, women were being granted the vote, and Montana had become the first state to elect a woman to Congress. Two months earlier, President Wilson had urged the Senate to pass a constitutional amendment that would grant women suffrage all over America. Athough it was a few votes short of being passed, it was clear that it was only a matter of time. New York had given women the vote a year earlier, but only those over thirty.

As well as a dozen canvassers for the Democrats, the Republicans, the Prohibitionists and the Socialists, a handful of newspapermen and photographers were positioned outside the candy store with their cameras raised.

'Why don't I just wait here with Luella?' Inez suggested at the corner of the block.

Ivory sighed and his round face slid downwards a fraction. 'Do we have to discuss this again?' he said warily. 'I thought we had a deal.'

It still hung between them, that day in July when Inez had gone to the music publisher and Ivory had followed her. As they had returned home in silence in Ivory's car, Inez had caught sight of her face, her eyes, her mouth in the reflection of the window. And yes, it was there already, all the lies and longing, all the regret and anger, all the disappointment and inertia, visible in the tiny creases at either corner of her mouth.

'You should get back to the parade,' she had said. 'You'll miss your spot.'

'I don't give damn about the parade,' he replied.

The car began to slow as it approached the apartment. Inez turned to her husband and looked him in the eye for the first time that day.

'Let's drive somewhere,' she had said. 'We need to talk.'

And so they had turned around, driven down to Battery and parked beneath the elevated railway. As the trains passed overhead and the sea lions barked in the aquarium, as Ivory's driver sat and smoked on a bench in the park, they agreed to tell each other the truth.

'I know,' he had said. 'I knew the first moment I saw her.'

They sat for a moment and each stared out at the chop of the bay and the stretch of Lady Liberty without actually seeing either. He had known about Luella for all this time and he hadn't said anything. Inez found it almost impossible to comprehend.

'But you see,' Ivory began, 'I've grown to . . . she's like my own, even though . . . she's clearly not.'

And Ivory Price, who thought he looked the same, but wasn't really, slowly, hesitantly, in statements and retractions, in anecdotes and muddled facts, admitted for the first time to anyone, anywhere, that he had been with another woman the night of the shooting. And what was more, there had been others.

'I see,' Inez had said eventually and turned away from him a fraction.

Outside, a gull rode on the breeze, wheeling and circling and finally hanging motionless. The driver stamped out his cigarette and lit another.

'So what shall we do?' she had asked him.

'Stay with me,' Ivory Price had said softly. 'I'll be a good husband. I'll love the baby like my own. I need you, Inez, not only, and this may sound shallow but is not intended to, not only for my politcal career but also . . . for myself. I love you. In fact I love you more every day. Let me be enough for you.'

Inez had looked at him, with his soft face and one eye that watered with the intensity of his own words. 'I'm sorry,' she had said simply. 'I can't.'

Ivory's shoulders had risen and fallen, risen and fallen. He took both her hands in his and held them so tightly that they began to hurt.

'I'm here. He isn't,' he had stated. 'And I need you, Luella needs you. Come back to us, Inez. I promise, I swear to you that I'll never, never go with another woman again.'

'And what if you do?'

'Then the deal's null and void.'

'And what if he comes looking for me?'

For a moment, the calm, collected, caring manner he had worked so hard to maintain fell. His reply was curt and not a little callous. 'He hasn't so far, has he?'

He let the comment, with all its spores of doubt, settle.

'Please, Inez – in my house, in my bed, in my life – be my wife again?'

On Amsterdam Avenue, the newspapermen saw the Price family hesitate on the corner on polling day. And so they picked up their bags, pulled the lens caps from their cameras, opened their notebooks and rushed towards them.

'Mrs Price,' one of them called out. 'Do you think your husband's going to win a seat?'

'Are the Republicans going to win this city?'

'Aren't you out on the campaign trail, Captain Price?'

Ivory turned to face them, smiled broadly and cleared his throat. Then he pulled out a speech that he had written earlier.

'If I may? I have two words for you to remember,' he said. 'Prosperity and stability. A vote for me will mean a vote for these fundamental necessities. If I get into office I vow to seek out and destroy any persons or organizations that oppose these principles. No tolerance for enemy aliens, subversive organizations or undesirables. Once the Germans have been defeated, we need to take on a more pressing adversary, the enemy within. I urge you all to fight the right fight with me, Ivory Price.'

The Republican canvassers, right on cue, burst into a polite smattering of applause.

'Are you a Wet or a Dry?' a journalist called out.

'A Dry most certainly,' he replied. 'I back Prohibition most wholeheartedly.'

'And what do you think of women's suffrage?'

He grinned but didn't comment.

'Mrs Price. What do you think?'

'It's about time,' she said.

Ivory's smile froze. 'Anyway,' he said. 'We have a moment, I think, for a photograph. Make it quick, fellas.'

With his patch over one eye and his walking stick, Price was instantly recognizable. He made it his policy always to stop for a photograph if a newpaperman asked him. And it had paid dividends. He had become one of the most famous, one of the most often profiled candidates up for election.

As the newpapermen hoisted their cameras on to their shoulders or repositioned their tripods, Ivory put his arm around his lovely wife's waist and held a smile. Half a dozen flashbulbs went off. Luella, startled by the light, began to cry. Inez picked her out of her pram, carried her inside the candy store and bought her a peppermint cane. The store owner, once he had handed her her change, went back to tearing off ballot papers. One by one he passed them out to voters after his daughter had scored out their name from a list.

'Keep seeing your husband's face in the paper,' the candy store owner told Inez. 'Yours too.'

'Not for much longer, hopefully,' she replied.

'But you look different in the flesh. Younger. Prettier.'

'Well, thank goodnesss for that. When did you open up?'

'Eight,' he answered. 'Even though it's gonna rain, I think there's going to be a good turnout. No one's falling sick any more.'

Over the last few weeks, the face-masks had come off. First their effectiveness was being called into question; it didn't seem to make any difference whether you wore one or not. And second, the Spanish flu in New York seemed to be on the wane. For the last two months Ivory had insisted that Inez stay indoors. She had often ignored him and taken Luella out for a walk in Central Park. I won't go near sneezers, she had assured him. We'll be fine.

And they were. Neither of them had caught it.

A space had been cleared on the counter and a pencil on a string hung from a hook. The counter's surface, its grooves and scores, were sparkled with a residue of sugar and yellow and orange sherbet. Two people, a man and a woman, were hesitating over their ballot papers.

Ivory was still out on the pavement, giving quotes to the newspapermen. He looked as if he would be some time.

'Can I see a ballot paper?' Inez asked the candy store owner. 'I've never seen one before.'

The candy store owner hesitated for an instant. 'It's not strictly allowed,' he said. 'But I suppose . . .' He tore one off, wrote 'spoiled' in large letters across it and then handed it to her.

Each candidate's name had a symbol beside it, an eagle for a Republican and a star for a Democrat. Ivory's name was in the last section, for election to the House of Representatives.

She felt the sudden pressure of a hand around her waist and turned.

'I'm afraid, Mrs Price,' Ivory announced, 'you're still too young to vote. But I'll buy you some candies if you like.'

The candy store owner smiled politely. A woman in the white sash of the suffragettes clicked her tongue in disapproval.

'Hope you don't mind me barging in like this,' Ivory said as he made his way to the front of the queue. Nobody objected, at least not publicly, and so, after his name was scored out, he took his ballot paper, rapidly marked it up with the pencil and posted it into the box.

'I hope I can count on your vote,' he announced to everyone. 'And if not, may the best man win. I'm much obliged to you all. Right. Must be off. Time to get back on the campaign trail.'

His car and driver were waiting for him across the street. Ivory nodded goodbye to the newspapermen and awkwardly climbed into the passenger seat. Inez watched as the car moved off, swung out into the traffic and headed down towards Columbus Circle and Fifty-Seventh Street.

Ivory was elected with a small majority. Although the mayor of New York, Al Smith, was a Democrat, the Republicans won both the House and the Senate. The election was, however, overshadowed by the news from Europe. In the early morning of 11

November, church bells all over New York began to ring. An armistice had been signed. The Great War was over.

In spring, the soldiers began to return from France, each division marching the length of Manhattan, their heads held high, the air above them filled with the flap of stars and stripes. Luella loved the victory parades and Ivory would take her and Mrs O'Leary with him when he took his place on the Republican Party's official Welcome Home stand.

It was here that Ivory met the widow of a former member of Congress. Ellen Finlay was twenty-two, an outspoken Prohibitionist who had just returned from France where she had spent six months making doughnuts for the troops at the front with the Salvation Army. Her husband was twenty years her senior but he had tragically been killed a week after the armistice in a road accident just outside Nantes. He had left her well-provided for, however, with a large fortune and a mansion on Riverside Drive.

As the soldiers filed by, she had dabbed her blue eyes with a handkerchief that Ivory had offered, pushed her soft blonde hair back under her hat and begun to tell him her life story. Halfway through the parade Mrs O'Leary declared she would walk home with Luella for a breath of air. Ivory told her he wouldn't be more than ten minutes behind her and yet he stayed on that stand long after the last soldiers had marched past and still Ellen Finlay was no further than her sixth birthday. Eventually, Ivory offered to drive her back to her mansion, and in between listing the names of all her ponies, in chronological order, she accepted. It was only when he kissed her, later, over a cup of English tea that she had brought all the way back from a shop in London, that she finally stopped talking and stared at him.

'I don't think you should have done that,' she said.

Ivory felt a rush from his heart to his face. She was right. He shouldn't have. After what had happened with Anna Denisova, he had sworn to himself that he would stop. And what was more he had his wife, to whom he had promised to be faithful. Yet, at that particular moment, just the thought of Inez made him flush with anger. What did he have to do to win her? Hadn't he given her everything? Hadn't he proved himself to her? Despite his injury, he was a success, a public figure, a successful businessman, and still she pushed him away.

Slowly, as he had recovered, she had begun to fall apart. He had watched her red hair fade, her skin grow pale, her body once so taut, her arms and legs so long and lean, begin to hang and drop as if they were weighed down with lead. Only a week before he had opened the liquor cabinet to pour himself a brandy and had discovered a new bottle of a brandy he hadn't ordered in the place of the old one. What was more, it was almost empty. And in some ways he was glad; he was relieved. If he couldn't be happy then neither should she.

Maybe, he considered briefly, she drank because she knew the state of his finances. Although it was unlikely that she had examined his bank statements, the campaign had cost four times what he had expected. Although Inez's inheritance had kept the company solvent and he had made a significant amount during the war, it wasn't enough to keep him living in the manner to which he was accustomed. Until he had made some clever investments or acted on some insider tips, his future prosperity was in question.

The one thing he was sure of, however, was that Inez's sordid little affair was over. That day in the car, he had informed her in no uncertain terms that if the piano player ever came anywhere near her, or if she made any attempt to contact him, he would have him thrown in prison and he would throw both her and the child on to the street. To his surprise she hadn't raised an objection, she hadn't sobbed and cried the way she used to. She had just nodded her head and begun to bite the ragged edges of her nails.

A cloud of blossom floated down from an apple tree outside the window of the mansion on Riverside Drive. Ivory raised his china cup to his mouth and took a sip. The tea was cold and tasted faintly of wet socks. He knew he should leave. His driver was waiting. Before he could rise and make his excuses, Ellen Finlay took the cup from his hands and placed it on one of a dozen small tables that were artfully arranged around the room, smoothed down her dress, took his face in her hands and kissed it.

'I'm no adulteress,' she whispered. 'I'm just bereaved.'

*

Inez stared out at the windsock on the runway and watched it snap and flap, snap and flap in a slow but regular rhythm. Out here in the office on the runway at Keyport, the high whine of the saw and the rumble of engines were barely audible. So the slap of the windsock in the wind was all there was, that and the tune in her head.

When she had first heard Ivory play 'Dancing with My Girl on the Amagansett Sands' on his Pianola, she was certain of two things: that Monroe had written it for her and that it would only be a matter of time before they would see each other again. But as the days and weeks rolled past, as the seasons chilled the air and then heated it back up again, the certainty she once felt had slowly faded. Maybe the song had been written by someone else. Maybe their experience had been duplicated by another couple who had their own love affair. But when she read the lyrics, which she kept folded up in a book beside her bed, she could not believe that was true.

Manhattan was full of returning soldiers, men who had lost any reserve they once had in French brothels, and who now spent their days lavishing their affection on the girls they left behind. And once or twice when she had caught sight of a shoulder in khaki or the back of a head in a campaign hat, and just for a moment she was so sure it was him, she had to take a deep breath and tell herself, no, no, it couldn't possibly be, he had deserted, he was no longer a soldier. And sure enough when the men felt the hot penetration of her eyes on the back of their necks and turned and glanced behind, she would see that it was not him at all but someone else entirely.

Keyport was her escape; twice a week she made the trip to the factory to bury herself in invoices and payslips, rotas and order books. A row of planes juddered in the sea wind on the small over-grown runway, their propellers gently spinning and the canvas of their wings straining on their struts. Price Aero had produced only a fraction of what it had been contracted to manufacture. But they were not the only aviation company that had been held up as they waited for their delivery of Liberty engines, the sole engine the War Department had authorized. Although thousands of training planes had now been delivered, only one reached France before the end of the war.

The workforce was slowly being reduced to its original size, and as the men came back from the war to fill their jobs, one by one the women were let go. Inez was sad to see them leave. They sang as they worked, they were honest and cheerful. A dozen had died in the flu epidemic and funds had been set up for their children. Inez was astonished at how much the workers donated; it was more, much more than each could possibly afford. Against the manager's advice, she had kept on three women, women who had extra dependants or had lost husbands at the front, as 'field workers'.

With the men's return, however, came a change of mood. The war had had a sobering effect on them; they saw their lives, their jobs, their futures in a different way. Also, prices had soared. Last week a dozen men and the three female field workers had come to her office and asked for a rise in wages and a shorter working day. Without consultation with the manager or with her husband, she had agreed.

Ivory rarely came out to the factory any more and did most of his business in his office in Manhattan or by telephone. Every evening he talked for hours about Red infiltration on the factory floor and the threat of Communism to the American way of life. General strikes had broken out all over America, halting production and stemming supplies. And so when the phone rang, Inez's hand hovered over the receiver for a moment before she answered it. He would be calling to override her, to overturn her decision, to inform her that she had no authority, no right and what was more that she had absolutely no place being out in Keyport at all. Maybe, she considered, she should let it ring. Maybe she should ignore it. But that would only postpone the inevitable. And so she took a deep breath and picked it up.

'Good afternoon,' she said.

'Call from Manhattan,' said the operator.

The line clicked but no one spoke. Her heart started to pound.

'Hello,' she said. 'Hello? It's a bad line. You'll have to speak up.'

Somewhere in Manhattan, a throat was cleared. 'I'm sorry,' said a woman. 'I think I have the wrong number. I'm looking for a Mr Ivory Price.'

'Who's calling?'

'Who? Just a friend,' the woman answered but wouldn't give her name.

Inez gave the caller her husband's office number and hung up. It was only after she had poured herself a brandy to steady her nerves that she thought about the call, about the way that the woman said her husband's name, in a breath, as if in a whisper in an ear. Inez stared at the palm that had held the receiver as if it held some sort of clue and then swallowed the brandy in one fiery mouthful. There it was, clear as day. Ivory had another woman again. All promises, all assurances, all those pledges had been broken. She was free to do whatever she liked.

The Russian Jewish market was closed on Saturday and only a few hawkers of potato *knishes* and *rugelach* pastries sat on the kerb or perched on stools beside their carts. Inez passed tailors, shoemakers and Abraham Stern's Russian bathhouse before she reached the Russian Club. She rang the bell. No one came and so, tentatively, she pushed the door open and stepped inside.

A board in the corridor was covered in notices written in the Cyrillic alphabet. The walls were painted brown and the tiles on the floor were cracked and dirty. A light hung from the ceiling, its shade a glass dish spotted with a dozen dead flies. From the basement came the sour smell of boiling meat and cabbage. Inez stood for a moment and listened. Apart from the clatter of pans in the kitchen, the lull and swell of voices came from a room on the left. She knocked twice and then opened the door.

The room was huge and hung with red flags and bunting. A samovar steamed in the corner and on every surface ashtrays overflowed with spent cigarettes. A group of men were playing cards around a small table. They turned at the heavy slam of the door and the man nearest rose to his feet and said something in Russian.

'I'm sorry . . . no one came. I'd like to leave a letter,' she said. 'For Andrei Dreslov.'

The Russian on his feet looked around the table and then shrugged. The card players shook their heads.

'We do not know a man by this name,' he said.

Inez blinked and began to fiddle with her gloves. 'I was told . . .' she began.

'If you would like to leave it here,' the man said. 'And if he happens to come here, it will be delivered. May I pass on your name?'

It sounded such an innocent request that for a moment she was speechless. What excuse could she give? She could think of none.

'It's Inez,' she said.

The Russian smiled and cocked his head to the side. 'Inez,' he said. 'Pretty name. Could it have been that I have seen your face in the newspaper?'

'No,' she replied. 'I don't think so.'

'I think so. I have a good memory for faces. You are the wife of . . . let me see now,' he said.

Inez took a deep breath and closed her eyes. 'Ivory Price,' she said. 'I'm Mrs Ivory Price.'

'Ah yes,' he replied. 'The man who makes aeroplanes and stood for election.'

Inez pushed the letter back into her bag. She couldn't leave it now. 'Good day,' she said and turned to go.

'Wait! If Mr Dreslov does reveal himself, what message shall I pass on?'

'Oh, nothing,' she answered. 'It's just . . . just a fund-raising issue.'

'You are looking for donations?'

'Always,' she said.

'For whom do you collect?'

Her mind went blank for an instant in the bright gaze of the man's eyes. She opened her mouth and said the first thing that came into her head. 'The Brooklyn Hebrew Orphan Asylum,' she pronounced. 'In fact, I'm on my way over there now.'

The Russian delved into his pocket and pulled out twenty dollars. 'May I?' he said.

After the smallest of hesitations, she took his money, tucked it into an envelope, pulled out a notebook from her purse and wrote out a chit.

'The flu epidemic,' she said as an explanation.

'Indeed,' he said. 'I shall look for Mr Dreslov. And if I find him, may I let him know how he may contact you?'

Inez swallowed twice, turned the chit over and wrote the telephone number of a diner on Fifty-Seventh Street that she had memorized. Underneath she wrote the words, Mondays 3 p.m.

Before she left, she looked up and caught sight of the piano in the corner. 'He plays,' she said. 'That's how . . . we know each other.'

The Russian smiled, revealing a large gap between his front teeth. But in his eyes there was a tiny glimmer, so small that Inez almost missed it, the minute sparkle of a sudden realization.

'A pleasure, Mrs Price,' he said with a low bow, as he held the door open so she could pass through unhindered. 'Good luck to you and your husband.'

28

A letter was waiting for Anna at the Manhattan General Post Office. The envelope was smudged with several sooty finger-prints and a few spots of grease, as if it had been lying around for a week or two on the desk of a regional official, or had been stuffed in the pocket of a greatcoat and then forgotten. Her name, the box number and the address of the post office, the contact address in America she had passed on so long ago, were written in a hand she didn't recognize.

Anna did not open the letter immediately, not there in the post office with its lines of people in queues for money orders or regis-tered letters and its pair of policemen at the door, not there with her hands trembling and her heart beating too fast. She turned, walked out through the main doors, crossed the street and headed into the City Hall Park. In the shade of the Hall of Records, she found an empty bench and sat down.

At first she held the letter to her face and just inhaled. Even though it had travelled thousands of miles, it still smelled of Russia: a sweet, almond smell, the smell of the sap of birch trees, the smell of summer sunshine on bare brown skin. In City Hall Park, a girl of about seven ran past and hid behind a statue. A man, her father, she assumed, strolled past, and then, pretending he hadn't seen her, walked on. As Anna watched, the girl's face fell and she looked as if she were about to cry. Anna felt a rise in her throat. It was just a game, she told herself, the father wasn't going to walk on, to leave the child behind for ever. Very soon he would turn and pretend to spot her and the game would resume. Anna closed her eyes and looked down at the letter again. Did she know what was coming? Later, she supposed she must have done.

As the sun dappled through the leaves on the tree, the world seemed benign. Birds sang, children played and the peanut seller on the corner turned the hot nuts in the sticky brown sugar. But then she slid her little finger underneath the flap of the envelope and very slowly she tore it open.

The letter came from a man called Sergei, that was all, no other name. Written on coarse paper in blue ink, it covered both sides of two pages. Her eyes scanned it quickly; the handwriting was accomplished and the tone was formal. A few words stood out – 'regret', 'unfortunately', 'brave' – but the rest was a blur. She forced herself to focus, to ignore the way her hands shook; she found the beginning of the letter and began to read.

Sergei had known Kima for three years. They had been officers in the same regiment at the front together, and while hundreds around them had died on the battlefield or of typhus, they had both survived. After the war they had returned to Petrograd together. When the Bolsheviks had seized power and Kima had joined the Greens, he had been sent to lead an uprising against the Red Army in a town sixty miles north of Leningrad. A tip-off had been given and the plot had been uncovered by the Cheka, the secret police, and the houses where Kima and thirty others had been living had been raided. The peasants who had put them up were shot one by one until the Greens gave themselves up. Kima was one of ten who came out of the woods where he had been hiding. He was taken to prison and held for three months. And then, by order of the Politburo Committee, Kima had been singled out and tortured. He regretted to inform her . . .

A cloud covered the sun. Anna ran her finger over the words as if they might disappear, as if the ink were merely a figment of her imagination, a legible nightmare.

How could it be that she had lived for so long in ignorance that her little boy was suffering? How could it be? How could it be that he was dead? How could it be that life carried on, that the world kept turning, regardless, indifferent to the fact that she would never kiss his cheek or hold him in her arms again? Had they tortured and killed him because of what she had done, or been accused of doing here, in America? And she suddenly felt plunged into emptiness. For months she had been constantly on the move, from a borrowed divan in Queens to a basement room in the Lower East Side and from an attic in Harlem to a small hotel room in the Bronx. Kima was her home, Kima was the future; now she had neither. She was stateless, rootless, lost. A sob caught in her throat, her chest began to burn, a cough rose inside to hollow her out, to tear at her lungs.

The letter began to blur before her eyes, the ink hit by the splash and blur of a sudden summer rain shower. And as the words blotched and ran, she read the final sentence.

'The final order came from Trotsky,' Sergei wrote. 'Based on information about you that had been wired from America.'

George du Blanc was on his way home from the Metropolitan Hospital on Blackwell's Island, where he worked as a doctor, when it started to rain. A pessimist by nature, he always carried an umbrella, no matter what the season. It was when he shook out the silk and pushed the lever until the spokes were taut that he caught sight of a woman doubled over on the bench, coughing, with a small white handkerchief covering her mouth. All the other people who had been strolling through the park or sitting on the benches had rushed to find shelter on the steps of the General Post Office or under the overhang of the newspaper kiosk, everybody else but her.

Although she was without a pram or a beau or a small child to watch, the woman was too well dressed, the doctor deduced, to be a derelict or a streetwalker. His mother had loved expensive clothes, and under her instruction he had learned the difference between factory and hand-made lace. The lace on her handkerchief, he could tell at three paces, was the latter.

The woman seemed unaware of the weather; her hair was plastered flat and her dress had been darkened a shade or two by the rain, and still she coughed. It seemed ungentlemanly, uncharitable, to walk past, to leave the woman to the elements while she was so clearly in a compromised state. Du Blanc paused for a moment, cleared his throat, and then he approached her.

'Madam,' he said, holding the umbrella over her head, 'I hope you won't think me too forward but may I offer you a little shelter?'

Anna glanced up quickly at the man whose sudden presence had stopped the rain, but found she was unable to remember a single word of English. He took this as an acceptance and, after placing the day's newspaper on the bench, sat down beside her.

'I'm sure it's only a passing shower,' he said.

As they sheltered under his umbrella, the woman's cough gradually subsided. And then she sat completely still and stared ahead, while her small hands, bare of gold and folded round a piece of paper, lay motionless in her lap. The doctor glanced down at her; the back of her neck was exposed and he felt a sudden wave of unexpected desire that he couldn't immediately own up to.

The rain kept falling; it pooled in puddles beneath their feet and it swirled along the gutters and down the wide-open mouths of the drains. And although there were at least six inches between them and their respectability was still intact, the doctor realized that the situation, the rain, the umbrella sheltering just enough space for the two of them, had created an intimacy that had not been his specific intention.

Anna's breath came more evenly now. The Bolsheviks. The Bolsheviks had done this. Trotsky, a man whom she had once trusted, a man whose own child she had brought back to him, had murdered her son. And what had been wired about her from America? She would not take this without a fight. She would not. Whoever had done this would pay dearly for it.

It was, just as George du Blanc had predicted, a passing shower. After fifteen minutes, the rain stopped, the birds started to sing once more and the air was filled with the earthy smell of rain on a city pavement. Neither, however, spoke a word or made a move, and they sat motionless under the umbrella as the sun came out and the shadows grew long. Finally, as the daylight began to fade, she opened her hand. In her palm was what was left of a crumpled letter. The ink had stained her fingers blue.

George du Blanc was forty-two. He had been born into a family of wealthy Jewish diamond dealers. Against his father's wishes, he had studied medicine rather than join the family business and had dedicated his life to providing medical treatment for the poor, rather than precious gems for the rich. A woman with whom he had once been in love, a woman whom he had taken out five times to the opera and for dinner and presented with gifts bought at cost price from his father's shop, had laughed when he had proposed marriage on the sixth date, and told him that apart from the fact she hardly knew him, he didn't look as if there was much worth discovering. The woman had married his second cousin in a large, extravagant wedding that he hadn't been invited to. Shortly after, he had given up his share of the family fortune to his younger brother who, with five children and a gambling problem needed the money, and he had become a doctor in a charity hospital. He was still unmarried.

When the woman in the park turned and looked up at him and told him something in a language that he was unable to translate, although he was at a loss for words, he was put at ease. Something was seriously wrong with her. He could tell immediately by the flush in her cheek and the tears in her eyes. This gave her, however, the kind of feverish beauty that he understood. He had none of the easy fluency of a man of his background, and was a habitual stutterer in all matters relating to relationships with women. Instead he immediately switched to the one role that he felt comfortable with.

'You look flushed,' he said. 'Would you mind if I checked your pulse? I am a doctor.'

Her wrist was limp, her arm was floppy but her heart raced faster than the second hand of his Elgin pocket watch. As he listened to its beat, he was aware of the pale skin underneath his finger. It was so soft, so smooth, so white. Her hair was almost dry now and fell in unruly curls around her face, but her brow still glistened with sweat.

'I think,' du Blanc said in as even a tone as he could, 'that you should have a full examination. Just to rule a few things out. Do you understand?'

The woman nodded and then pushed a strand of her hair back underneath a pin. As she did so, the lace-edged handkerchief fell

318

out of her sleeve on to the damp grey gravel of the path. They both stared at it, at the spots of blood that patterned its creases like the tiny coloured droplets on the paisley shawl that his mother used to wear.

Great sorrow and great joy often seem to overlap. Babies are born a day or two after their grandparents die, good fortune such as a run of luck on the horses or an unexpected inheritance comes a heartbeat after terrible news such as the collapse of a mine or the admission of an infidelity, and love and loss become inextricably linked. The human heart, it seems, thrives on both extremes at once; we never feel more vital than in moments such as these. But these sudden peaks and unexpected troughs can have unforeseen consequences, launching us on to routes and paths we never thought we'd take.

When George du Blanc realized that the beautiful woman on the bench had all the signs of advanced TB, the desire he had felt was quickly superseded by devastation. And yet what was once sure to remain as an impulse never acted upon, a brief dalliance with a possible outcome that he would be too cautious to chase, now became an overwhelming compulsion. Tuberculosis was highly contagious, of course, but only from the sputum. He knew the prognosis, he knew her life expectancy was short. He knew he would lose her but that only made him want her more.

'Oh,' he said softly. 'I'm so very, very sorry.'

Anna Denisova turned and looked for the first time at the man with whom she had been sitting in close proximity. She had been aware of the weight of him on the wood of the bench beside her, his hand holding the umbrella and the pressure of his finger on her wrist, but she had not assembled him into a whole person.

The man with the umbrella was tall and gaunt with greying hair and a large nose. He was not handsome or stylishly dressed or in good physical shape, but there was something in his eyes, an openness, a kindness that shone through the slightly unfortunate arrangement of his face. And what was more, he was looking at her with such gentleness that she had to swallow down the lump that rose again in her throat, and look away.

'Why are you sorry?' she asked, her English finally returning.

319

He swallowed and scratched his whiskers. Didn't she know?

'This is not the appropriate setting for that particular conversation,' he began. 'Would you care to join me for a light supper?'

She glanced around at the park and shivered. Her legs felt weak, her body limp. The thought of climbing up the stairs to the elevated train and returning home alone with the weight of her wretchedness was too much to bear.

'I hope,' the man beside her stuttered, 'I hope you will not think of my offer as disrespectful? I am . . . a doctor. But if you would rather not. . .'

'No,' she answered softly, 'I would rather.'

He folded the umbrella, stood up and offered his arm. A motorized cab appeared and he hailed it. After he had helped her climb inside, he rushed back to the bench, pulled out a rubber glove from his briefcase and picked up the lace handkerchief. Then he wrapped it up as well as he could in newspaper, dropped it into a surgical sack and placed it in his bag for incineration at the hospital later. Once he had climbed back inside the cab, he gave an address in Murray Hill.

A bed was hastily made up in the spare room, should she care to rest a little, by the Polish woman who came every evening and cooked him dinner. A bath was run and a Chinese silk dressing gown, a gift he had never worn, was offered. Anna accepted everything without question. It seemed too much effort to refuse. Later, when she had bathed and had picked at a plate of food and was lying in bed with a cup of tea on the bedside table, he came to her room and knocked on the door.

'Please?' she said. 'Come in.'

'How are you?' he asked as he sat on the edge of the bed.

'I feel a little better,' she replied. 'Why are you doing this?'

He smiled and stared down at his hands. 'It's what I do,' he said. 'I'm a doctor.'

'But you don't even know me.'

'That's something that we can change,' he said and looked at her expectantly. 'I'm George, George du Blanc, all the way from New Jersey.'

'Anna,' she responded. 'Anna Denisova from St Petersburg, Russia.'

But when she offered him her tiny hand, he blinked and looked away.

'Anna,' he said softly and took the hand in his. 'I am afraid you really should be in a sanitarium, as far away as possible from the city.'

She cocked her head and examined his face. 'Why?' she asked.

But deep down she knew why. And so when he said the word it was a relief.

'I was told it was bronchitis,' she said.

'Sometimes the symptoms . . .' he began. 'But in actual fact . . . I suppose you could, if you liked, stay here for a little while.'

His hand still held hers. It seemed as if he did not want to let it go.

'Are you sure?' she asked.

'Very sure,' he replied.

She shrugged. The world had ceased to make any sense earlier that afternoon. What did it matter? 'Then I will stay,' she answered. 'For a little while.'

The doctor sat back, his shoulders relaxed. 'It's for the best,' he said softly.

The Polish woman was despatched to Anna's hotel with a key and detailed instructions. The bill was paid and a suitcase containing all her belongings was brought back. Life that had been so difficult for so long was now simple. She didn't have to worry about having to move on, about money, about being discovered. For hours Anna would feel herself again, calm, together, collected. She could make conversation, she could taste the food in her mouth and she knew where she was. And then from nowhere she would be hit by a wave of grief so strong it would pull her under and she would forget everything but Kima. Once, when she opened her eyes in the dead of night, she found the doctor there, watching over her.

'You cried out,' he said by way of explanation.

'My son is dead,' she said in Russian.

He looked puzzled. He didn't understand. But she didn't have the words, the English words.

'Drink this,' he said and gave her a spoonful of liquid. When she woke it was morning and he was gone.

Anna felt transparent, as if the fabric of her had become faded and worn. Sometimes she would find herself crying and couldn't remember when she started. Sometimes she would catch herself listening to her own heartbeat or staring at her face in the mirror. How long did she have left? The doctor wouldn't tell her. Life, she realized, is all we have, life and love.

The affair was like no other she had ever experienced. Locked away in a three-storey townhouse beside the small gated park, she let herself be cared for, nursed, adored. It was a place of soft edges and warm baths, of muffled footsteps on wooden floors that were covered in Turkish rugs. She felt submerged, crystallized, a glass dahlia inside a paperweight. The only point of focus was the doctor.

'Anna,' he said. 'I want you to marry me.'

'I can't,' she replied.

'Why not?' He pulled back and stared at her. Was she married already?

'I don't believe in it,' she replied. 'No contracts, no promises, no expectations. This, this is enough.'

When she gave him permission to kiss her, undress her, his hands shook so much that he was unable to undo the tiny pearl buttons of her bodice. At every stage, he paused and stared into her eyes. Was she all right? Was she happy? Was he doing what she wanted? And so she took his hands and guided them to her breast, to her mouth, to the place between her legs until they both knew that his questions were being answered in every nerve ending, in every tremble, in every shiver.

And so she was sad when George left in the morning for the hospital and happy when she heard the slam of the front door and his feet on the hall stairs in the early evening. To feel his kiss on her head, to soak up the heat of his breath on her neck, to mould her body around his, was to numb the ache in her chest.

But did she love him? There was so much she couldn't and wouldn't tell him. She thought back over the last few years – the night she had spent with Dante Faccini, the day she had met Noah Serginov in the park, her first meeting with Winter Hare and that hotel room where Ivory Price had shot himself – and she knew that she could never breathe a word of her past to her sweet doctor. And yet the longer she spent with him, the more questions he began to ask. And the longer she stayed in one place, the more likely it was that she would be found. Anna knew that it was only a matter of time before the glass around her began to shatter; when it did, she would have to act, if not for herself, then for her son, for her beautiful boy, for Kima. Until that day, however, the world outside receded into nothing more than the distant rattle of homecoming parades and the occasional bang of a firecracker.

'Been another postal bomb,' the doctor told her one morning as he read the paper over breakfast. 'Didn't reach its intended target, a judge. Instead it blew a postmistress's hands clean off. These people! Where do they all come from?'

Later that same morning the front doorbell rang. It was the postman with a parcel addressed to the doctor. Normally she would have thought nothing of it, she would have left the parcel on the hall table with the rest of the doctor's letters. But as she closed the door, she noticed a smell, a smell she recognized. The parcel was small but heavy. According to the postmark, it had been mailed in Hoboken. She held it to her face and inhaled. And there it was, stronger this time, the unmistakable smell of nitroglycerine.

29

When the doorbell rang at 2 a.m., Monroe climbed out of bed and switched on the light. The house on Tenth Street was deadly quiet.

'You want me to answer that?' Monroe shouted.

Pokolitov didn't reply. He opened the Russian's bedroom door gently and peered inside. The bed was empty but the window that led on to the fire escape was wide open. The bell rang again and a knuckle rapped on the wood. Monroe hurried down the stairs and opened the front door.

Standing halfway down the stoop was a man with pitted skin and pale blue eyes. In one hand he held a bottle of spirits and in the other the narrow wrist of a coloured girl, a streetwalker by the look of her.

'Where's Pokolitov?' he asked in Russian. And then he strode straight past him through the open door. 'You think I was the Immigration Service come to arrest you and ship you off to Ellis Island?'

'He's not here,' Monroe said in English. 'I'm sorry. Who are you?'

The man spun round on his heel and examined him. 'You must be the American lapdog,' he said in Russian. 'Pokolitov!' he shouted. 'You can come out now!'

The streetwalker looked around and began to finger a bunch of dusty silk flowers on the mantelpiece. In the glow of the electric light, although she only looked about sixteen, her face suggested that she had lived every one of the years twice over already. Her companion flopped down on the divan and lit a cigarette.

'Excuse me,' Monroe said, 'but it's the middle of the goddam night!'

'Isn't this the city that never sleeps?' the man replied.

The slam of a door on the first floor made them all turn and look up. Pokolitov was standing at the top of the stairs.

'Noah Serginov. My old friend,' he said in stuttering English. 'Next time you tell us you are going to come. Ah . . . but at least you brought us some liquor.'

'Sorry, boys,' he said. 'This is for the lady. Nice place you have.'

Pokolitov looked around, as if for the first time, at the pink drapes and the surfaces cluttered with ornaments, and nodded. 'Very nice. When did you arrive back?' he asked, reverting to Russian again. 'I thought you were in Sweden.'

'I arrived back this morning from Stockholm,' Noah Serginov replied. 'I bring you an order. You are to cease all operations immediately. Do you know how much money you have spent?'

Pokolitov looked uncomfortable. 'You need to spend money to make money,' he said. 'It takes time. These things cannot be done overnight.'

'We don't have time,' Noah announced. 'You are to return to Russia as soon as you can. But listen, we can talk in the morning. I need to take this young lady upstairs. Where can I sleep?'

Pokolitov scratched his beard and then looked pointedly at Monroe.

The divan in the parlour had not been shipped to Westchester by the owner for a reason. It was unevenly stuffed with straw and horse-hair and the seat sloped back into a hollow. The upholstery smelled of mothballs, sour milk and mould. Monroe pulled a sheet over himself and closed his eyes but could not fall asleep. He turned one way and was suffocated by pillow, he turned the other and felt himself slowly slide into the hollow. And so he lay on his back and stared up at the ceiling. The piano still stood against the wall but he had barely touched it for weeks. His plan hadn't worked. Although a woman, he had been told by Von Hofe, had asked for him at the publishing company several months earlier and been given his forwarding address, Inez hadn't written to him, as he hoped she might, care of the Russian Club on Hester.

It was the not knowing that was so hard to live with. If he could discover that she had decided to stay with her husband then at least he could try to forget her. But every time he remembered that stolen afternoon and all the plans they had made, he felt sure that somehow, surely, she still felt something.

A girl's scream rang out. He threw off the blanket and ran up the stairs. Pokolitov's door was still firmly closed.

'Hey,' he said at the door to the room that had previously been his. 'Is everything all right?'

He tried the handle. It was locked. From inside the room, he could hear the sound of a girl's sobbing.

'What's going on in there?' he yelled.

The door opened suddenly. Noah stood naked in the doorway. Behind him the girl lay half dressed and spread-eagled on the bed; a long red stripe ran down her back.

'What have you done?' Monroe said.

The Russian shrugged. 'She said she liked it,' he said.

Monroe picked up a blanket and tried to throw it around the girl's shoulders. She clambered off the bed and cowered in the corner. There was a deep gash along her cheek.

'You have her,' Noah Serginov said. 'I was finished anyway.'

'It's all right,' Monroe assured the girl. 'I'm not going to hurt you.' He pulled out Inez's silk scarf and used it to try to stop the bleeding. And then he half-carried, half-guided the girl down the stairs and out of the house.

'I'm going to take you to the hospital,' he told her. 'Or a doctor.'

A taxicab bumped along Tenth Street towards them. Monroe hailed it and asked the driver to take them to the nearest medical facility. He took some persuading but eventually agreed to take them to a hospital in Brooklyn. But when Monroe turned to help the girl climb inside, she had gone.

'You don't need to worry about these people,' the cab driver said. 'They can look after themselves. That's what you pay 'em for. You want to go somewhere else?'

'Frankly, I'd rather walk anywhere than get into a car with you,' Monroe replied and slammed the door. The driver yelled something unintelligible and then drove off.

It was a humid May night, the air warm and sticky. Monroe couldn't face going back into the townhouse and so he started to walk, north. Block after block he paced, the buildings growing taller and taller, the streets more and more silent. Finally he reached the park, a blot of pure, dense dark in the perpetual glow of the city. He walked along its perimeter until he reached the block where Inez lived. Would she be awake too? All the windows were dark, nothing lit but the harsh over-bright glare of the lobby. And so he turned left, walked round Columbus Circle and then headed up Broadway until it crossed Amsterdam Avenue.

San Juan Hill looked more sinister than he remembered it. Empty bottles, screws of greasy paper and cigarette butts spilled out of the bashed-up dustbins that lay on their sides in the middle of the pavement. He kept walking, increasing his pace a little when he passed the huddle of a sleeping body lying beneath a handcart. The bar where he had drunk beer with Edward had shut up shop; one of the windows was boarded up, the other papered over. He paused for a moment and wondered if he should turn back. On the next block, however, he could hear the sound of conversation and laughter, and he could see the bright patch of reflected light from an apartment on the top floor on the roof of the black car that was parked on the kerb.

And then the music started: the slide of a trumpet, the clatter and rattle of a drum, the chime of a piano. Monroe closed his eyes and for a minute or two he just listened. The band played a rag and then broke into something else, music that sounded on the brink of falling apart, the trumpet yelled and swooned, the drums cantered and stopped, cantered and stopped, the piano began to stride and broke into a trill before shifting back into a melody. A voice started to sing. He cocked his head and listened. It was Edward, he was sure of it. Monroe pushed down his hat and started to run. The bell didn't work and so he stood in the street and yelled up.

'Hey, Edward. It's me, Monroe!'

A bottle fell from an open window and smashed on the pavement. Inside, the music kept on playing. He tried again. A few windows were yanked open. In the distance a siren wailed.

'Edward!' he yelled once more.

Two arms grabbed him from behind. He smelled sweat and fear, rum and adrenalin.

'Hey, baby,' a voice whispered in his ear, 'you a faggot?'

'No! I'm looking for Edward Mackenzie,' he insisted. 'He's a friend of mine.'

There was a pause and Monroe steeled himself for the first blow. It didn't come. The arms loosened their grip. A face, a young man's, peered into his. It took Monroe a moment to recognize him.

'Little Joe?' he asked. 'Is that you?'

Little Joe was no longer little. He had a scar along his jawline and wore a pair of heavy boots. Three other boys of his own age, about seventeen, stared at him.

'He knew my brother,' he said by way of explanation. 'Worked down on Tin Pan Alley.'

The party was still in full swing up above, oblivious of what was happening in the street. But Monroe was suddenly aware that there were other people watching from behind curtains and from fire escapes. A couple of doors slammed down the block. Little Joe's friends started to drift away.

'You shouldn't be here,' Little Joe pointed out. 'This here is San Juan Hill.'

'I just need to know,' Monroe said. 'Where's Edward? Did he make it back from France?'

Little Joe whistled and then gave a little smile. 'You missed the victory parade?' he replied. 'Joined the Hell-Fighters and fought beside the French. Came back with a medal the size of a silver dollar pancake. He's a star player now. At the Marshall Hotel. And he plays at all those high-society parties for the Clef Club. Doing one for the American Red Cross on Saturday night.'

'He is?' Monroe said.

'He sure is,' Little Joe confirmed. 'Got a wife and a kid and a car and a place in Harlem. Got to pay the bills somehow, I guess.'

Monroe had to swallow down the bitter taste of envy that rose in his mouth. He had pictured plenty of different scenarios for Edward but he had never imagined this one.

'That's—' he began, 'that's a swell piece of news. You must be as proud as punch. And what are you doing?'

'Got a job on the railways,' Little Joe said. 'You still down on the Alley? You got that girl yet?'

'Hell, no,' he said. 'Still working on it.'

A group of men appeared on the far corner with shirts thrown over their vests. One of them called out to Little Joe.

'You better beat it,' Little Joe told Monroe. 'A friend of my brother's just got back from France. Took a trip out of town on the sniff of a job and got strung up and lynched by white folk. Hadn't even changed out of his uniform.'

For a moment Monroe didn't answer. He wondered if Joe knew about what had happened to Edward at Camp Upton.

'That's terrible,' said Monroe.

One of the men coughed and took a step towards them.

'But it's good to see you again, Little Joe. The Marshall Hotel. I'll find him. Thanks!'

Monroe turned on his heel and started to run, and he did not stop until he reached the wide, seemingly endless canyon of Eighth Avenue that drifted with litter blown all the way up from Washington Market.

Pokolitov was eating a boiled egg and reading the paper by the time Monroe arrived back at the townhouse early the next morning. The bedclothes on the divan had been put away and there was no trace of Noah Serginov. It was as if the night before had never happened.

'Good morning,' he said. 'Come in and have some breakfast. Would you like me to boil you an egg?'

'No, thank you,' Monroe replied.

'Tea?'

'No,' he said.

'Well, at least sit down, my friend.'

Monroe did not sit down. Even though he had rehearsed what he wanted to say several times over as he had paced the streets of Chelsea, now he was here, in front of Pokolitov, he found that his mind blanked, he forgot his carefully conceived argument, and all his tactfully phrased reasons eluded him.

'Listen, I've been doing a lot of thinking recently,' he said, 'and I've decided that it's time to move on. I'd like to thank you for all you've done for me but I think it's for the best.'

'For the best,' repeated Pokolitov. He put down his teaspoon and leaned back in his chair. 'You think so?'

'Yes,' said Monroe. 'I do. You're leaving town. I should go.'

'Did I say I was leaving?' asked Polkolitov. 'Of course you must do what you want. I wish you luck.'

'And about those bank accounts?'

'We can close them down,' Pokolitov replied. 'It is not a problem.'

And with that Pokolitov turned back to the paper and continued to scoop out the remains of his egg.

Monroe paused and wondered what he had been so worried about. It had been easy.

'Right,' he said. 'I'll just collect my things.'

The Georgian didn't answer. He seemed to be too engrossed in a newspaper article.

Ten minutes later, Monroe stood by the door in the suit, shoes and with the hat that Pokolitov had bought him, with his suitcase packed.

'So you're sure that I can . . .'

'Keep it all? Of course!' Pokolitov assured him. 'A gift. A souvenir. So where will you go?'

'I have a few ideas,' Monroe said. 'Nothing concrete. As yet.'

'And are you still Andrei Dreslov? Just in case . . . just in case someone comes looking for you at the Russian Club?'

Pokolitov smiled. There was a crumb of boiled egg in his beard. He licked his lips and folded his hands over his belly. A slick of sweat had appeared on his top lip.

'A woman for example?' he added. 'Are you sure you wouldn't like an egg? Or two? It won't take more than a few minutes.'

Two eggs jostled in a pan. The samovar rattled. A blackbird sang in the tree outside.

'It is easy to think that we have many chances in life,' Pokolitov said as he brought tea and salt to the table. 'That in matters of love

330

or luck we may sin and be forgiven, we may be lost and then found again, we may err and then redeem ourselves, over and over again, but in truth when we come to it, and believe me, we all will eventually, we realize that all those other little incidents that happened before were only minor distractions.'

He blinked several times as he lifted the eggs from the pan of water with a spoon and carefully placed them on a small plate in front of Monroe.

'And once you have lost that very thing you thought was always yours,' he went on, 'through carelessness or a weakness of will, you realize that you can never claim it back. That it is gone. Please eat.'

'I'm not hungry.'

Pokolitov smiled at him. His eyes were bloodshot. 'We have a saying in Georgia. When a friend cooks you an egg, you should work up an appetite,' he said.

Monroe picked up a spoon.

'The girl with red hair,' Pokolitov said softly. 'She came looking for you at the Russian Club.'

Monroe stood up, knocking over the chair he had been sitting on with a crash. 'What!' he exclaimed. 'Why didn't you say something?'

Pokolitov shrugged. 'A random name, a random place, a random outcome. What kind of a plan was it?' he asked. 'A very poor one.'

'I thought she'd write. If she'd written me a letter then someone would have passed it on. That's what they do for me at the Russian Club.'

'Women! So unpredictable!'

'Did she leave any way of contacting her? When was it? Why didn't you tell me?'

Pokolitov didn't answer. Instead he picked up an egg, cracked it and began to peel it. Outside, the knife-grinding cart drove by, ringing its bell.

'I, too, have one final chance,' he said. 'In my life I have sacrificed many things, many friendships, many women, many opportunities. When I came from Georgia to St Petersburg as a young man, people laughed at me. But not any more.'

331

Monroe was only half listening. 'I'm going up there,' he said. 'I'm going to go and see her and explain.'

Without warning, Pokolitov's hand shot out and grabbed Monroe's wrist. 'You see, another bad plan,' he said. 'I am going to help you. In fact, it is all arranged.'

'What are you talking about?' Monroe stared down at the Georgian's hand. It gripped like a vice.

'One chance,' Pokolitov said.

Finally, he looked up at Monroe. And then with his other hand, he plucked a card from his pocket.

'An American Red Cross dinner,' Pokolitov articulated slowly. 'Hosted in memory of her husband by Mrs Ellen Finlay. Take a look.'

He released Monroe's wrist. Hesitantly, Monroe took the invitation and read it. 'How did you get this?'

'There will be lots of people there, businessmen, industrialists, investors,' Pokolitov enthused. 'One of our bankers will make the introductions. It is to be the last big social event of the season. Everybody will be there.'

'How did you get this?' he asked again.

Pokolitov paused, then snatched the invitation back.

'Your young lady, of course,' he replied. 'She was very obliging. You come with me, translate, and I shall organise a lovers' tryst.'

Monroe closed his eyes. He was so angry he could feel the blood beating through his temples. He focused on breathing, in and out. Inez had come looking for him and had found the Georgian. What had he told her? And what had she given him in return? It was obvious that Pokolitov had used her for his own purposes. He tried to picture her and realized he had almost forgotten the configuration of her face. Instead he remembered fragments: the line of her nose, the sound of her laugh, the sweet scent of her neck. It had been so long, so very long since he had seen her.

'Of course,' Pokolitov said, 'if you have changed your mind about the girl—'

'No, I'll do it,' he said softly. 'When?'

'Saturday!' Pokolitov answered brightly.' I shall leave a message for her today. Remember you do this not just for me but for the Russian people.'

Pokolitov held out his hand. Reluctantly, Monroe shook it.

'It was business, my friend,' Pokolitov said. 'And information is another form of currency.'

'What about that man?' Monroe asked, 'the man who came in the middle of the night, What was his name? I thought he told you to stop everything.'

'Noah Serginov?' Pokolitov laughed. 'He is just a boy. A stupid boy. He doesn't know what he is saying.'

30

As soon as Inez set eyes on Mrs Ellen Finlay, the host of the fund-raising dinner for the American Red Cross, she knew for certain. She wore a black evening dress cut above the ankle and carried a small white dog. Although Ivory greeted her formally, and explained to Inez that they had met at one of the victory parades, the woman looked and laughed, a giggle really, as if she'd just been caught with her finger in the honey pot.

'I was in California for a small vacation,' she started suddenly as if they had been in the middle of a conversation but it had been broken off. 'Until last Tuesday. It was divine but a little lonely on my own.'

Her eyes slid to the entranceway beyond and her face stretched into a proprietorial smile. 'You will have to excuse me,' she said. 'I must just go and meet Mr . . . oh heavens, what is his name? Lovely to talk to you at last.' And she laughed again and touched Inez on the arm before she moved away. Inez had not spoken a single word.

'Why exactly did you want to come here tonight?' Inez asked Ivory when the hostess was out of earshot.

Ivory turned to her and raised his eyebrows. He had no idea that she suspected anything, no idea at all. 'Inez,' he said, 'you're the wife of a representative now. And this is just the right sort of social event to be seen at. The Vanderbilts are expected as well as the Guggenheims and the Astors.'

Inez didn't reply. Now the war was over, the parties were more lavish, more extravagant and more numerous than before. There were thousands of new millionaires in the city, people made rich by corned beef or barbed wire or munitions. And the lights of Times

Square, the lights of Broadway, and lights inside the towers and townhouses burned more brightly than ever.

'Is that a new dress?' Ivory asked her. 'You been downtown again?'

'No,' she replied. 'I haven't been for a week or two.'

'You used to go all the time,' he countered.

'Captain Price! I thought it was you!'

A middle-aged man in evening dress strode up and shook her husband's hand.

'And how are you?' he asked.

'In fine fettle,' Ivory replied. 'Fit enough, I'd say, to wage a war on the fanatics, Reds and anarchists that remain on our shores.'

'Good show, old man. What a blow.'

Ivory never explained what had happened to him, even when he was asked directly. He would suggest that it was the result of something slightly clandestine, leaving people to guess that his injury was connected with espionage. And then he would launch into his vociferous support for the Immigration Service's decision to round up any Reds they found and imprison them on Ellis Island. 'A dangerous lot,' he would state. 'Best place for them.'

'Do you agree with deportation?' the man in evening dress asked.

'Absolutely,' Ivory insisted. 'It's something that I personally have campaigned for.'

And he went on to decry the well-to-do women, the humanitarians and social workers, who had insisted on sailing to Ellis Island in their dozens to check up on the detainees and the conditions in which they were being held.

'Do the Reds care about the people they murder and maim, about all the Americans whose minds they are poisoning with notions of Communism? I think not. If I were governor of New York, and one day I hope that will be the case, I would get rid of all enemy aliens before they blow us all to kingdom come. And mark my words, that day will come, sooner, much sooner than you think.'

And then they both laughed, even though it was certainly no laughing matter.

'Have you met my wife?' Ivory asked. But when he turned to where Inez had been standing only moments before, she was gone.

The lower rooms of the villa were completely empty of furniture, apart from a dining room where a dozen tables were laden with crockery and silverware that had been polished and buffed to a high shine. It would seem, Inez thought, like a sacrilege to touch them, to smudge their reflective surfaces with hands and mouths and food. A few gilt chairs had been placed around the walls and several vases of flowers unfolded on mantelpieces. To have such an enormous space and to have virtually nothing in it spoke of more wealth than she had ever seen before.

'Drink, madam?'

A waiter offered her a glass. Since Prohibition had been enforced in January, every party or gathering was dry, with glasses of orange juice and lemonade instead of wine or sherry. She took a glass of lemonade and lingered over a severe portrait of an ancestor that peered out above the inglenook fireplace. When the waiter had gone, Inez pulled a small flask of gin from her handbag and poured about a third of it into her glass. The drink was sweet and so strong it made her eyes sting. But it was just what she needed if she was going to survive the rest of the evening.

From the ballroom next door came the sound of live music, a jazz band, and the hum of conversation. She drained her glass and cautiously looked out into the hallway. Ivory wasn't there, the coast was clear.

The ballroom was so large that it seemed even emptier than the rest of the villa. A chandelier hung from a central rose on the ceiling and was reflected back a dozen times from the mirrors that flanked the walls. A grand piano stood in the corner guarded by twin sentries of two huge potted palms.

The band stopped playing to introduce themselves and explain that they had been hired from the Clef Club. And then a drummer, trumpet player and piano player raced through a series of dance tunes. As they played, however, few of the guests paid any attention.

'I bought a huge section of the Trans-Siberian Railway,' a

gentleman was boasting beside her. 'And the world rights to any platinum.'

'Russia is a new market,' another man agreed. 'Great place to invest if you want to see a quick profit.'

'I heard that it will be like Mexico all over again,' another gentleman added. 'I spoke to a fellow earlier about it. Very affable he was, too.'

Inez felt the gin flow through her, reaching her fingers, her toes, the depths of her belly. She closed her eyes and just listened to the music, to the uninhibited blast of it.

'Inez!' came Ivory's voice. She opened her eyes. He was standing right in front of her.

'Where have you been? That was extremely embarrassing. That was the governor I was talking to, for Christ's sake, a man in whose shoes I hope one day to stand. If you would come with me now, I'll introduce you.'

'No,' she replied. 'I'm staying here. I'm listening to the music.'

Ivory looked around the ballroom and smiled and nodded to a few of the other guests. And then Inez stepped around him so she had a clear view of the band again.

'Have you been drinking, Inez?' he asked. 'Oh, my God, you have. I don't believe it.'

He swallowed and ran his forefinger and thumb down his nose in an action Inez had seen many times before. The hostess suddenly appeared at his elbow. Had she been watching the whole exchange? Probably, Inez supposed.

'Is everything all right?' said Ellen Finlay. 'Do you need anything?'

'A cup of black coffee,' he said. 'And then, Inez, I think I should send you home.'

'Oh, my,' said Ellen Finlay. 'You're feeling poorly, what a pity.'

'I'm not in the least poorly,' Inez snapped.

'How could you?' he said. 'You make a mockery of everything I stand for.'

'Shall I get you a chair?' asked Ellen Finlay. 'Maybe you should sit down. If you're feeling poorly.'

Inez looked at the hostess, at the spots of rouge on both cheeks which did nothing to define the rounded surfaces of her face, at the yellow hair that was turning dark at the roots, at the little white dog that stood listlessly at her ankle, and suddenly felt sorry for her.

'I feel very well, thank you,' she said and pulled out her flask of gin and took a long swig. 'Or I will after I drink more of this.'

There was a brief pause before Ivory uttered those five little words that said more than he could surely have intended.

'What did I tell you?'

Inez had thought that her life could never be fixed; it was a broken thing without spare parts. She had messed it up, not only for herself but for her daughter. She had arrived an hour early at the diner on Fifty-Seventh Street just in case. Coffee was brought to her without her actually ordering it and the owner kept asking if she wanted him to call her a cab. It was quite clearly a bad choice. She was too conspicuous; she knew that she could never come here again. The minutes dragged past until she looked at her watch and it was already half past three. So that was it. It was over. She had adjusted her hat, left a dollar under her saucer and was about to leave when finally the phone rang, once, twice, three times. When she picked up, her hand was shaking so much that she could barely hold the receiver.

'Monroe.' She closed her eyes. 'I've missed you so much.'

It was not Monroe, however, but the man she had met in Hester Street, a man who introduced himself as Pokolitov.

'I'm sorry,' she whispered. 'I don't know what came over me.'

For a moment neither of them spoke.

'I am sorry, too. I wish with all my heart,' Pokolitov replied eventually, 'that I was he.'

'He's just a friend,' Inez tried to explain. 'He is – he was – a song-writer. And I heard this song and it sounded like it had been written about us a long time ago and I thought, I thought . . . Anyway, the name of the person who wrote it was Andrei Dreslov, which is not his name but I thought that this person might at least know something.'

Inez swallowed. What was she saying? 'I should go,' she said.

'Wait a moment,' said the caller. 'I will look for the man you seek. But it will take time. Who knows where he might be? Michigan? Mexico? Milwaukee? But I have contacts all over America with the Russian community. If he is here, I will find him for you.'

'Thank you,' she said. 'Maybe – please don't be offended – I can pay you.'

'There is no need,' he said, but paused.

There was something he wanted. She started to twist the cable around her fingers.

'Are you sure there's nothing I can do?'

'I tell you what. Let us meet and discuss it,' he said. 'There may be something after all. Name a place and a time and I will be there.'

'It will have to be somewhere anonymous,' she began. 'Somewhere discreet.'

'Of course,' he agreed.

They met a week later in Lord and Taylor's, at eleven o'clock exactly on the sixth floor. It was a calculated risk; Inez knew that although the Salon would be full, the shop floor would be empty. Over a rack of fur coats, he told her that if she could provide him with guest lists to dinners and details of any social engagements that her husband was invited to attend, he could use these for business purposes.

'That's all?' she asked. 'Why, of course.'

'How shall we communicate?' he said. 'I suppose I am right in thinking that you would not like anyone to know.'

For a moment Inez floundered. There had to be a means of doing it so there was no way that Ivory would ever find out. She looked around the shop floor. And then she remembered the pneumatic terminal next to the stairs. She pressed the foot pump once and a canister fell out. The single silk stocking with a hole in it was still inside.

They took the lift and descended to the ground floor in silence. When the bell rang and the attendant slid the doors open, Inez announced that she would like to go back up again, to the tenth-floor dining rooms. Pokolitov placed his hat on his head and stepped out. Two nannies with young children climbed in and requested the toy department. The Russian was fingering a pair of bright blue lady's leather gloves on the nearest counter when the doors closed once more. He glanced up and with a barely discernible nod of his head, he bade her goodbye.

Once a week Inez had made her way up to the sixth floor and, when there was nobody around, had pressed the foot pump of the pneumatic terminal. Quickly, she would pull out the note that was waiting for her in the brass canister, push a bundle of dinner party invitations and the list of guests inside and press the pump again to send it back inside the tube. The notes she had received in return were maddeningly vague. Scrawled in poor English, they spoke of leads in Pittsburgh and sightings in Chicago.

Her trips to Lord and Taylor's, however, always seemed to make her husband happy. Maybe the guilt, should he have any, was diluted in direct proportion to how much money she spent. And so once she had done what she had set out to do, she spent liberally, buying new hats, dresses, shoes, gloves, most of which were put away in the closet and never worn. After this party, there were no more social events until the autumn season: she had skipped her usual weekly trip to the department store. She did not pick up Pokolitov's most recent note.

As the band launched in to a foxtrot, Ivory looked at his wife; although she claimed she had developed a new interest in fashion, she didn't seem to care what she wore any more. If only she returned a little of what he had offered. If only she hadn't forced him to find solace in another woman. If only she loved him like he still loved her. He looked at his watch.

'Inez, the driver is waiting outside,' he said. 'I'd like you to go home.'

'Let me listen to one more song,' she replied. 'And then I'll go.'

A waiter tapped Ivory on the shoulder and told him that he had a phone call.

'Could I request that someone sees her to the car?' Ivory asked the hostess.

340

'The butler?' Ellen suggested.

'I can do it,' Inez replied. 'Thank you.'

'But promise me you'll go straight home?' Ivory insisted.

Inez shrugged and then nodded. 'That's what I said. After the next song.'

'Good,' said Ivory. 'Very good.'

The piano player finished the song and launched into the next. This time he began to sing. He had a rich mellow voice that carried above the murmur of business deals and gossip that filled the ballroom.

'I like this one,' said Ellen Finlay. '"Dancing on the Sand at . . ." Where is it?'

'Amagansett,' said Inez. 'It's Amagansett.'

And as she said the words she looked across the room. Standing beneath a potted palm, staring straight at her, was Monroe Simonov.

31

Anna climbed out of the taxicab and gave the driver a generous tip. Her bag was heavy and although she had had plenty of practice at making it look weightless, that evening she seemed to have lost the knack. And yet she had lost none of her carriage, her dignity, the sense that she was someone.

'Good evening, madam,' said a butler at the door. 'May I take your coat?'

'Many thanks,' she replied.

She handed it to him. Underneath, she wore her scarlet dress.

'Your bag?' he offered.

'No, thank you,' she replied. 'Not the bag. I prefer to carry it with me.'

The villa was huge and imposing but decorated, Anna decided, with so little taste that it looked cheap. The rooms were swarming with well-dressed people, with bankers, by the look of them, and industrialists, politicians and judges. A waiter offered her a glass of lemonade. It was cool and sweet and she was glad of it. She was weaker now than she had ever been; the night sweats were worse and she woke up feeling drained. She felt a cough rise up in her throat. No, she thought, not now, not here. She took a deep breath and slowly, painfully, it subsided.

The doctor's voice suddenly came into her head: Anna, you must rest; Anna, you must lie down; Anna, come here. He would be home now; he would call out her name, walk through the empty rooms and then find her letter.

A woman rushed past but stopped when she saw her.

'I don't believe we've met . . .?' she began.

'It's Anna,' she replied. 'Anna Denisova.'

The woman pushed back a curl of blond hair from her forehead. By the way her hands fidgeted and her eyes darted to the door and back again, Anna doubted if she would remember it later.

'Pleasure,' the woman said. 'Mrs Ellen Finlay. And you're a friend of . . .?'

Anna smiled and said the first name that came into her head. 'Ivory Price,' she said.

'Splendid,' the woman said, her face freezing almost imperceptibly. 'He was just here . . .'

Anna had not expected this. How could she have been so stupid? Months ago she had picked up a newspaper and spotted his picture. He had survived the gunshot wound and had become a politician. She had been filled with relief. But she didn't want to meet him, not here, not now. That would ruin everything. She realized she would have to work faster than she would have liked. And then she looked up and saw a face she was not expecting, a face she had not seen for many years.

After she had disposed of the parcel that had arrived at the doctor's house, dropping it from one of the Chelsea Piers into the Hudson River, Anna had made the trip to the safe house in Hoboken. Once more she walked along the docks, once more she had rung the bell in the faceless tenement and waited, and once more she was not certain, exactly, of who or what she would find inside.

Winter Hare seemed unsurprised to see her and greeted her with a kiss that smelled of garlic and home-made alcohol.

'I heard you were dead,' she said.

'I lost two fingers,' he said, holding up a hand with missing digits.

'How did you find me?' she asked as she removed her gloves.

Winter Hare sighed and then he riffled through some papers on the mantelpiece and handed her a piece of paper with the name of the hotel in the Bronx at the top. In clumsy writing, the Polish maid's she supposed, was her full name and the name and address of the doctor.

'It was quite by chance,' he explained. 'One of our members

found a job working on the desk. He recognized your name. Since you failed to return to Russia, I was given the order to assassinate, if not you, then those who were sheltering you.'

Outside it started to rain. The sky was a metallic grey and the room was almost completely dark. And still Winter Hare didn't make a move to turn on the light. Tears welled up from behind her eyes.

'Did you really think that I was the one,' said Anna, 'the one who gave all those names to the Americans?'

Winter Hare shrugged.

'Someone betrayed me,' she said softly. 'And my son.'

'Pokolitov said that he had proof,' said Winter Hare. 'He said that you were in the pay of that American. That you were his lover and you argued over money and then you shot him in the face. What was he called? Price?'

'What did you say? That name?'

'Price?'

'No. The other?'

'Who? Pokolitov?'

She turned and stared at Winter Hare. 'Pokolitov's here?' she said softly. 'In New York?'

'Why, yes. He gave me a telegram to send to St Petersburg with all the details. You were sentenced in absentia.'

Anna tried to stay calm but she was shaking. 'For how long,' she asked, 'for how long has Pokolitov been here?'

'In America?' Winter Hare's shoulders fell. 'I followed his instructions. I took your letters, I gave them to him. I don't know what he did with them.'

'No wonder there were never any for me in return,' she replied bitterly. 'And do you know where I might find him?'

Winter Hare shook his head. 'He is going back to Russia any day now. He could have left already. Noah Serginov has been put in charge of the American operation.'

Anna sat down. She tried to remember why she had come. 'I need to clear my name,' she said. 'I need you to stop targeting my friend.'

Winter Hare shrugged. 'I just do what I am told,' he said.

'I have never passed on any names, dates or addresses. Do you believe me?'

Winter Hare massaged the stumps where his two fingers had been. He did believe her. 'I suppose if you were to volunteer, to put yourself forward, you might have a good case . . . in fact you might be just the sort of person we need for a job we are setting up.'

Anna Denisova stood up. 'You know I won't . . .'

'You won't what? he repeated.

She sighed. 'Nothing,' she replied. 'So, what do you want me to do?'

'Wait here. Let me speak to Serginov,' he said. 'And then I shall pass on his instructions.'

It was true. Pokolitov was in New York. He was standing just a few feet away from her at the top of the stairs. His hair was greying and his stance was a little more stooped than she remembered it but was him, Le Brouillon. She was certain, also, that he didn't know that she had seen him. She placed her bag on the bottom step and then wandered over to a window and gazed out. As she did so, she heard him come down the stairs and head for the front door.

'Your coat, sir,' the butler said at the door.

'No coat,' he replied. 'Just an umbrella.'

Pokolitov quickly extracted one from the stand and then turned and hurried down the front steps. Anna put down her glass and slowly moved to the entrance. Tadeus was walking away as quickly as he could down Riverside Drive. And she suddenly saw him for what he was and had been all along: a coward, a liar, a fraud.

Without her bag or her coat, Anna's body felt lighter. She took the steps two at a time and set off along the street behind him. She didn't see Ivory Price stroll out of the ballroom behind her. She didn't know that he watched her deposit the bag and put down her empty glass. She had no idea that he wasn't surprised to see her, that in fact he had been expecting her.

32

Edward was halfway through the song when he looked over at his old friend, Monroe Simonov. He was staring across the room at the woman. Her head was lit from behind; it was impossible to see the expression on her face, but while everyone around her was moving, she stood completely still.

Monroe had turned up out of the blue at the Marshall Hotel the day before while Edward had been playing his afternoon set. Afterwards Edward had bought him a drink – there was whisky behind the bar if you knew who to ask – and Monroe had explained in fits and starts how he had run into Little Joe in San Juan Hill.

'And what were you doing in San Juan Hill?' Edward asked. 'All by yourself?'

'I thought I heard you playing,' he replied. It was as if all those years had never happened. He rubbed his face with his hands and sighed. 'I'm in a mess, Edward, you have no idea.'

Edward told him to slow down and tell him everything. And so Monroe told him what had happened after the fight at Camp Upton, how he had gone to Mexico with the Italians and come back again, how he had changed his name and become a Russian.

'So you're Communist, too?' Edward asked.

'Thinking about it,' he said. 'I saw what it was like for you during the war, the way they treated you.'

Edward shrugged and examined his fingers. The joint on one of them, the little finger, wouldn't bend any more. He would never be as good a player as he was before the fight at Camp Upton, but he had learned to play with it. Otherwise he had come back from the war without a scratch.

'Things are changing,' he said. 'I got a medal.'

'You were fighting for the French, don't forget,' Monroe pointed out. 'The American Army wouldn't let a black man fight beside a white.'

'They still seem to have a problem with us,' he agreed. 'But not as much as they have with the Reds.'

They sipped their drinks in silence for a moment. Monroe had changed, Edward had noticed. His clothes looked new and his shoes were polished but there was something rougher around the edges that hadn't been there before.

'How's Bessie?' Monroe asked.

'Still beautiful,' he replied.

'She still singing?'

'Got a headliner spot waiting for her,' he told him proudly. 'Starting right after Christmas. And the baby, the baby almost tears my heart out. If only she would stop crying all night.'

'Isn't that what they do?'

He laughed. 'Sure,' he said. 'You still writing songs?'

Monroe smiled and flexed his fingers.

'All I used to care about,' he said softly, 'was music. And then I met her . . . Edward, I need to ask you a favour.'

And so here he was, playing Monroe's song, while the woman Monroe loved, the woman Monroe had loved for years, stood and listened.

As Monroe watched her across the ballroom, Inez took the smallest of steps forward. Monroe felt something inside him begin to rise. And then she stopped; a man, the man he recognized as her husband, was shouting in her ear, insisting on something. He put his hand around her waist and began to try to guide her away. A coat was being placed around her shoulders. She was leaving. So that was it. The end. At least now he was sure. Monroe glanced down and turned round. He didn't want her to see him like this. Edward finished the song and launched into another.

From the front door, however, there was a sudden commotion. A policeman ran in to the ballroom, breathless and red-faced, and switched on all the lights. A woman started to scream in the hallway so he had to shout.

'Please evacuate the building,' the policeman yelled. 'As fast as you can. We're about to turn off the power as a precaution. Don't panic!'

'Bomb scare,' a voice shouted through the door. 'Everybody out.'

In an instant, almost everyone in the room began to crush towards the door. As they pushed and shoved and swore and sobbed, only one person walked the other way through the ballroom, away from the door.

'Monroe? The song . . . I heard the song,' she began.

'I wrote it for you,' he replied.

'I know,' she whispered.

The villa was plunged into darkness. Monroe reached out and touched her face, the curls of her hair, the curve of her cheek. And then she stepped forward, her coat fell off her shoulders and she put her arms around him.

A servants' door had been opened next to the fireplace. The band were gathering up their instruments and leaving. In only a matter of minutes, the villa was surrounded by policemen and firemen, detectives and journalists, and the air was full of flashing lights and sirens, loud-hailers and raised voices.

'Monroe,' Edward shouted from the door. 'This way.'

They both followed him out through the servants' entrance, through the basement kitchen and up on to a side street. A crowd of people, guests and neighbours, were standing well back behind some hastily erected police tape. Mrs Ellen Finlay was being comforted by Ivory Price. Hundreds of Riverside Drive's residents had lifted their curtains and were peering out into the night. Nobody, however, could see anything in the yellow beam of the policemen's torches, but if the tip-off was correct, a bag, the one singled out and illuminated at the bottom of the stairs, might detonate at any moment.

It would be late the next morning before the bomb specialist finally arrived from Chicago where he had been investigating a series of mail bombs that had been sent to judges, senators and police commissioners. With a sheen of sweat on his face and shaking hands, he would carefully, tentatively, open the bag. Inside, however, he wouldn't find a bomb or any kind of explosive device, just a portrait of a young boy taken in a photographic studio in St Petersburg, some ladies' lace undergarments and a tattered copy of *Das Kapital* by Karl Marx.

The night before, however, as the guests and neighbours were herded into Riverside Park until they were a safe distance away, many of them decided to wait to see what would happen. When after an hour nothing had happened and it started to rain, they began to look for their drivers and head back to their apartments on the Upper East Side or Fifth Avenue, or their clubs in Midtown.

Monroe, Inez and Edward had walked together towards Broadway. The rain looked like fine mist in the city's night-time incandescence and the streets shone. In her thin evening dress, Inez shivered.

'You left your coat?' Monroe asked.

'Here, take my scarf,' said Edward and put it around her shoulders.

'Thank you,' she said.

'You want a lift anywhere?' Monroe asked Edward when he had hailed a cab.

'I can walk to Harlem from here,' he replied. 'Goodbye, Monroe. And good luck.'

'I owe you,' said Monroe.

'Well, I still owe you a coat, remember?' he laughed. 'Keep the scarf and let's call it quits.'

Hester Street was quiet at night. The market stalls were empty and the hawkers' carts were all stored under fire escapes and tucked away in doorways. In the Russian Club they could hear the sound of a dozen men playing chess in the meeting room. Monroe led Inez up the stairs to the Tsar's Room. While she waited outside, he drew the curtains and lit half a dozen candles.

'You can come in now,' he said.

'It's beautiful,' Inez whispered. 'Where is it?'

'It's the Winter Palace. In St Petersburg.'

Inez gazed out through painted windows at the River Neva, at the Palace Square and the gilded dome of St Isaac's Cathedral.

'It's as if we're in another place, in another life,' she said.

And then she felt Monroe's arms around her and his breath on her neck.

'Stay with me,' he whispered. 'Stay with me now. In this life.'

Inez turned around and her mouth found his mouth. And one by one, their clothes fell on to the floor like so many discarded shadows.

Later, they lay on the bed and stared up at the ceiling, at the gold leaf and the scudding Russian clouds that flickered in the candlelight.

'Do you remember,' she whispered, 'the first time we met? You were playing and I was singing.'

'Of course I do. And do you remember,' he said, 'how you danced on the beach?'

Inez started to laugh.

'And that policeman,' Monroe said. 'He thought we were spies . . .'

'Signalling to the Germans. In semaphore . . .'

'You said I had eyes the colour of Taconic Mountain slate.'

'Did I?' she replied. 'I don't remember.'

A candle flickered and then went out. Early morning light was beginning to spill under the curtains. Inez rested her head on Monroe's shoulder. He lifted his arm and pulled her close and then a little closer still.

'What are we going to do?' she said softly.

'We'll go west,' Monroe whispered. 'To California. We'll start again, all of us.'

'But what on earth are we going to live on?'

'The truth,' answered Monroe. 'We could just about live on that.'

He kissed the top of her head. She leaned up on her elbow and looked at him.

'You start,' she said. 'Tell me something you've never told me before.'

He sighed deeply. 'Well, all right,' he said.

She was suddenly filled with apprehension. What did he have to tell her?

'Here goes. Inez, you're not a singer.'

She laughed. 'Is that all?'

'That's all. Your turn.'

Inez sat up, took both Monroe's hands and held them to her mouth. She kissed each in turn.

'Go on,' he said. 'Spit it out.'

'Luella,' she said. 'She's yours.'

As the expression on his face shifted from shock to pure unmasked joy to desolation, there was a sudden commotion on the stairs outside; the blast of whistles and raised voices. Inez pulled a sheet around her body as the door burst open. A couple of men, one with a raised baton, rushed into the room.

'Two more in here!' he yelled.

'Get dressed,' the other shouted. 'You're under arrest. Understand?'

'What?' said Monroe.

'This one speaks English,' the first one said. 'Well, do understand this, you filthy Red.' He raised his baton and brought it down on Monroe's shoulder.

'Stop!' yelled Inez. 'What on earth do you think you're doing? You're not even a policeman.'

'American Protective League. We got a warrant to round up Commies,' he told her. 'Get your shoes on or would you rather go barefoot?'

'Wait,' she said. 'I'll put them on. But let me tell you something. You're making a mistake.'

'Leave the lady,' Monroe said to the man without a baton. 'She has nothing to do with this.'

'We got to take everyone on the premises,' he replied.

'On whose orders?' she asked.

'From the top. The whole city's gonna be cleaned up. Starting right here.'

'Name?' the other ordered, pulling a crumpled piece of paper and a pencil out of his pocket.

'I'm not saying a word without a lawyer present,' Monroe said.

The baton was raised again.

'Don't hit him!' said Inez. 'His name's Andrei. Andrei Dreslov.'

'You?' he asked Inez.

'Suzette,' she said, looking at Monroe. 'It's Suzette Kinross.'

33

The press conference had been arranged for 9 a.m. at the corner of Riverside Drive and West Ninety-Seventh Street. The whole block had been cordoned off and two dozen policemen urged the curious to move along. Ivory Price had not been home all night; he had been holed up in his club, preparing.

'As you can see,' he told the waiting reporters, referring to the evening clothes he still wore, 'last night, sleep eluded me. I suppose we should have expected it. Reds have infiltrated our country, Communists have disrupted our industry by instigating strikes and walk-outs. And now this – cold-blooded murder. What would have happened if we had not been given a tip-off?'

'But the bomb didn't actually detonate, did it?' a reporter suggested.

'Thankfully, no,' he agreed. 'But if it had, dozens, maybe hundreds of the city's finest and their loved ones would have been butchered. Even the target showed how callous these people are. To bomb the home of a widow who so recently lost her husband at the front shows what kind of people we are dealing with.'

'And how is Mrs Ellen Finlay?' one of the journalists asked.

'Traumatized, naturally. But the last thing I heard she was being comforted by friends at the Ritz Carlton.'

'Say, Mr Price,' another journalist shouted out. 'I hear there was a raid last night. How many did you arrest.'

'About sixty-five,' he replied.

'And do you have files on all these people?'

'Most of them,' he answered. 'These aren't just some random immigrants, if that's what you're thinking. These are hard-nosed radicals. Let me name some figures. Just this month, thirty letter bombs and one explosive device. Who knows what else they have planned?'

'Where are they now?' another asked. 'Ellis Island?'

'That's right,' he said. 'In a top-security unit. We have to show these people, these aliens, that this kind of terrorism will not be tolerated. We must act swiftly, decisively, with finality. There is no going back. That is why I have made a personal request to the mayor to take unprecendented action. We must deport them all.'

Ivory Price climbed into his car and immediately headed south to Battery where another group of photographers were waiting to snap him as he boarded a boat with the Chief of Police. As the bow skipped over the churning black water of the bay, Ivory looked back at the city and felt happy. In his head he tried out adjectives that might one day be applied to his career: meteoric, stratospheric, spectacular. By the time they reached the quay at Ellis Island, he had written his own biography, first a Republican representative and then the governor of New York.

'Your list is extensive,' the Chief of Police had told him. 'Names, dates, involvement with specific groups. How on earth?'

'I have contacts,' he replied. 'These Russians aren't averse to a little palm grease. That was how we knew about the bomb – the tip-off came from an insider.'

He rubbed his hands. It was a clear summer day and the sky was a luminous blue.

'And how is your wife?' the Chief of Police asked.

It was an innocent enough question but one that he hadn't asked himself for a while. She had promised him that she would go straight home, hadn't she? He had no reason to presume that she had done otherwise.

'Very well,' he said without missing a beat. 'Probably fast asleep. Have you ever met a women yet who rises earlier than you?'

The policeman nodded and agreed that his wife only rose before nine if she had an appointment booked with her hairdresser.

The men sat on benches in the Great Hall. Most of them, Ivory noticed, looked shabby and unkempt, in grubby caps and worn-out boots. Several hunched forward and sucked on cigarettes, others pushed their hats over their faces and snoozed.

'A motley lot,' he said.

A call came through for him from the governor's office. He decided to take it in private. Now he would get the praise he deserved.

'It wasn't a bomb,' the governor said. 'It was just a bag.'

'What?' Ivory replied. 'Are you sure?'

'Of course I'm sure. But if this gets out, and I can't guarantee that it won't, then the whole operation is going to make us all look like a bunch of fools.'

'Surely we can still deport them?'

'Are you out of your mind? Public opinion would not allow it. You haven't given any kind of press conference, have you?'

Ivory's face began to flush. Should he deny it? His words would be all over the papers in a couple of hours anyway.

'You what?' the governor yelled. 'On whose authorization? Mr Price, although you have had some success on the political spectrum, I'd urge you to drop any idea that you will go any further up the ladder. As for any deportation orders, unless we see a serious act of terrorism in the next twenty-four hours, and I mean serious with several deaths and multiple injuries, I will not only give a press conference overturning your announcement, but I will also recommend that you are removed immediately from office for gross incompetence. Good day, Mr Price.'

His hand was shaking when he finally hung up the phone. It was worse, much worse than he had ever anticipated. Would the governor give a press conference contradicting everything he had announced? If so, he would have to face the full bombardment of the press when he arrived back from Ellis Island. All he wanted to do was to leave as quickly as possible.

'Mr Price?' the Chief of Police said. 'Would you like to see the women now?'

'Of course,' he replied. 'But we'll have to make it swift.'

'Let me show you what the cat dragged in.'

Inez was being held in a small dormitory with six other women, none of whom spoke English. Two, just in their teens, were being comforted by a couple of older women in headscarves. Even though it was summer, it was chilly in the cell and Inez was glad of Edward's scarf. A few hours earlier, some stale bread and a pitcher of water had been placed on the floor by a guard. No one had touched it.

When the door was unlocked and two men stepped in with a list of names, Inez was staring out of the tiny window above her head, thinking about Luella, wondering if Mrs O'Leary had given her breakfast yet, imagining how she would react when she met Monroe. What would she tell Luella's beloved nanny? How could she explain the situation? A name was read out but it didn't register. A heavy silence descended.

'Suzette Kinross?'

She turned and there, standing in the doorway, next to the guard, was Ivory. He lowered his head, closed his eyes and shook his head.

'Are you all right?' asked the Chief of Police. 'You know this woman?'

Ivory opened his eyes wide and stared at Inez. And then he laughed. 'Know her?' he said. 'Of course I don't know her. What are you suggesting?'

34

When the rain started to fall, Pokolitov had paused to put up a huge black umbrella. And then he walked south, block after block, through the Eighties, the Sixties, the Forties and Twenties. In the past Anna would have kept pace easily; she used to walk practically the length of Manhattan and back almost every day. But she was tired, she was weak, and she struggled to keep up. Finally he turned left at Tenth Street and she watched from the end of the block as he let himself into a large, well-appointed townhouse.

It was way past midnight and she had been trailing him for almost an hour. The rain had stopped now but although it wasn't cold, she was shivering. Her head, however, was burning. She would wait, she decided, until she had regained something of her strength, until her courage had returned.

The house across the street was for sale. Shutters had been drawn across every window and the main door was heavily padlocked. The mailbox was completely full and so handfuls of letters had been shoved under the door and become stuck. Anna pulled one out. The name on the envelope was Miss Patty Devine. The window next to the small door underneath the stoop shattered with just two small taps of her heel. She pulled the shoe back on and then reached through the broken window and quickly unlocked it.

Miss Patty Devine's furniture was shrouded in white sheets and a layer of dust covered every surface like fine grey snow. The house had clearly been empty for several years. What had happened to her? Had she died? Maybe she had moved to South America, Anna told herself, to live in splendour as the lover of a Brazilian diplomat. As she crept from room to room, however, she was continually startled; there were mirrors on every wall and round every corner, and when she caught sight of the flicker of movement from the corner of her eye, she would almost cry out in terror before she realized that it was nothing but her own image bouncing back at her, the only living person in a house full of ghosts.

On the other side of the road, a light in a room on the first floor was extinguished. She was still shivering; the shoulders and hem of her red dress were wet through. She undid the side fastening and stepped out of it. Luckily, her corset was still dry. It was fortunate that Anna Denisova had lost so much weight in the last few months that her clothes fell around her body with a few inches to spare. Since she had decided that she would never carry dynamite in her bag again, she had been looking for another way. She had learned how to sew in Siberia; there were no tailors or dressmakers to fix, alter and make her dresses, just bales of harsh linen and needles and thread. And so she had taken her corset apart herself and remade it with eight small pockets big enough to carry one stick each, all of which could be wired up to a battery and a timer that Winter Hare had given her.

The plan had been to transfer the dynamite to her bag at the party, wire up and set the timer, then leave. Winter Hare had assured her that a tip-off would be given and that nobody would be hurt. It was a show, that was all, Winter Hare had told her. Just a show. Of what, he wasn't sure.

Anna wrapped herself up in a dust sheet, lay down on a divan in the parlour and tried to sleep. Her feet were cold and there was nothing she could do to warm them. She suddenly missed the tight embrace and the soft kiss of her darling doctor almost more than she could bear. In the hours before dawn, her mind went over and over her life. Why had Pokolitov arranged for her escape from Siberia if he had been the one who had betrayed her in the first place? Why had he made her believe he would look after Kima in return for her services in America? And what was his involvement in the plot to assassinate her? She saw now that he had toyed with her, used her and thrown her away as if she were worth nothing.

She woke with a start as another handful of mail was shoved beneath the front door. She dressed quickly – what if the mailman had spotted the broken window? – but before she left everything the way she had found it and let herself out, she set the timer.

Although a gramophone was blasting out a recording of Caruso in the house next door, number 59, Tenth Street was deadly quiet. When she finally rang the bell it sounded, long and sonorous, somewhere deep inside the building.

Sunlight streamed through the front door and made Tadeus Pokolitov look older than he really was, redrawing the crags and hollows of his face. As she watched him come down the stairs, rubbing his eyes, she was struck by how often she had imagined this moment. It was nothing like the way she had envisaged. He looked frailer, more pathetic than she had expected.

'Anna?' Pokolitov's face blanched. He tried to swallow down his shock but he couldn't hide it.

'What a grand house,' she said as she stepped inside. 'My, you've come up in the world, Tadeus. Why didn't you tell me you were here, in New York?'

He swayed on his feet. He seemed unable to come up with an explanation.

'Is it really you?' he said at last.

'Well, aren't you even going to greet me?'

When he leaned forward to kiss her, his jacket caught on the umbrella stand and something tore. As he untangled himself from the spokes, he tried to regain something of himself.

'How lovely to see you,' he said. 'Still so elegant. America has been good for you, you look a little rounder. Please come in, sit down. I shall make you some tea.'

'I don't want tea,' she said.

When she kissed his lips, at first he did not respond. But then, slowly, hesitantly, he opened his mouth and kissed her back.

All night Pokolitov had lain and listened for the sound of the blast. It never came. He fell asleep shortly before dawn and dreamed he heard it not once but over and over again. He woke in a cold sweat and a foul temper. After depositing the gold in American banks and after creaming off a large sum for himself he had raised a lot of money for the new government. Now he was being ordered to hand over power to Noah Serginov and return to Russia immediately. Russia was in a state of civil war, there was disease, famine, anarchy. And he had grown used to his life in America, to the townhouse on Tenth Street and the Russian Club on Hester. He loved the sound of jazz and the cut of his new suit. For most of his life he had woken up wondering if he would have enough to eat or if he would find a bed to sleep in. He didn't want to do that any more.

Instead, he had bought a ticket on a steamer to Argentina and intended to clear his the bank accounts and leave. The party was his last chance to secure a little more money. And with Monroe translating, he had raised several hundred thousand dollars by selling off Russia's natural resources to greedy, naïve Americans. All he had to do was put the cheques in the bank and wait for them to clear.

When he saw Anna Denisova at the bottom of the stairs in that huge villa on Riverside Drive, however, he was filled with remorse. She looked so small, so fragile and still so beautiful that he wondered why he could ever have felt threatened by her.

But when he had arrived in America he had put the past behind him. He was powerful, he was ruthless, he was strong; Anna Denisova was his one weakness. And that, he told himself, was something that he could not tolerate. Even though he had recruited her to the cause, someone had been handing information over to the Americans and it didn't take too much imagination to deduce that it could have been her. In effect, he had signed her death sentence himself.

He watched from above as she put down her bag. Since she had gone underground, he had heard she was working for the Italians, transporting explosives all over America. The bag was bulky and it looked heavy. He broke into a cold sweat. It was a bomb, he was sure of it. Why else would she be here? Despite himself, he was shocked by the audacity of it. To blow up one or two people, judges or policemen, seemed acceptable. To blow up a villa where dozens of industrialists and politicians and millionaires had gathered was going too far.

As he left the villa, he felt a slight stab of regret about leaving

Monroe Simonov, but it couldn't be helped. People die every day, he told himself as he walked the blocks back down to Tenth Street, both the innocent and the guilty. And now here she was, Anna Denisova, without, he had checked, her bag.

'Anna,' he whispered. 'It's been so long.'

'Almost nine years. Hold me. Don't let me go.'

'I looked for you,' he said. 'I never stopped looking.'

When she didn't reply, he pulled back an inch and gazed down at her. Her eyes were red, the whites yellow, but she was still as striking as ever.

'How I loved you,' she said.

'I loved you too,' he replied.

Maybe, he considered briefly, despite all that he had done, they could make it work. Maybe he could take her with him to Argentina? Maybe they could make a new life together. He inhaled the smell of her, the smell that brought back so many memories. And then he noticed something else, the tiniest tick of a clock. He thought nothing of it. He ran his hand down her waist. There was something hard beneath her dress, something that didn't feel like any corset he had ever felt before.

'No,' Anna said. 'You didn't.'

Above Central Park the air trembled. In Midtown, the windows of the newly constructed skyscrapers rattled in their frames and threatened to break. Down in the Village, the birds, pigeons, sparrows and starlings rose up in a darkening cloud, as Tenth Street hiccuped with a sudden shudder, a blast of smoke and showering stone that plumed the streets all the way from Greenwich Avenue to the Bowery with wreaths of grey.

When the smoke cleared, it revealed a gap between numbers 57 and 61. A whole house gone – as if suddenly extracted like a rotten tooth – leaving nothing more than a pile of rubble and the flitter of a pile of mail that had been delivered that morning and hadn't yet been opened. The buildings on either side still clung on to something of their absent neighbour on their party walls: an elegant marble fireplace with a huge Greek Revival over-mantel mirror – the glass now shattered – on what had been the ground floor, lilac floral wallpaper and a red silk-fringed shade on the floor above. Four stairs without balustrade leading up to an attic room with a modest grate and wash-hand basin – the shaving brush still in its holder – both spectacularly suspended. And hanging skew-whiff upon the opposite wall a photographic studio portrait of a pretty woman in a large hat.

On the street outside, a man was sitting in a pool of his own blood and the blood of his secretary whom he had been taking out for a cup of mid-morning tea and who now kept repeating, 'Two sugars please, two sugars please'; a messenger boy was crawling away from the wreckage of his bicycle; an old woman with a bag of groceries clutched the base of a lamppost and mouthed a single word in a language that wasn't English. And then the air was full of sirens as dozens of emergency service workers and Jesuit priests from the seminary a few streets away arrived, their arms bulky with blankets and Bibles.

'Number 59,' the cop announced to the crowd at the hastily erected barrier, 'Number 59 is gone. Survivors?' He shook his head and looked away. 'In all my twelve years on the beat,' he went on, his bright blue Irish eyes so sharp-focused and creased with it all they resembled melting ice, 'this is the most shocking scene I have ever witnessed.'

His colleague, a hefty middle-aged Italian, was sent on clean-up duty and would pick things out of the rubble he wouldn't even mention to his wife, for fear of upsetting her delicate nature and giving her bad dreams. And one by one he would label body parts, some so damaged and torn up that they put him in mind of the butcher's bucket despite himself, and some still perfect, apart from the cleanest, kindest cuts that had severed them from their owners with one stroke, so that he couldn't stop himself from imagining these parts being cared for, being kissed and bathed and manicured by mothers and wives and lovers, and he felt loath to let them go. Once labelled and numbered, wrapped up and tied, however, he would place them as gently as sleeping babies into the van.

It was the dirty hand that he couldn't forget. He tried to wipe it clean with his handkerchief but the dirt was so ingrained that he heard his dear dead mother's voice telling him that nothing short of a long, hot, soapy bath would remove it. He had wept a little then. It was a woman's hand, a beautiful hand, a delicate hand with long white ringless fingers. Slowly he ran his own finger along the long lines of the palm and, when he was sure that no one was looking, held the severed wrist to his face, inhaled and caught the faintest trace of French perfume.

And then he felt as filled with guilt as he lay wide awake next to his sleeping wife as if he'd committed some unforgivable act of infidelity. And maybe, in fact, he had.

35

By September, a boat had been found. It wasn't the most suitable vessel in the ocean, it was true, but it was seaworthy. A paddle-steamer, it had been a pleasure boat before it had been taken over by the army and used to transport troops across the Atlantic to the front. Several hundred more 'undesirables' had been sent from Pittsburgh, Buffalo and Philadelphia, and the boat was anchored at a pier in South Brooklyn with its steam up, all ready to sail.

'A present for Lenin,' the mayor was quoted as saying. 'They're all going back to Russia where they belong.'

The bomb on Tenth Street had roused public anger to such a degree that a deportation order seemed like the obvious solution. Ivory Price declined to comment but the photograph that had been taken of him that night in his evening clothes was reprinted many times. Mrs Ellen Finlay, whose house, she said, was never the same again, had moved south to Florida. Mrs Ivory Price, it was rumoured, had been so upset by the evening that she had become a recluse. As for the child, she seemed to spend all her time with her nanny.

Monroe saw Inez once, a few days after he had heard the news about the boat, on the other side of the Great Hall. He broke out of the queue for lunch and headed to where she was being held in a side room.

'There's been a mistake,' he told the guard. 'This woman isn't Russian. She has no political allegiances. And she has a child. She shouldn't be in here.'

'Back in the line,' the guard said as he manhandled Monroe away from the doorway.

'Take your hands off me!' he yelled.

'Another one for the lock-up,' shouted the guard as three more men in uniform grabbed Monroe by both arms and legs.

'It's all right,' Inez shouted. 'Don't worry. Everything is going to be all right. Please don't hurt him.'

As he sat out the hours on a cold stone floor of a cell in Ellis Island, Monroe clung to the memory of her face as she lay in his arms in the Tsar's Room. And the thought of her both comforted and pained him. He had a child? Why hadn't she told him before? And what had he done? He had inadvertently got her involved in something that had nothing to do with her. If he'd known what was about to happen, he asked himself, would he have taken the risks, would he have followed the same actions? But still he felt the resonance inside him like a major chord. For the few hours they had been alone together, he had felt more alive, more blessed, more joyous than he could ever have believed possible.

Dozens of detainees asked to see lawyers and attorneys, or at least their families. Few requests were granted. When Suzette Kinross, however, asked to see the representative, Ivory Price, he arrived the following day.

'Let us both out of here,' Inez asked Ivory when she was sure the guard was out of earshot. 'This is ridiculous. You know we shouldn't be in here. Poor Luella, she must be missing me so much.'

'What were you doing with him?'

'What do you think I was doing with him?'

'Tell me.'

Inez looked at her husband, at his eye blotched with exhaustion, at his mouth which could not stay still but shifted around his face as if trying to disguise what he was really thinking.

'You want to know? Why, so you can feel vindicated?'

He clenched and unclenched his fists but said nothing.

'The same,' she said eventually, 'the same things you did with Ellen Finlay. Or are you going to deny it?'

Ivory inhaled sharply, as if her words were actual blows that had hit him hard and low. As he caught his breath again, he looked up and out of the window. A line of male detainees were being herded on to a small boat. Another line stood waiting on the quay. Second from the front was the figure of the piano player.

Inez was standing at the other side of the room staring at the door. He strolled over to where she was standing and positioned himself a few inches away.

'You know he's a card-carrying Communist?' he whispered. 'A Murdering Red, as they are otherwise known. Goes by the name of Andrei Dreslov. What was his name before that? Monroe Simonov. Wanted for desertion. Who knows who else he has been. And what he might or might not have done. I mean, how well do you even know this man?'

'He's just a songwriter,' Inez replied. 'I know him.'

She turned to face him. Her hair fell in curls around her shoulders, the skin beneath her eyes was smudged with blue but her face was so open, so unmasked, that he suddenly saw beyond the front she presented to the world and knew without any doubt that she was lost to him.

For a moment or two, neither spoke. He swallowed twice and clenched his teeth. And then his eyes ran over her face, back and forth, as if trying to memorize it for later.

'You see,' Ivory said, his mouth turning down slightly at the corners. 'The trouble is, I don't think you understand the seriousness . . . there's nothing I can do now.'

'Maybe he'll get a short prison term,' she said. 'But with a good lawyer.'

'I don't mean . . .' he said. 'I don't mean just for him.'

At the time, it had seemed like such a wonderful proposition: in return for a considerable sum, more even than he could actually afford, there would be a detonation, a terrorist act in which he himself would be personally caught up. With ample warning, however, a telephone call put through from an accomplice on the street outside, there would be no casualties, just a lot of collateral damage. Ellen had never liked that house and besides, it was insured to the hilt. Afterwards he would milk every drop he could out of it. He knew how to wear the mantle of the victim to its fullest effect; he would be governor within five years.

And it had seemed to go so smoothly. The party, the phone call, the evacuation. But he had been tricked; he had been swindled by that filthy Russian, Noah Serginov, a man who had been in the pay of the American Protective League for years. Now there was a name he'd never forget. There was no detonation, no explosion. At least not there and not then.

'Tell them who I am,' Inez demanded. 'If you don't, I will.'

'You really think that would help?' he hissed. 'You were found in the Lower East Side in bed with a Red, remember? The papers would have a field day. All that stuff they wrote about the indefatigable Mrs Ivory Price, the supportive wife, the loving mother. I'd have to divorce you, of course, and you'd be left with nothing'

'Listen, ' Inez insisted. 'You can get me out of here, you could if you wanted to.'

'And if somebody twigged that Miss Suzette Kinross was really Mrs Ivory Price? I'm just surprised you haven't been recognized already.'

'Please, Ivory,' she begged. 'Please.'

'I am an elected member of Congress,' he replied. 'It's impossible. I'd never live a thing like this down. It would ruin me. I'm sorry.'

Inez's eyes were wide with shock. 'I can't!' she said. 'I can't go to Russia!'

'Isn't this what you want? To be together?'

Inez stared at her husband, at the man who would not meet her eye but fixed his gaze on the radiator, and started to shake. Her breath came in gusts. Tears spilled from her eyes.

'But my little girl,' she gasped. 'My little girl!'

Ivory did not want to feel anything. He wished he could freeze his heart with pure cocaine. He tried to take her hand. It was balled into a fist. He tried to hold her gaze but her eyes were both blind with grief. He tried to put his arm around her, but she pushed it off. Gradually, however, her shoulders stopped shaking, her tears were blinked away and she wiped her face with the back of her sleeve.

'When does the boat leave?' she asked.

'Tonight,' he said.

Inez pulled Edward's scarf around her shoulders and closed her eyes. Outside she could hear the slap of water against the quay and the splutter of a boat engine. A chain was rattled, a gate clanked shut, a key was turned. Was this her punishment? Was this the price she had to pay for all the wrong choices, for all the mistakes she had made: to be exiled, to be banished? As the low-pitched blast of a ship's siren rang out across the bay, she pulled in a breath and gradually let it out. It would not break her; it would not destroy a single spark of the love she felt for Monroe, she would not let it. And when she met Ivory's gaze at last, her face was almost calm.

'Look after Luella for me,' she said. 'And tell her I'm coming back. We both are.'

EPILOGUE

As the boat blunt-nosed its way out of Jamaica Bay and into the Atlantic, a crescent moon rode high above, its points both pick-sharp. Down below, most of the passengers sat cross-legged or lay curled up on the lower deck: some were in the mood for a celebration and sang Russian songs or openly jeered at the guards – one for every man and woman – who had been sent to accompany them. Others lay mute on the sacking they had been given to lie on, the memory of the tears of their wives and children who had gathered on the Brooklyn quay still so acute that it would be days before they would be able to sleep.

Over four thousand miles away, a telegram from the governor of New York arrived in St Petersburg. It was placed on the desk in an office in the Winter Palace but blew on to the floor and was trampled underfoot for a week or two before anyone actually picked it up and read it. Outside, the rain that had been falling for hours momentarily ceased. An emaciated man staggered along the Embankment with a wooden window frame that he intended to burn on his shoulders. A dog pulled at the remains of a dead horse. A gunshot sounded somewhere close by. The railways were at a standstill, the morgue was full. And all over the city, portraits of Lenin gazed triumphantly into empty rooms.

Half a dozen gulls glided on the tailwind from the boat, dipping down and soaring up again like kites. But one by one they tipped their wings and turned, to head back along the fraying white line of the boat's wake, back to the coast, back to the lights of Martha's Vineyard and Nantucket that glittered softly in the velvet of the night.

AUTHOR'S NOTE AND ACKNOWLEDGMENTS

In 2001, five weeks after 9/11, I moved to New York with my family and lived there for a few years. Sometimes, on a Sunday, we'd go for a walk downtown, past the scar where the two towers once stood, and through the financial district.

It was here, passing along Wall Street, that I read there had been another act of terrorism over eighty years earlier. In 1920, a horse and cart loaded with explosives stopped outside JP Morgan bank. When the bomb was detonated, it killed over thirty people, injured many more and caused $2 million of damage. This happened at the height of what was known as the Red Scare. Although no one was ever charged, the atrocity was blamed on anarchists and Communists, the so-called, 'enemy within'.

It's easy to think that you know a city; you know its streets, subway system and weather patterns. And yet when I looked back at the beginning of the twentieth century I found I barely knew New York at all. I began to read up on the period and discovered a city full of exiled Russian revolutionaries and militant Italian anarchists. I also read about the so-called Russian Ark, a ship filled with deported Russians and undesirable aliens that sailed for Petrograd in 1919 labelled as 'a Christmas present for Lenin'.

The Songwriter is a book about a period of New York history that I wanted to explore. It seemed to me that the heady music of jazz was echoed in the idealism and ambition of what was then still a very new nation. My characters are mostly invented but contain elements of certain well-known figures of the time such as Inessa Armand, Alexandra Kollontai and Irving Berlin. Although much of what happens in the book is based on fact, I imagined settings, songs and events.

Thank you Simon Trewin, Jessica Craig and Ariella Feiner at United Agents, plus Zoe Pagnamemta; Caroline Westmore and Roland Philipps at John Murray, and Morag Lyall who copy-edited with such skill. Thanks are also due to the Scottish Arts Council who awarded me a travel bursary to visit St Petersburg and the Royal Literary Fund who supported me with a fellowship.

I'd also like to thank my family, especially my mother who always stepped in to help, my children Theo and Frances; my friends especially Sara Pinto, Miranda France, who enlightened me about Argentina, and Alison Hayes and Louis White whose energy and generosity was always an inspiration. Also thanks to Anne Robertson who taught me how to play the piano and Annie Armstrong for helping me keep everything in order. Lastly, my thanks to Paul.

Read more ...

Amitav Ghosh

SEA OF POPPIES

An epic seafaring adventure set against the backdrop of the Opium Wars

Deeti is a widow to opium, saved from her husband's funeral pyre by the low-caste Kalua, who has been waiting for her. Paulette is the orphaned daughter of a French botanist and Jodu, the son of her wet nurse, is the only link to her past. A bankrupt raja is chased from his estates which fall into the hands of an avaricious opium dealer. Fate throws these characters, and a host of others, together as a motley crew on an old slaving ship, the *Ibis*.

Set against the backdrop of the Opium Wars, this unlikely dynasty is what makes *Sea of Poppies* so breathtakingly alive – an absorbing masterpiece from one of the world's finest storytellers.

'Profoundly moving' *The Times*

'A remarkably rich saga' *Guardian*

'It is the sheer energy and verve of Amitav Ghosh's storytelling that binds this ambitious medley' *Daily Mail*

Order your copy now by calling Bookpoint on 01235 827716 or visit your local bookshop quoting ISBN 978-0-7195-6897-8
www.johnmurray.co.uk

Read more ...

Lloyd Jones

MISTER PIP

Shortlisted for the Man Booker Prize

Winner of the Commonwealth Writers' Prize

On a lush island in the South Pacific, civil war threatens daily life.
Thirteen-year-old Matilda and her friends haven't seen the inside of a
classroom for months until the village recluse emerges to breathe life
back into an old book. Surrounded by the constant threat of violence,
their new teacher introduces the children to a boy named Pip and a
man called Mr Dickens. But on an island at war, the power of stories
can have deadly consequences.

'Haunting and morally complex' *Sunday Times*

'A brilliantly nuanced examination of the power of imagination'
Financial Times

'One of the best books of the year!' Isabel Allende

*Order your copy now by calling Bookpoint on 01235 827716 or
visit your local bookshop quoting ISBN 978-0-7195-6994-4
www.johnmurray.co.uk*

Read more . . .

Beatrice Colin

THE LUMINOUS LIFE OF LILLY APHRODITE

Decadent, tantalizing Berlin in a Germany torn apart by war at the turn of the twentieth century

The illegitimate, orphaned daughter of a cabaret dancer, Lilly Nelly Aphrodite's early life is one of reinvention. Transformed from maid to war bride via tingle-tangle nightclub girl, she lands in the heart of the glamorous motion picture world and quickly becomes one of Germany's leading silent film stars.

But when she falls in love with a Russian director, she has no idea that the affair will span decades, cross continents and may ultimately cost her everything.

'The storytelling is masterful and the language magical . . . a rich book, in both its prose and in the strength of its characters' *Sunday Times*

'Full of suspense, this is an all-feeling novel, seductively and dramatically told' *Daily Mail*

'An exceptional novel' *Sunday Herald*

Order your copy now by calling Bookpoint on 01235 827716 or visit your local bookshop quoting ISBN 978-1-84854-031-6 www.johnmurray.co.uk